ORANGE CROWS ™

WRITTEN BY JAMES PERRY II
ART BY RYO KAWAKAMI

HAMBURG // LONDON // LOS ANGELES // TOKYO

Orange Crows Volume 1
Written by James Perry II
Art by Ryo Kawakami

Lettering - Lucas Rivera
Cover Design - Louis Csontos

Editor - Lillian Diaz-Przybyl and Hope Donov
Pre-Production Supervisor - Vicente Rivera, Jr.
Print-Production Specialist - Lucas Rivera
Managing Editor - Vy Nguyen
Senior Designer - Louis Csontos
Senior Designer - James Lee
Senior Editor - Bryce P. Coleman
Senior Editor - Jenna Winterberg
Associate Publisher - Marco F. Pavia
President and C.O.O. - John Parker
C.E.O. and Chief Creative Officer - Stu Levy

A **TOKYOPOP** Manga

8/10/10   10.99
TOKYOPOP and 🐸 are trademarks or registered trademarks of TOKYOPOP Inc.

TOKYOPOP Inc.
5900 Wilshire Blvd. Suite 2000
Los Angeles, CA 90036

E-mail: info@TOKYOPOP.com
Come visit us online at www.TOKYOPOP.com

ISBN: 978-1-4278-1228-5

First TOKYOPOP printing: February 2009
10 9 8 7 6 5 4 3 2 1
Printed in the USA

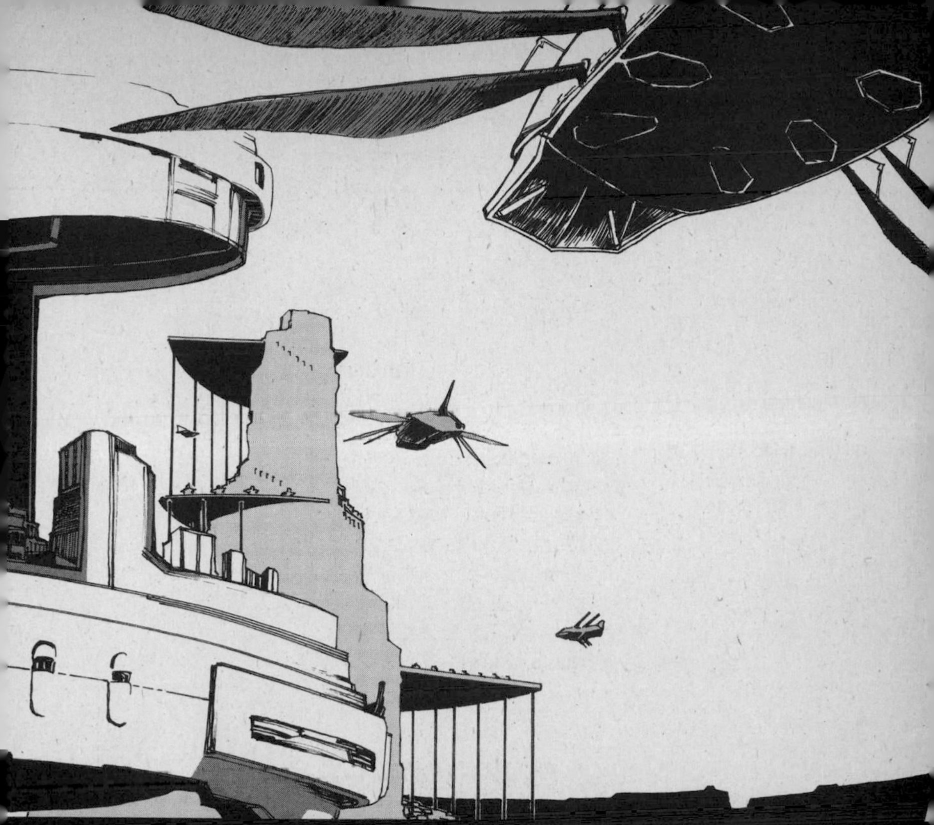

TABLE OF CONTENTS

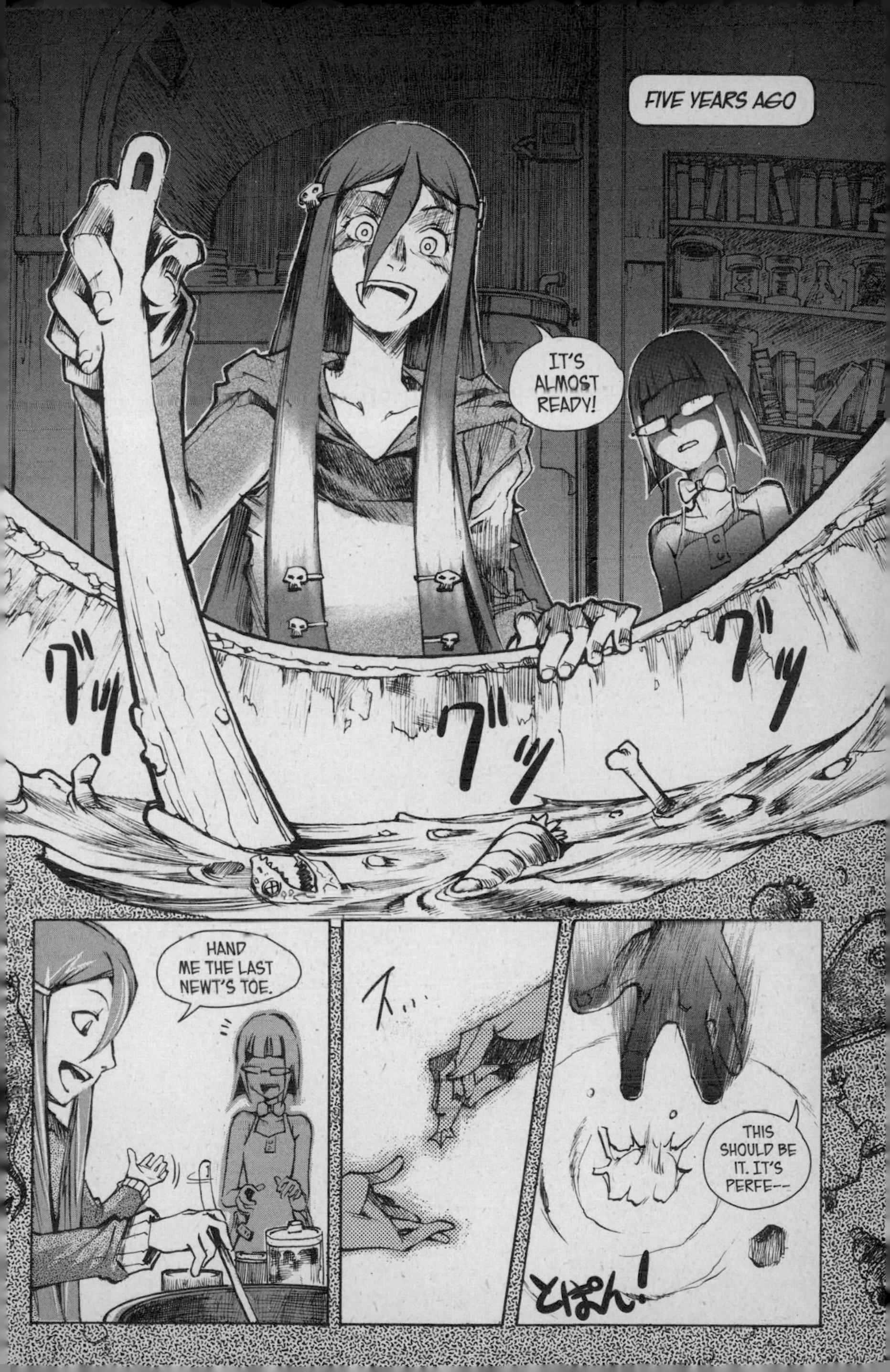
FIVE YEARS AGO
IT'S ALMOST READY!
ヴッ
ヴッ
ヴッ
HAND ME THE LAST NEWT'S TOE.
ス…
THIS SHOULD BE IT. IT'S PERFE--
とぷん!

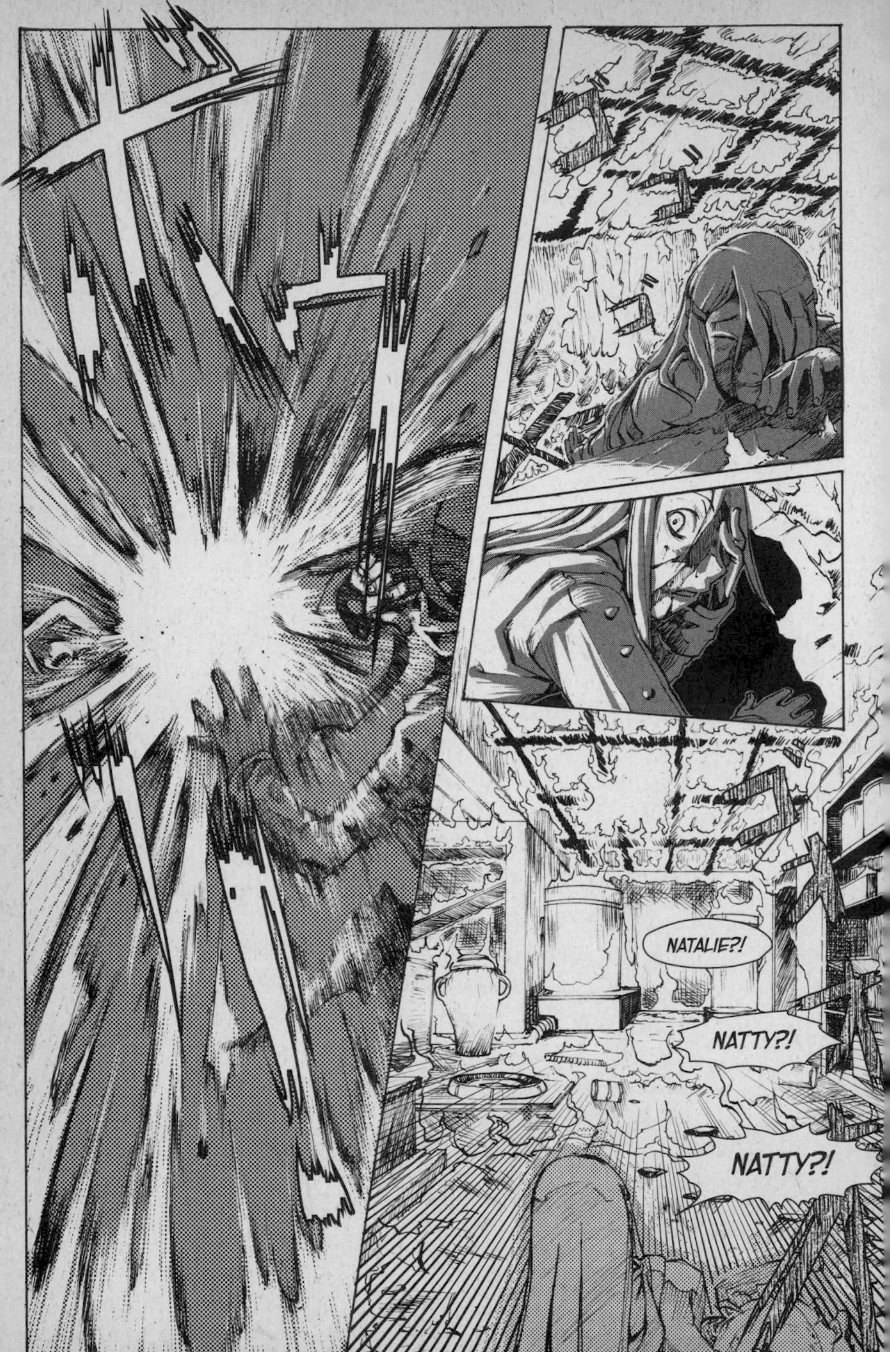
NATALIE?!
NATTY?!
NATTY?!

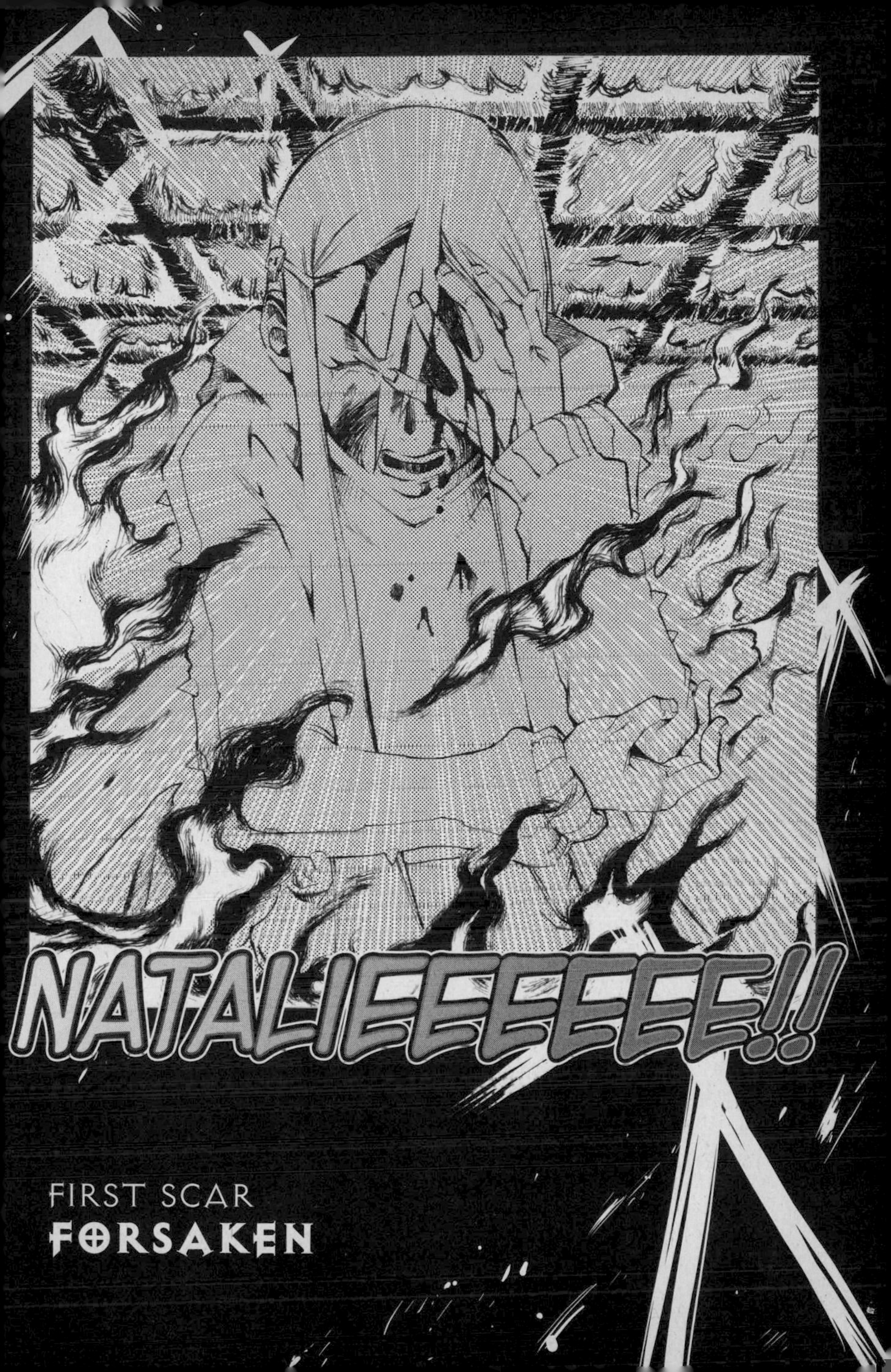
NATALIEEEEEE!!

FIRST SCAR
FORSAKEN

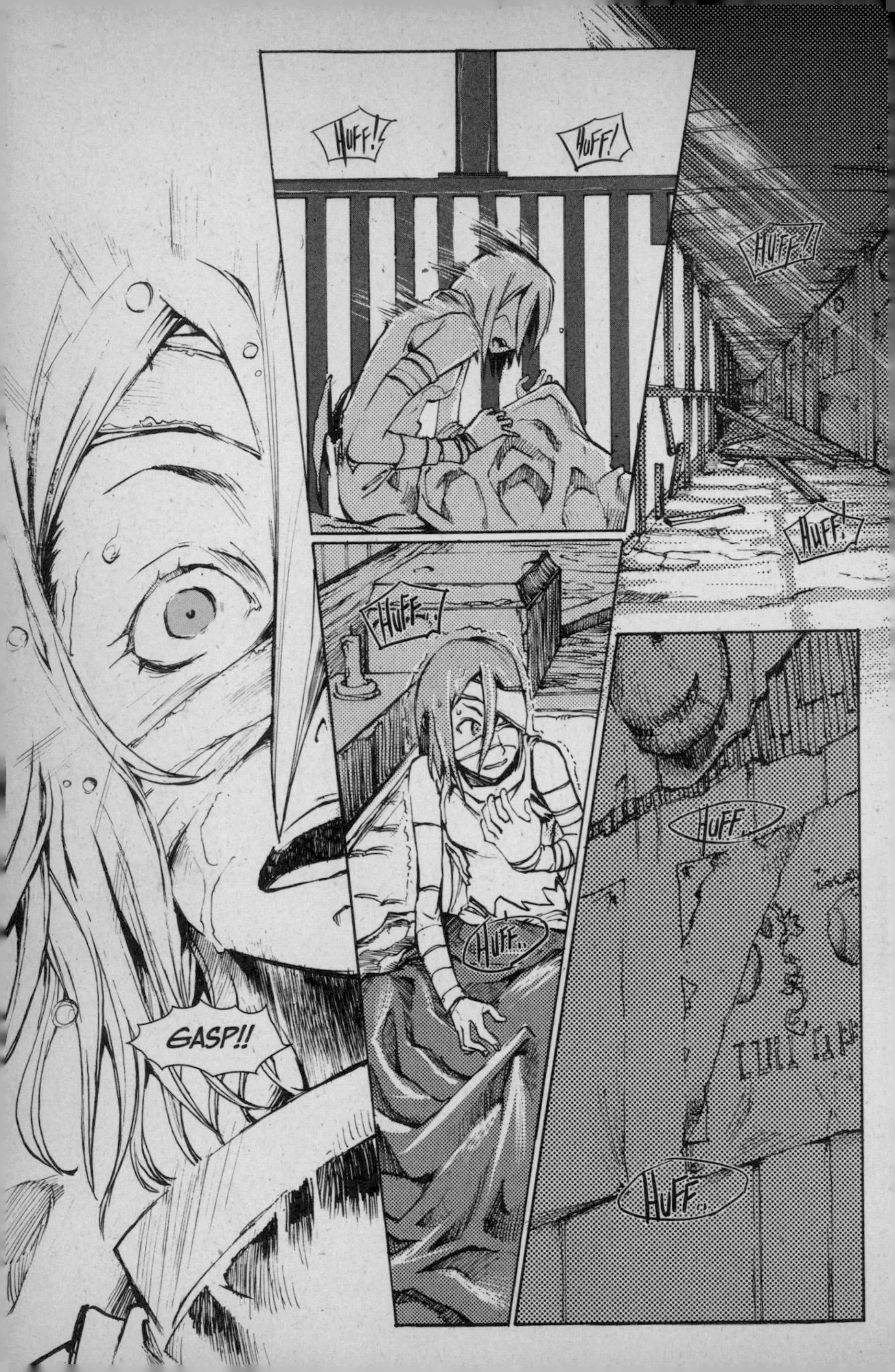
HUFF!
HUFF!
HUFF!
HUFF!
HUFF...
HUFF...
HUFF...
HUFF...
GASP!!

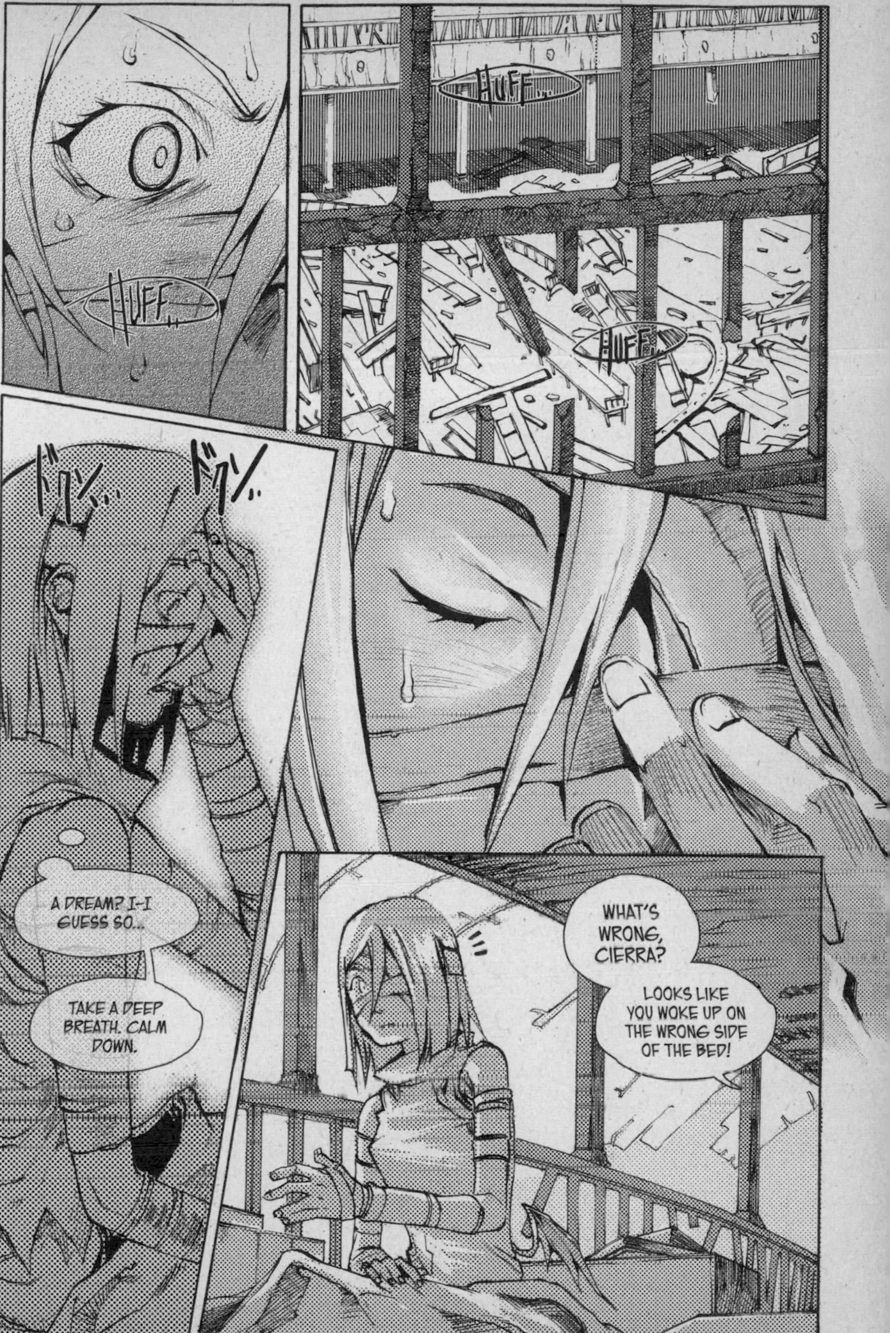
HUFF...
HUFF...
HUFF...
WHAT'S WRONG, CIERRA?
LOOKS LIKE YOU WOKE UP ON THE WRONG SIDE OF THE BED!
ドクン...
ドクン...
A DREAM? I-I GUESS SO...
TAKE A DEEP BREATH. CALM DOWN.

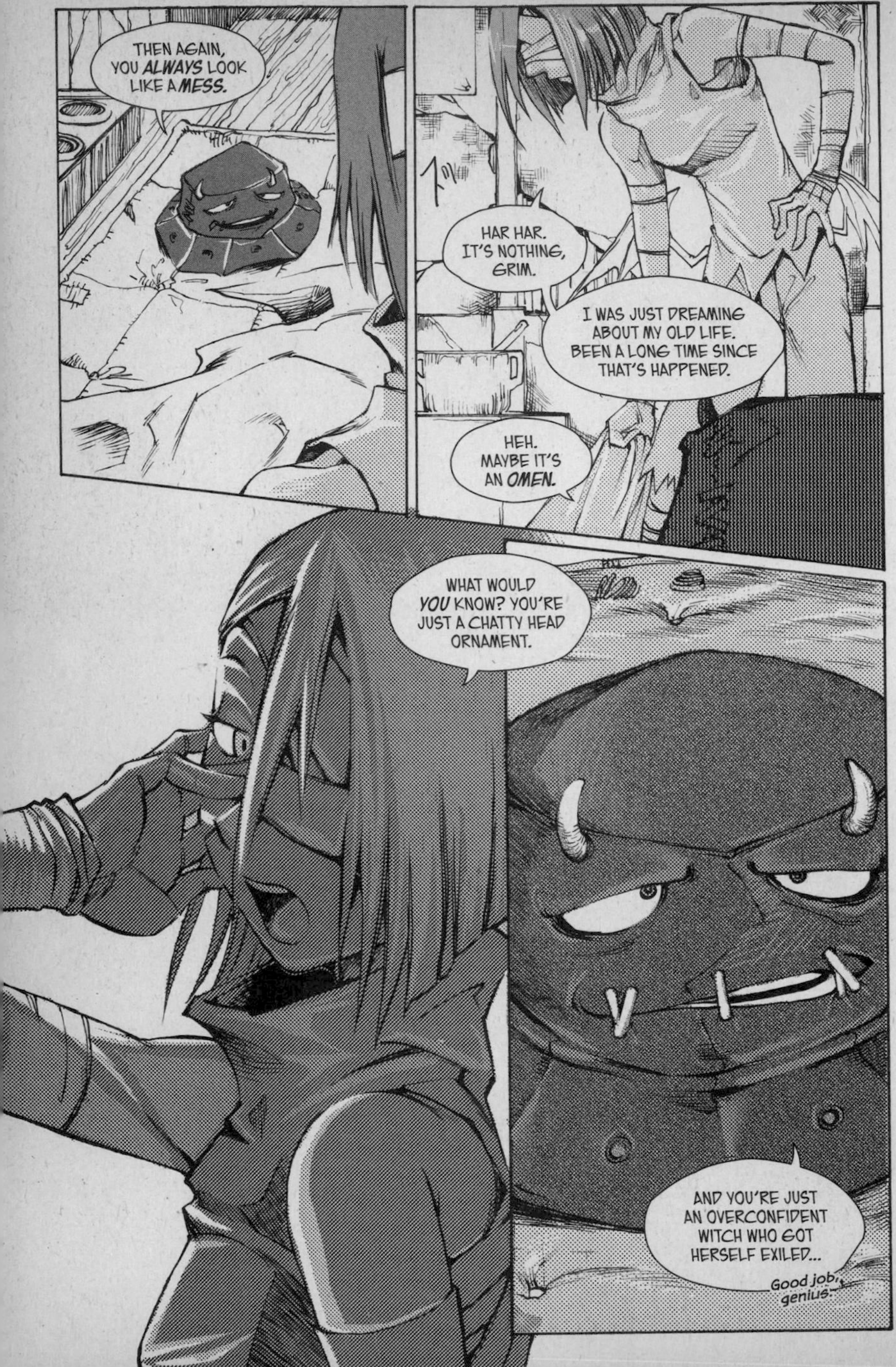
THEN AGAIN, YOU *ALWAYS* LOOK LIKE A *MESS.*
HAR HAR. IT'S NOTHING, GRIM.
I WAS JUST DREAMING ABOUT MY OLD LIFE. BEEN A LONG TIME SINCE THAT'S HAPPENED.
HEH. MAYBE IT'S AN *OMEN.*
WHAT WOULD *YOU* KNOW? YOU'RE JUST A CHATTY HEAD ORNAMENT.
AND YOU'RE JUST AN OVERCONFIDENT WITCH WHO GOT HERSELF EXILED...
Good job, genius.

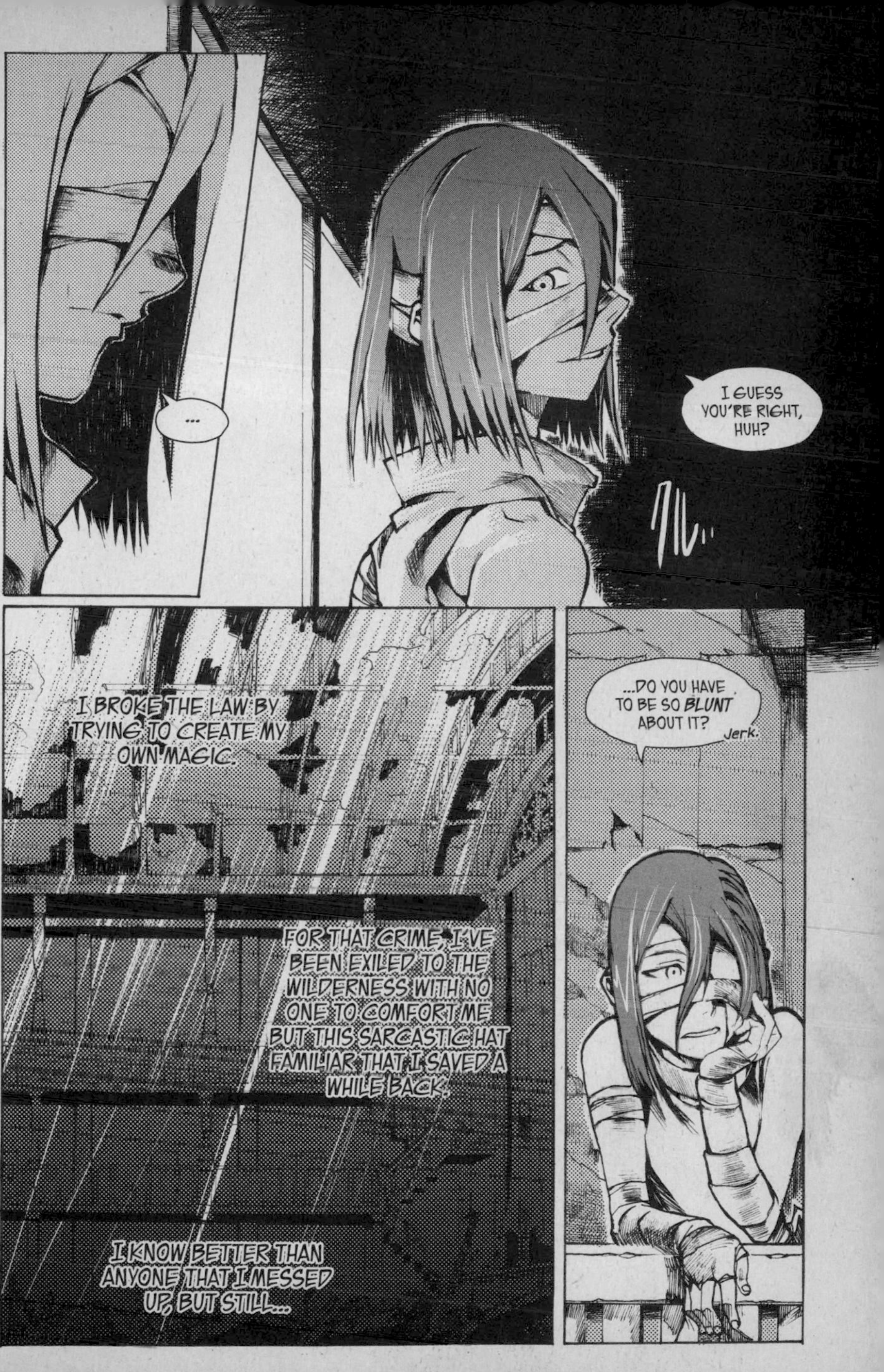
...
I GUESS YOU'RE RIGHT, HUH?
I BROKE THE LAW BY TRYING TO CREATE MY OWN MAGIC.
FOR THAT CRIME, I'VE BEEN EXILED TO THE WILDERNESS WITH NO ONE TO COMFORT ME BUT THIS SARCASTIC HAT FAMILIAR THAT I SAVED A WHILE BACK.
I KNOW BETTER THAN ANYONE THAT I MESSED UP, BUT STILL...
...DO YOU HAVE TO BE SO BLUNT ABOUT IT?
Jerk.

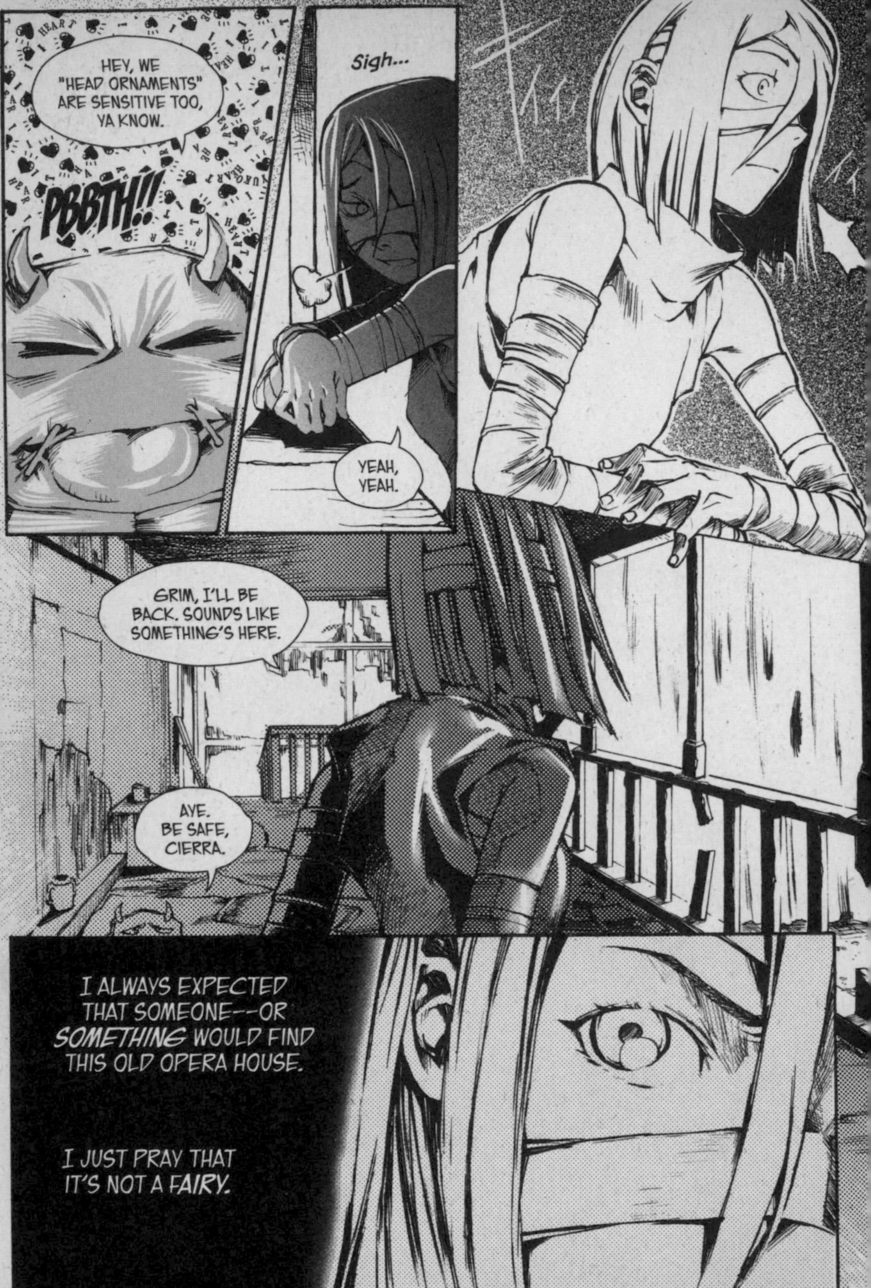

HEY, WE "HEAD ORNAMENTS" ARE SENSITIVE TOO, YA KNOW.
PBBTH!!
Sigh...
YEAH, YEAH.
GRIM, I'LL BE BACK. SOUNDS LIKE SOMETHING'S HERE.
AYE. BE SAFE, CIERRA.
I ALWAYS EXPECTED THAT SOMEONE--OR SOMETHING WOULD FIND THIS OLD OPERA HOUSE.
I JUST PRAY THAT IT'S NOT A FAIRY.

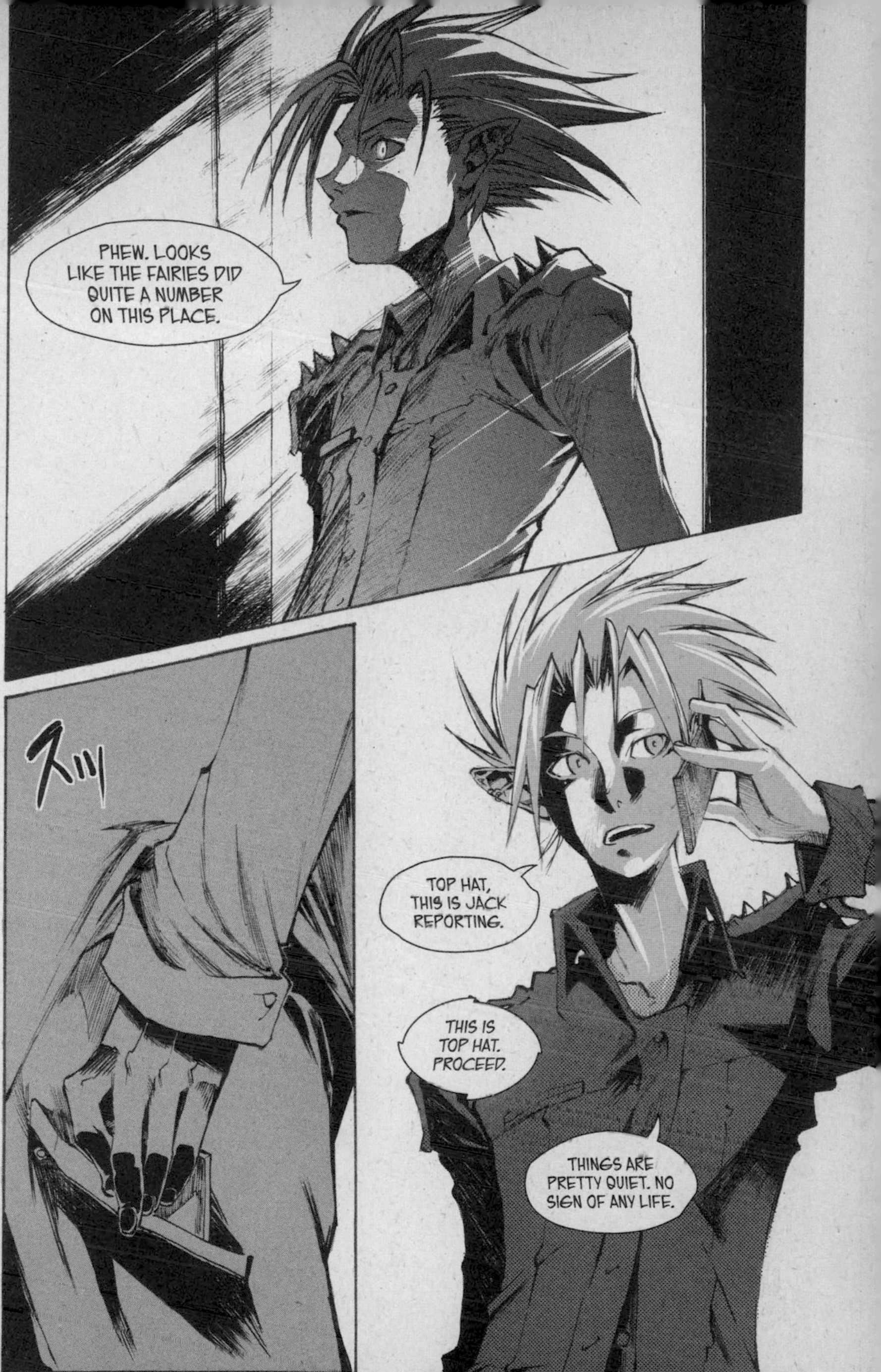
PHEW. LOOKS LIKE THE FAIRIES DID QUITE A NUMBER ON THIS PLACE.
TOP HAT, THIS IS JACK REPORTING.
THIS IS TOP HAT. PROCEED.
THINGS ARE PRETTY QUIET. NO SIGN OF ANY LIFE.
スッ

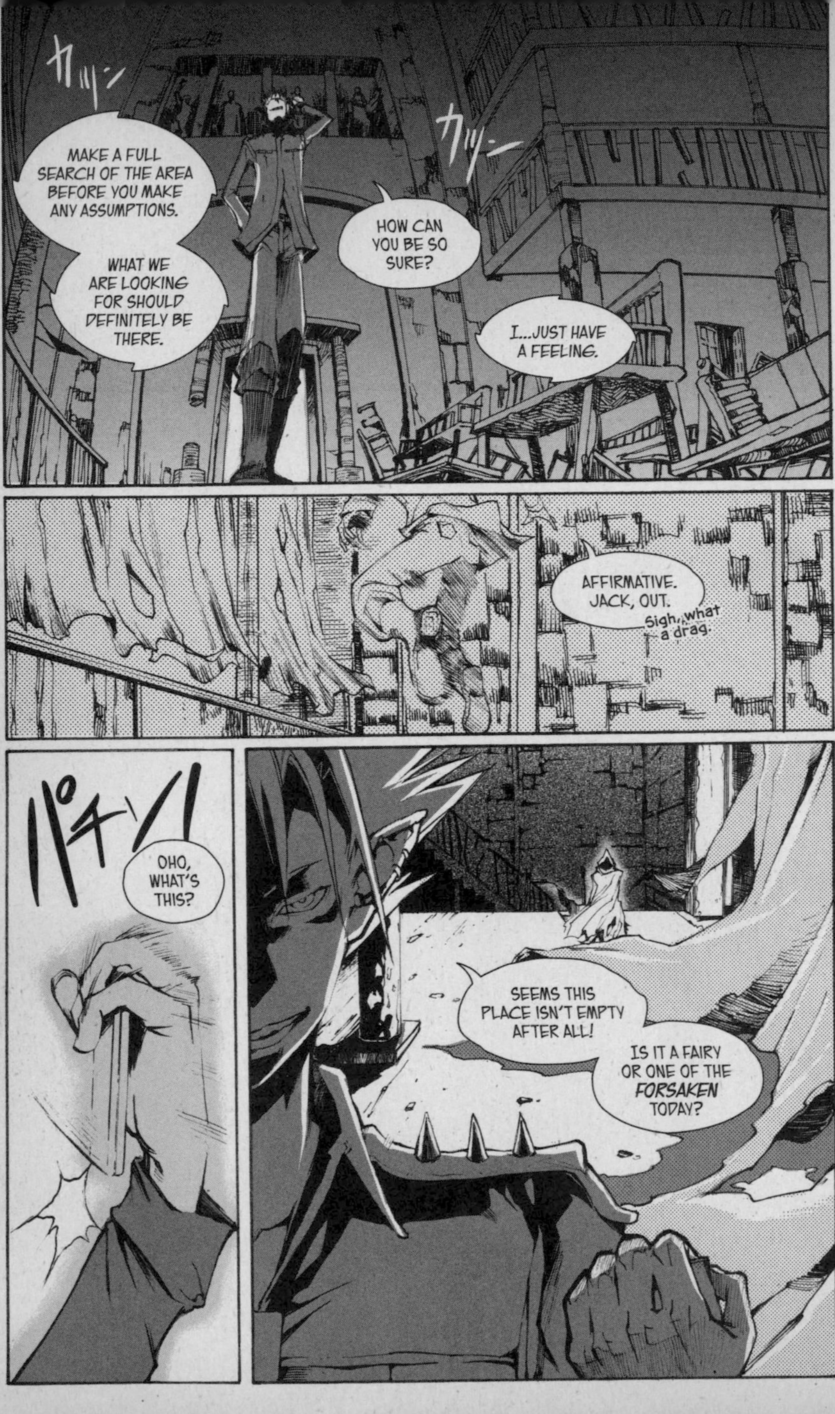
カッーン
MAKE A FULL SEARCH OF THE AREA BEFORE YOU MAKE ANY ASSUMPTIONS.
WHAT WE ARE LOOKING FOR SHOULD DEFINITELY BE THERE.
カツーン
HOW CAN YOU BE SO SURE?
I...JUST HAVE A FEELING.
AFFIRMATIVE. JACK, OUT.
Sigh, what a drag.
パチン
OHO, WHAT'S THIS?
SEEMS THIS PLACE ISN'T EMPTY AFTER ALL!
IS IT A FAIRY OR ONE OF THE *FORSAKEN* TODAY?

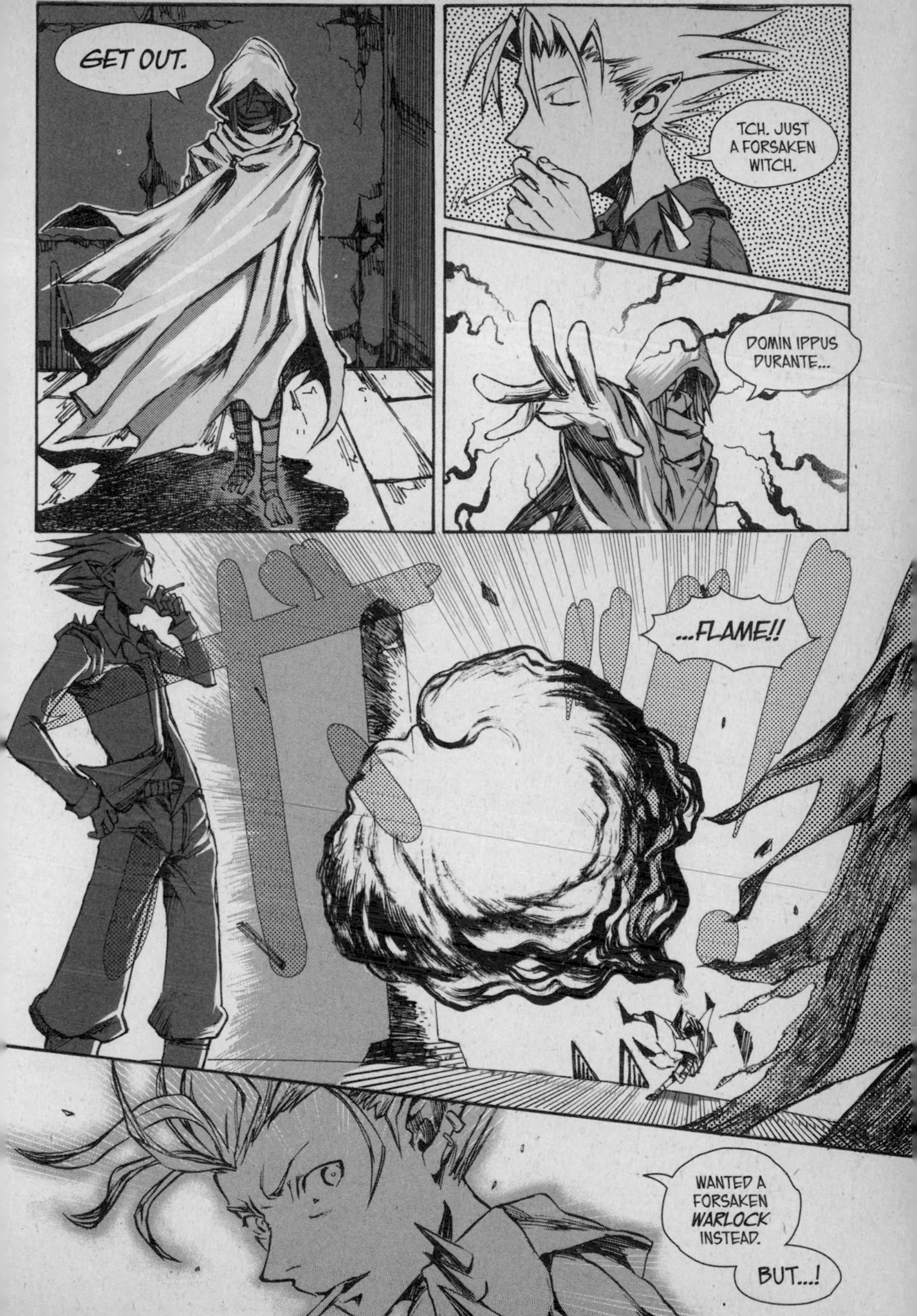
GET OUT.
TCH. JUST A FORSAKEN WITCH.
DOMIN IPPUS DURANTE...
...FLAME!!
WANTED A FORSAKEN WARLOCK INSTEAD.
BUT...!

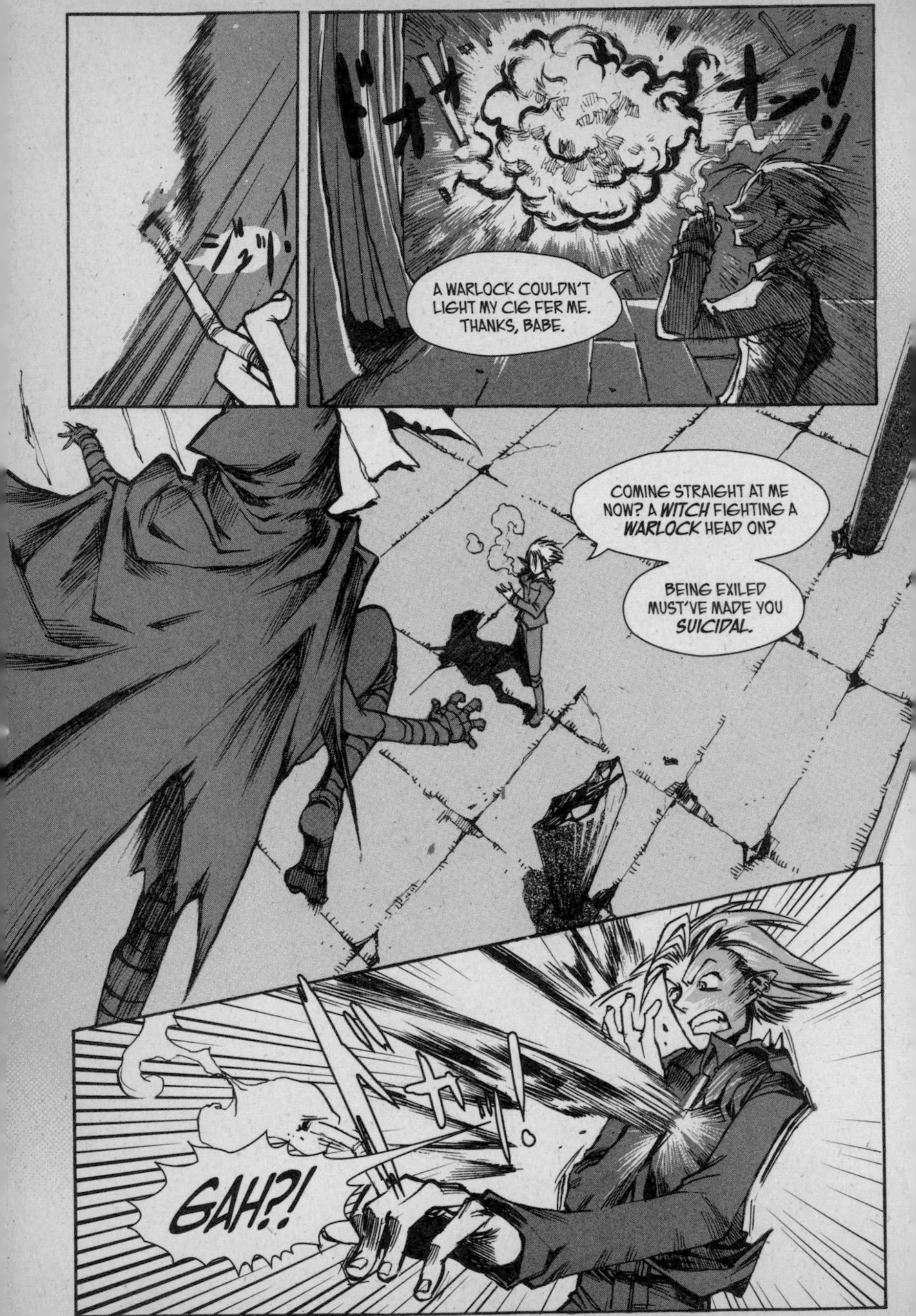
A WARLOCK COULDN'T LIGHT MY CIG FER ME. THANKS, BABE.
COMING STRAIGHT AT ME NOW? A WITCH FIGHTING A WARLOCK HEAD ON?
BEING EXILED MUST'VE MADE YOU SUICIDAL.
GAH?!

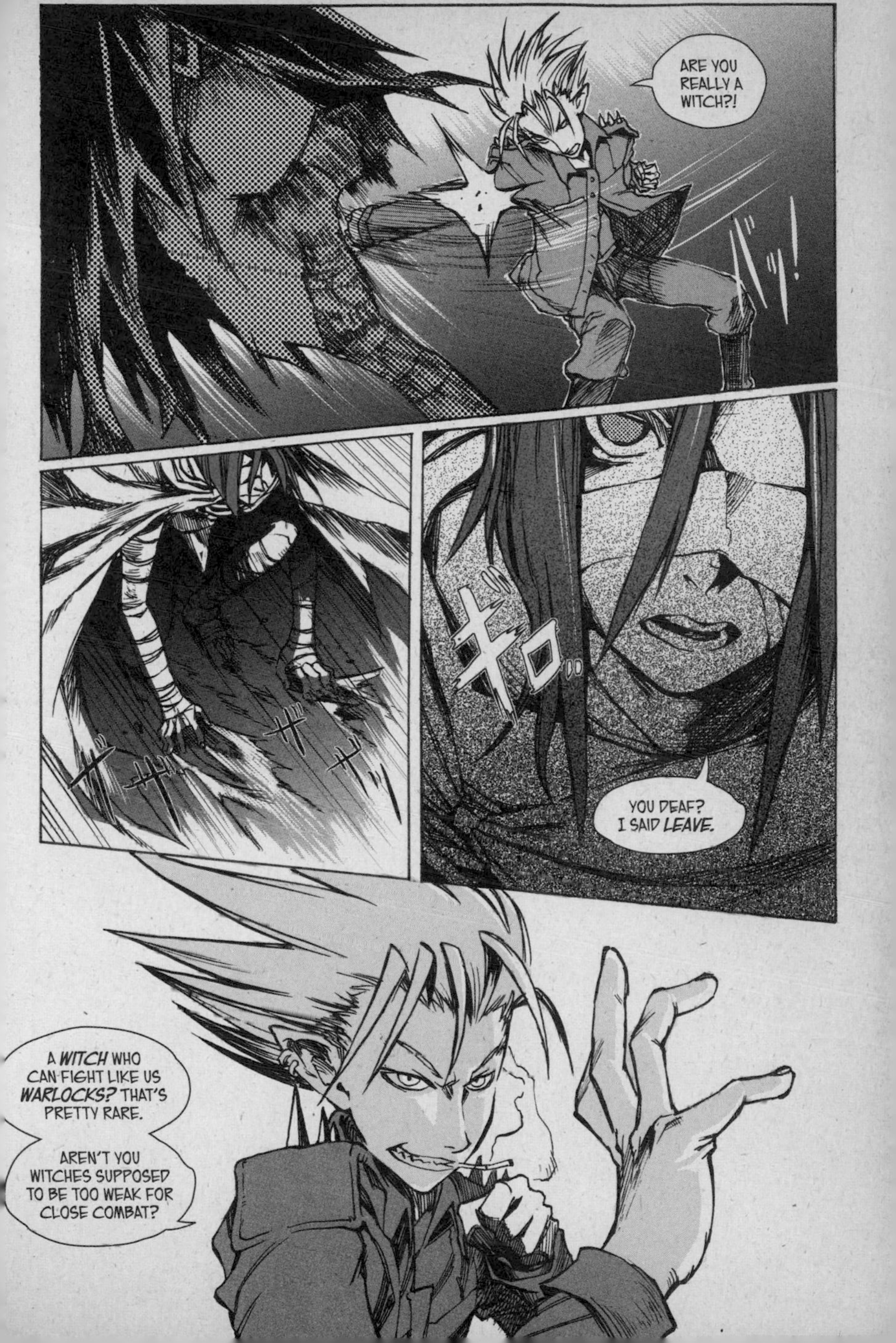
ARE YOU REALLY A WITCH?!
バッ!
ギロ
YOU DEAF? I SAID LEAVE.
ザ ザ ザ ザ
A WITCH WHO CAN FIGHT LIKE US WARLOCKS? THAT'S PRETTY RARE.
AREN'T YOU WITCHES SUPPOSED TO BE TOO WEAK FOR CLOSE COMBAT?

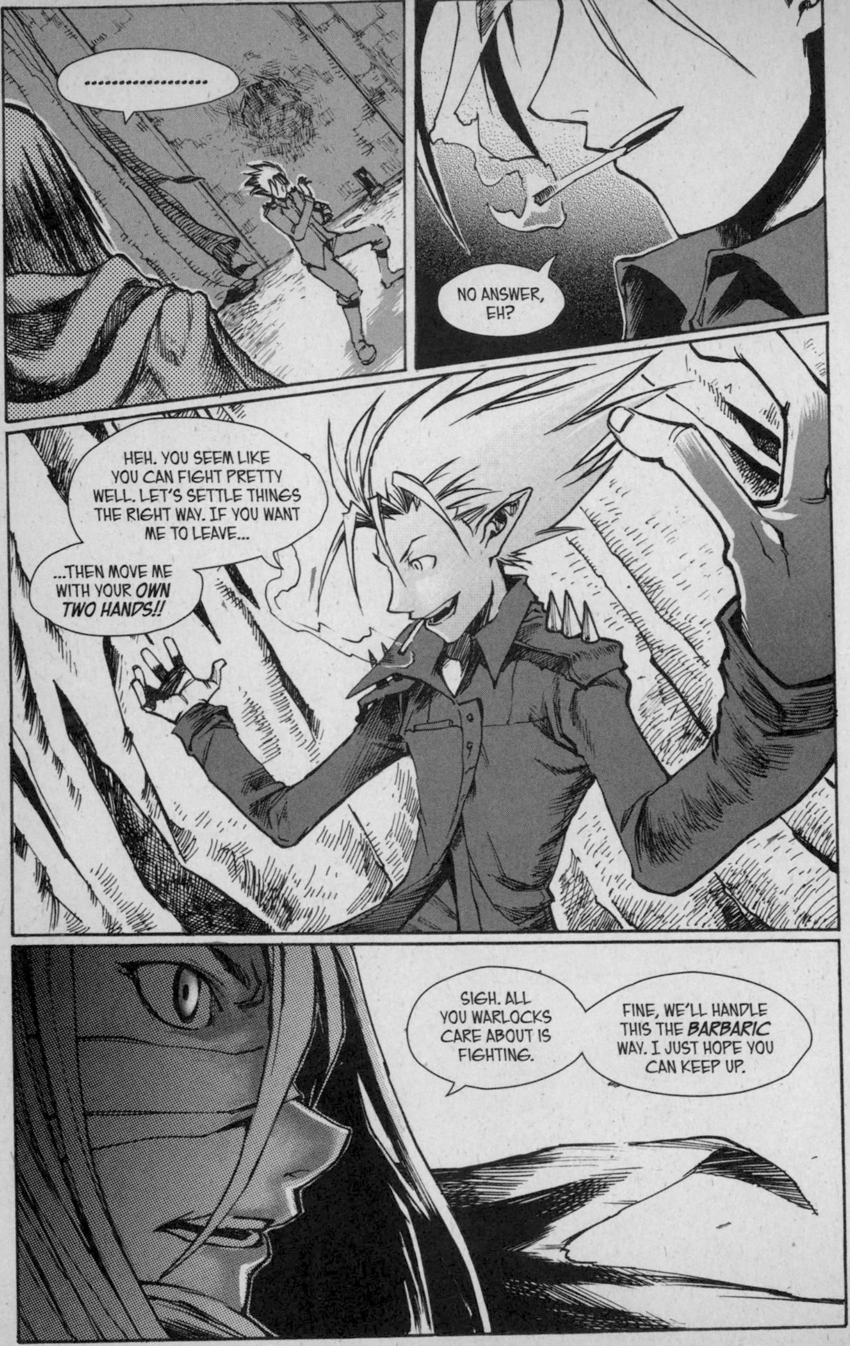

....
NO ANSWER, EH?
HEH. YOU SEEM LIKE YOU CAN FIGHT PRETTY WELL. LET'S SETTLE THINGS THE RIGHT WAY. IF YOU WANT ME TO LEAVE...
...THEN MOVE ME WITH YOUR *OWN TWO HANDS!!*
SIGH. ALL YOU WARLOCKS CARE ABOUT IS FIGHTING.
FINE, WE'LL HANDLE THIS THE *BARBARIC* WAY. I JUST HOPE YOU CAN KEEP UP.

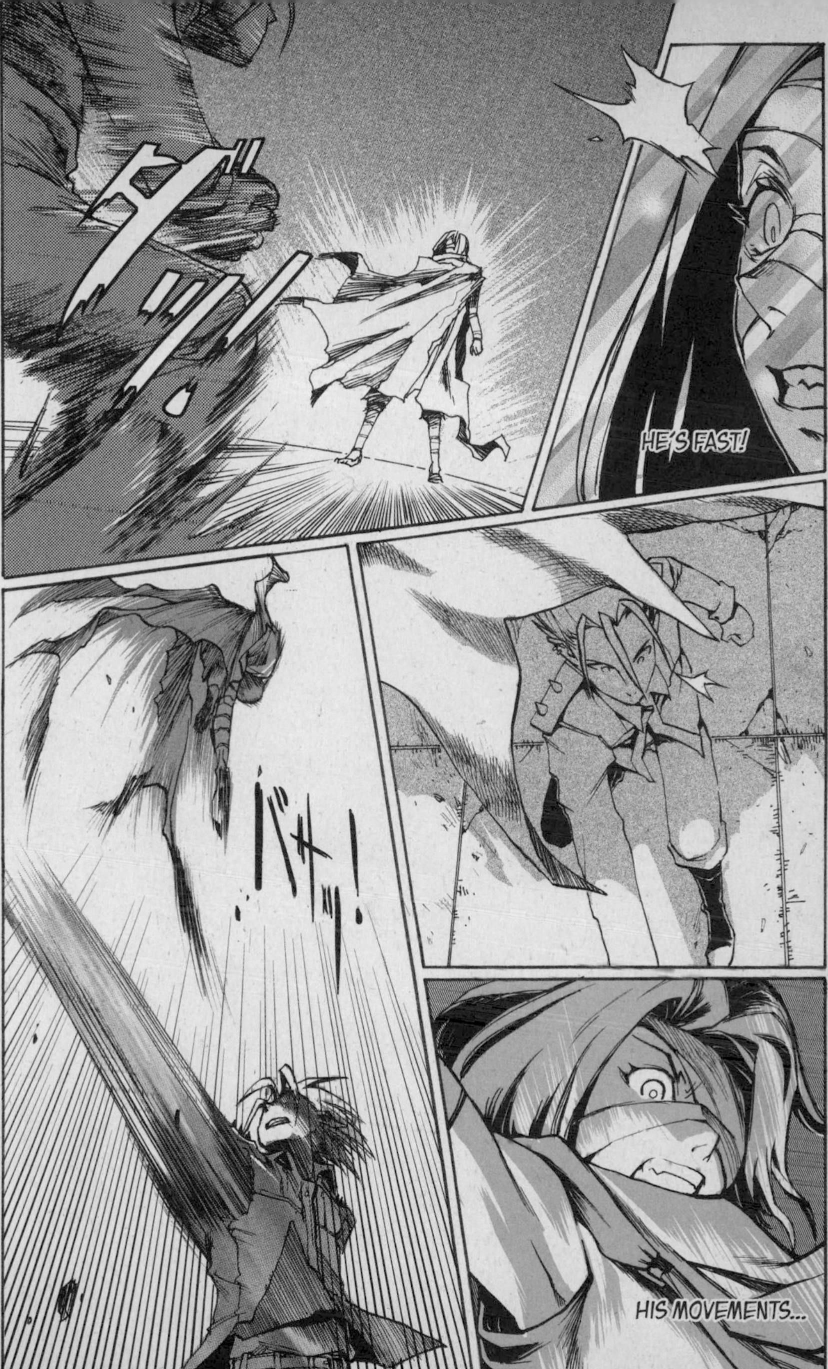
HE'S FAST!
ダッ
HIS MOVEMENTS...
バサッ!

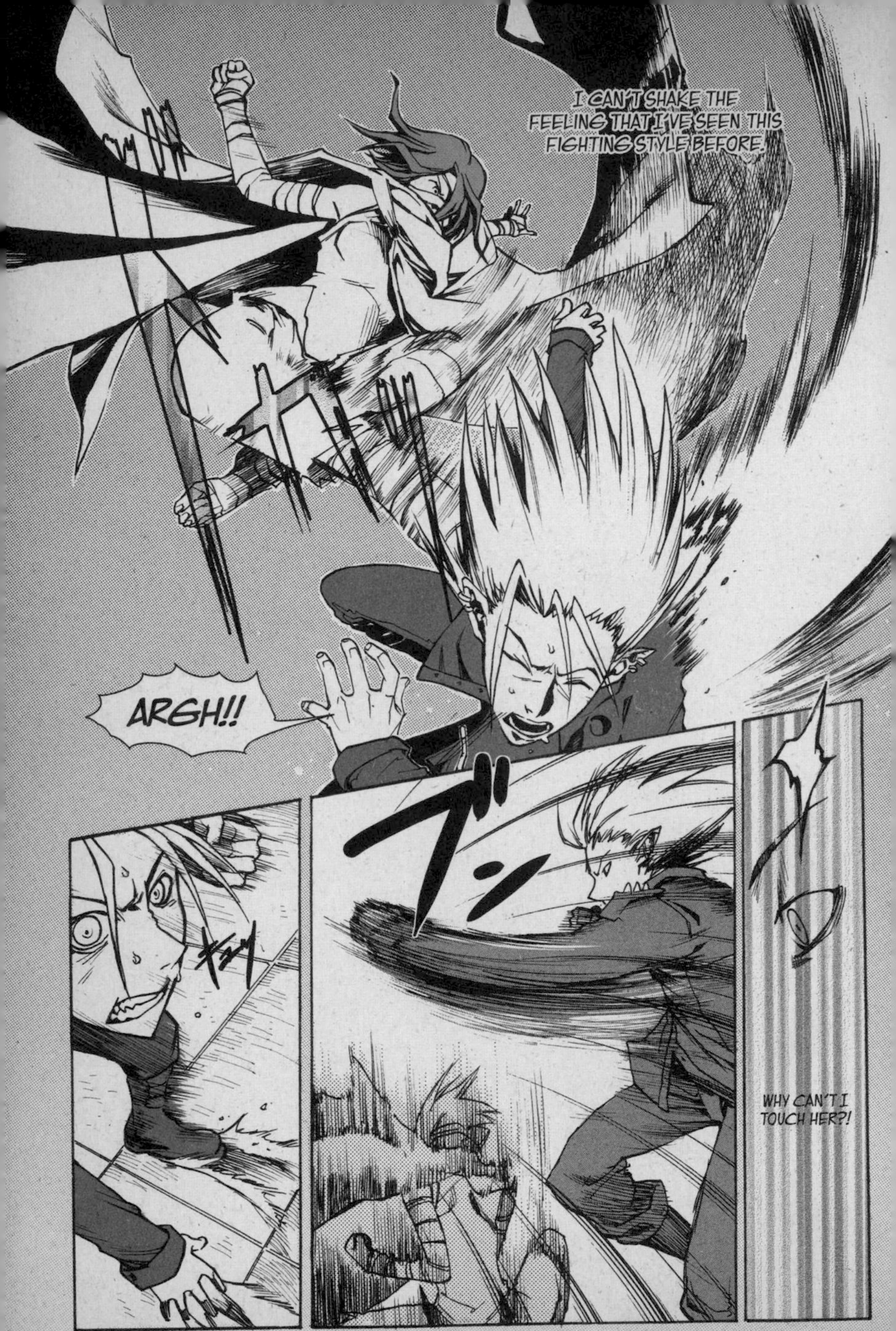

I CAN'T SHAKE THE FEELING THAT I'VE SEEN THIS FIGHTING STYLE BEFORE.
ARGH!!
WHY CAN'T I TOUCH HER?!

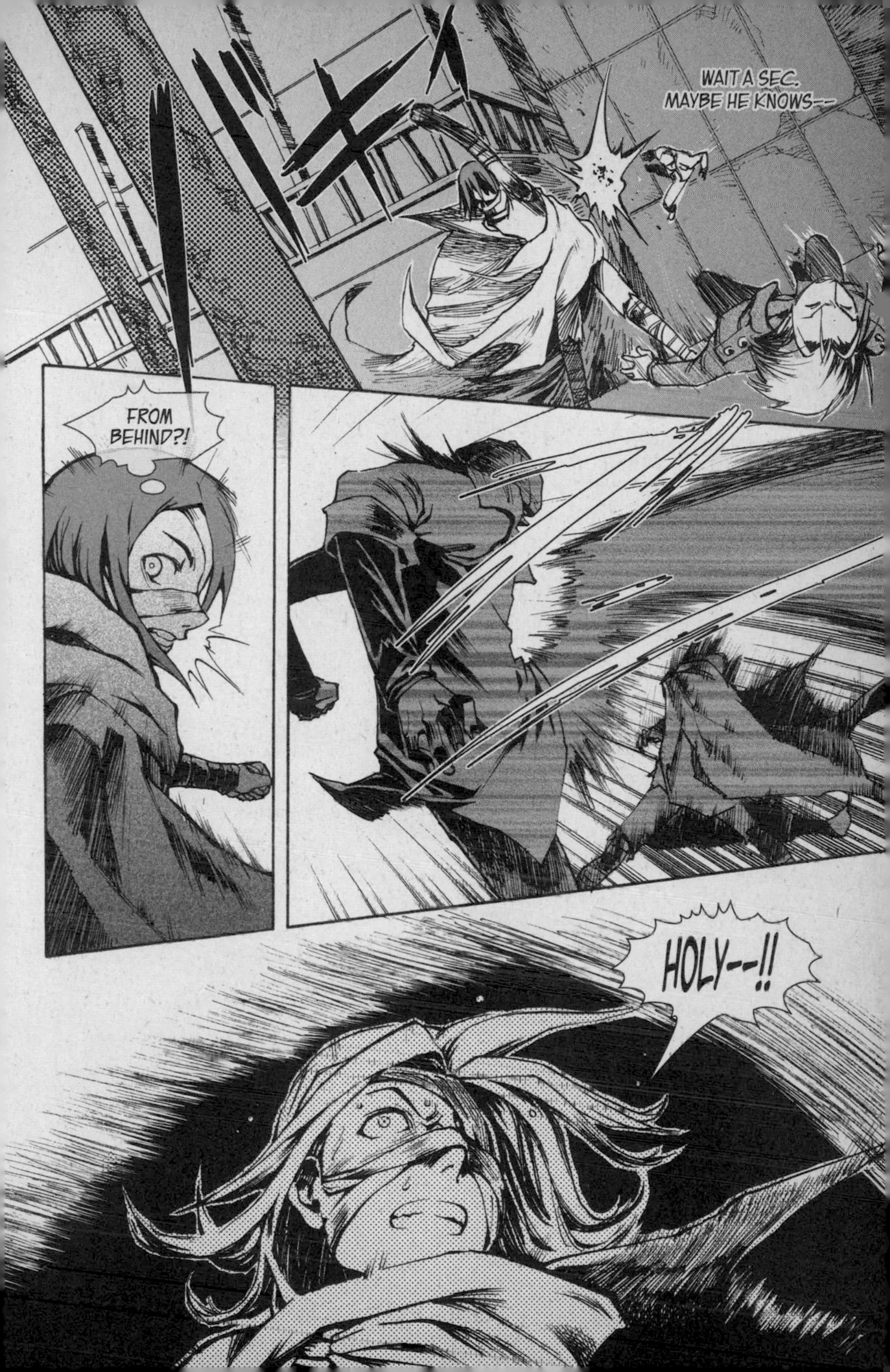
WAIT A SEC. MAYBE HE KNOWS--
FROM BEHIND?!
HOLY--!!

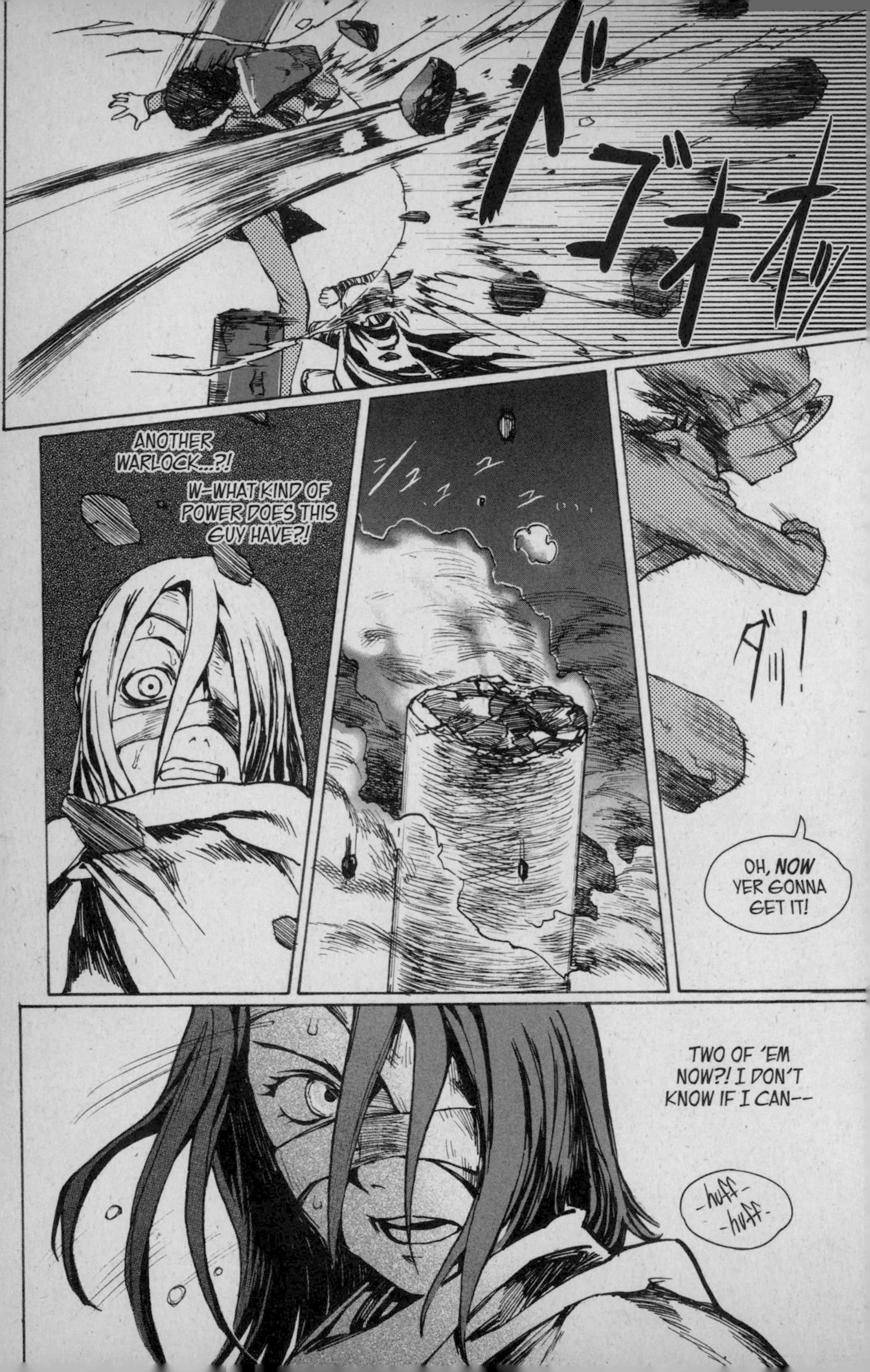
ズゴオッ
ダッ!
OH, **NOW** YER GONNA GET IT!
ANOTHER WARLOCK...?!
W-WHAT KIND OF POWER DOES THIS GUY HAVE?!
TWO OF 'EM NOW?! I DON'T KNOW IF I CAN--
-huff- -huff-

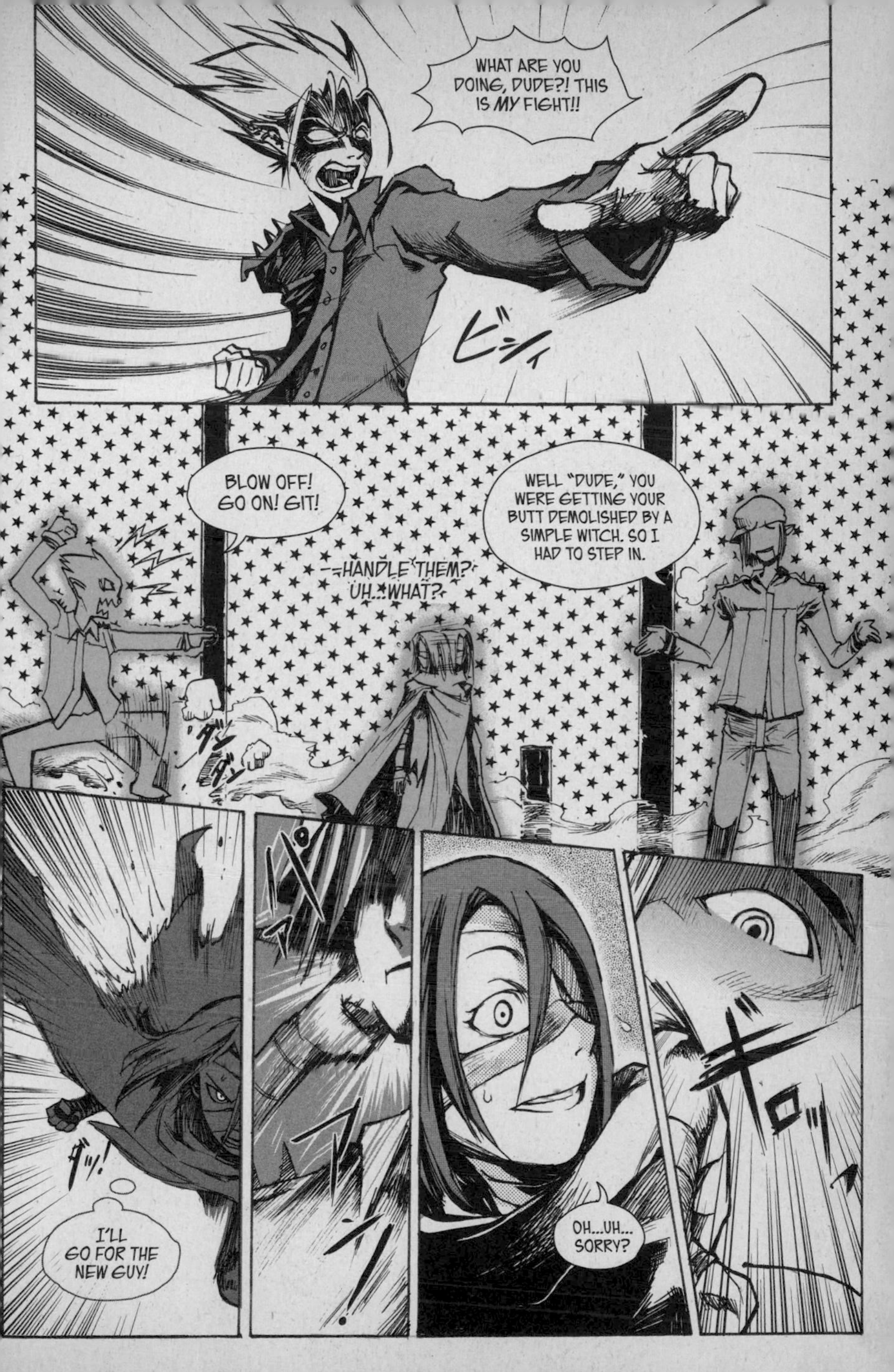
WHAT ARE YOU DOING, DUDE?! THIS IS MY FIGHT!!
WELL "DUDE," YOU WERE GETTING YOUR BUTT DEMOLISHED BY A SIMPLE WITCH. SO I HAD TO STEP IN.
--HANDLE THEM? UH...WHAT?
BLOW OFF! GO ON! GIT!
OH...UH... SORRY?
I'LL GO FOR THE NEW GUY!

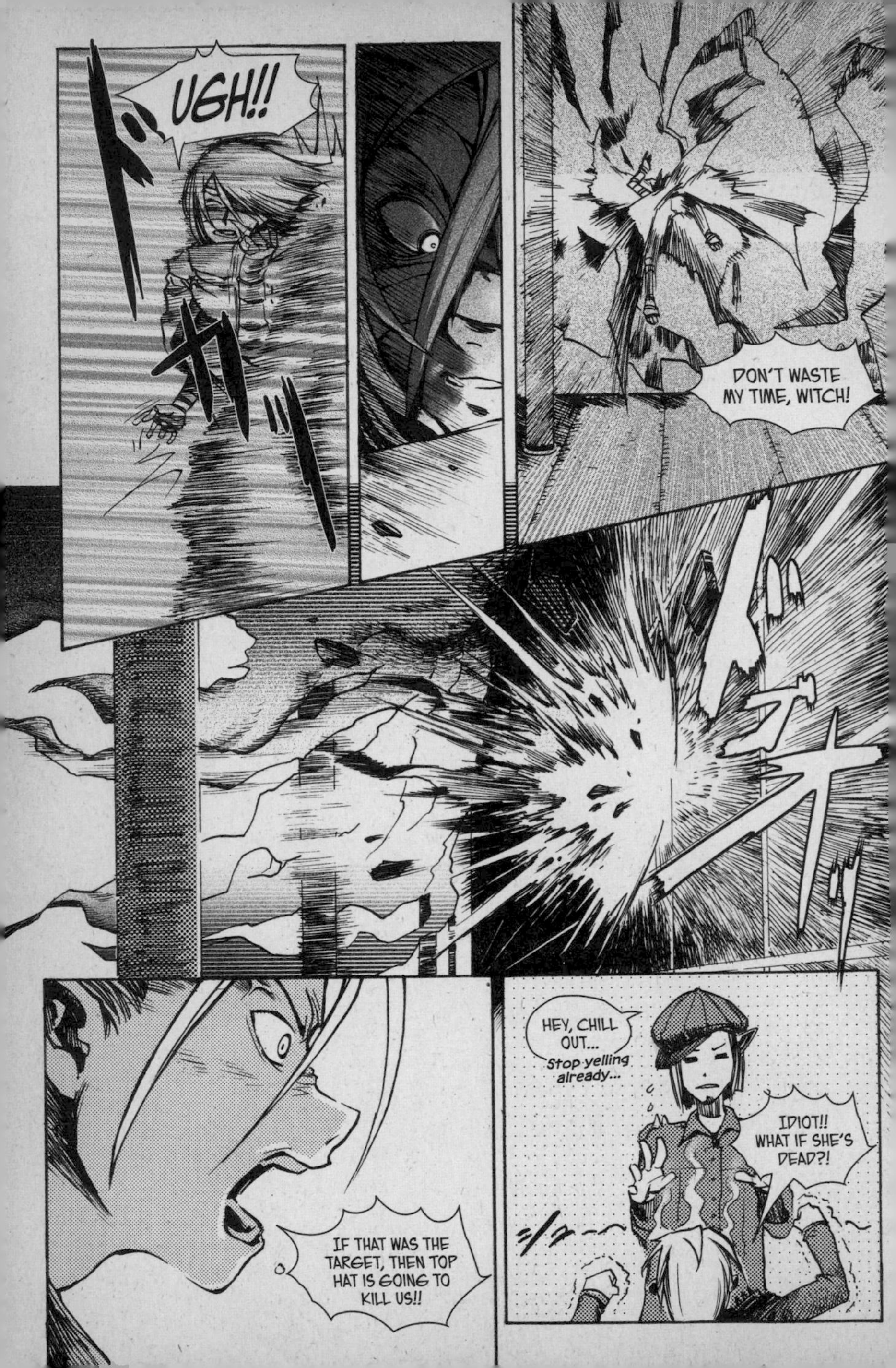
DON'T WASTE MY TIME, WITCH!
UGH!!
HEY, CHILL OUT...
Stop yelling already...
IDIOT!! WHAT IF SHE'S DEAD?!
IF THAT WAS THE TARGET, THEN TOP HAT IS GOING TO KILL US!!

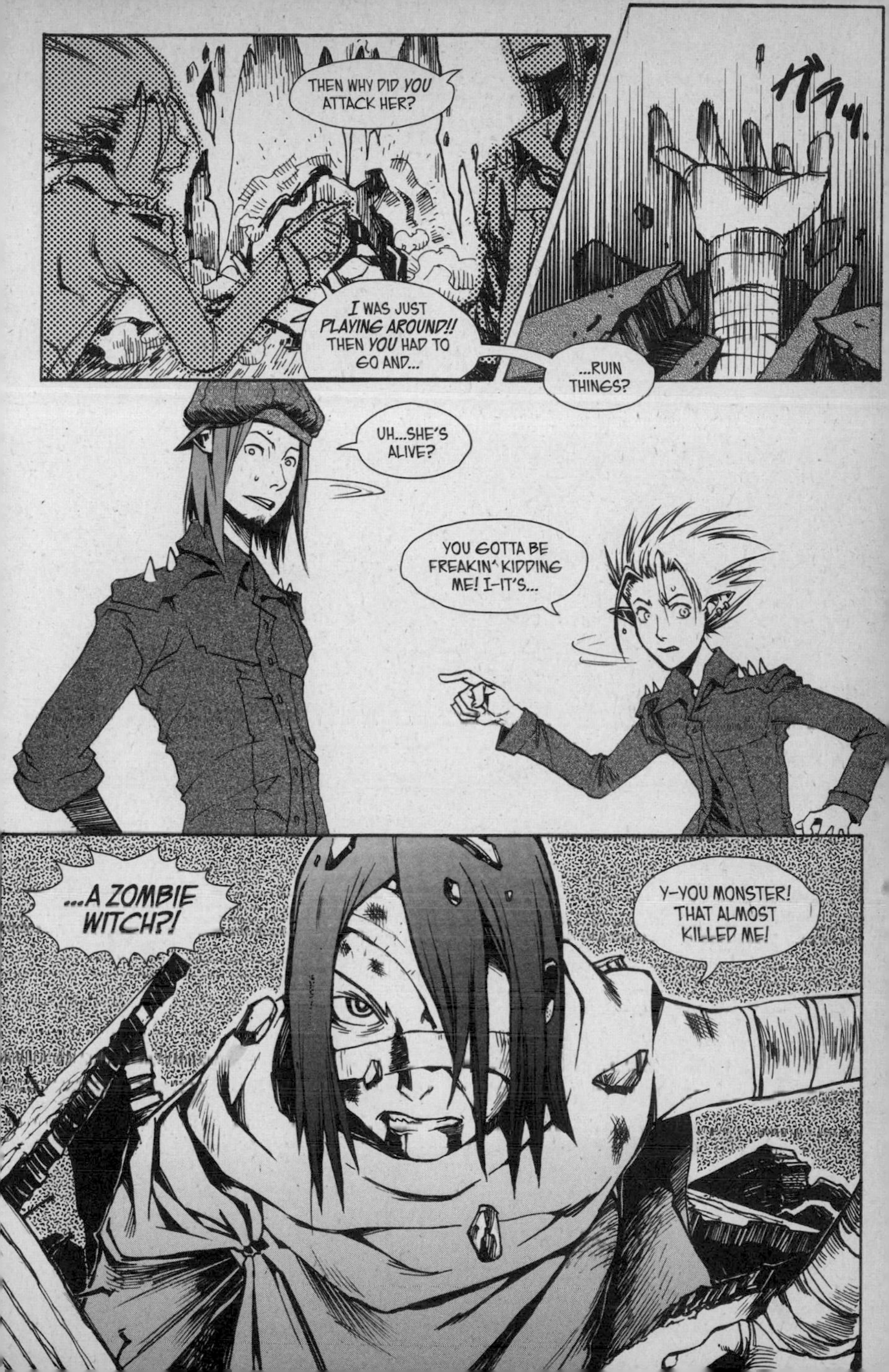
ガラッ
THEN WHY DID YOU ATTACK HER?
I WAS JUST PLAYING AROUND!! THEN YOU HAD TO GO AND...
...RUIN THINGS?
UH...SHE'S ALIVE?
YOU GOTTA BE FREAKIN' KIDDING ME! I-IT'S...
...A ZOMBIE WITCH?!
Y-YOU MONSTER! THAT ALMOST KILLED ME!

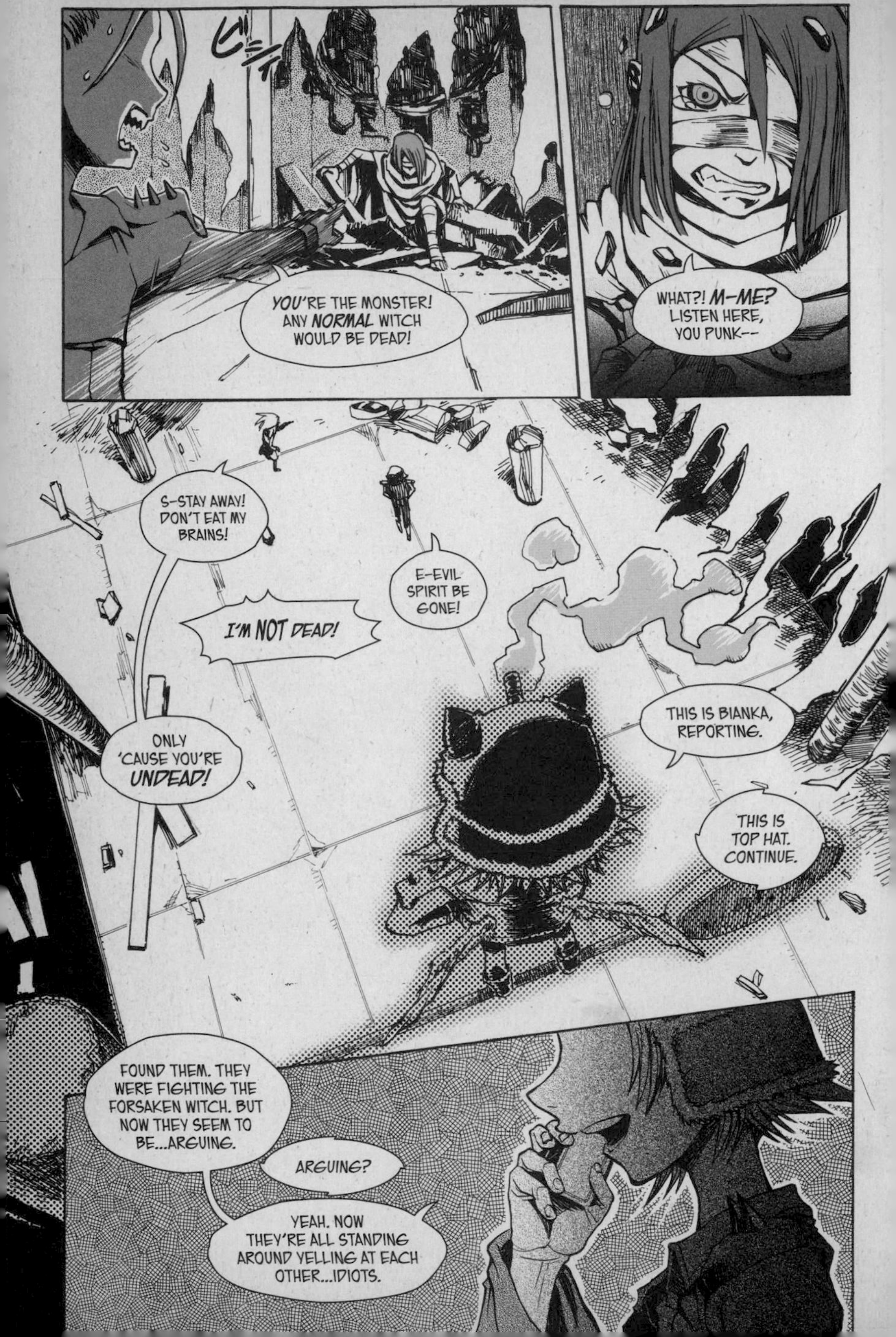

YOU'RE THE MONSTER! ANY NORMAL WITCH WOULD BE DEAD!
WHAT?! M-ME? LISTEN HERE, YOU PUNK--
S-STAY AWAY! DON'T EAT MY BRAINS!
E-EVIL SPIRIT BE GONE!
I'M NOT DEAD!
ONLY 'CAUSE YOU'RE UNDEAD!
THIS IS BIANKA, REPORTING.
THIS IS TOP HAT. CONTINUE.
FOUND THEM. THEY WERE FIGHTING THE FORSAKEN WITCH. BUT NOW THEY SEEM TO BE...ARGUING.
ARGUING?
YEAH. NOW THEY'RE ALL STANDING AROUND YELLING AT EACH OTHER...IDIOTS.

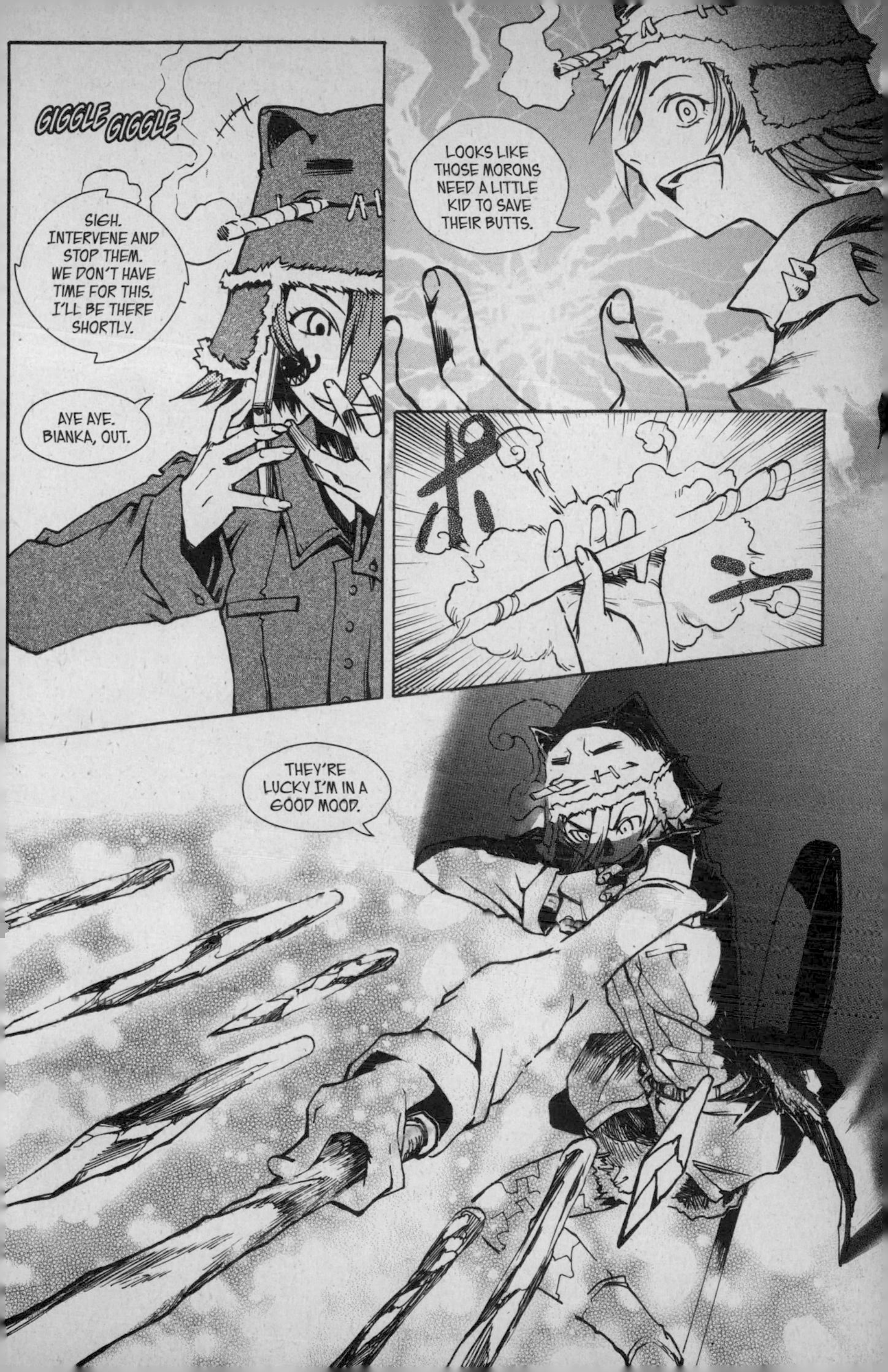
GIGGLE GIGGLE
SIGH. INTERVENE AND STOP THEM. WE DON'T HAVE TIME FOR THIS. I'LL BE THERE SHORTLY.
AYE AYE. BIANKA, OUT.
LOOKS LIKE THOSE MORONS NEED A LITTLE KID TO SAVE THEIR BUTTS.
THEY'RE LUCKY I'M IN A GOOD MOOD.

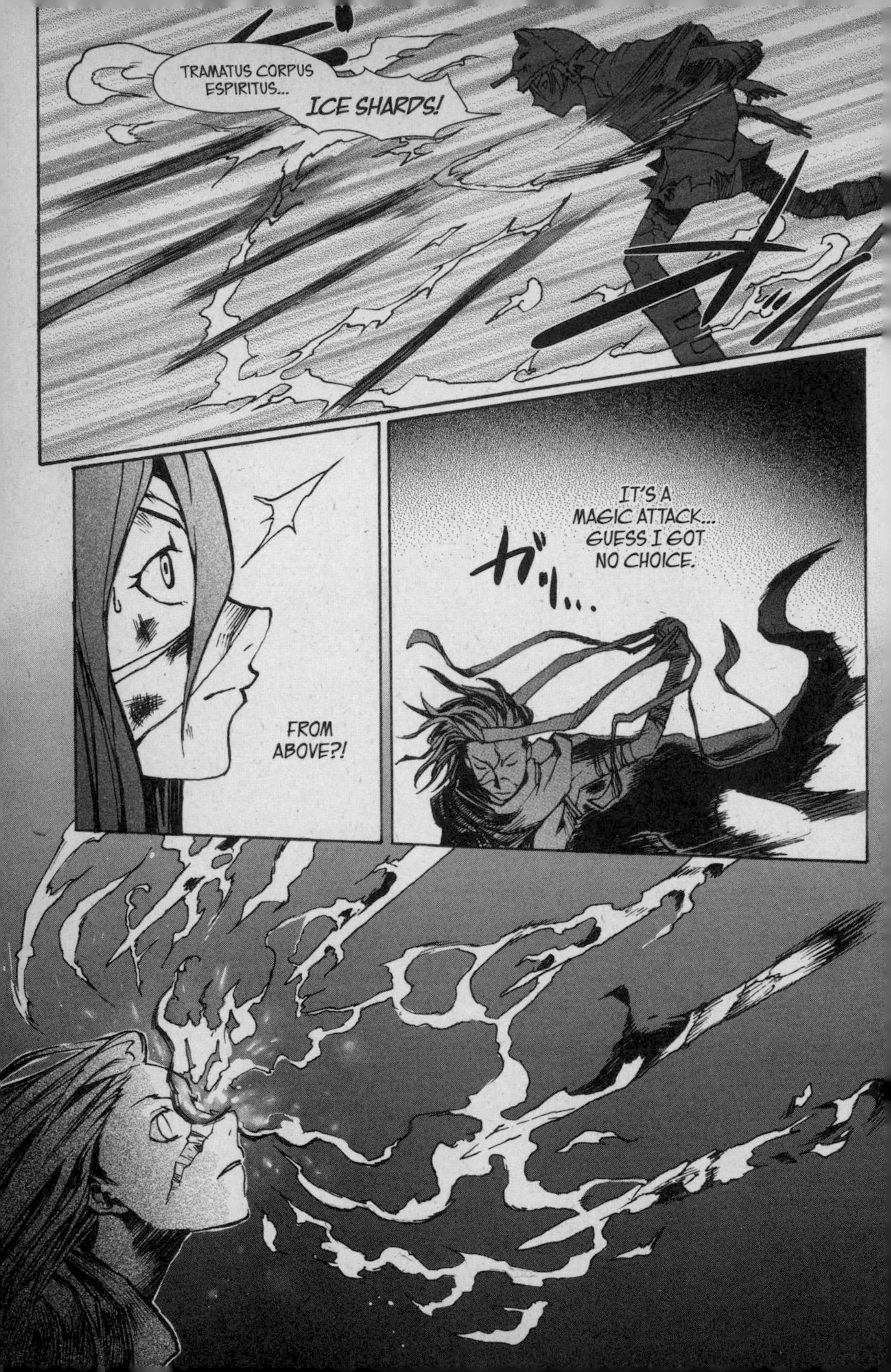
TRAMATUS CORPUS ESPIRITUS... ICE SHARDS!
IT'S A MAGIC ATTACK... GUESS I GOT NO CHOICE.
ガッ...
FROM ABOVE?!

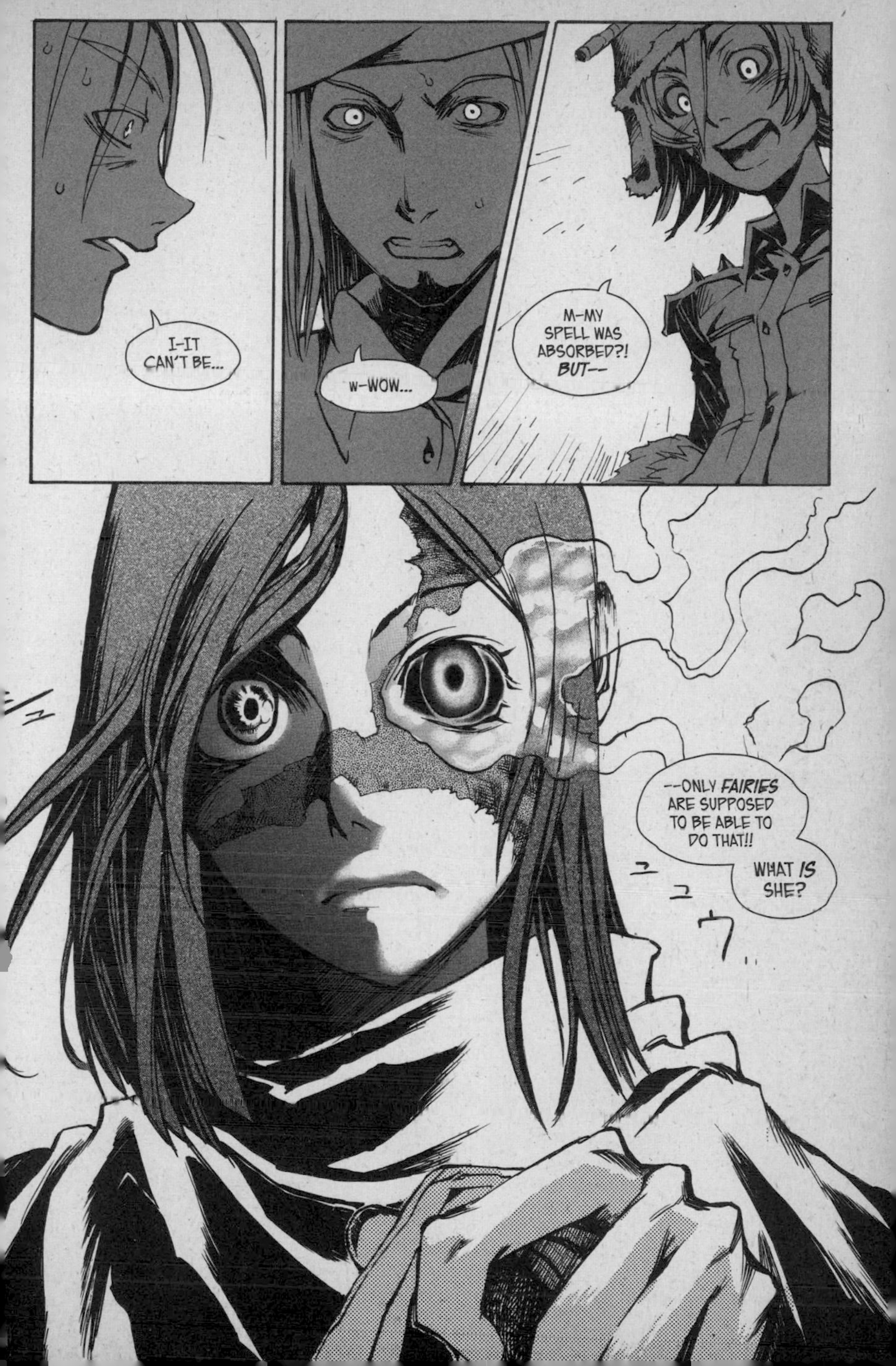
M-MY SPELL WAS ABSORBED?! BUT--
W-WOW...
I-IT CAN'T BE...
--ONLY FAIRIES ARE SUPPOSED TO BE ABLE TO DO THAT!!
WHAT IS SHE?

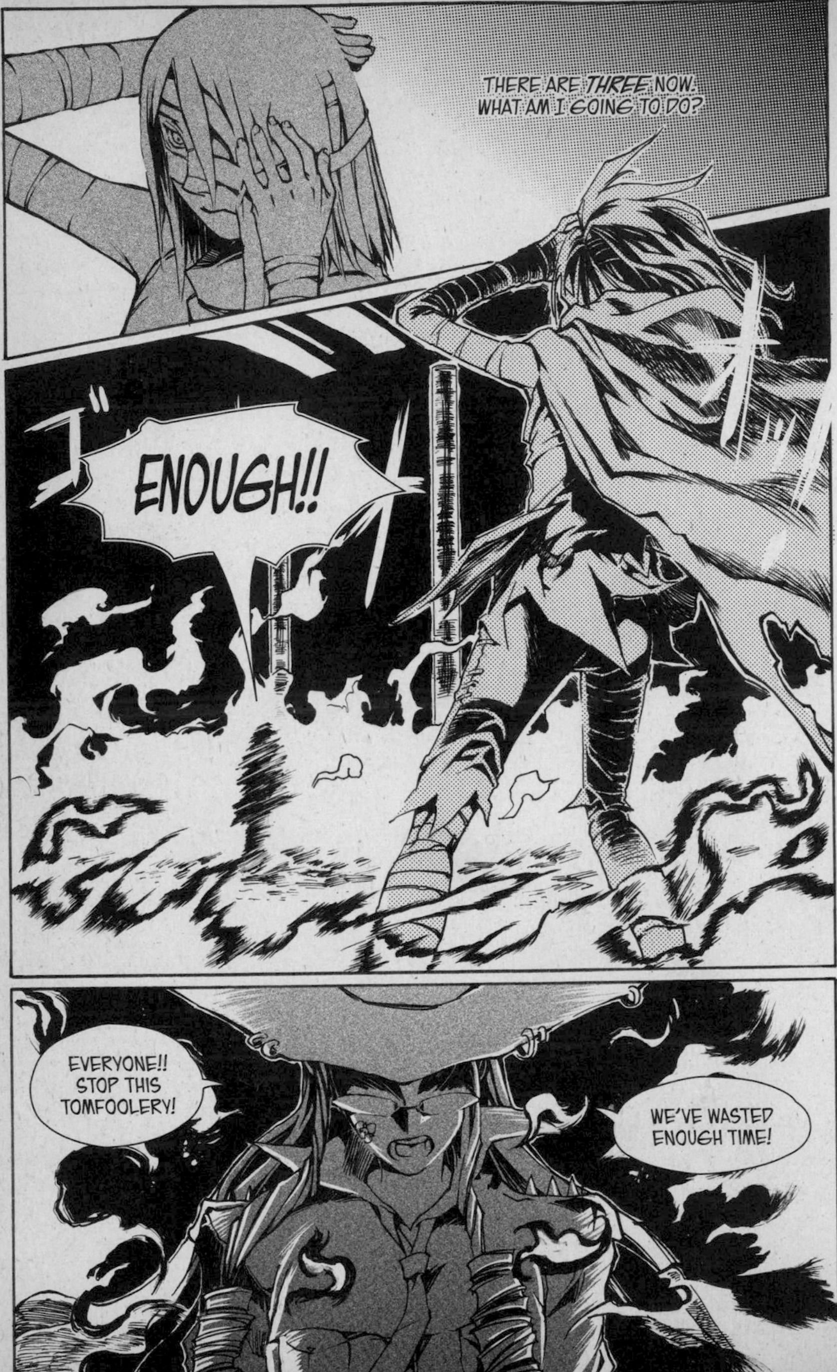
THERE ARE THREE NOW. WHAT AM I GOING TO DO?
ENOUGH!!
EVERYONE!! STOP THIS TOMFOOLERY!
WE'VE WASTED ENOUGH TIME!

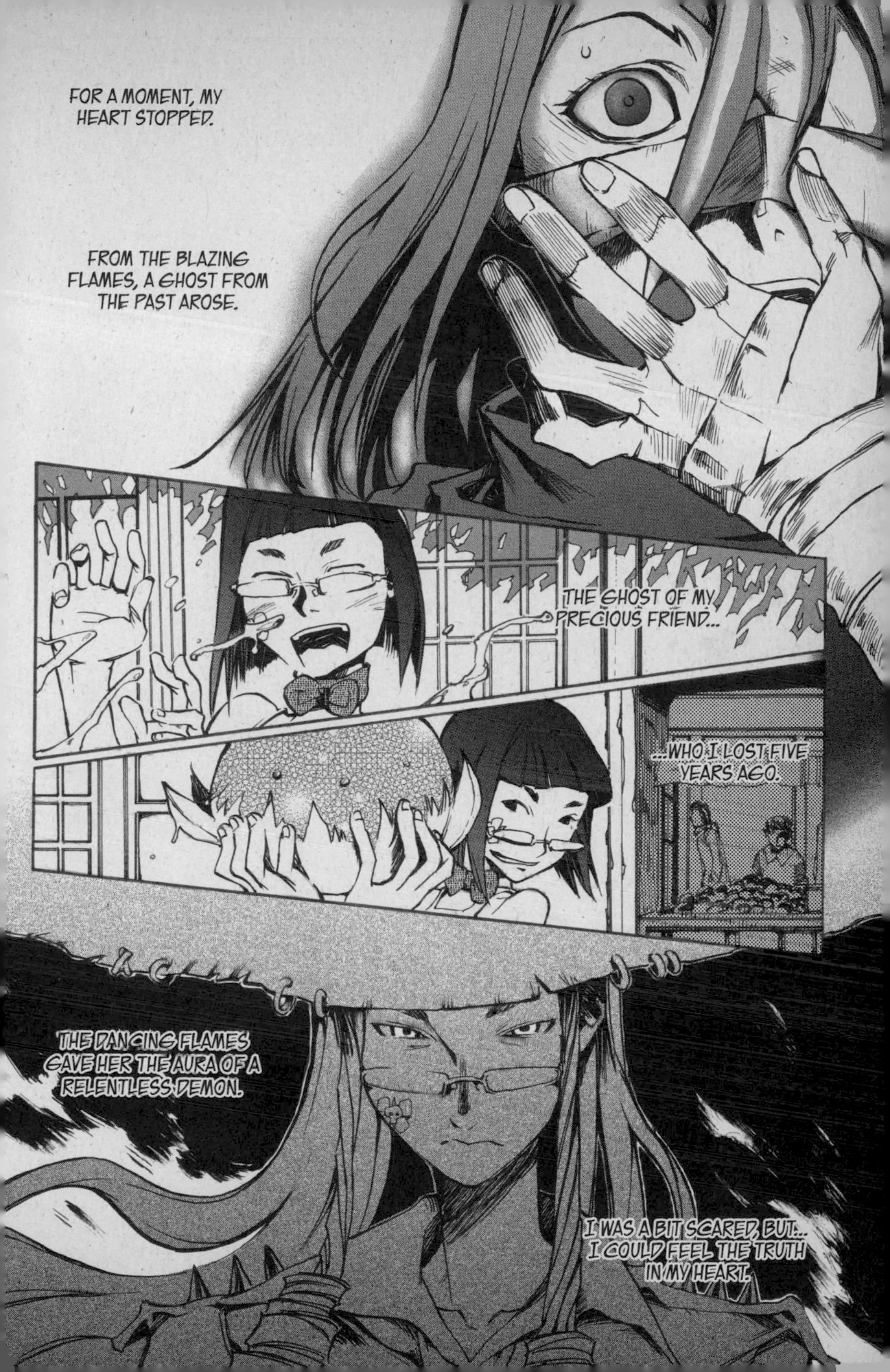
FOR A MOMENT, MY HEART STOPPED.
FROM THE BLAZING FLAMES, A GHOST FROM THE PAST AROSE.
THE GHOST OF MY PRECIOUS FRIEND...
...WHO I LOST FIVE YEARS AGO.
THE DANCING FLAMES GAVE HER THE AURA OF A RELENTLESS DEMON.
I WAS A BIT SCARED, BUT... I COULD FEEL THE TRUTH IN MY HEART.

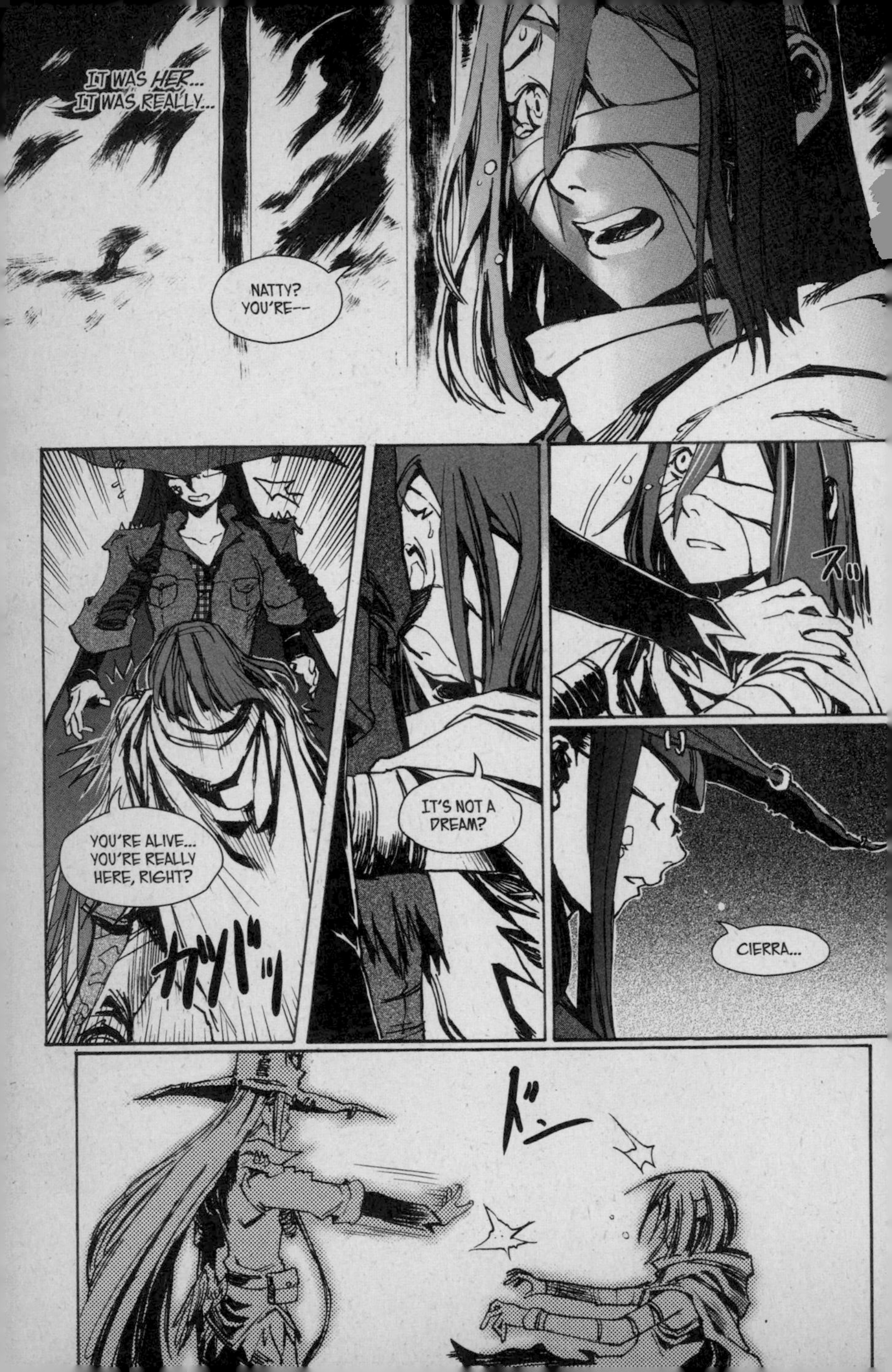
IT WAS HER...
IT WAS REALLY...
NATTY? YOU'RE--
CIERRA...
IT'S NOT A DREAM?
YOU'RE ALIVE... YOU'RE REALLY HERE, RIGHT?

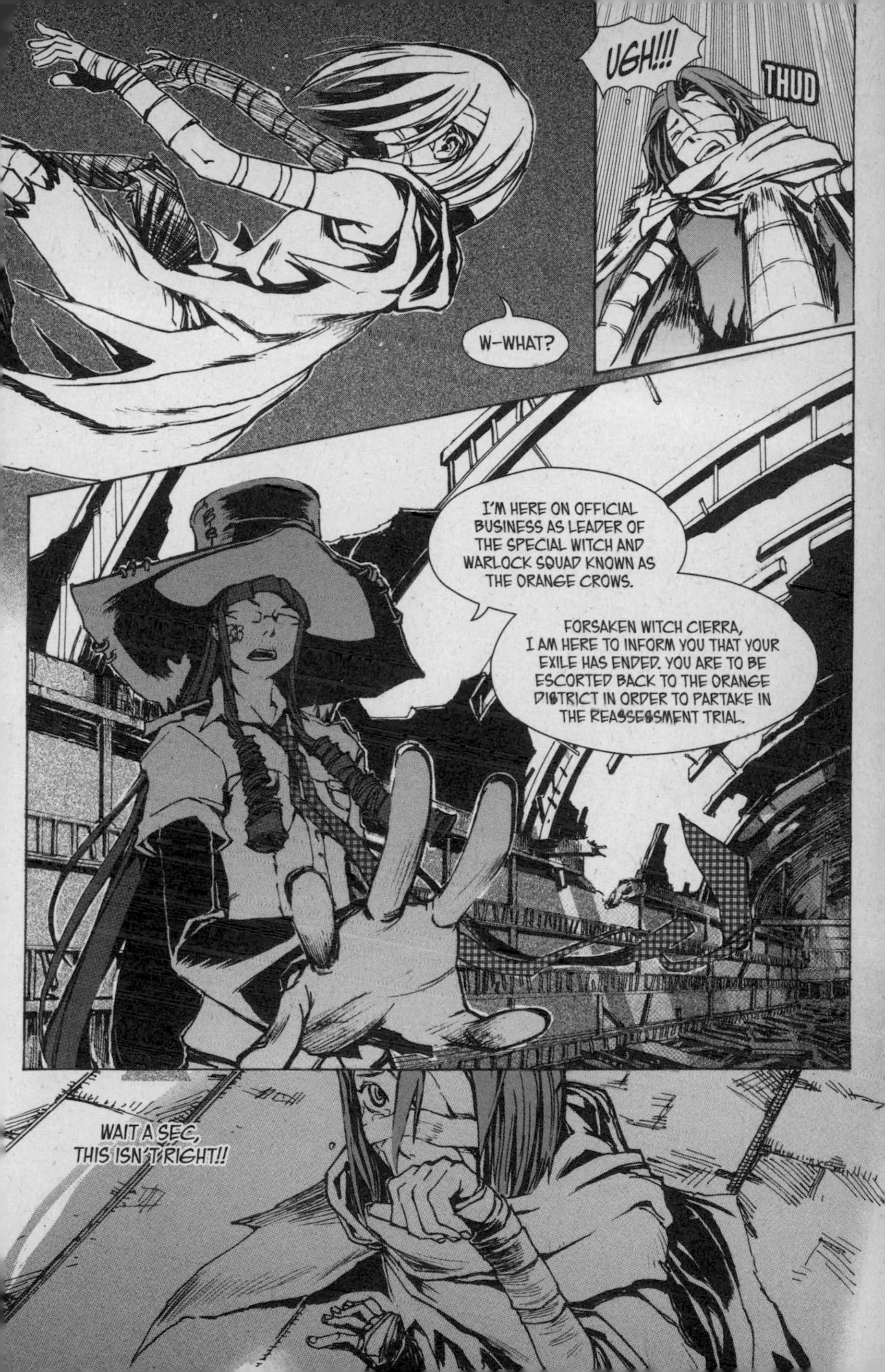
UGH!!!
THUD
W-WHAT?
I'M HERE ON OFFICIAL BUSINESS AS LEADER OF THE SPECIAL WITCH AND WARLOCK SQUAD KNOWN AS THE ORANGE CROWS.
FORSAKEN WITCH CIERRA, I AM HERE TO INFORM YOU THAT YOUR EXILE HAS ENDED. YOU ARE TO BE ESCORTED BACK TO THE ORANGE DISTRICT IN ORDER TO PARTAKE IN THE REASSESSMENT TRIAL.
WAIT A SEC, THIS ISN'T RIGHT!!

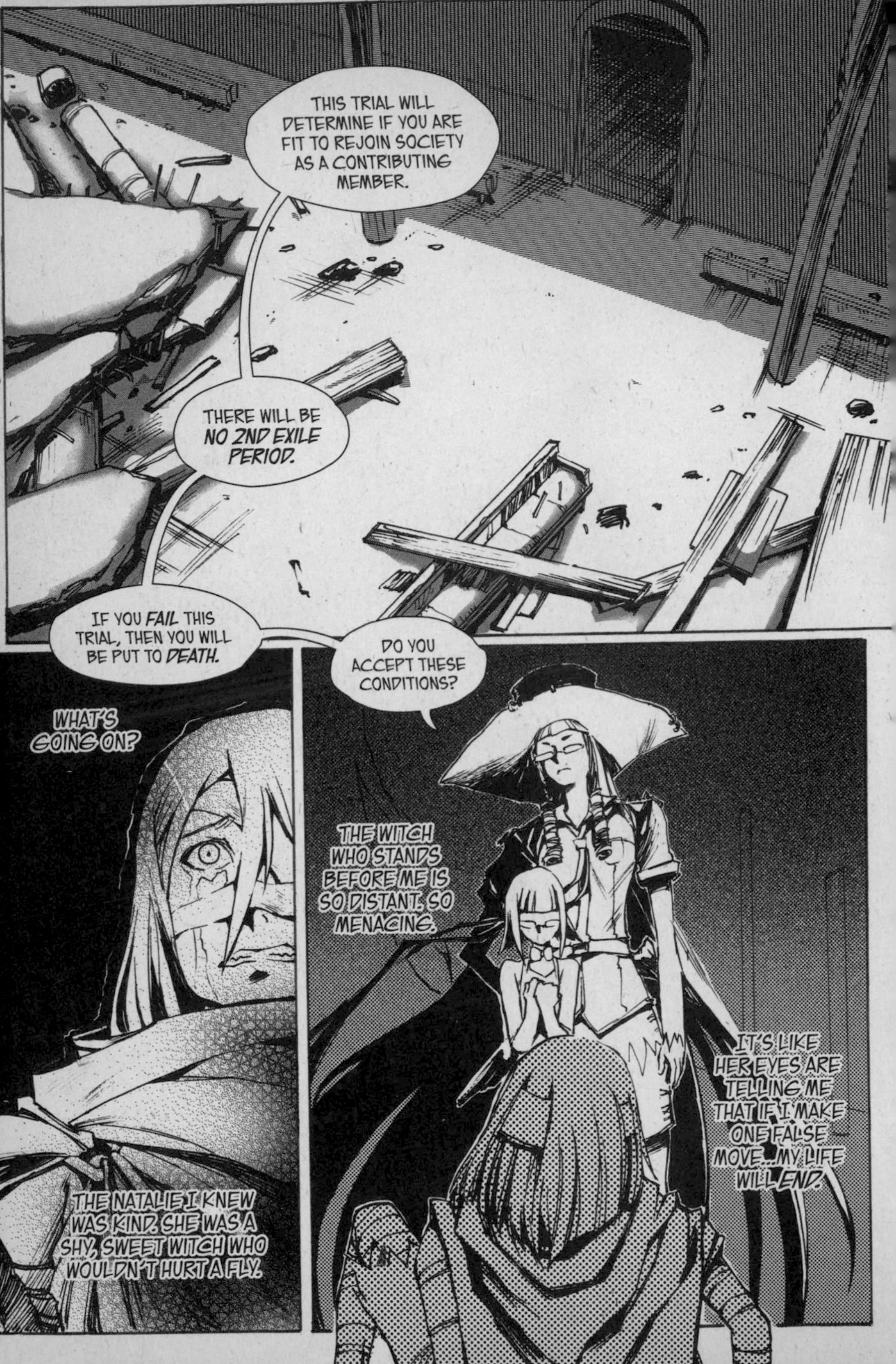
THIS TRIAL WILL DETERMINE IF YOU ARE FIT TO REJOIN SOCIETY AS A CONTRIBUTING MEMBER.
THERE WILL BE NO 2ND EXILE PERIOD.
IF YOU FAIL THIS TRIAL, THEN YOU WILL BE PUT TO DEATH.
DO YOU ACCEPT THESE CONDITIONS?
WHAT'S GOING ON?
THE NATALIE I KNEW WAS KIND. SHE WAS A SHY, SWEET WITCH WHO WOULDN'T HURT A FLY.
THE WITCH WHO STANDS BEFORE ME IS SO DISTANT. SO MENACING.
IT'S LIKE HER EYES ARE TELLING ME THAT IF I MAKE ONE FALSE MOVE...MY LIFE WILL END.

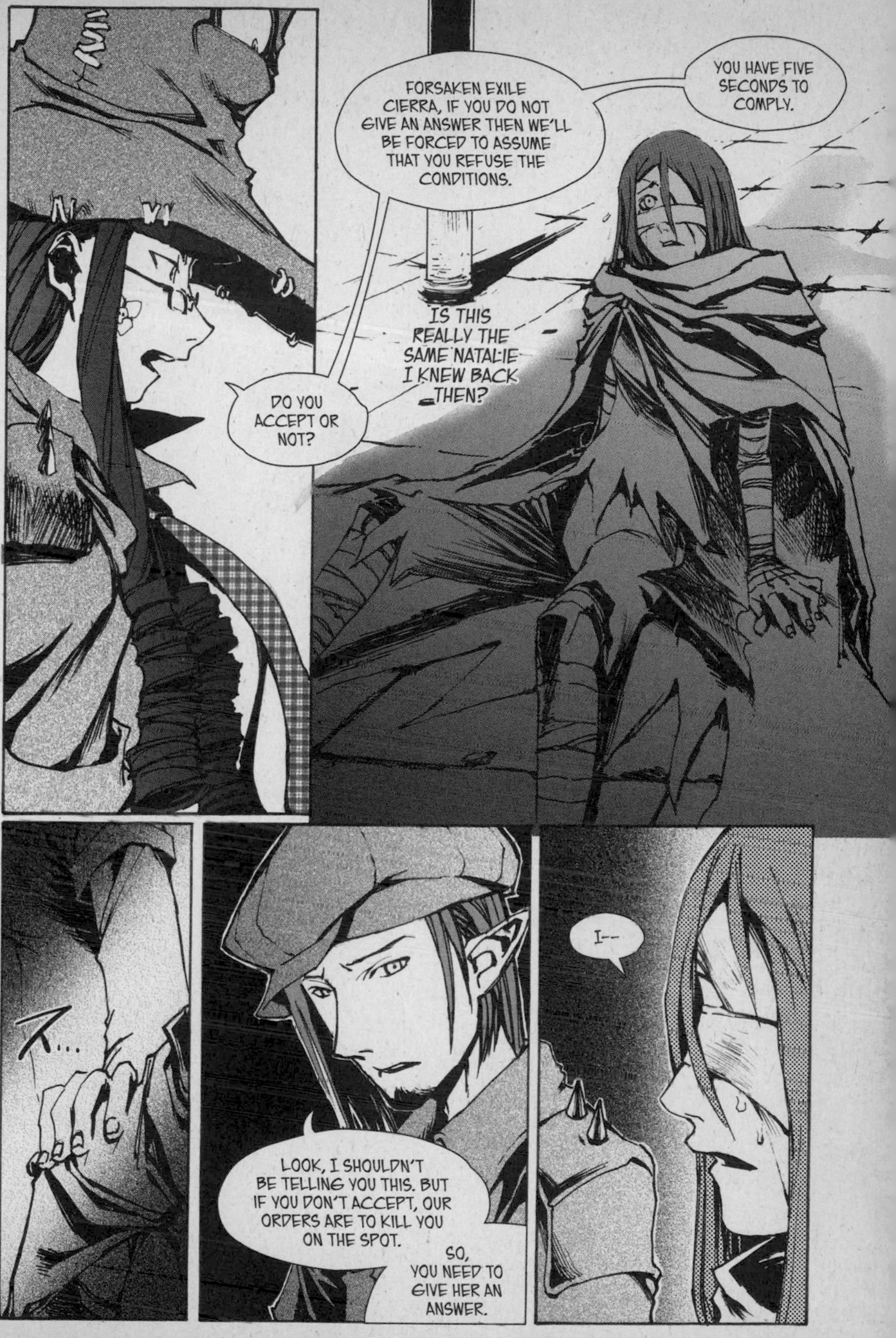
FORSAKEN EXILE CIERRA, IF YOU DO NOT GIVE AN ANSWER THEN WE'LL BE FORCED TO ASSUME THAT YOU REFUSE THE CONDITIONS.
YOU HAVE FIVE SECONDS TO COMPLY.
IS THIS REALLY THE SAME NATALIE I KNEW BACK THEN?
DO YOU ACCEPT OR NOT?
I--
LOOK, I SHOULDN'T BE TELLING YOU THIS. BUT IF YOU DON'T ACCEPT, OUR ORDERS ARE TO KILL YOU ON THE SPOT.
SO, YOU NEED TO GIVE HER AN ANSWER.

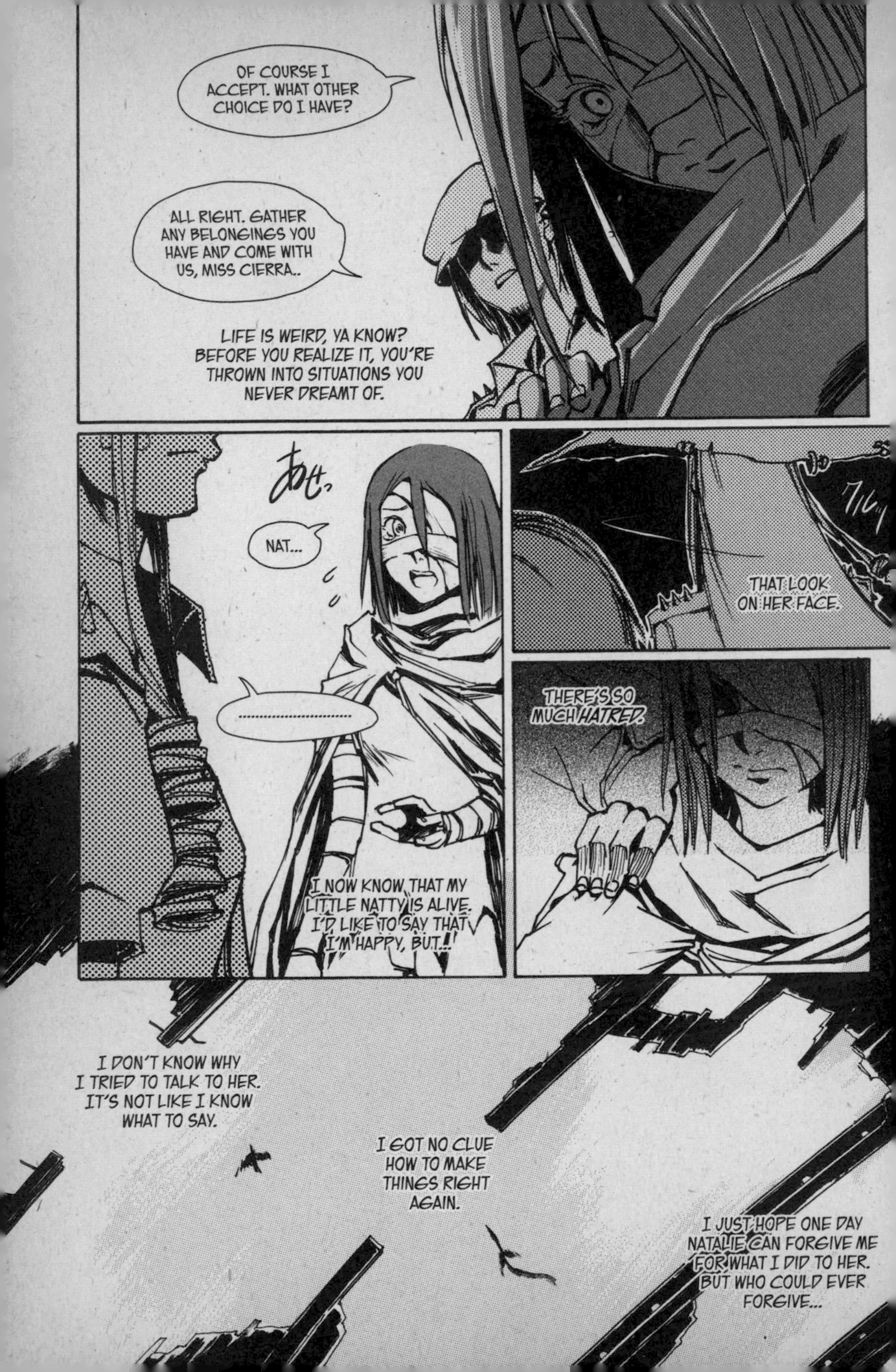
OF COURSE I ACCEPT. WHAT OTHER CHOICE DO I HAVE?
ALL RIGHT. GATHER ANY BELONGINGS YOU HAVE AND COME WITH US, MISS CIERRA..
LIFE IS WEIRD, YA KNOW? BEFORE YOU REALIZE IT, YOU'RE THROWN INTO SITUATIONS YOU NEVER DREAMT OF.
THAT LOOK ON HER FACE.
THERE'S SO MUCH HATRED.
あせっ
NAT...
....
I NOW KNOW THAT MY LITTLE NATTY IS ALIVE. I'D LIKE TO SAY THAT I'M HAPPY, BUT...
I DON'T KNOW WHY I TRIED TO TALK TO HER. IT'S NOT LIKE I KNOW WHAT TO SAY.
I GOT NO CLUE HOW TO MAKE THINGS RIGHT AGAIN.
I JUST HOPE ONE DAY NATALIE CAN FORGIVE ME FOR WHAT I DID TO HER. BUT WHO COULD EVER FORGIVE...

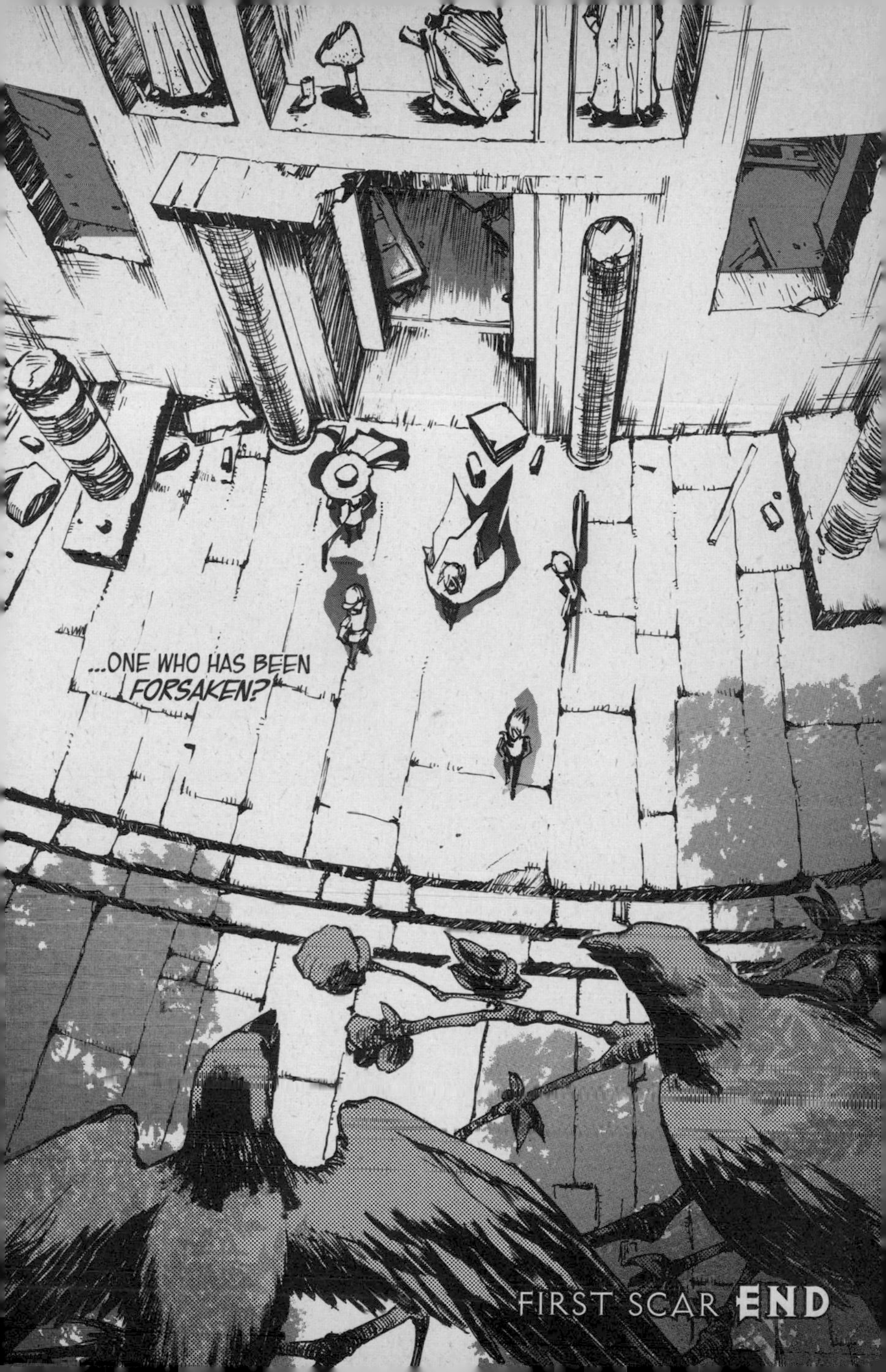
...ONE WHO HAS BEEN FORSAKEN?
FIRST SCAR END

QUEEN BIANKA'S CRASH COURSE

CHAPTER ONE: S.W.S.

FIRST UP I'M GOING TO TEACH YOU ABOUT THE SPECIAL WITCH AND WARLOCK SQUADRON, USUALLY CALLED THE S.W.S. THESE ARE ELITE WITCHES AND WARLOCKS WHO TAKE CARE OF SPECIAL MISSIONS OUTSIDE OF THE DISTRICT. NOT JUST ANYONE CAN DO THIS! WE'RE THE CREAM OF THE CROP! LOW CLASS'VE HEARD OF US, BUT RARELY GET TA SEE US. SO I'M NOT SURPRISED THAT CIERRA DIDN'T REALIZE WHO SHE WAS FIGHTIN'. WE USUALLY DEAL WITH THE HIGH CLASS BY ORDER OF THE DISTRICT MAYOR.

MISSION LIST

1. PROTECTING THE DISTRICT FROM FAIRIES

2. ESCORTING IMPORTANT AIRSHIPS

3. DELIVERING IMPORTANT INFO INBETWEEN DISTRICTS

4. MORE THAT I WON'T MENTION NOW

BUT IT'S ALL PRETTY BORING IF YA ASK ME. I SIGNED ON TA BLOW STUFF UP! SOMETIMES WE COME ACROSS A FORSAKEN OR TWO WHO CAN ACTUALLY PUT UP A FIGHT. AND WHENEVER WE DO GET IN A PINCH, QUEEN BIANKA IS THE ONE TA SAVE THE DAY!

IF YA EVER NEED A HAND, CALL ON THE QUEEN!

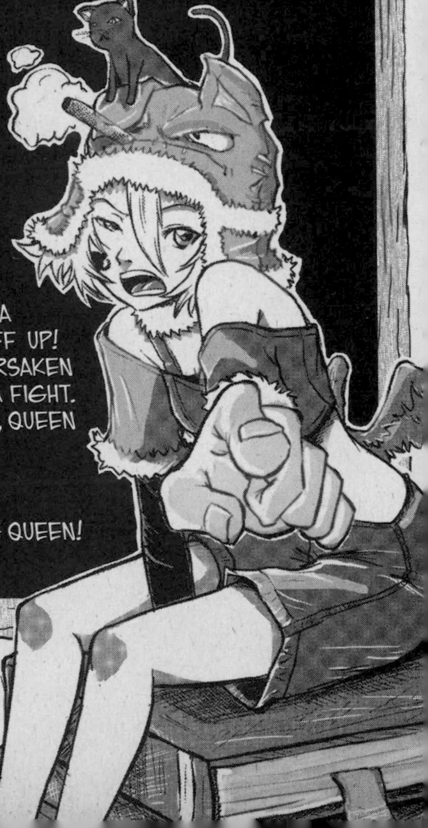
LISTEN UP! TIME FOR THE FIRST INSTALLMENT OF Q.B.C.C.!

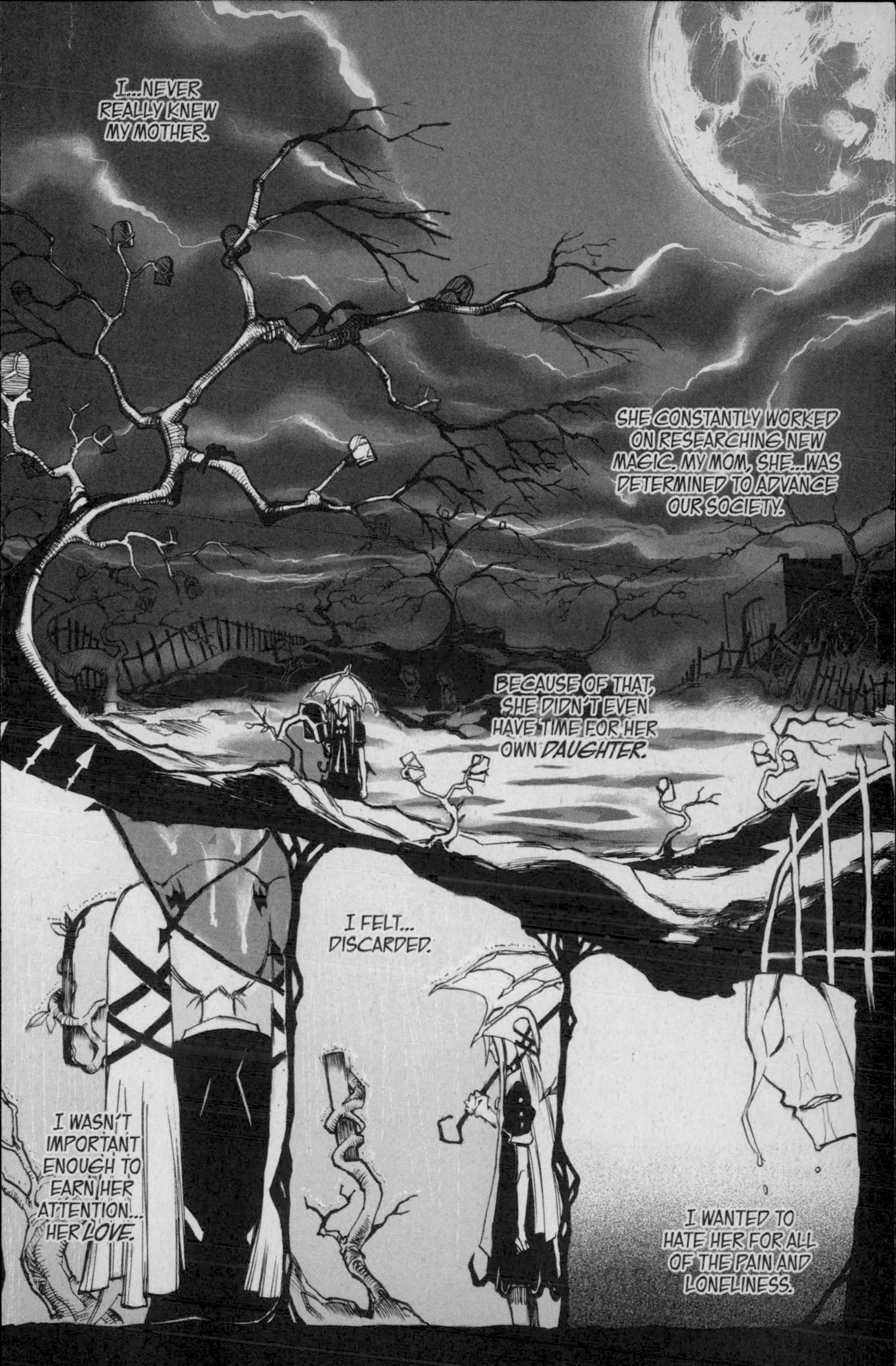
I...NEVER REALLY KNEW MY MOTHER.
SHE CONSTANTLY WORKED ON RESEARCHING NEW MAGIC. MY MOM, SHE...WAS DETERMINED TO ADVANCE OUR SOCIETY.
BECAUSE OF THAT, SHE DIDN'T EVEN HAVE TIME FOR HER OWN DAUGHTER.
I FELT... DISCARDED.
I WASN'T IMPORTANT ENOUGH TO EARN HER ATTENTION... HER LOVE.
I WANTED TO HATE HER FOR ALL OF THE PAIN AND LONELINESS.

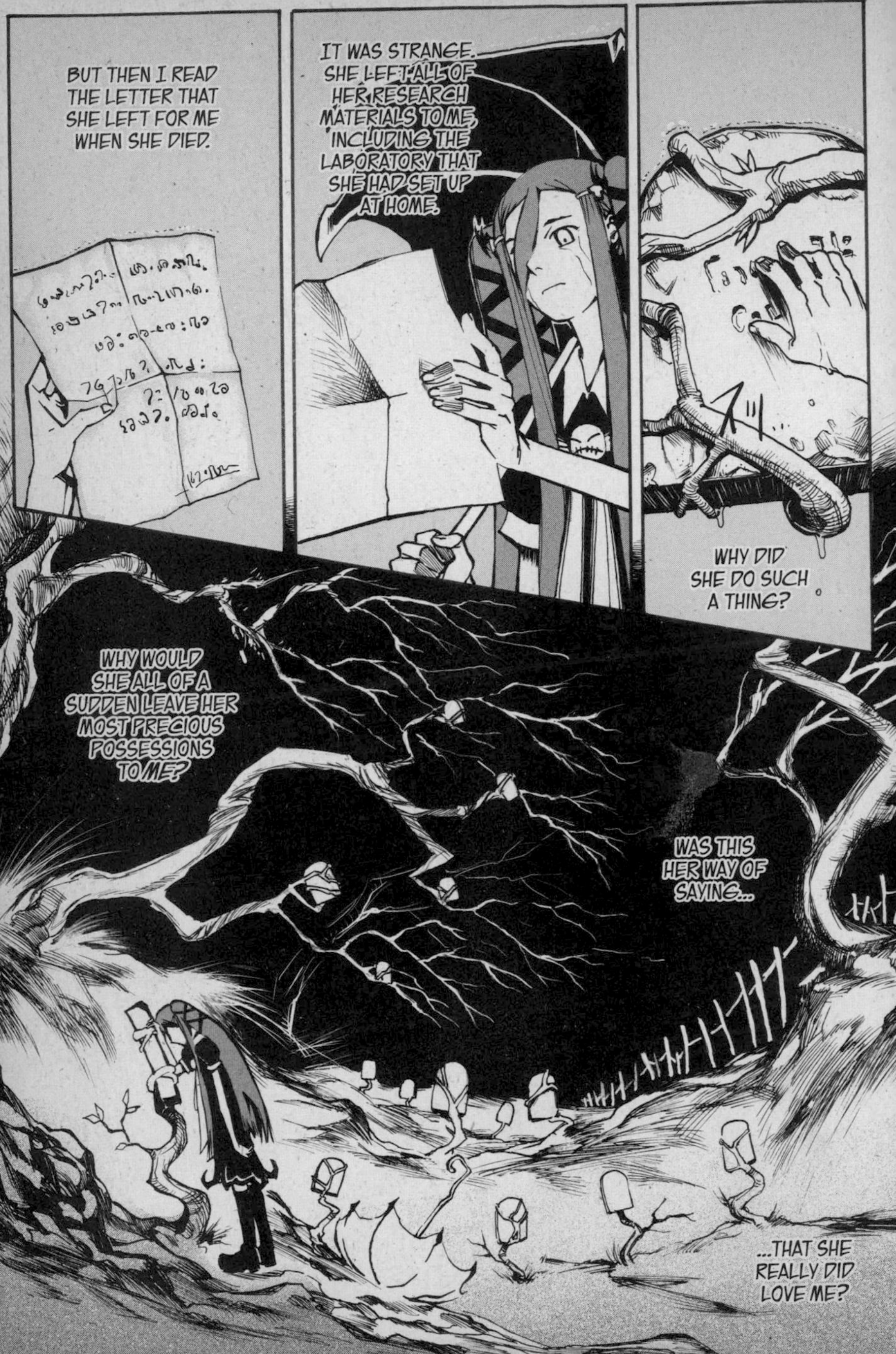
BUT THEN I READ THE LETTER THAT SHE LEFT FOR ME WHEN SHE DIED.
IT WAS STRANGE. SHE LEFT ALL OF HER RESEARCH MATERIALS TO ME, INCLUDING THE LABORATORY THAT SHE HAD SET UP AT HOME.
WHY DID SHE DO SUCH A THING?
WHY WOULD SHE ALL OF A SUDDEN LEAVE HER MOST PRECIOUS POSSESSIONS TO ME?
WAS THIS HER WAY OF SAYING...
...THAT SHE REALLY DID LOVE ME?

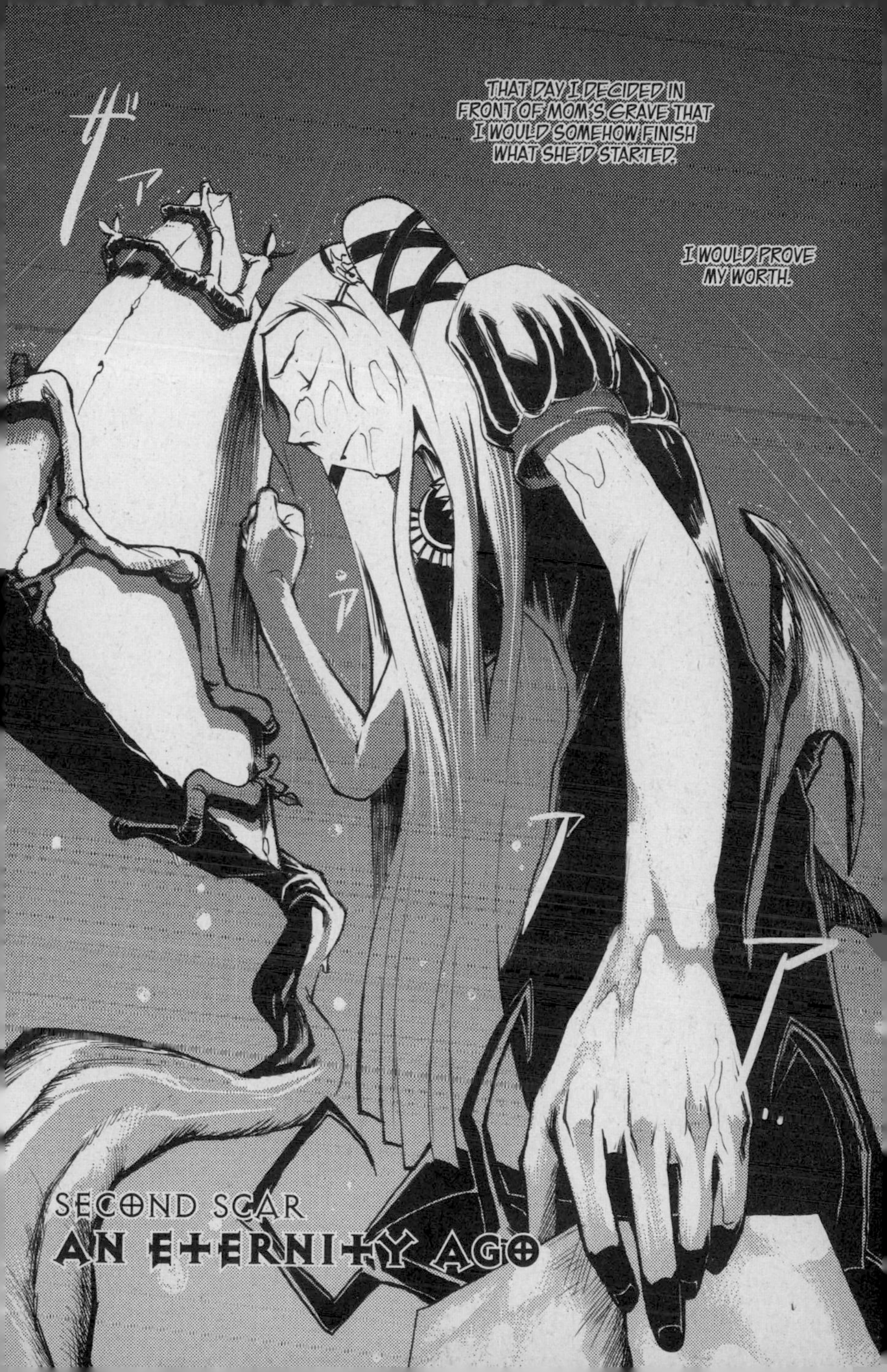
THAT DAY I DECIDED IN FRONT OF MOM'S GRAVE THAT I WOULD SOMEHOW FINISH WHAT SHE'D STARTED.
I WOULD PROVE MY WORTH.
SECOND SCAR
AN ETERNITY AGO

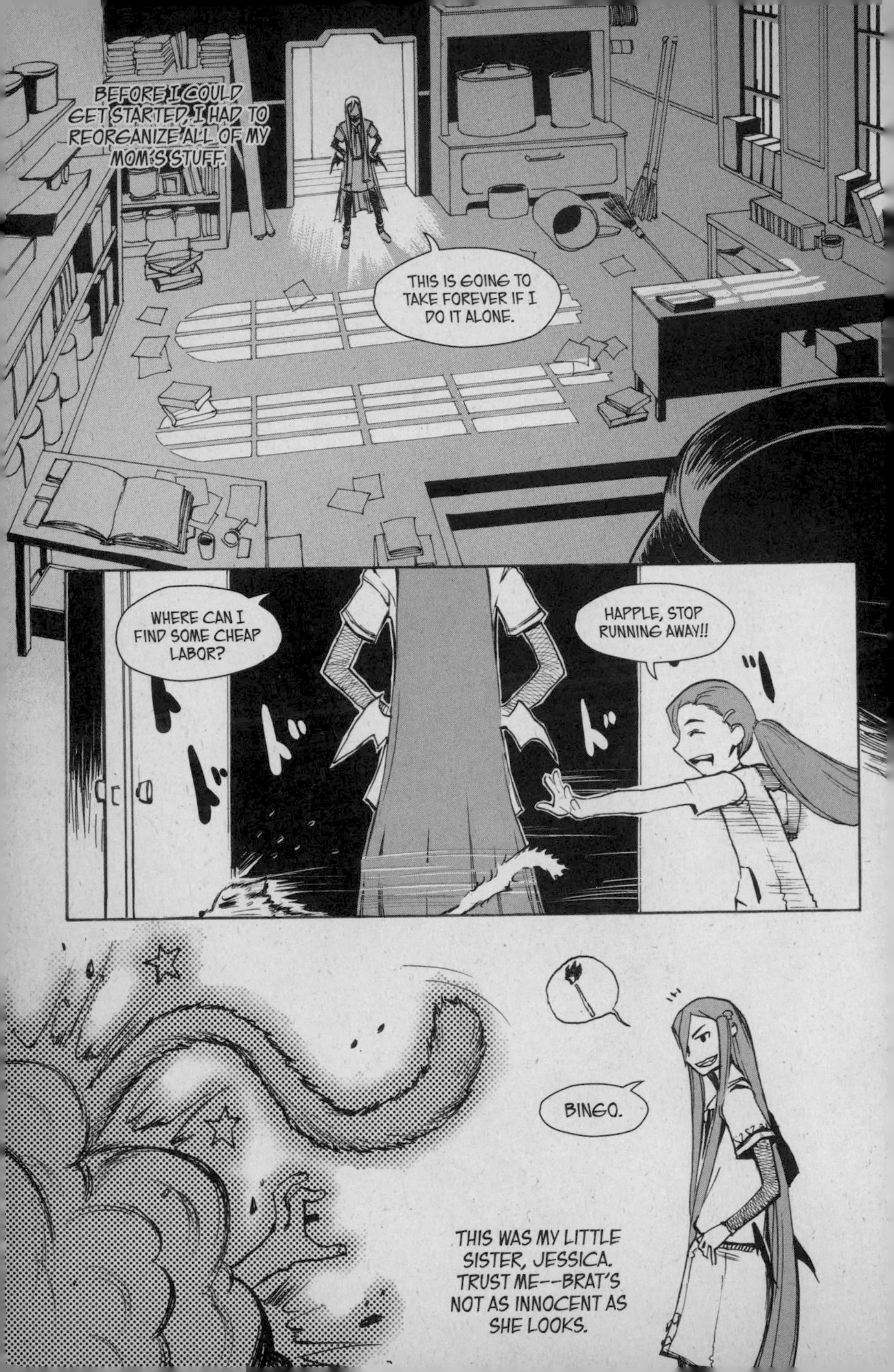
BEFORE I COULD GET STARTED, I HAD TO REORGANIZE ALL OF MY MOM'S STUFF.
THIS IS GOING TO TAKE FOREVER IF I DO IT ALONE.
WHERE CAN I FIND SOME CHEAP LABOR?
HAPPLE, STOP RUNNING AWAY!!
BINGO.
THIS WAS MY LITTLE SISTER, JESSICA. TRUST ME--BRAT'S NOT AS INNOCENT AS SHE LOOKS.

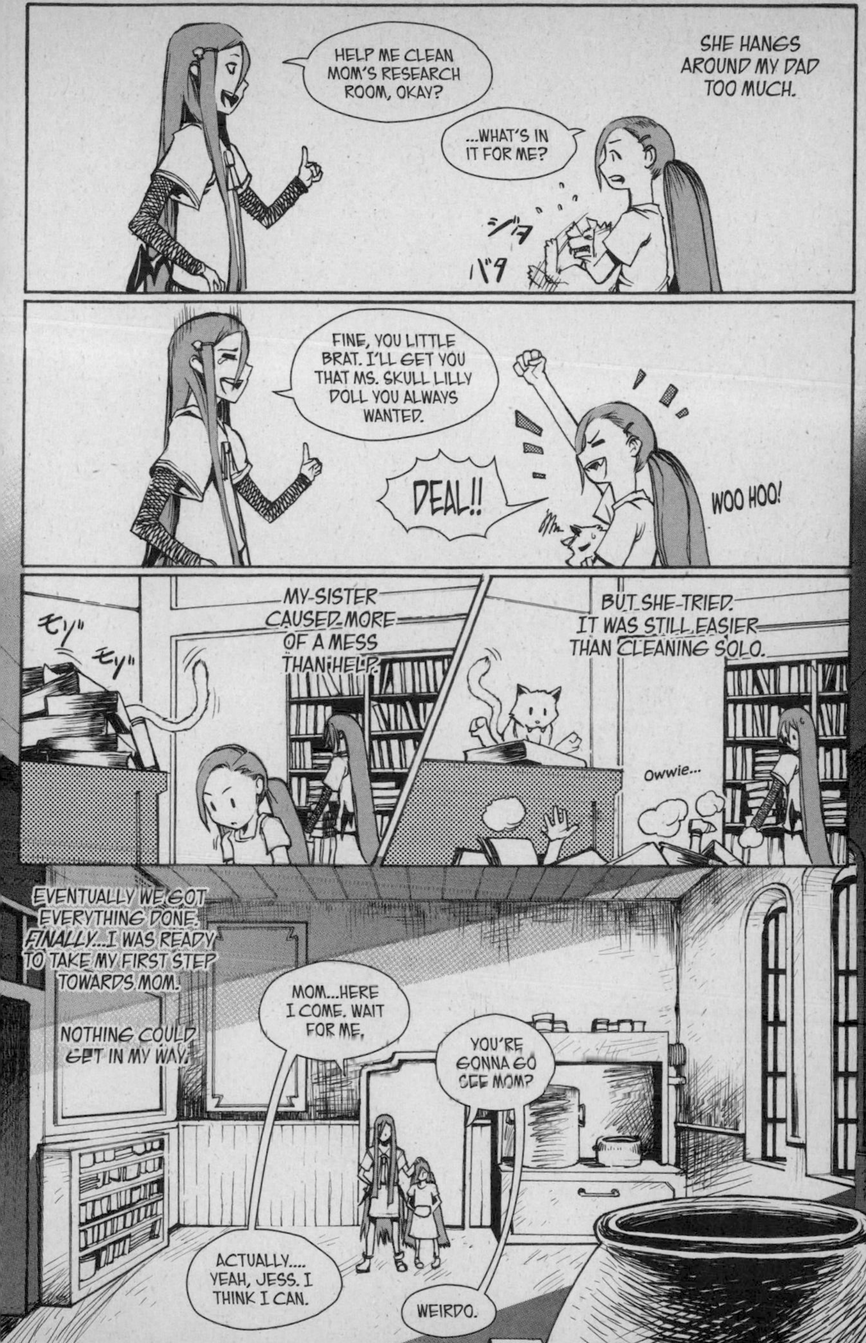
HELP ME CLEAN MOM'S RESEARCH ROOM, OKAY?
SHE HANGS AROUND MY DAD TOO MUCH.
...WHAT'S IN IT FOR ME?
ジタ
バタ
FINE, YOU LITTLE BRAT. I'LL GET YOU THAT MS. SKULL LILLY DOLL YOU ALWAYS WANTED.
DEAL!!
WOO HOO!
モゾ
モゾ
MY SISTER CAUSED MORE OF A MESS THAN HELP.
BUT SHE TRIED. IT WAS STILL EASIER THAN CLEANING SOLO.
Owwie...
EVENTUALLY WE GOT EVERYTHING DONE. FINALLY...I WAS READY TO TAKE MY FIRST STEP TOWARDS MOM.
NOTHING COULD GET IN MY WAY.
MOM...HERE I COME. WAIT FOR ME.
YOU'RE GONNA GO SEE MOM?
ACTUALLY.... YEAH, JESS. I THINK I CAN.
WEIRDO.

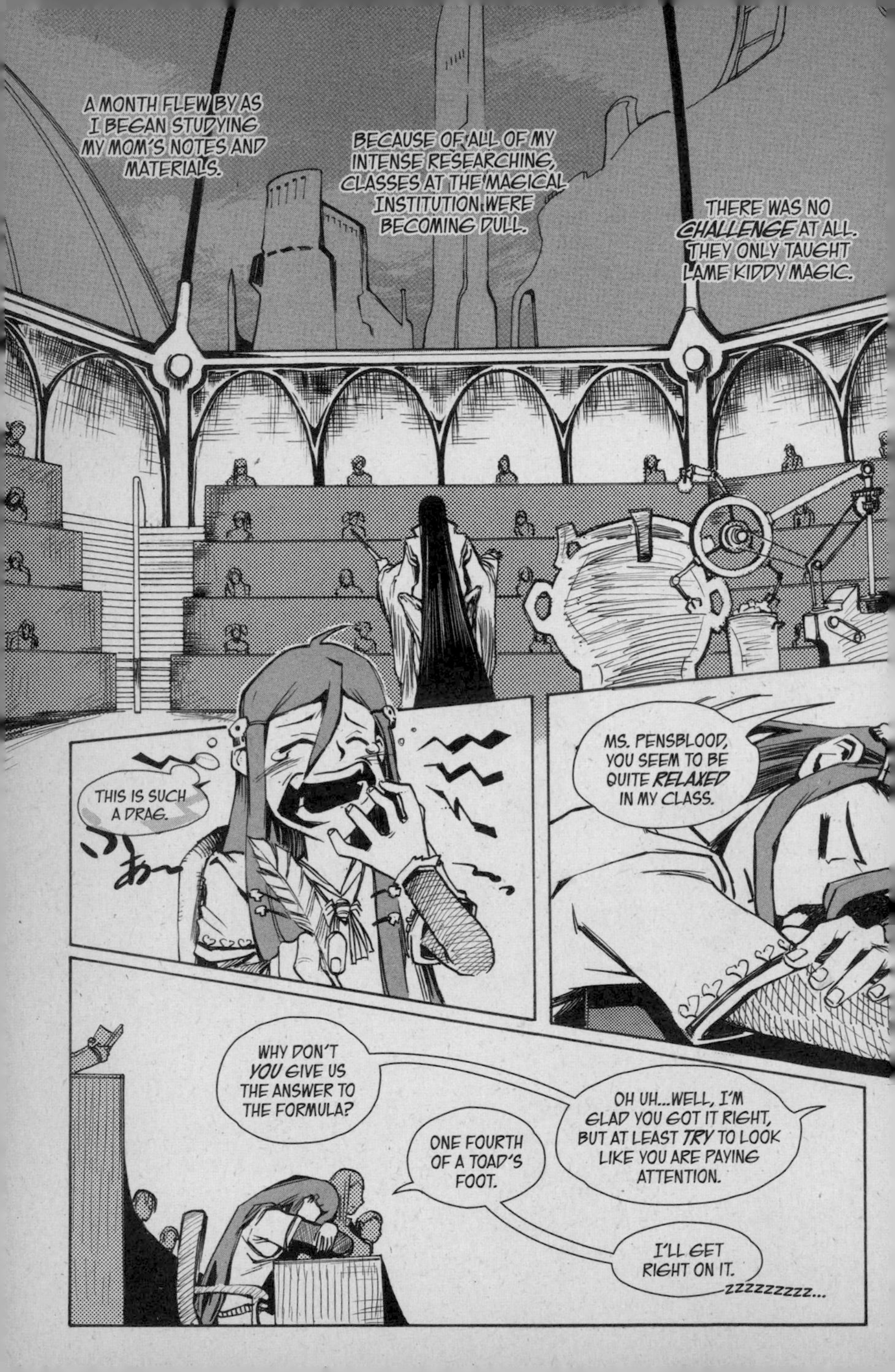
A MONTH FLEW BY AS I BEGAN STUDYING MY MOM'S NOTES AND MATERIALS.
BECAUSE OF ALL OF MY INTENSE RESEARCHING, CLASSES AT THE MAGICAL INSTITUTION WERE BECOMING DULL.
THERE WAS NO *CHALLENGE* AT ALL. THEY ONLY TAUGHT LAME KIDDY MAGIC.
THIS IS SUCH A DRAG.
ふあ～
MS. PENSBLOOD, YOU SEEM TO BE QUITE *RELAXED* IN MY CLASS.
WHY DON'T *YOU* GIVE US THE ANSWER TO THE FORMULA?
ONE FOURTH OF A TOAD'S FOOT.
OH UH...WELL, I'M GLAD YOU GOT IT RIGHT, BUT AT LEAST *TRY* TO LOOK LIKE YOU ARE PAYING ATTENTION.
I'LL GET RIGHT ON IT.
ZZZZZZZZZ...

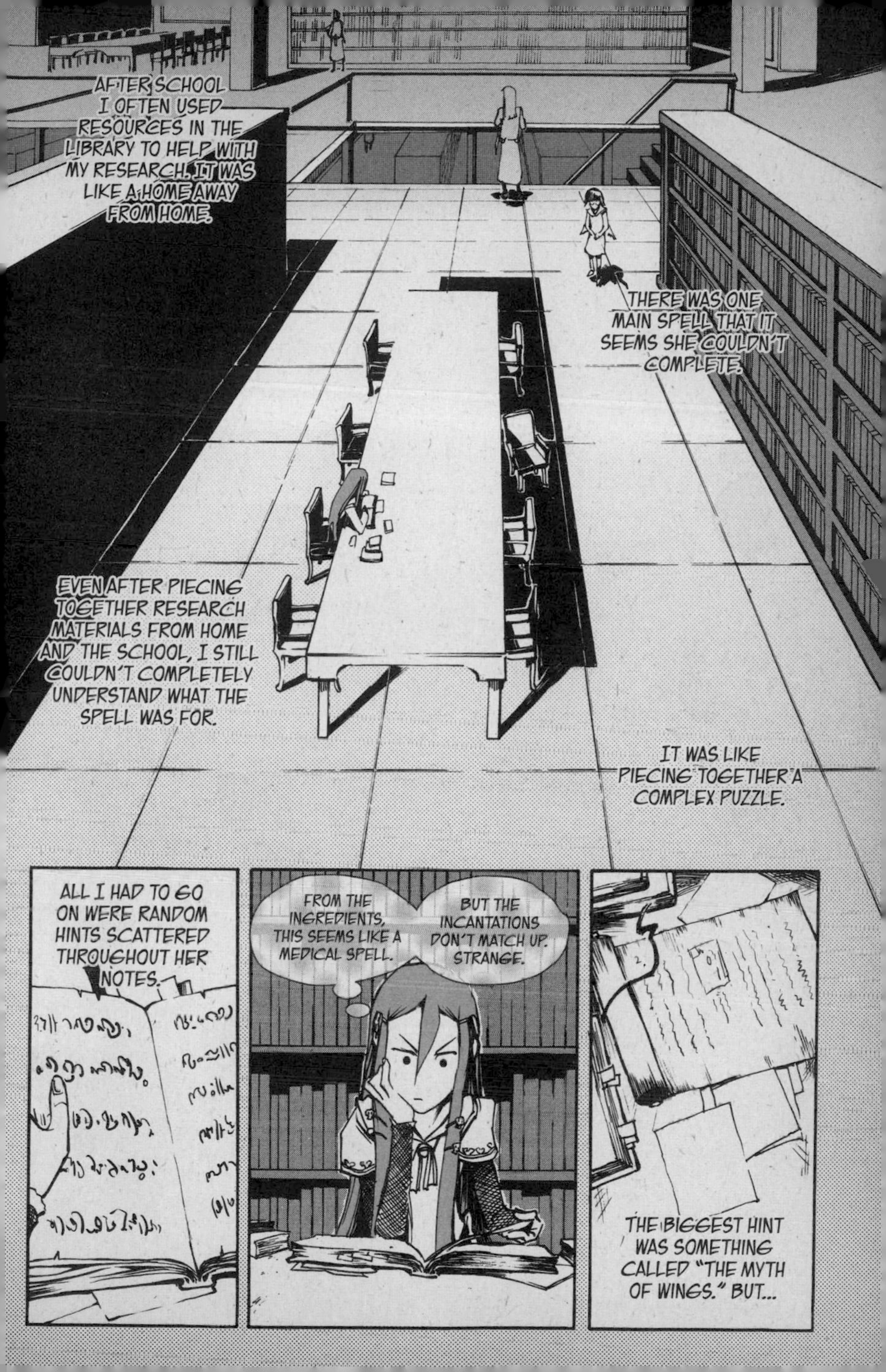

AFTER SCHOOL I OFTEN USED RESOURCES IN THE LIBRARY TO HELP WITH MY RESEARCH. IT WAS LIKE A HOME AWAY FROM HOME.
THERE WAS ONE MAIN SPELL THAT IT SEEMS SHE COULDN'T COMPLETE.
EVEN AFTER PIECING TOGETHER RESEARCH MATERIALS FROM HOME AND THE SCHOOL, I STILL COULDN'T COMPLETELY UNDERSTAND WHAT THE SPELL WAS FOR.
IT WAS LIKE PIECING TOGETHER A COMPLEX PUZZLE.
ALL I HAD TO GO ON WERE RANDOM HINTS SCATTERED THROUGHOUT HER NOTES.
FROM THE INGREDIENTS, THIS SEEMS LIKE A MEDICAL SPELL.
BUT THE INCANTATIONS DON'T MATCH UP. STRANGE.
THE BIGGEST HINT WAS SOMETHING CALLED "THE MYTH OF WINGS." BUT...

*T*here was a legend that witches had a great desire to fly, and therefore the gods bestowed magnificent wings upon them. They learned to what great heights they could climb, and realized that there was no limit to where they could reach.

From the greatest height in the world, the witches peered down on the vast land below them and were awestruck by its immenseness. Each tribe wanted to possess it all, and none were willing to share. Thus, a war broke out that shook the land and caused great destruction.

As punishment for their greediness, the gods decreased the size of the witches' wings, stripping away their ability to fly. The witches did not learn their lesson, and continued to destroy each other. The gods then sent the demonic Fairies, who feasted on the souls of witches. There was much pain and anguish, and many suffered. But hope was not completely lost.

A poor witch child from a small, nameless tribe rose from the bloodstained lands and lent her knowledge and wisdom. This witch child, later to be known as the first Queen Witch, united the quarreling tribes against the flightless black beasts, pushing them back.

She created order and returned peace, but our wings were never restored to their previous splendor by the gods. This devastating loss was the price of our greed and selfishness.

This is why witches have wings. We are reminded of the mistakes our ancestors made through these beautiful yet useless things.

-Myth of Wings. Tome of History, Chapter 757

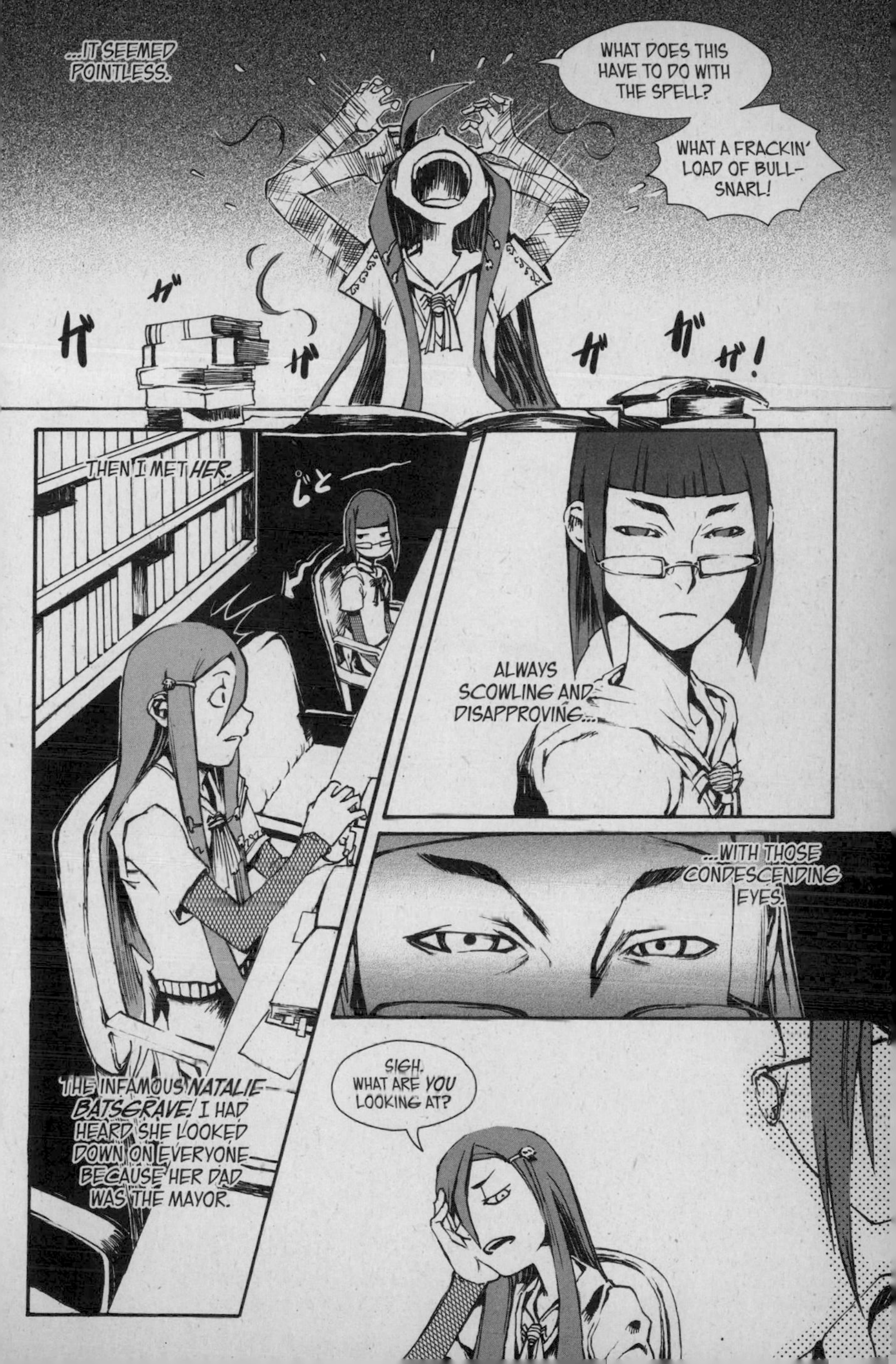
...IT SEEMED POINTLESS.
WHAT DOES THIS HAVE TO DO WITH THE SPELL?
WHAT A FRACKIN' LOAD OF BULL-SNARL!
ガ ガ ガ ガ ガ ガ!
THEN I MET HER.
じと——
ALWAYS SCOWLING AND DISAPPROVING...
...WITH THOSE CONDESCENDING EYES.
THE INFAMOUS NATALIE BATSGRAVE! I HAD HEARD SHE LOOKED DOWN ON EVERYONE BECAUSE HER DAD WAS THE MAYOR.
SIGH. WHAT ARE YOU LOOKING AT?

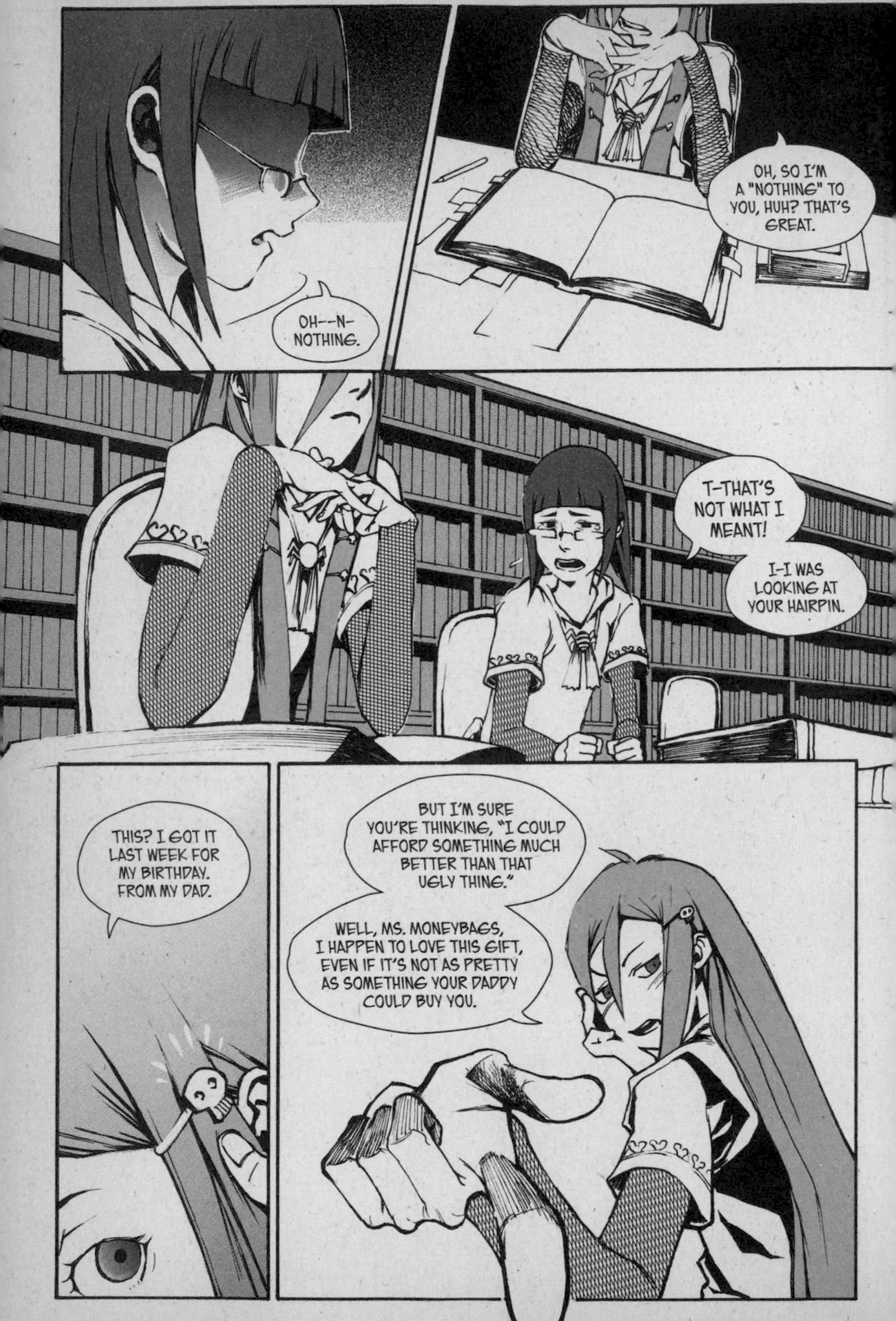
OH--N-NOTHING.
OH, SO I'M A "NOTHING" TO YOU, HUH? THAT'S GREAT.
T-THAT'S NOT WHAT I MEANT!
I-I WAS LOOKING AT YOUR HAIRPIN.
THIS? I GOT IT LAST WEEK FOR MY BIRTHDAY. FROM MY DAD.
BUT I'M SURE YOU'RE THINKING, "I COULD AFFORD SOMETHING MUCH BETTER THAN THAT UGLY THING."
WELL, MS. MONEYBAGS, I HAPPEN TO LOVE THIS GIFT, EVEN IF IT'S NOT AS PRETTY AS SOMETHING YOUR DADDY COULD BUY YOU.

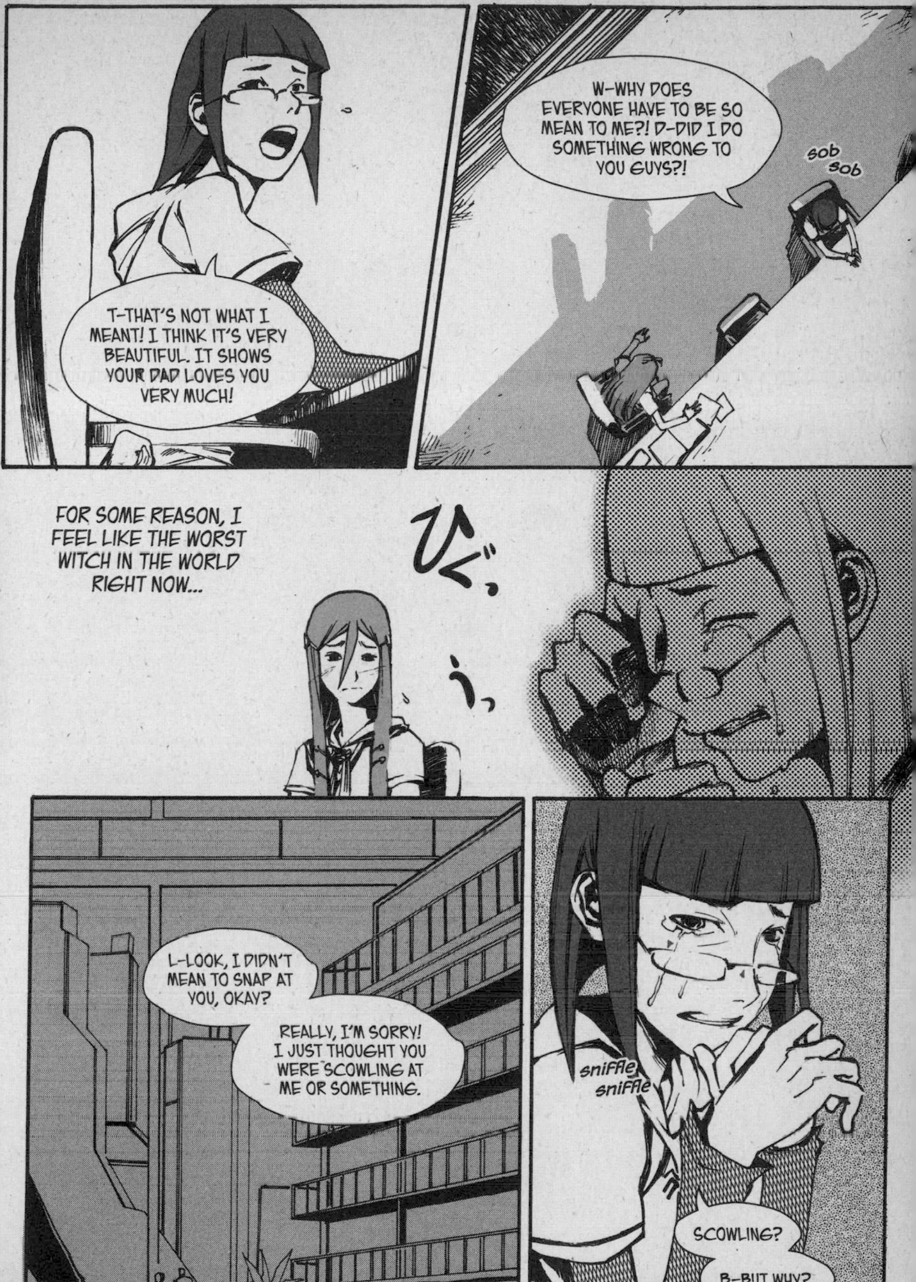
T-THAT'S NOT WHAT I MEANT! I THINK IT'S VERY BEAUTIFUL. IT SHOWS YOUR DAD LOVES YOU VERY MUCH!
W-WHY DOES EVERYONE HAVE TO BE SO MEAN TO ME?! D-DID I DO SOMETHING WRONG TO YOU GUYS?!
sob sob
FOR SOME REASON, I FEEL LIKE THE WORST WITCH IN THE WORLD RIGHT NOW...
ひぐっ
うっ
L-LOOK, I DIDN'T MEAN TO SNAP AT YOU, OKAY?
REALLY, I'M SORRY! I JUST THOUGHT YOU WERE SCOWLING AT ME OR SOMETHING.
sniffle sniffle
SCOWLING?
B-BUT WHY?

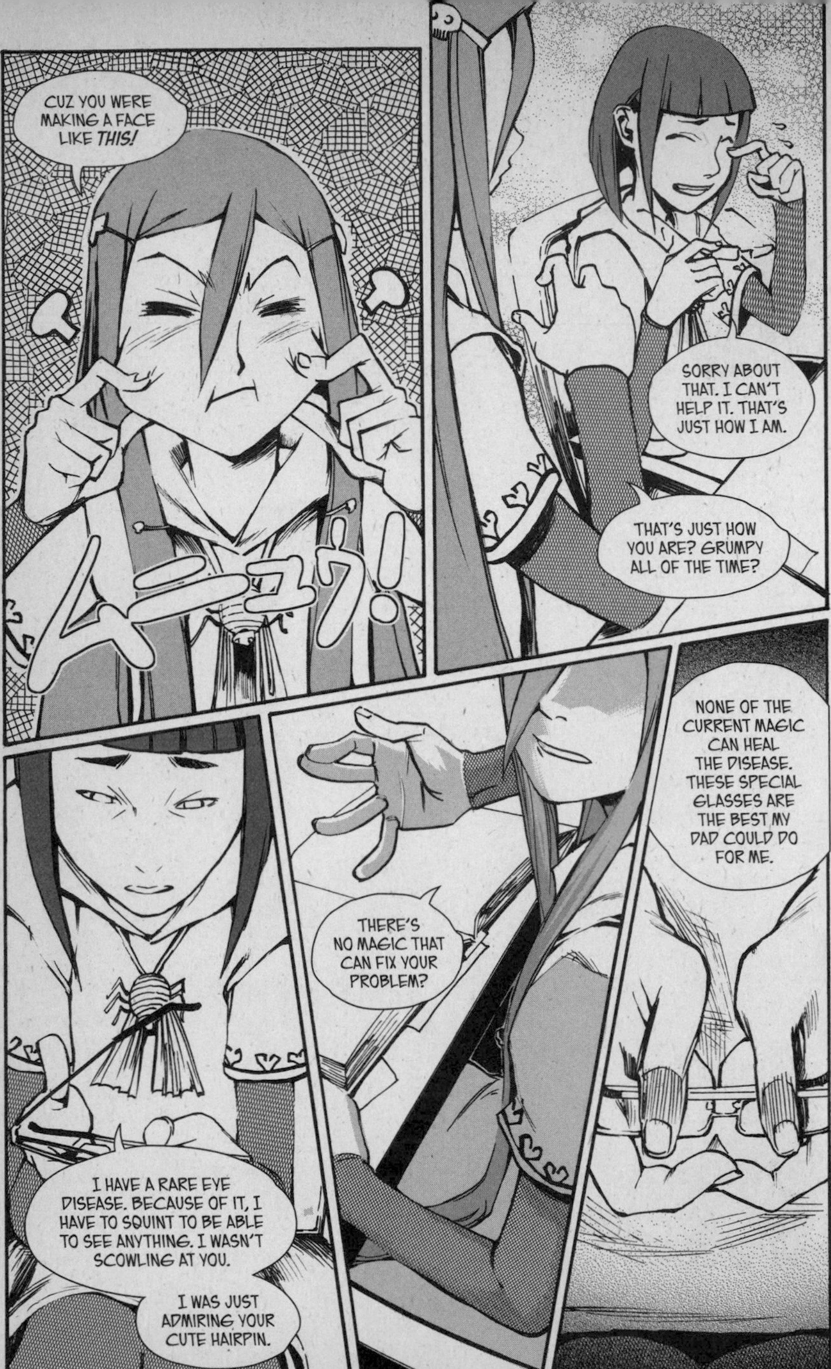
CUZ YOU WERE MAKING A FACE LIKE *THIS!*
ムニュウ!
SORRY ABOUT THAT. I CAN'T HELP IT. THAT'S JUST HOW I AM.
THAT'S JUST HOW YOU ARE? GRUMPY ALL OF THE TIME?
I HAVE A RARE EYE DISEASE. BECAUSE OF IT, I HAVE TO SQUINT TO BE ABLE TO SEE ANYTHING. I WASN'T SCOWLING AT YOU.
I WAS JUST ADMIRING YOUR CUTE HAIRPIN.
THERE'S NO MAGIC THAT CAN FIX YOUR PROBLEM?
NONE OF THE CURRENT MAGIC CAN HEAL THE DISEASE. THESE SPECIAL GLASSES ARE THE BEST MY DAD COULD DO FOR ME.

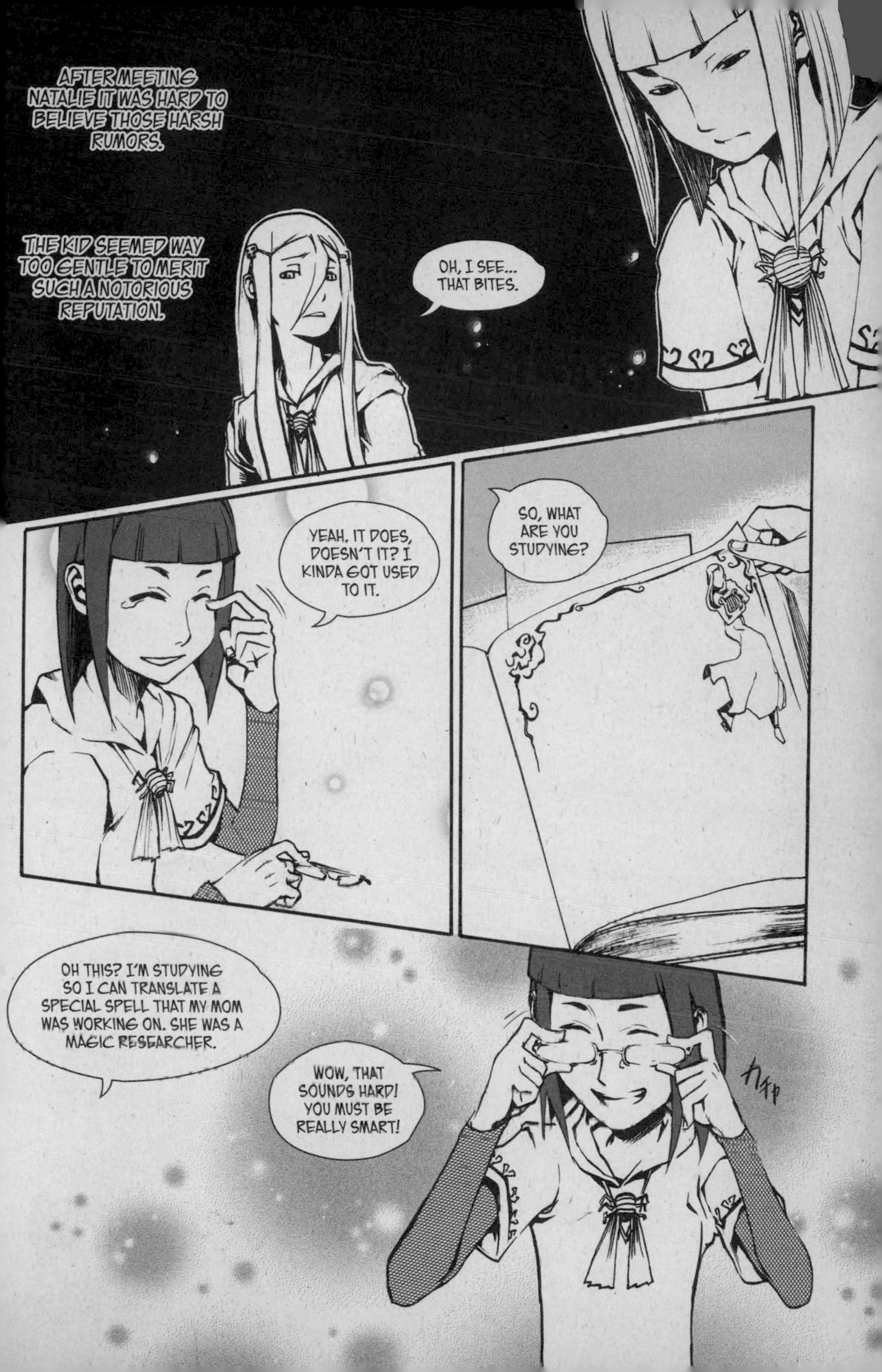
AFTER MEETING NATALIE IT WAS HARD TO BELIEVE THOSE HARSH RUMORS.
THE KID SEEMED WAY TOO GENTLE TO MERIT SUCH A NOTORIOUS REPUTATION.
OH, I SEE... THAT BITES.
YEAH. IT DOES, DOESN'T IT? I KINDA GOT USED TO IT.
SO, WHAT ARE YOU STUDYING?
OH THIS? I'M STUDYING SO I CAN TRANSLATE A SPECIAL SPELL THAT MY MOM WAS WORKING ON. SHE WAS A MAGIC RESEARCHER.
WOW, THAT SOUNDS HARD! YOU MUST BE REALLY SMART!

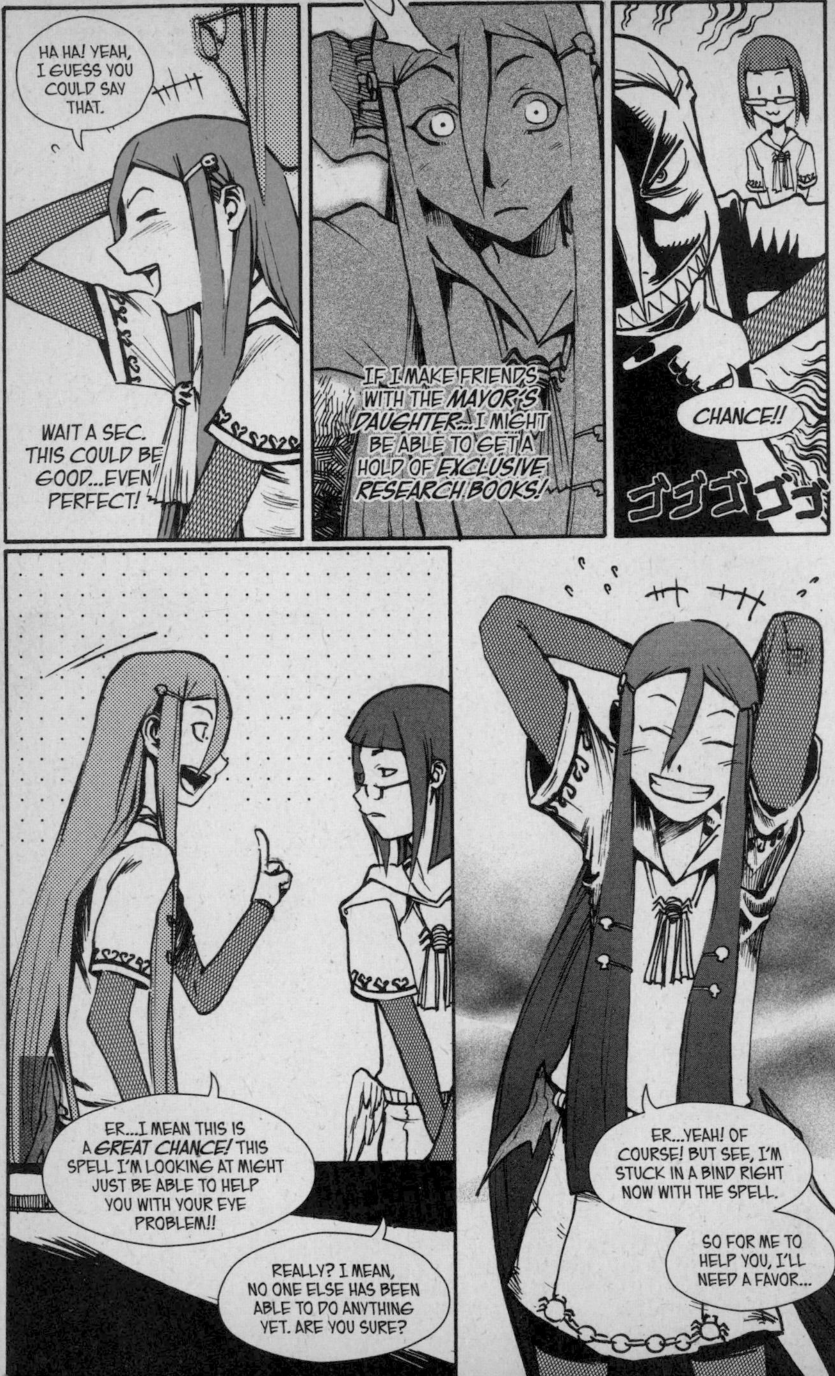
HA HA! YEAH, I GUESS YOU COULD SAY THAT.
WAIT A SEC. THIS COULD BE GOOD...EVEN PERFECT!
IF I MAKE FRIENDS WITH THE *MAYOR'S DAUGHTER*...I MIGHT BE ABLE TO GET A HOLD OF *EXCLUSIVE RESEARCH BOOKS!*
CHANCE!!
ゴゴゴゴゴ
ER...I MEAN THIS IS A *GREAT CHANCE!* THIS SPELL I'M LOOKING AT MIGHT JUST BE ABLE TO HELP YOU WITH YOUR EYE PROBLEM!!
REALLY? I MEAN, NO ONE ELSE HAS BEEN ABLE TO DO ANYTHING YET. ARE YOU SURE?
ER...YEAH! OF COURSE! BUT SEE, I'M STUCK IN A BIND RIGHT NOW WITH THE SPELL.
SO FOR ME TO HELP YOU, I'LL NEED A FAVOR...

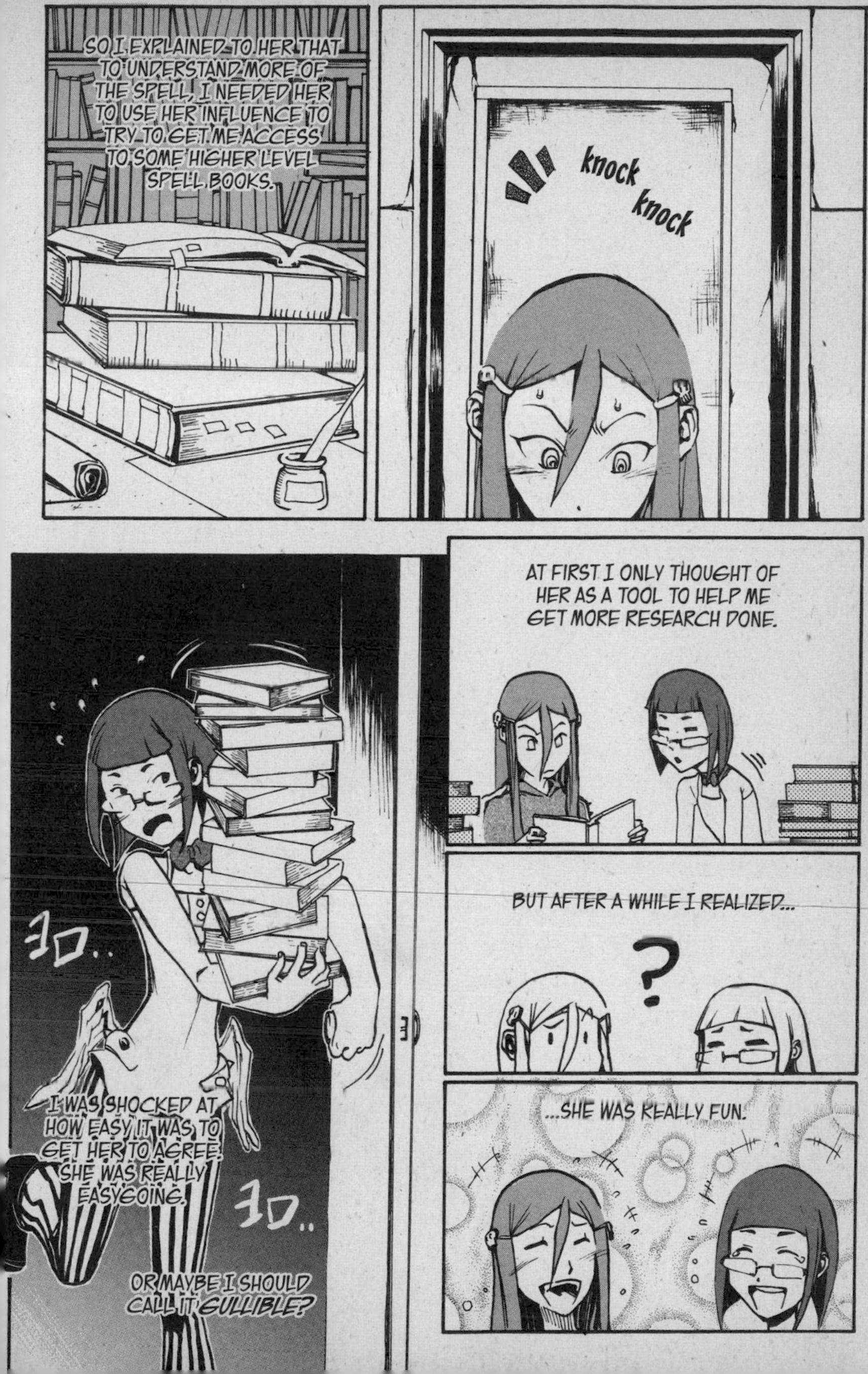
SO I EXPLAINED TO HER THAT TO UNDERSTAND MORE OF THE SPELL, I NEEDED HER TO USE HER INFLUENCE TO TRY TO GET ME ACCESS TO SOME HIGHER LEVEL SPELL BOOKS.
knock knock
I WAS SHOCKED AT HOW EASY IT WAS TO GET HER TO AGREE. SHE WAS REALLY EASYGOING.
OR MAYBE I SHOULD CALL IT GULLIBLE?
AT FIRST I ONLY THOUGHT OF HER AS A TOOL TO HELP ME GET MORE RESEARCH DONE.
BUT AFTER A WHILE I REALIZED...
?
...SHE WAS REALLY FUN.

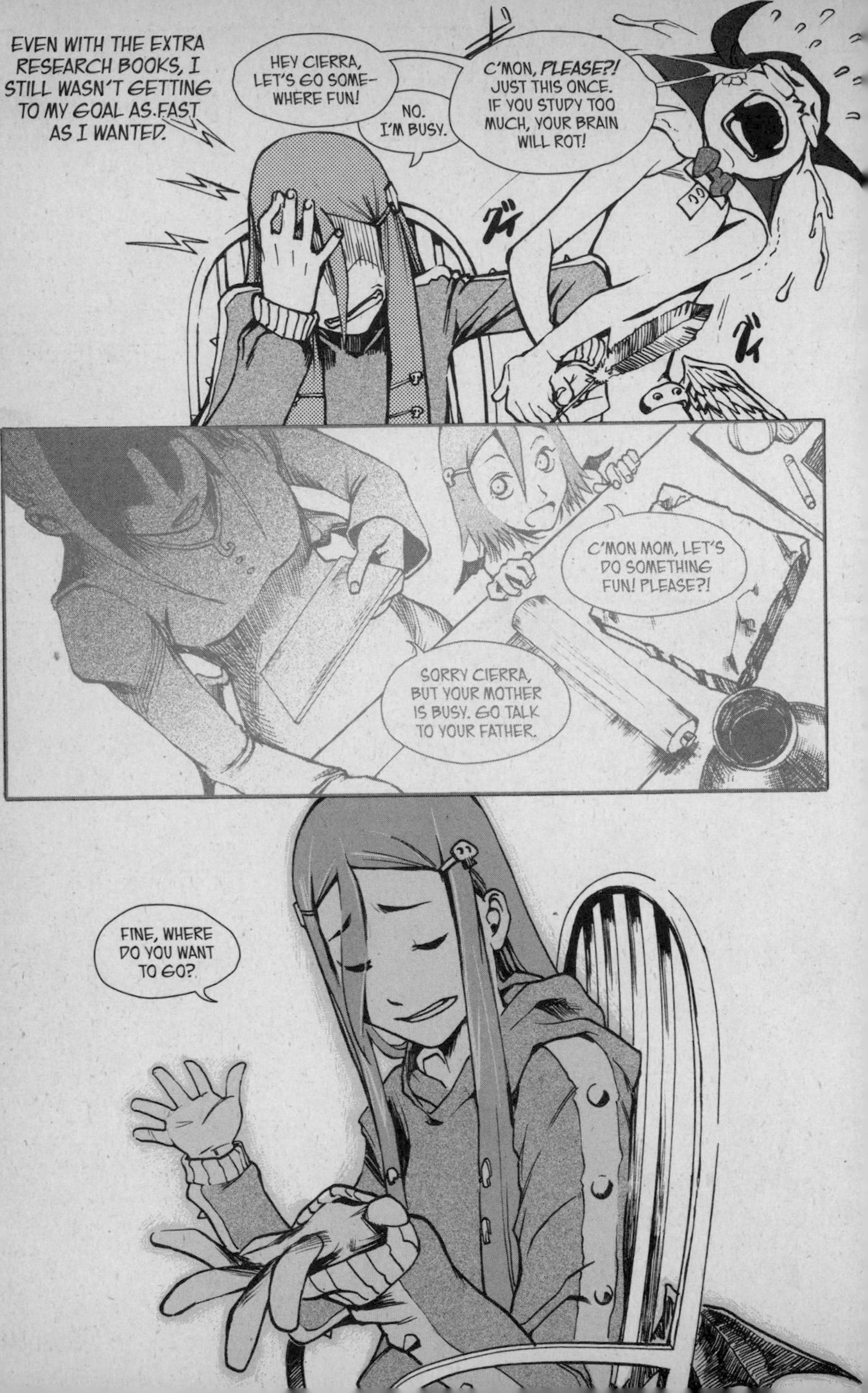
EVEN WITH THE EXTRA RESEARCH BOOKS, I STILL WASN'T GETTING TO MY GOAL AS FAST AS I WANTED.
HEY CIERRA, LET'S GO SOME-WHERE FUN!
NO. I'M BUSY.
C'MON, PLEASE?! JUST THIS ONCE. IF YOU STUDY TOO MUCH, YOUR BRAIN WILL ROT!
C'MON MOM, LET'S DO SOMETHING FUN! PLEASE?!
SORRY CIERRA, BUT YOUR MOTHER IS BUSY. GO TALK TO YOUR FATHER.
FINE, WHERE DO YOU WANT TO GO?

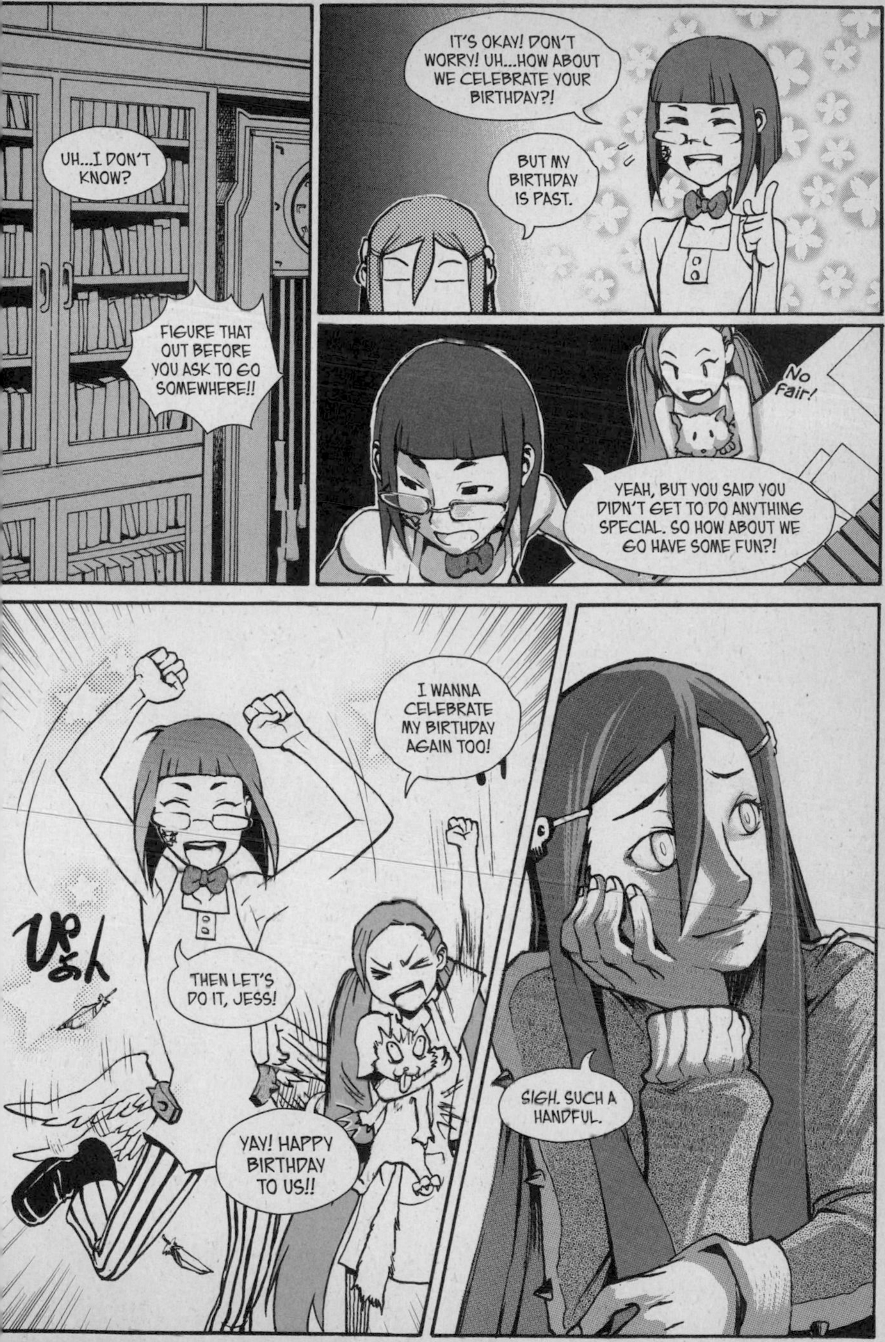
UH...I DON'T KNOW?
FIGURE THAT OUT BEFORE YOU ASK TO GO SOMEWHERE!!
IT'S OKAY! DON'T WORRY! UH...HOW ABOUT WE CELEBRATE YOUR BIRTHDAY?!
BUT MY BIRTHDAY IS PAST.
No Fair!
YEAH, BUT YOU SAID YOU DIDN'T GET TO DO ANYTHING SPECIAL. SO HOW ABOUT WE GO HAVE SOME FUN?!
I WANNA CELEBRATE MY BIRTHDAY AGAIN TOO!
ぴょん
THEN LET'S DO IT, JESS!
YAY! HAPPY BIRTHDAY TO US!!
SIGH. SUCH A HANDFUL.

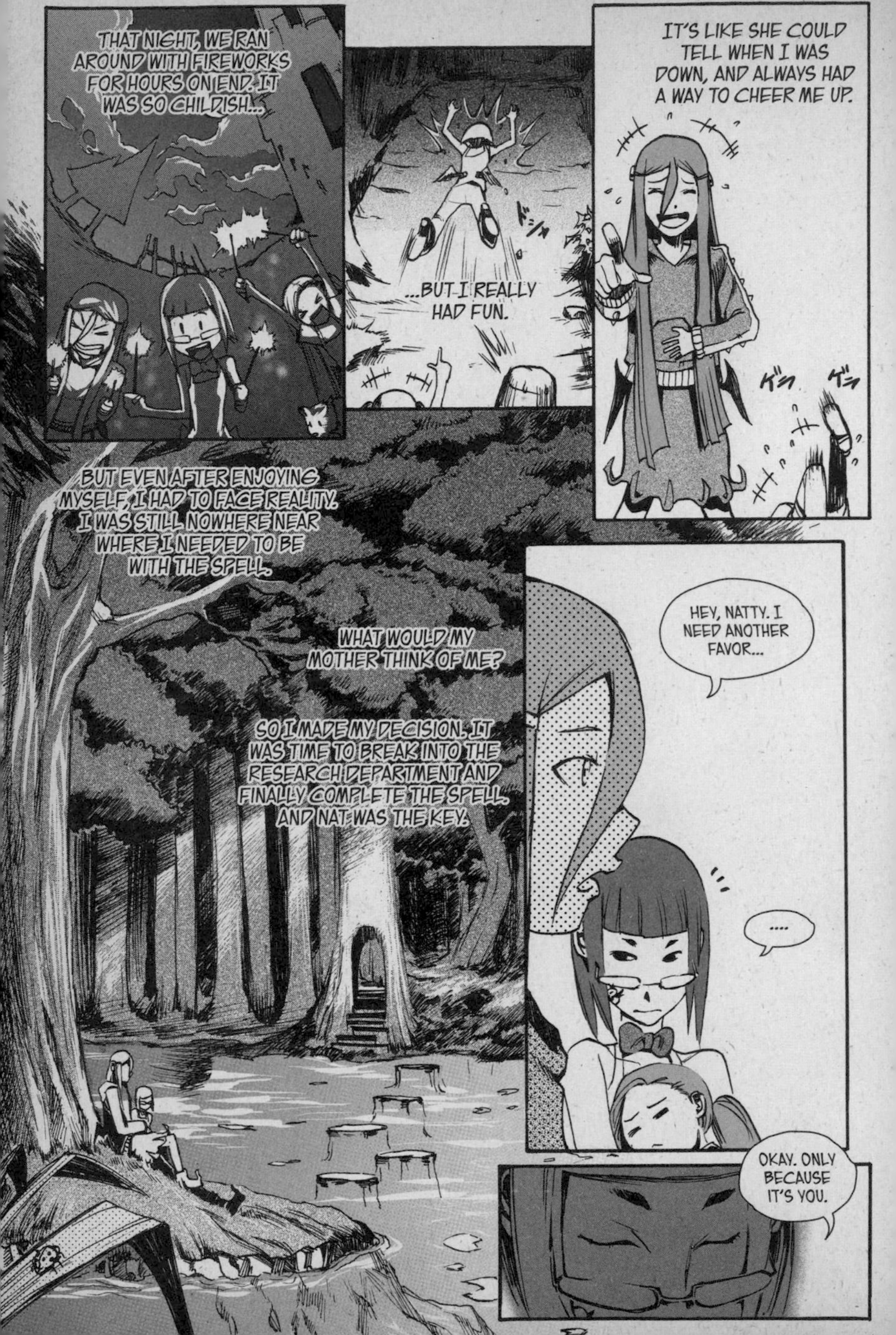
THAT NIGHT, WE RAN AROUND WITH FIREWORKS FOR HOURS ON END. IT WAS SO CHILDISH...
...BUT I REALLY HAD FUN.
IT'S LIKE SHE COULD TELL WHEN I WAS DOWN, AND ALWAYS HAD A WAY TO CHEER ME UP.
BUT EVEN AFTER ENJOYING MYSELF, I HAD TO FACE REALITY. I WAS STILL NOWHERE NEAR WHERE I NEEDED TO BE WITH THE SPELL.
WHAT WOULD MY MOTHER THINK OF ME?
SO I MADE MY DECISION. IT WAS TIME TO BREAK INTO THE RESEARCH DEPARTMENT AND FINALLY COMPLETE THE SPELL. AND NAT WAS THE KEY.
HEY, NATTY. I NEED ANOTHER FAVOR...
....
OKAY. ONLY BECAUSE IT'S YOU.

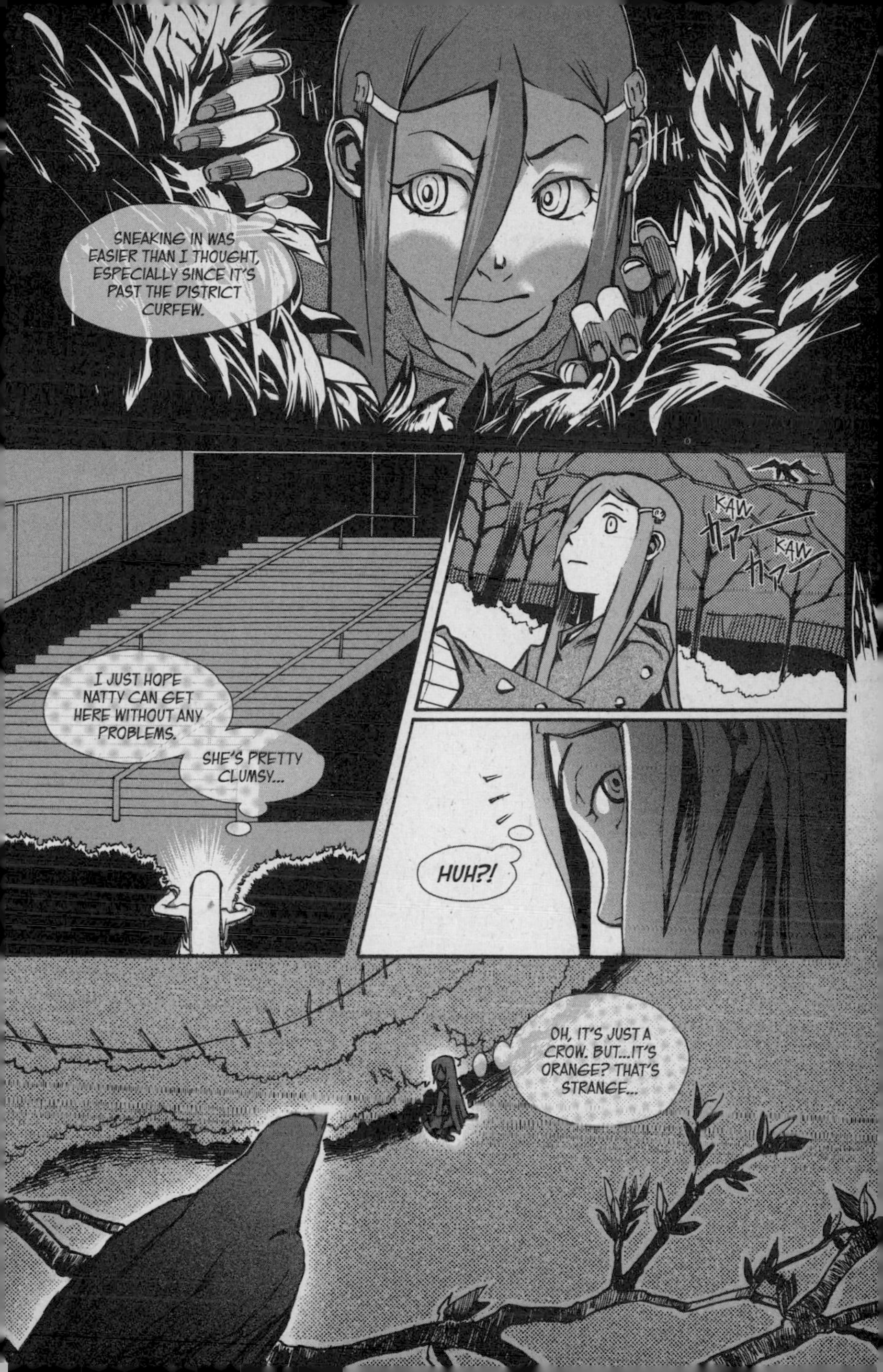
SNEAKING IN WAS EASIER THAN I THOUGHT, ESPECIALLY SINCE IT'S PAST THE DISTRICT CURFEW.
I JUST HOPE NATTY CAN GET HERE WITHOUT ANY PROBLEMS.
SHE'S PRETTY CLUMSY...
KAW
KAW
HUH?!
OH, IT'S JUST A CROW. BUT...IT'S ORANGE? THAT'S STRANGE...

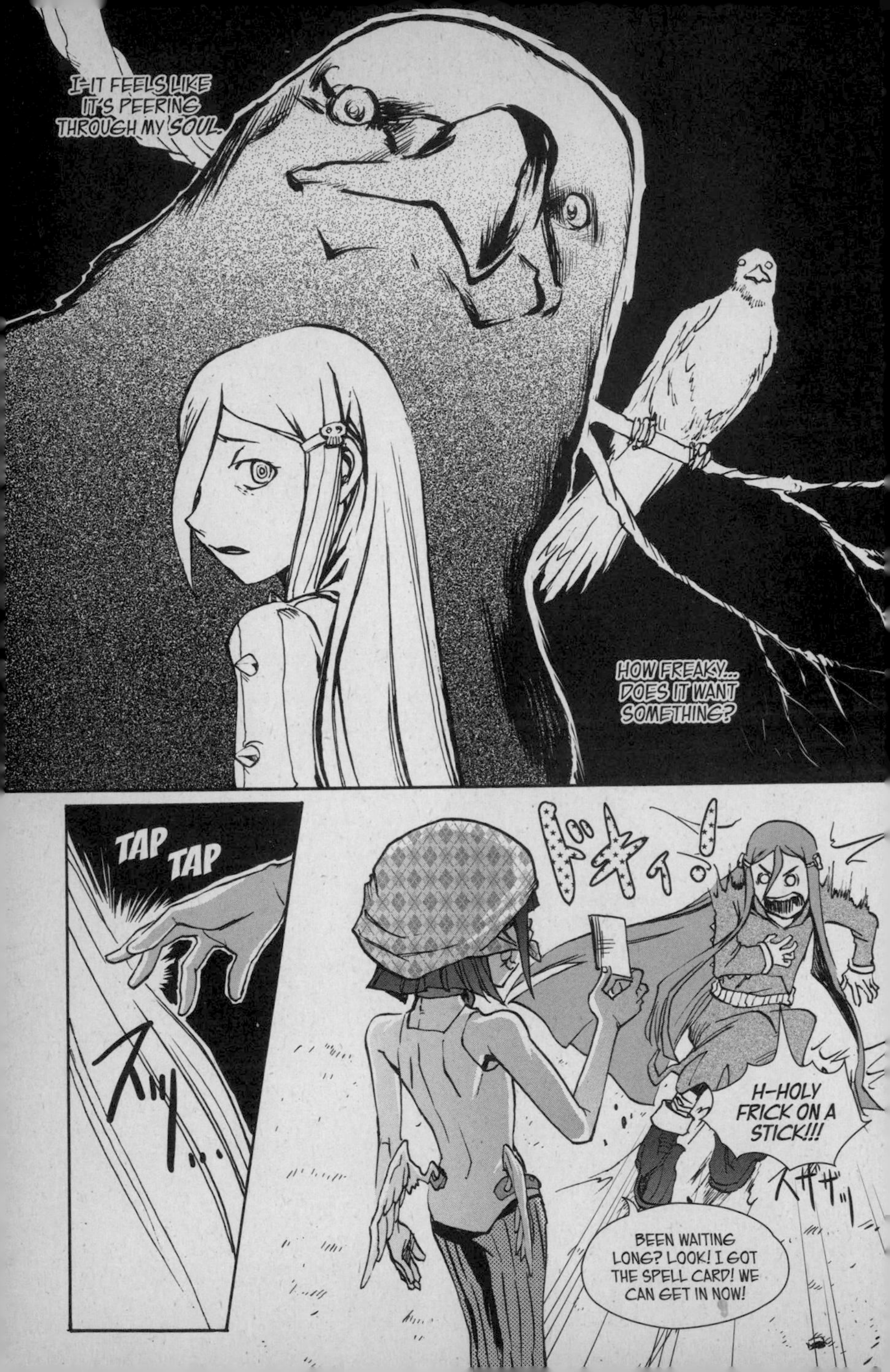
I-IT FEELS LIKE IT'S PEERING THROUGH MY SOUL.
HOW FREAKY... DOES IT WANT SOMETHING?
H-HOLY FRICK ON A STICK!!!
BEEN WAITING LONG? LOOK! I GOT THE SPELL CARD! WE CAN GET IN NOW!
TAP TAP

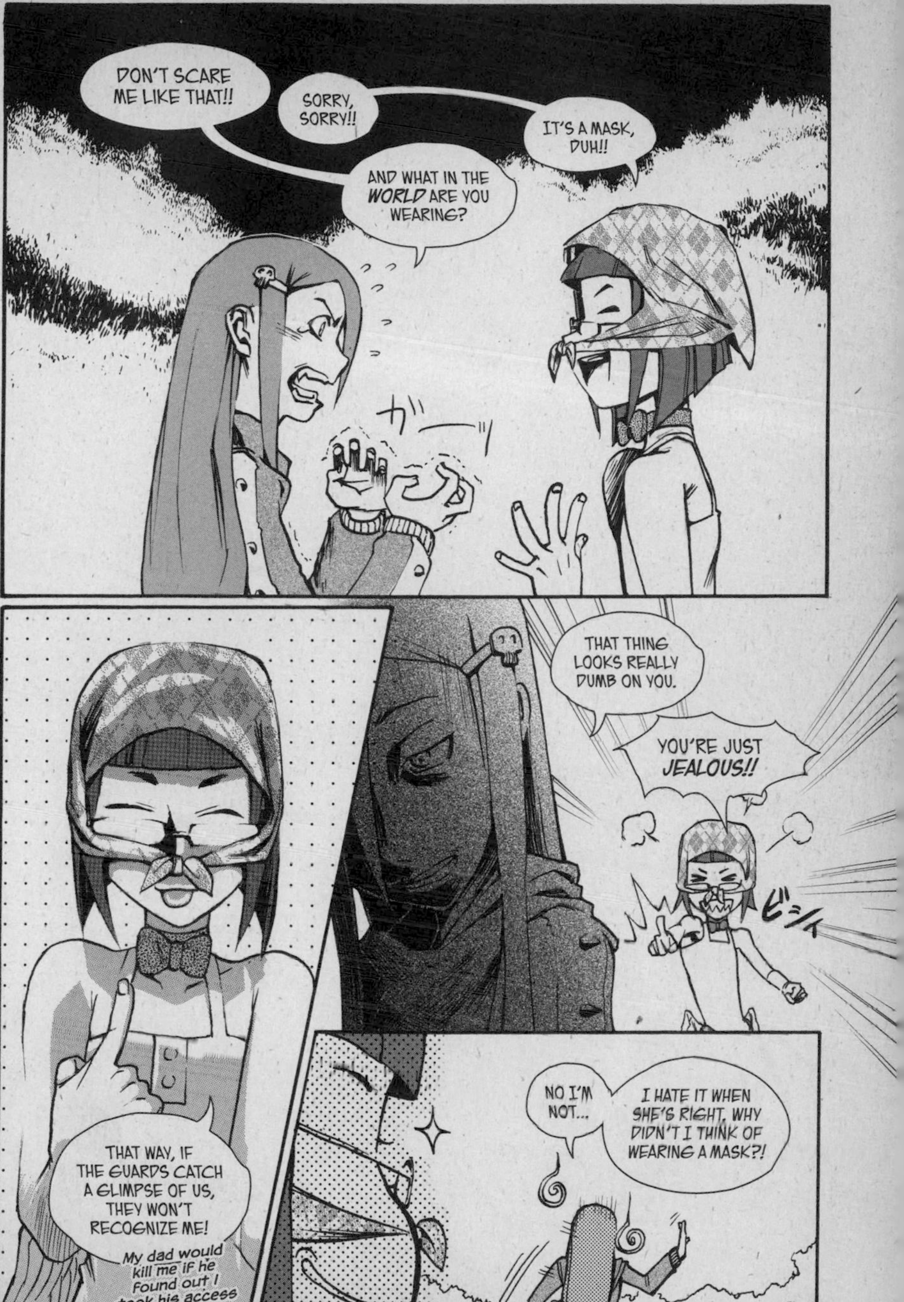

DON'T SCARE ME LIKE THAT!!
SORRY, SORRY!!
AND WHAT IN THE ***WORLD*** ARE YOU WEARING?
IT'S A MASK, DUH!!
THAT WAY, IF THE GUARDS CATCH A GLIMPSE OF US, THEY WON'T RECOGNIZE ME!
My dad would kill me if he found out I took his access spell card.
THAT THING LOOKS REALLY DUMB ON YOU.
YOU'RE JUST ***JEALOUS!!***
NO I'M NOT...
I HATE IT WHEN SHE'S RIGHT. WHY DIDN'T I THINK OF WEARING A MASK?!

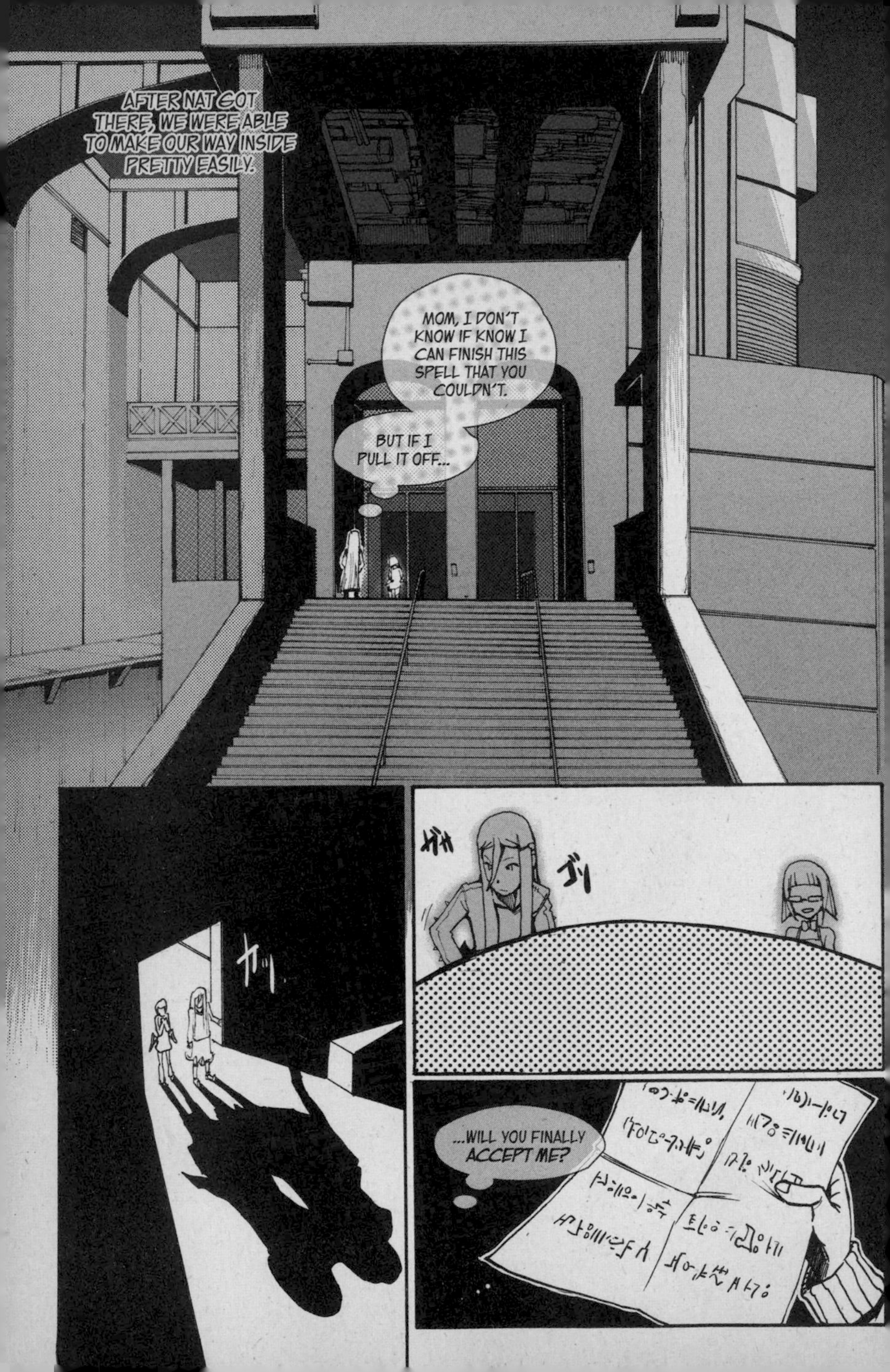
AFTER NAT GOT THERE, WE WERE ABLE TO MAKE OUR WAY INSIDE PRETTY EASILY.
MOM, I DON'T KNOW IF KNOW I CAN FINISH THIS SPELL THAT YOU COULDN'T.
BUT IF I PULL IT OFF...
...WILL YOU FINALLY ACCEPT ME?

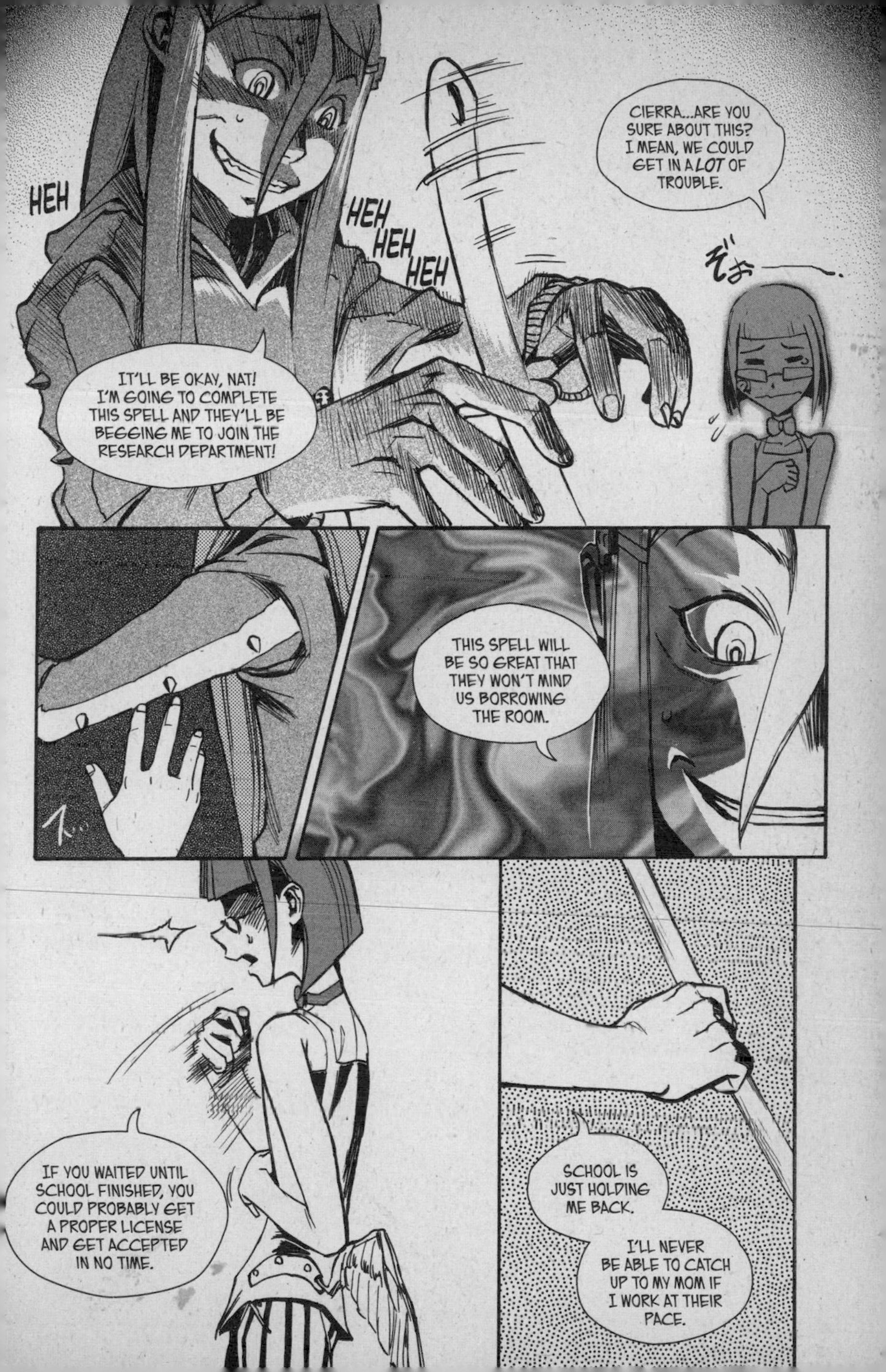
CIERRA...ARE YOU SURE ABOUT THIS? I MEAN, WE COULD GET IN A *LOT* OF TROUBLE.
HEH
HEH HEH HEH
ぞぉ
IT'LL BE OKAY, NAT! I'M GOING TO COMPLETE THIS SPELL AND THEY'LL BE BEGGING ME TO JOIN THE RESEARCH DEPARTMENT!
THIS SPELL WILL BE SO GREAT THAT THEY WON'T MIND US BORROWING THE ROOM.
IF YOU WAITED UNTIL SCHOOL FINISHED, YOU COULD PROBABLY GET A PROPER LICENSE AND GET ACCEPTED IN NO TIME.
SCHOOL IS JUST HOLDING ME BACK.
I'LL NEVER BE ABLE TO CATCH UP TO MY MOM IF I WORK AT THEIR PACE.

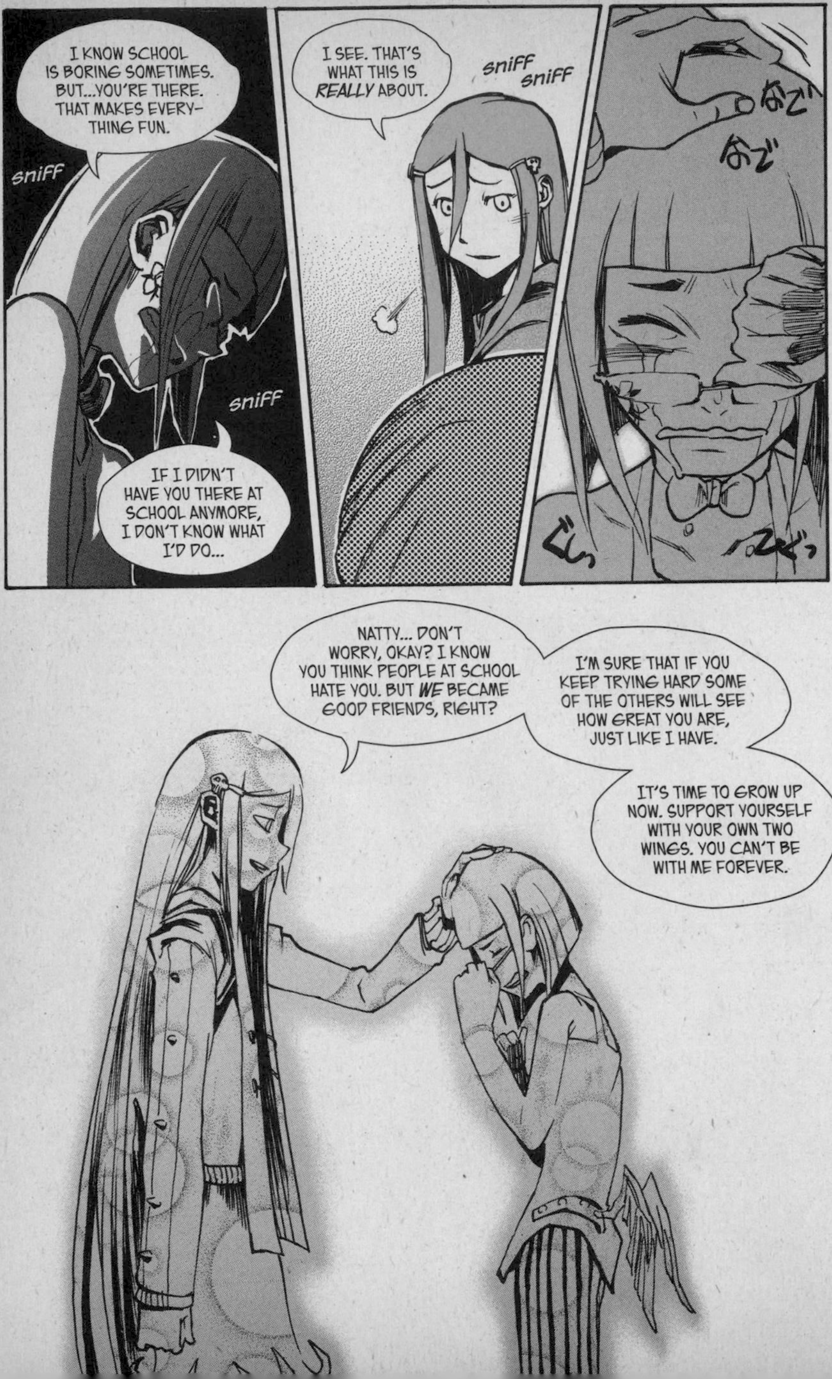
I KNOW SCHOOL IS BORING SOMETIMES. BUT...YOU'RE THERE. THAT MAKES EVERY-THING FUN.
sniff
sniff
IF I DIDN'T HAVE YOU THERE AT SCHOOL ANYMORE, I DON'T KNOW WHAT I'D DO...
I SEE. THAT'S WHAT THIS IS *REALLY* ABOUT.
sniff sniff
なで
なで
ぐしっ
NATTY... DON'T WORRY, OKAY? I KNOW YOU THINK PEOPLE AT SCHOOL HATE YOU. BUT *WE* BECAME GOOD FRIENDS, RIGHT?
I'M SURE THAT IF YOU KEEP TRYING HARD SOME OF THE OTHERS WILL SEE HOW GREAT YOU ARE, JUST LIKE I HAVE.
IT'S TIME TO GROW UP NOW. SUPPORT YOURSELF WITH YOUR OWN TWO WINGS. YOU CAN'T BE WITH ME FOREVER.

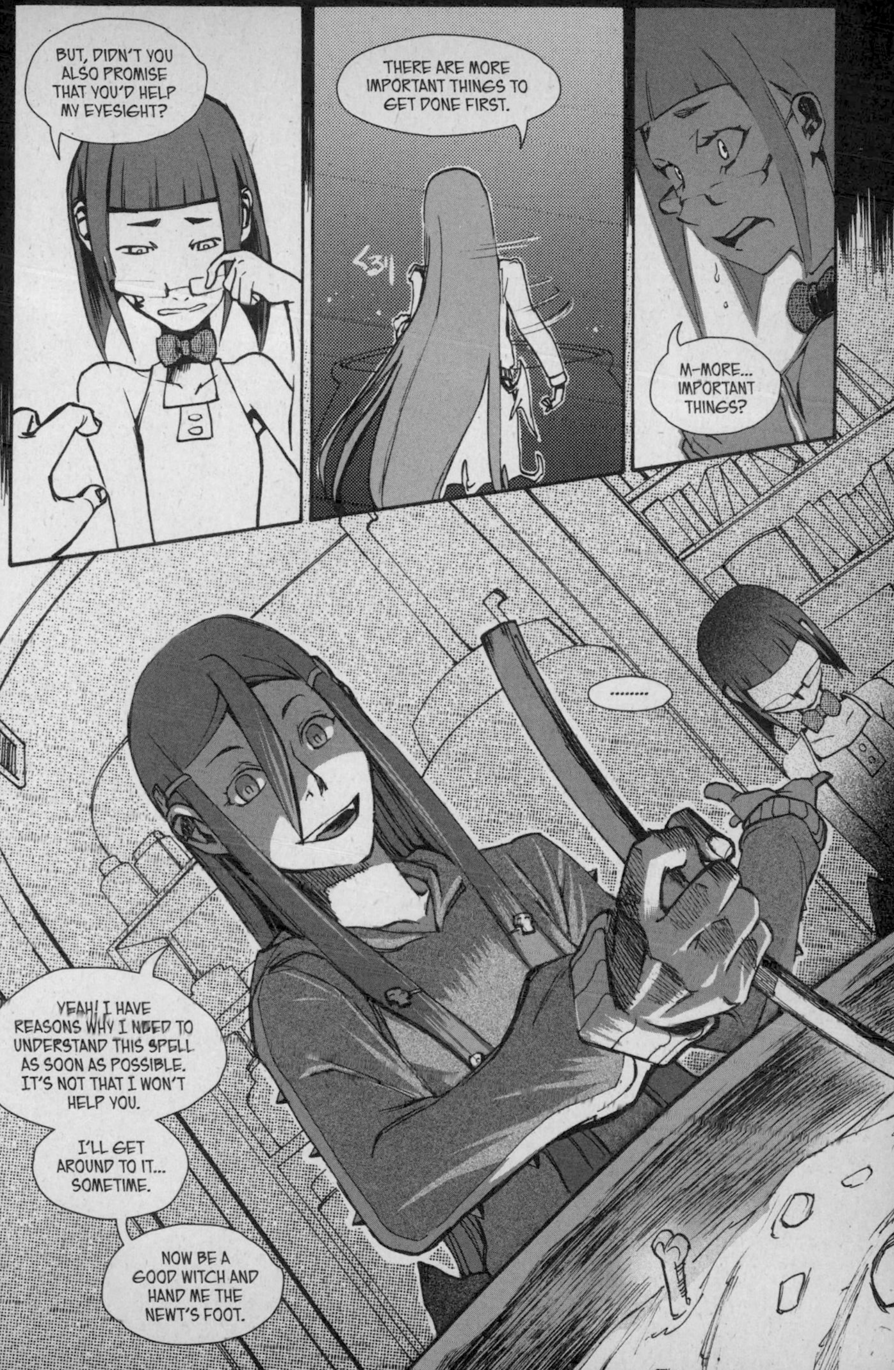
BUT, DIDN'T YOU ALSO PROMISE THAT YOU'D HELP MY EYESIGHT?
THERE ARE MORE IMPORTANT THINGS TO GET DONE FIRST.
M-MORE... IMPORTANT THINGS?
....
YEAH! I HAVE REASONS WHY I NEED TO UNDERSTAND THIS SPELL AS SOON AS POSSIBLE. IT'S NOT THAT I WON'T HELP YOU.
I'LL GET AROUND TO IT... SOMETIME.
NOW BE A GOOD WITCH AND HAND ME THE NEWT'S FOOT.

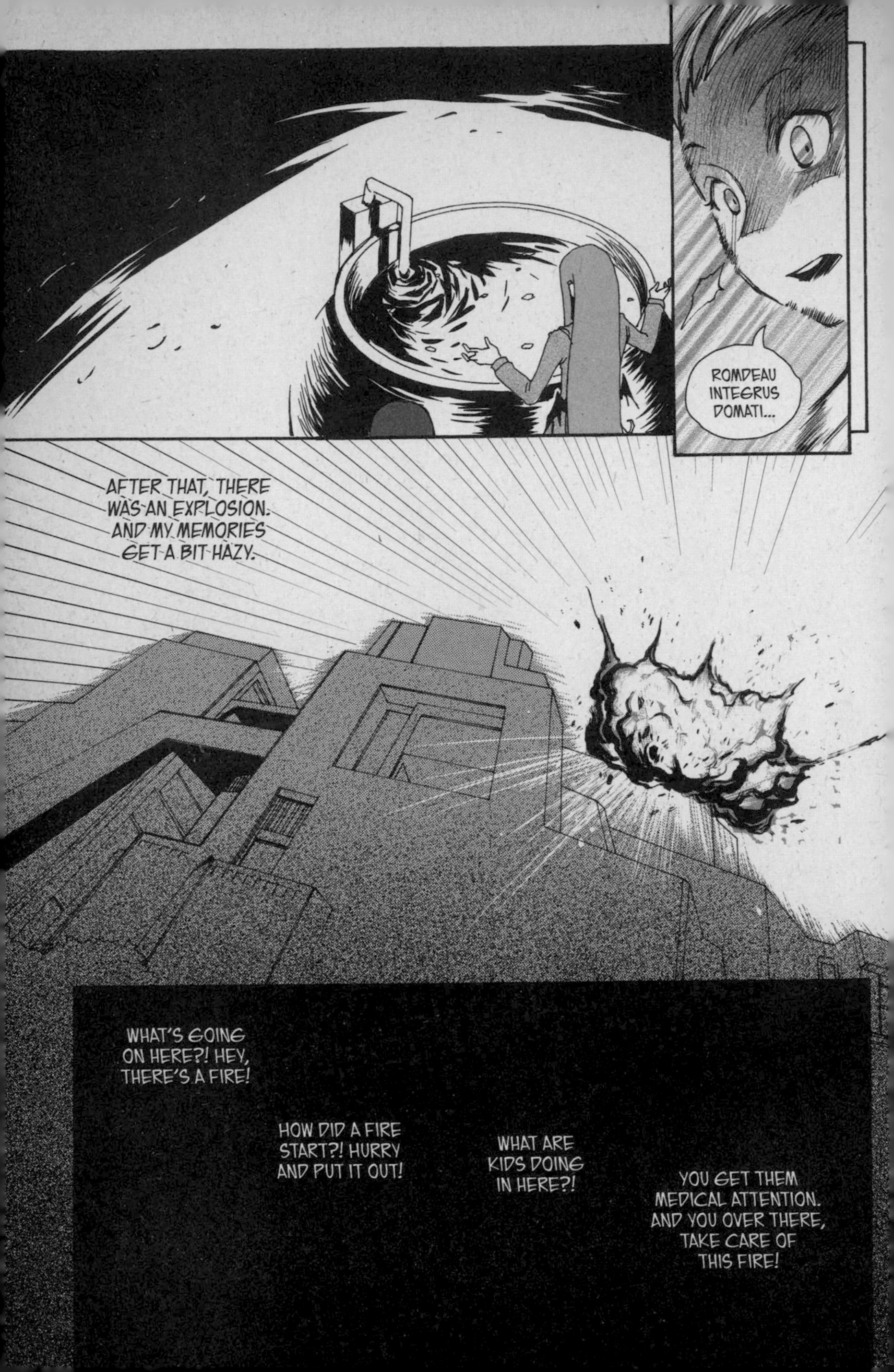
ROMDEAU INTEGRUS DOMATI...
AFTER THAT, THERE WAS AN EXPLOSION. AND MY MEMORIES GET A BIT HAZY.
WHAT'S GOING ON HERE?! HEY, THERE'S A FIRE!
HOW DID A FIRE START?! HURRY AND PUT IT OUT!
WHAT ARE KIDS DOING IN HERE?!
YOU GET THEM MEDICAL ATTENTION. AND YOU OVER THERE, TAKE CARE OF THIS FIRE!

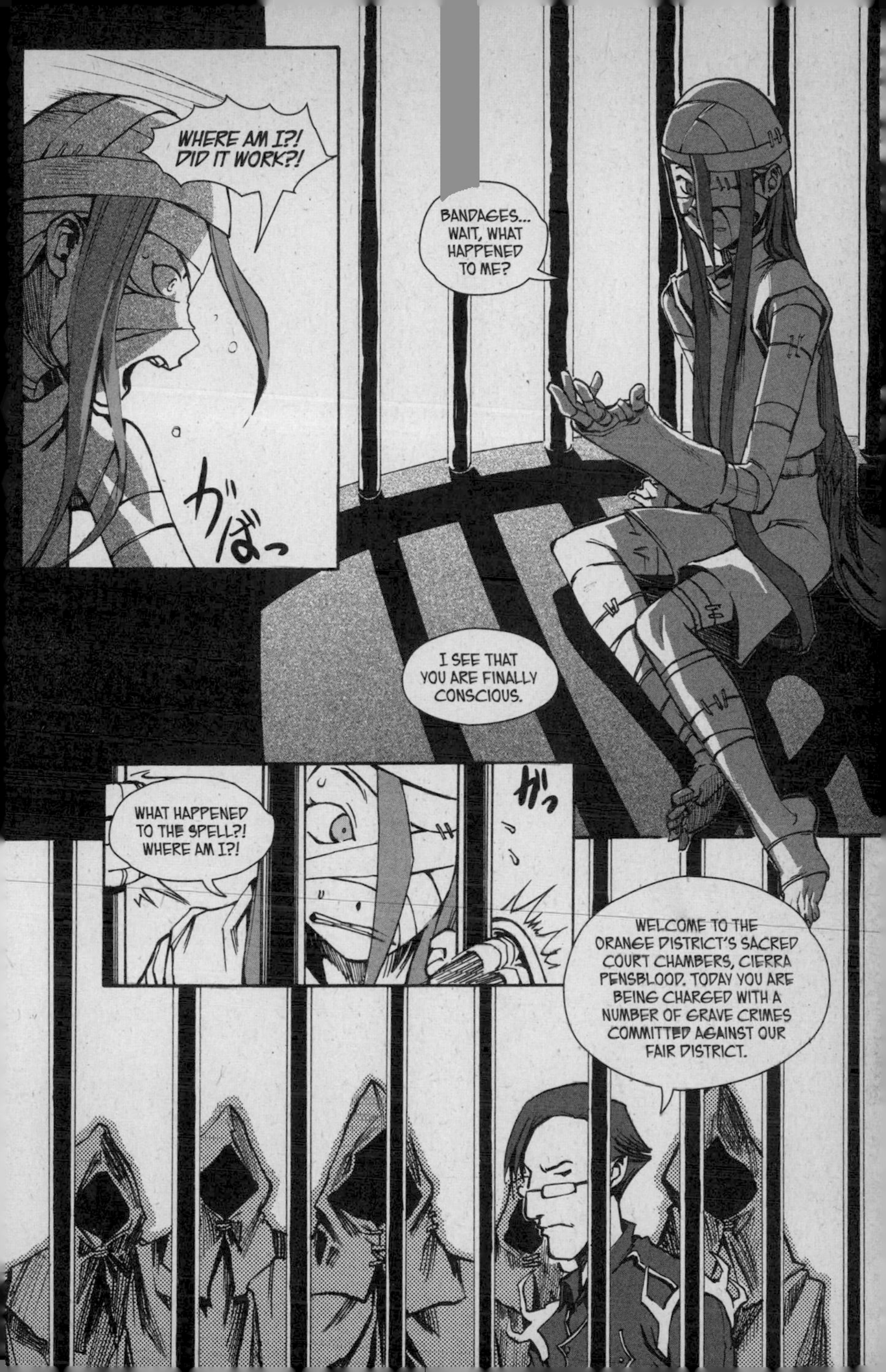
WHERE AM I?! DID IT WORK?!
がばっ
BANDAGES... WAIT, WHAT HAPPENED TO ME?
I SEE THAT YOU ARE FINALLY CONSCIOUS.
WHAT HAPPENED TO THE SPELL?! WHERE AM I?!
がっ
WELCOME TO THE ORANGE DISTRICT'S SACRED COURT CHAMBERS, CIERRA PENSBLOOD. TODAY YOU ARE BEING CHARGED WITH A NUMBER OF GRAVE CRIMES COMMITTED AGAINST OUR FAIR DISTRICT.

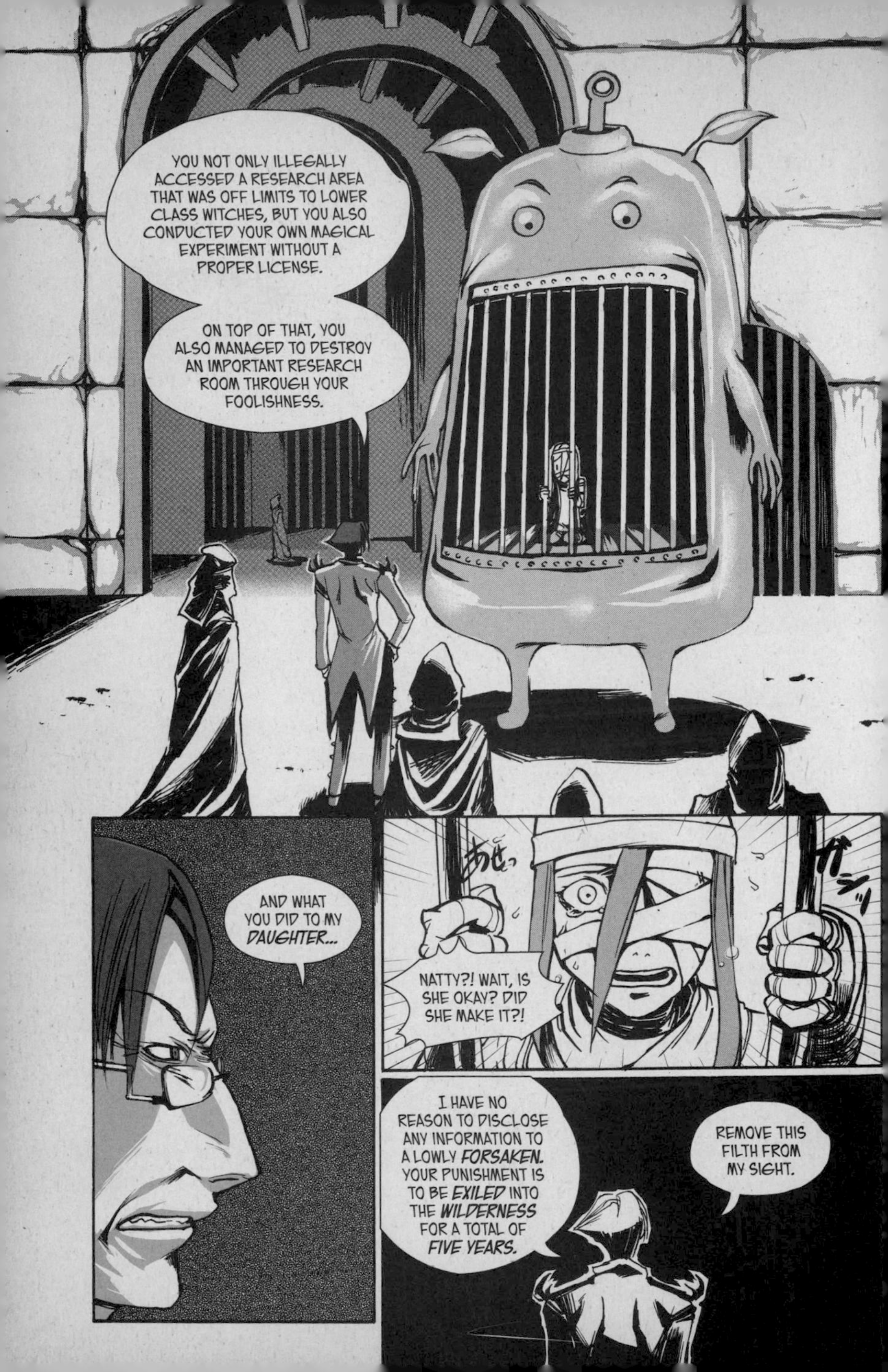
YOU NOT ONLY ILLEGALLY ACCESSED A RESEARCH AREA THAT WAS OFF LIMITS TO LOWER CLASS WITCHES, BUT YOU ALSO CONDUCTED YOUR OWN MAGICAL EXPERIMENT WITHOUT A PROPER LICENSE.
ON TOP OF THAT, YOU ALSO MANAGED TO DESTROY AN IMPORTANT RESEARCH ROOM THROUGH YOUR FOOLISHNESS.
AND WHAT YOU DID TO MY *DAUGHTER...*
あせっ
ガシッ
NATTY?! WAIT, IS SHE OKAY? DID SHE MAKE IT?!
I HAVE NO REASON TO DISCLOSE ANY INFORMATION TO A LOWLY *FORSAKEN.* YOUR PUNISHMENT IS TO BE *EXILED* INTO THE *WILDERNESS* FOR A TOTAL OF *FIVE YEARS.*
REMOVE THIS FILTH FROM MY SIGHT.

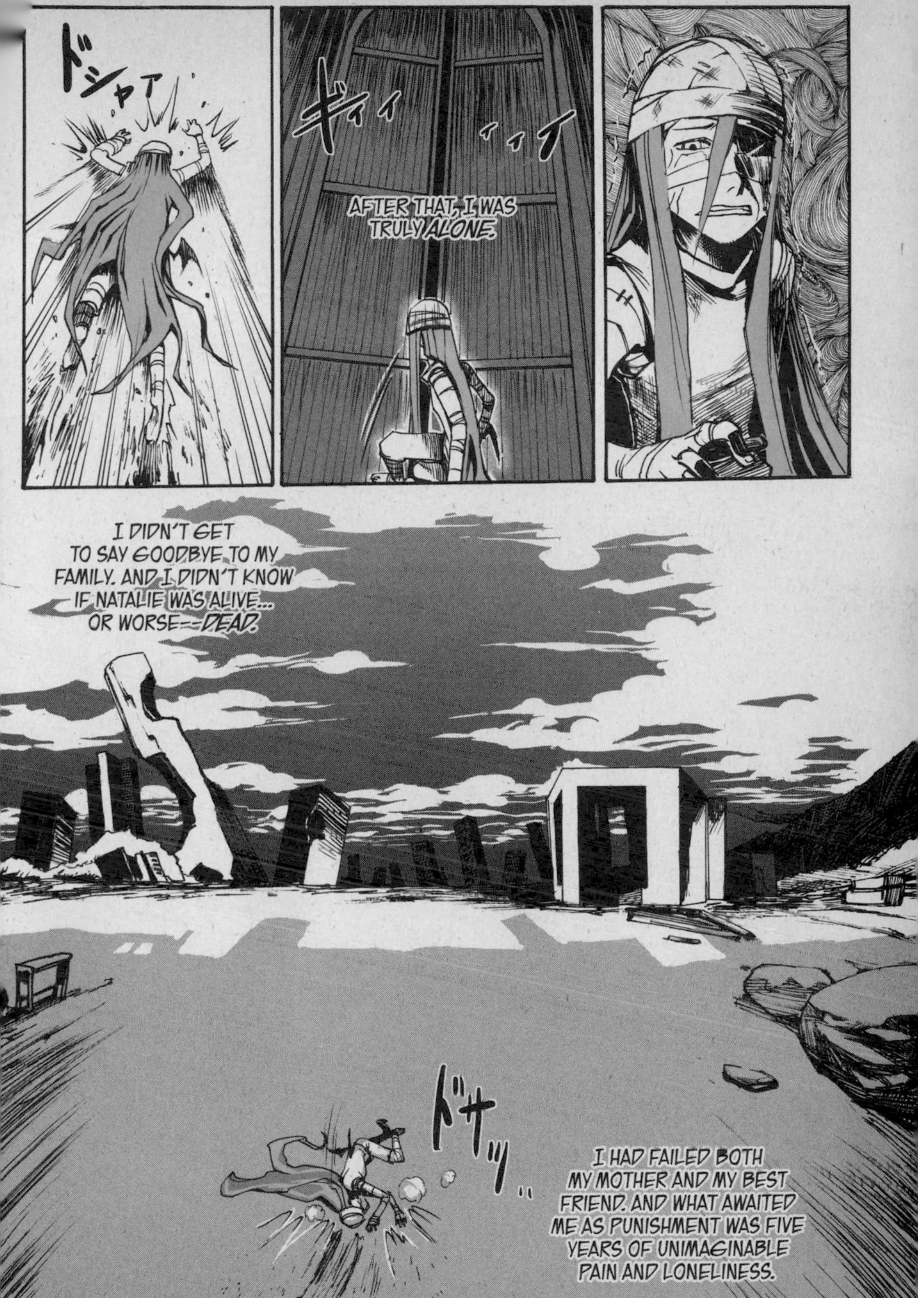
ギィイ
ィィイ
AFTER THAT, I WAS TRULY ALONE.
ドシャア
I DIDN'T GET TO SAY GOODBYE TO MY FAMILY. AND I DIDN'T KNOW IF NATALIE WAS ALIVE... OR WORSE--DEAD.
ドサッ..
I HAD FAILED BOTH MY MOTHER AND MY BEST FRIEND. AND WHAT AWAITED ME AS PUNISHMENT WAS FIVE YEARS OF UNIMAGINABLE PAIN AND LONELINESS.
SECOND SCAR END

QUEEN BIANKA'S CRASH COURSE

CHAPTER TWO: WILDERNESS

THE WILDERNESS IS THE NAME WE GIVE THE DANGEROUS AREAS OUTSIDE OF THE PROTECTION OF THE DISTRICTS. THIS IS WHERE WITCHES AND WARLOCKS WHO HAVE MESSED UP AND BEEN FOUND GUILTY ARE SENT INTO EXILE. THERE ARE LOTS OF DANGEROUS CREATURES AND MONSTERS OUT THERE. HERE ARE A FEW...

MONSTER LIST

1. FAIRIES
2. ROTTING DURLOPS
3. DRAGONS
4. MORE CREATURES THAN I CARE TA COUNT

THE WORST OF THE WORST ARE THE FAIRIES. THE AVERAGE WITCH OR WARLOCK WOULD BE DEAD IN SECONDS IF THEY TRIED TA FIGHT AGAINST A FAIRY ONE ON ONE. TA BE HONEST, BEING EXILED IS PRACTICALLY A DEATH SENTENCE. ONLY 2 OUT OF 10 FORSAKEN ACTUALLY LIVE LONG ENOUGH TA SEE THE END OF THEIR EXILE.

HERE'S THE LOWDOWN...*DON'T MESS UP.*

IF YOU ARE FOUND GUILTY, YOU'RE AS GOOD AS DEAD!

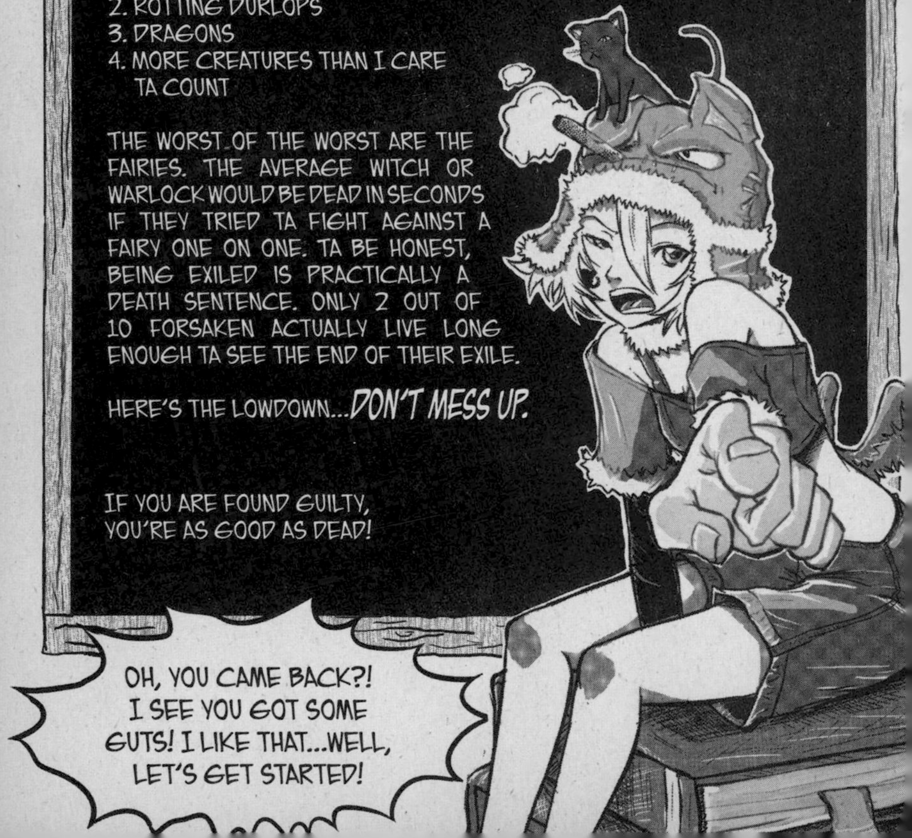
OH, YOU CAME BACK?! I SEE YOU GOT SOME GUTS! I LIKE THAT...WELL, LET'S GET STARTED!

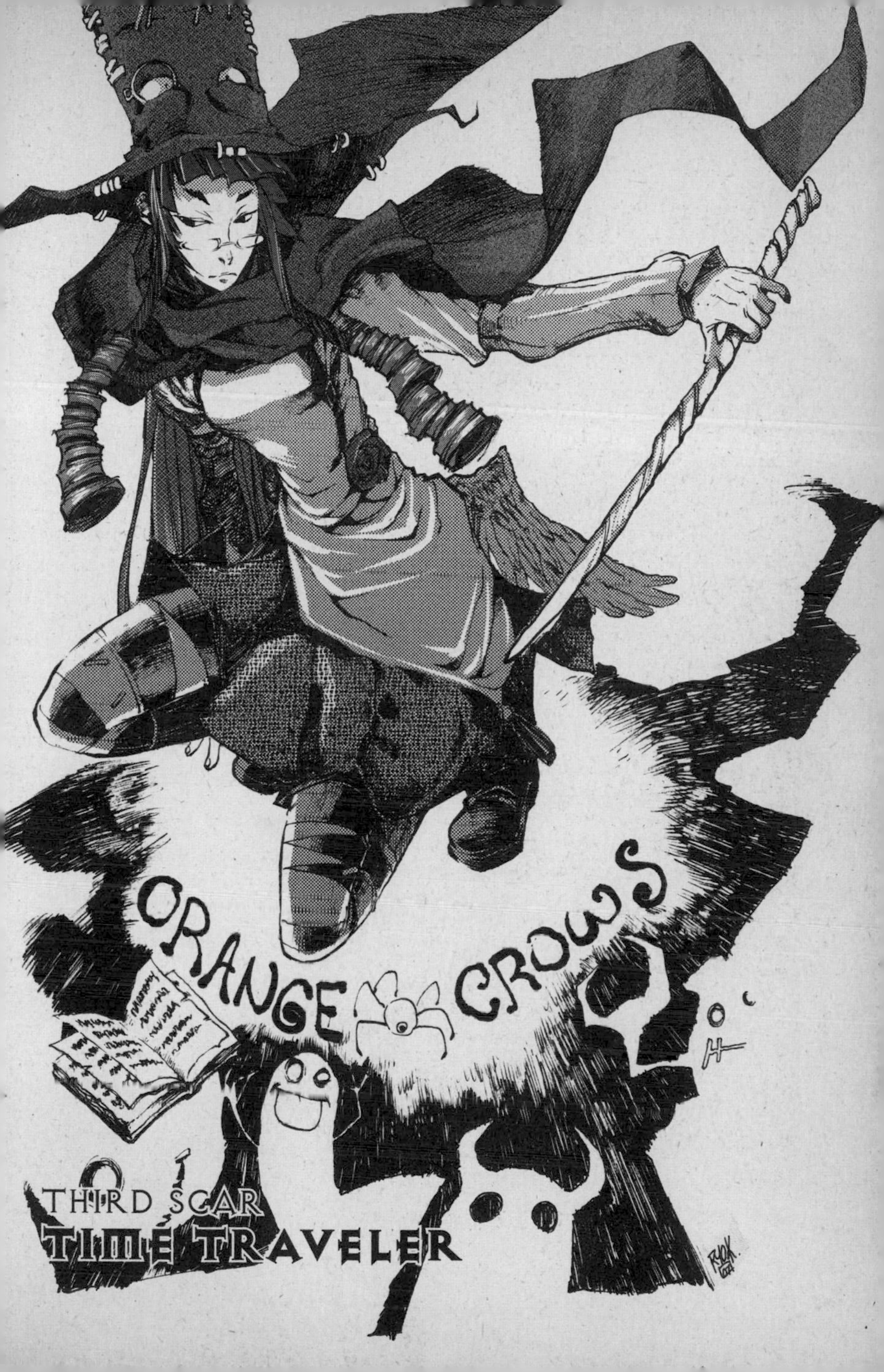
ORANGE CROWS
THIRD SCAR
TIME TRAVELER

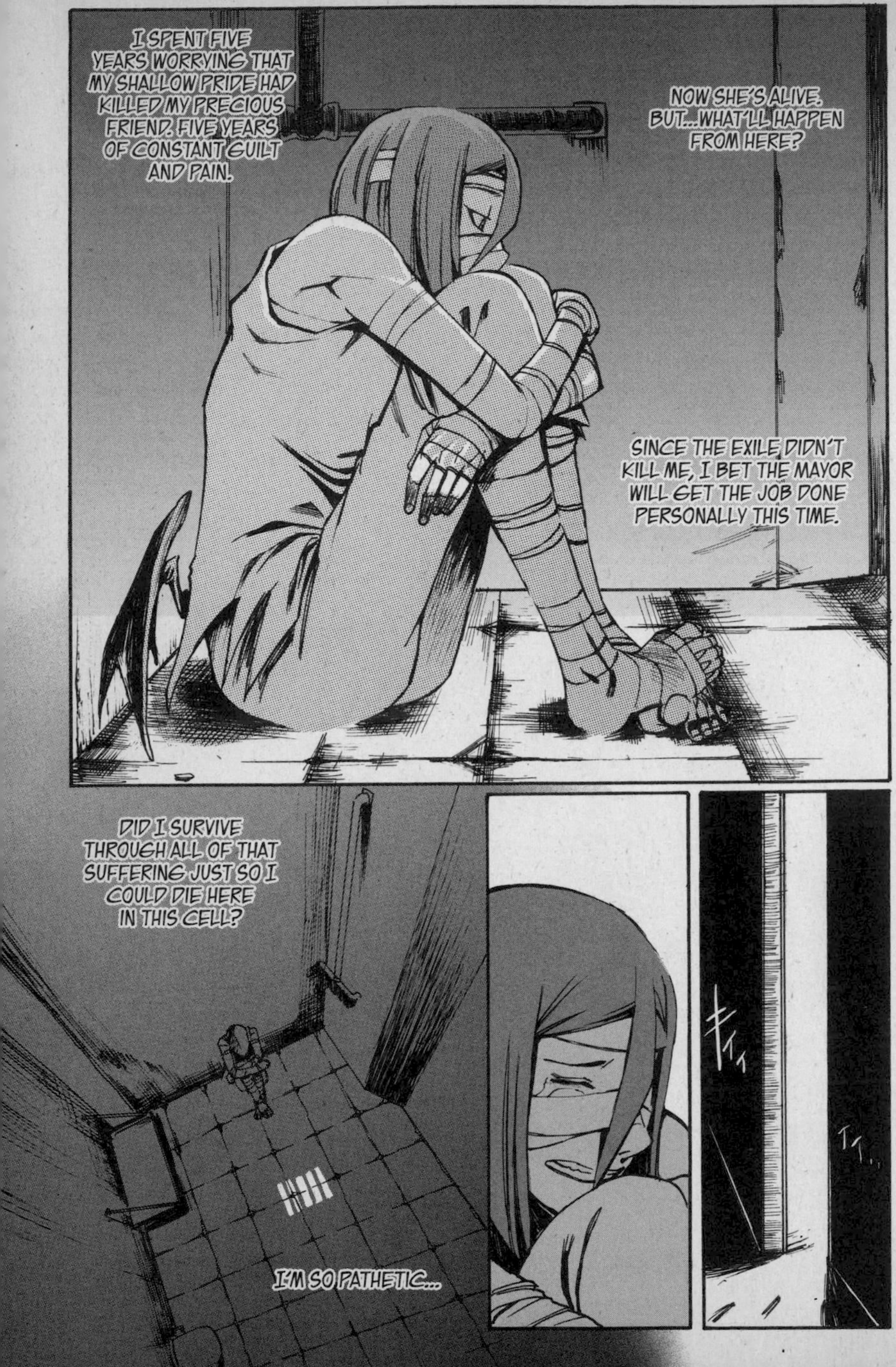
I SPENT FIVE YEARS WORRYING THAT MY SHALLOW PRIDE HAD KILLED MY PRECIOUS FRIEND. FIVE YEARS OF CONSTANT GUILT AND PAIN.
NOW SHE'S ALIVE. BUT...WHAT'LL HAPPEN FROM HERE?
SINCE THE EXILE DIDN'T KILL ME, I BET THE MAYOR WILL GET THE JOB DONE PERSONALLY THIS TIME.
DID I SURVIVE THROUGH ALL OF THAT SUFFERING JUST SO I COULD DIE HERE IN THIS CELL?
I'M SO PATHETIC...

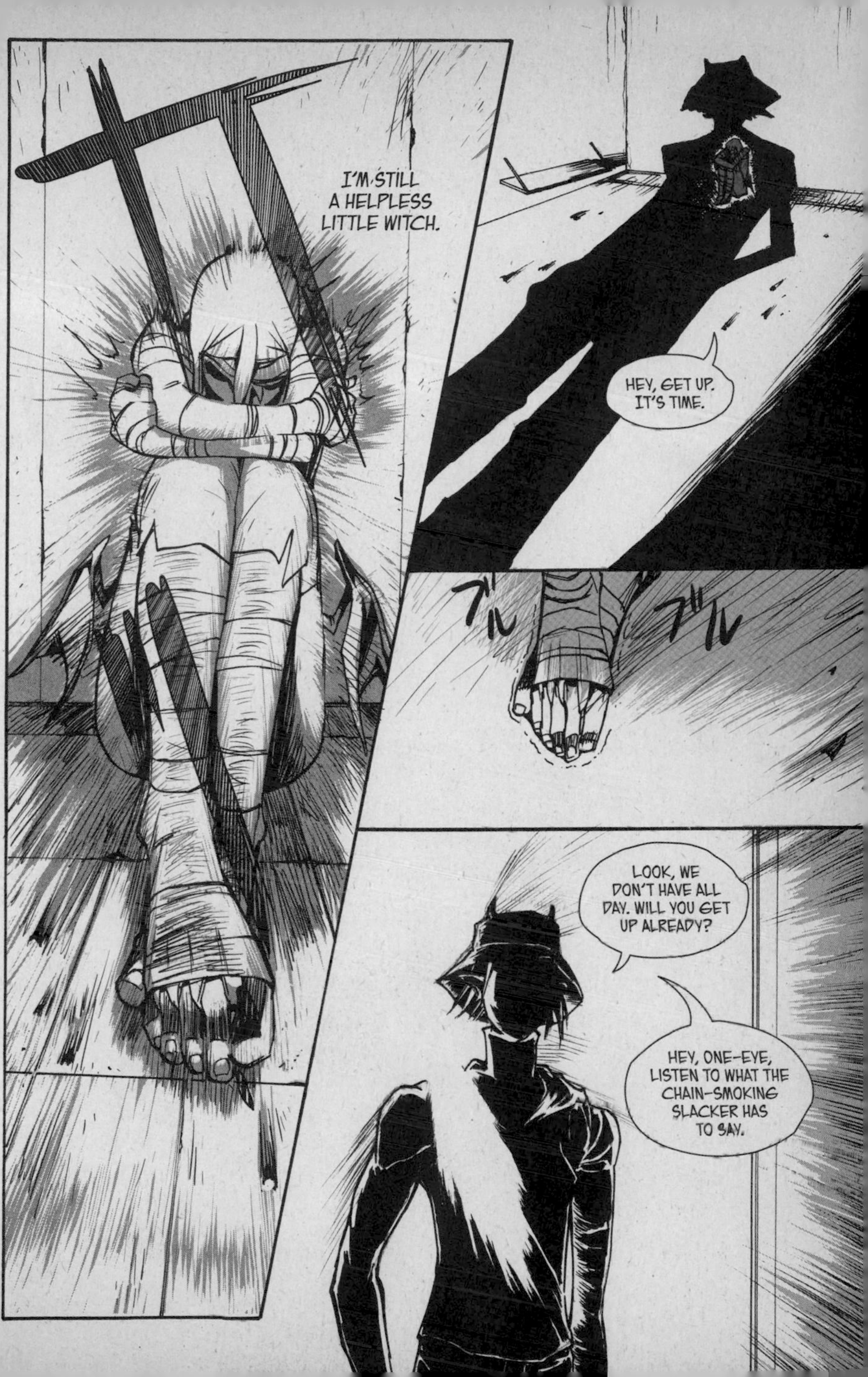
HEY, GET UP. IT'S TIME.
ブル
ブル
LOOK, WE DON'T HAVE ALL DAY. WILL YOU GET UP ALREADY?
HEY, ONE-EYE, LISTEN TO WHAT THE CHAIN-SMOKING SLACKER HAS TO SAY.
I'M STILL A HELPLESS LITTLE WITCH.

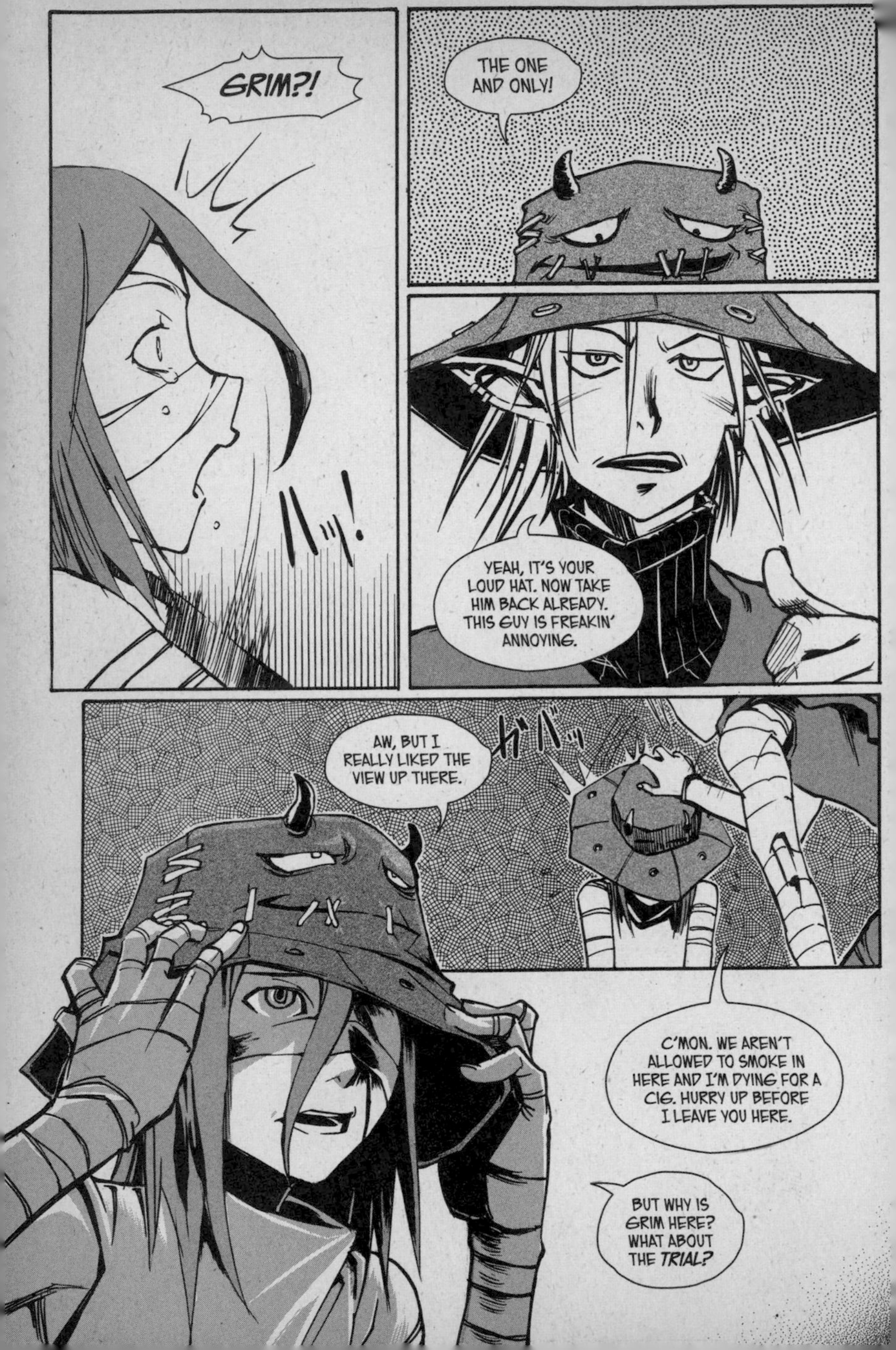
GRIM?!
ハッ!
THE ONE AND ONLY!
YEAH, IT'S YOUR LOUD HAT. NOW TAKE HIM BACK ALREADY. THIS GUY IS FREAKIN' ANNOYING.
AW, BUT I REALLY LIKED THE VIEW UP THERE.
ガバッ
C'MON. WE AREN'T ALLOWED TO SMOKE IN HERE AND I'M DYING FOR A CIG. HURRY UP BEFORE I LEAVE YOU HERE.
BUT WHY IS GRIM HERE? WHAT ABOUT THE *TRIAL?*

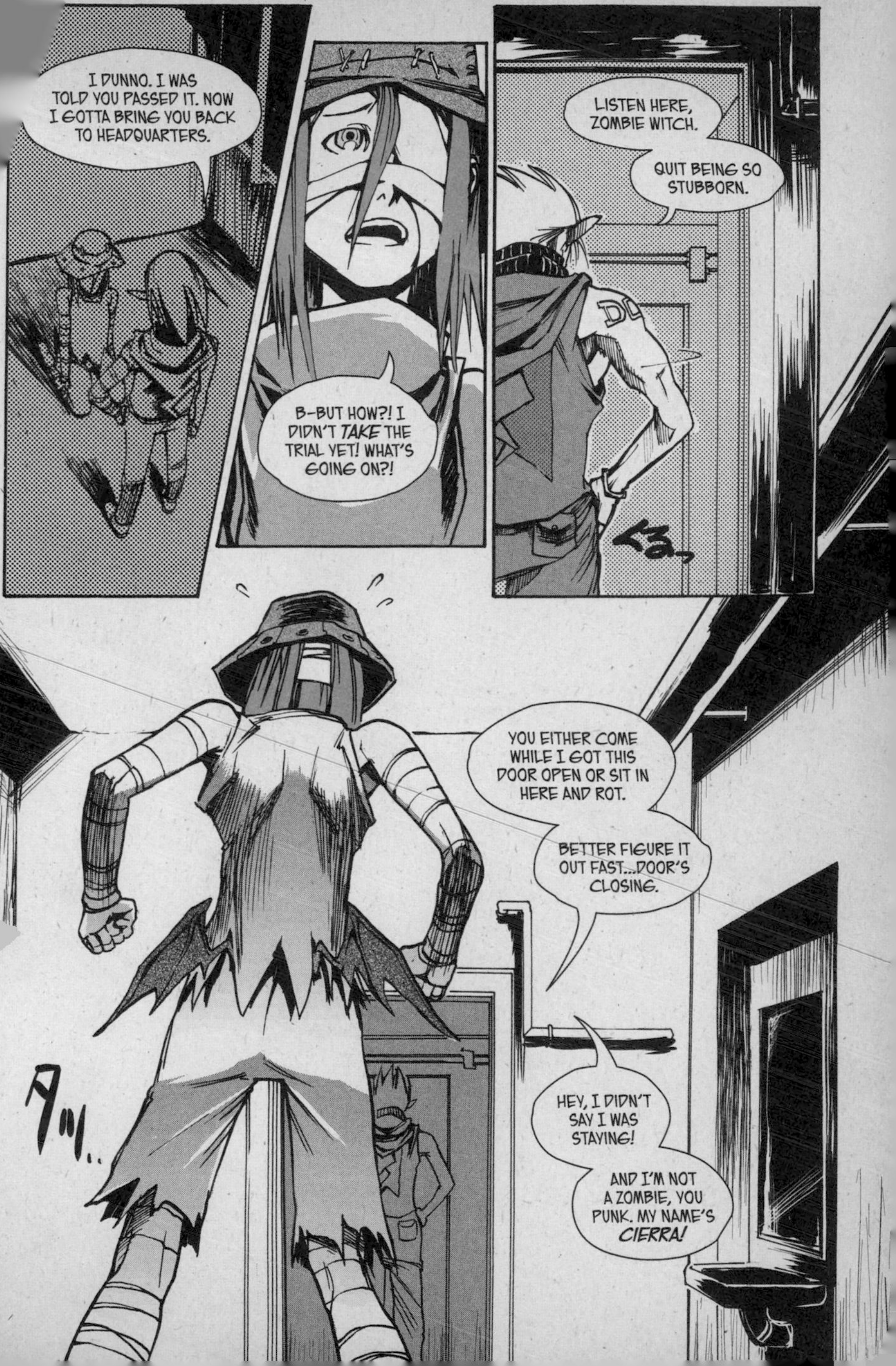
I DUNNO. I WAS TOLD YOU PASSED IT. NOW I GOTTA BRING YOU BACK TO HEADQUARTERS.
B-BUT HOW?! I DIDN'T *TAKE* THE TRIAL YET! WHAT'S GOING ON?!
LISTEN HERE, ZOMBIE WITCH.
QUIT BEING SO STUBBORN.
くるっ
YOU EITHER COME WHILE I GOT THIS DOOR OPEN OR SIT IN HERE AND ROT.
BETTER FIGURE IT OUT FAST...DOOR'S CLOSING.
HEY, I DIDN'T SAY I WAS STAYING!
AND I'M NOT A ZOMBIE, YOU PUNK. MY NAME'S ***CIERRA!***

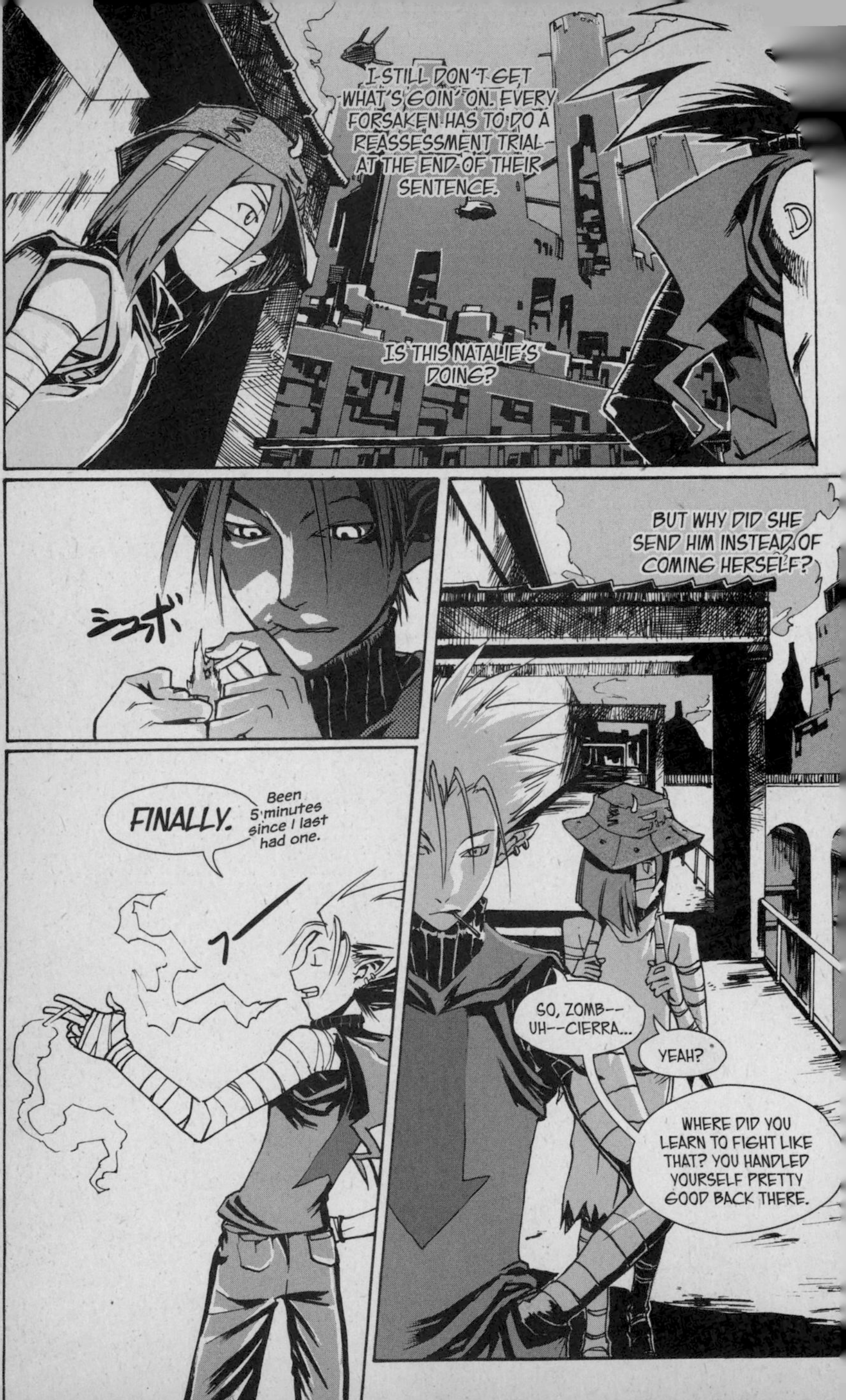
I STILL DON'T GET WHAT'S GOIN' ON. EVERY FORSAKEN HAS TO DO A REASSESSMENT TRIAL AT THE END OF THEIR SENTENCE.
IS THIS NATALIE'S DOING?
BUT WHY DID SHE SEND HIM INSTEAD OF COMING HERSELF?
SO, ZOMB-- UH--CIERRA...
YEAH?
WHERE DID YOU LEARN TO FIGHT LIKE THAT? YOU HANDLED YOURSELF PRETTY GOOD BACK THERE.
シュッボ
FINALLY.
Been 5 minutes since I last had one.
フー

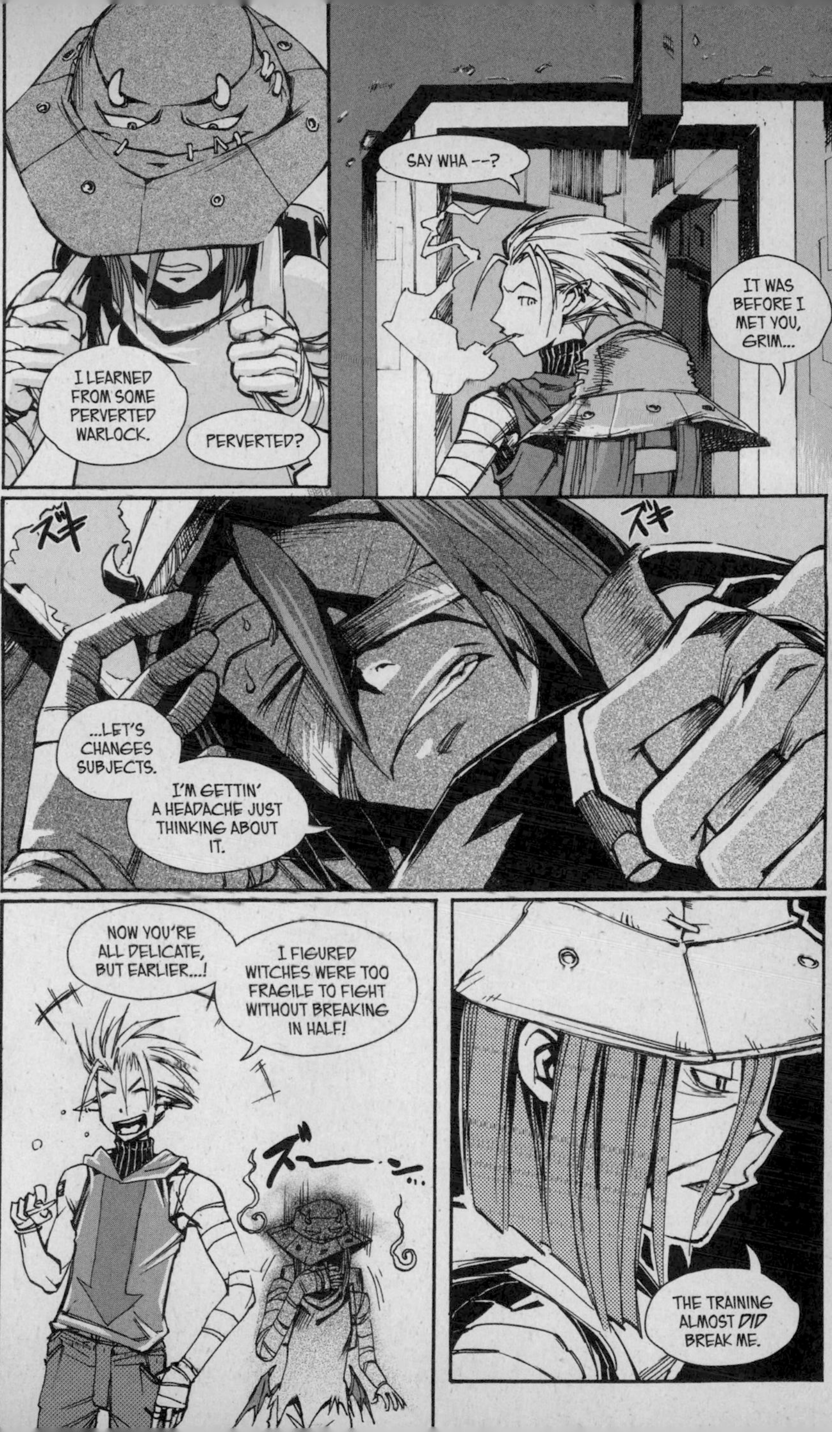
SAY WHA --?
IT WAS BEFORE I MET YOU, GRIM...
I LEARNED FROM SOME PERVERTED WARLOCK.
PERVERTED?
ズキ
ズキ
...LET'S CHANGES SUBJECTS.
I'M GETTIN' A HEADACHE JUST THINKING ABOUT IT.
THE TRAINING ALMOST *DID* BREAK ME.
NOW YOU'RE ALL DELICATE, BUT EARLIER...!
I FIGURED WITCHES WERE TOO FRAGILE TO FIGHT WITHOUT BREAKING IN HALF!
ズーン...

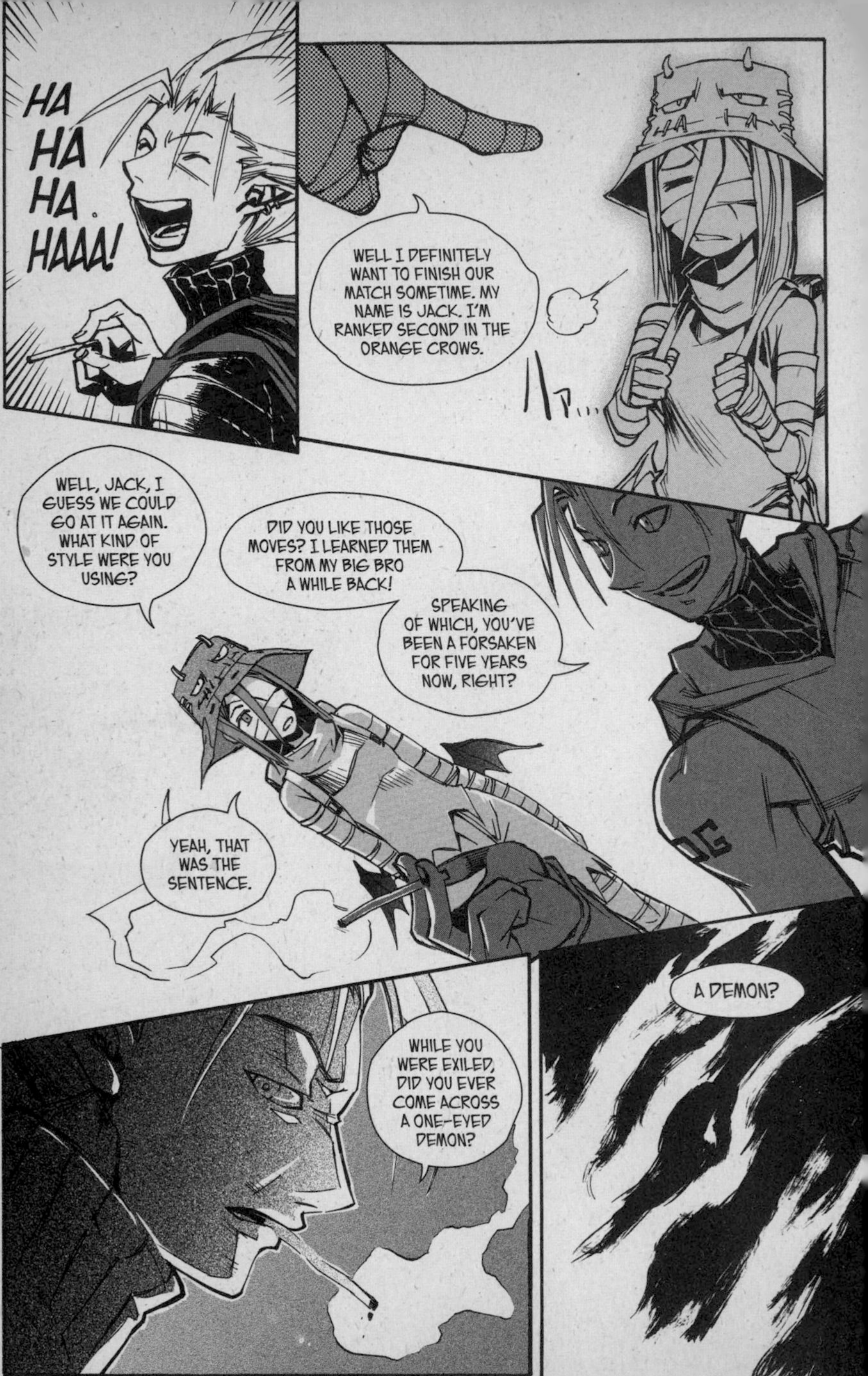
HA HA HA HAAA!
WELL I DEFINITELY WANT TO FINISH OUR MATCH SOMETIME. MY NAME IS JACK. I'M RANKED SECOND IN THE ORANGE CROWS.
WELL, JACK, I GUESS WE COULD GO AT IT AGAIN. WHAT KIND OF STYLE WERE YOU USING?
DID YOU LIKE THOSE MOVES? I LEARNED THEM FROM MY BIG BRO A WHILE BACK!
SPEAKING OF WHICH, YOU'VE BEEN A FORSAKEN FOR FIVE YEARS NOW, RIGHT?
YEAH, THAT WAS THE SENTENCE.
WHILE YOU WERE EXILED, DID YOU EVER COME ACROSS A ONE-EYED DEMON?
A DEMON?

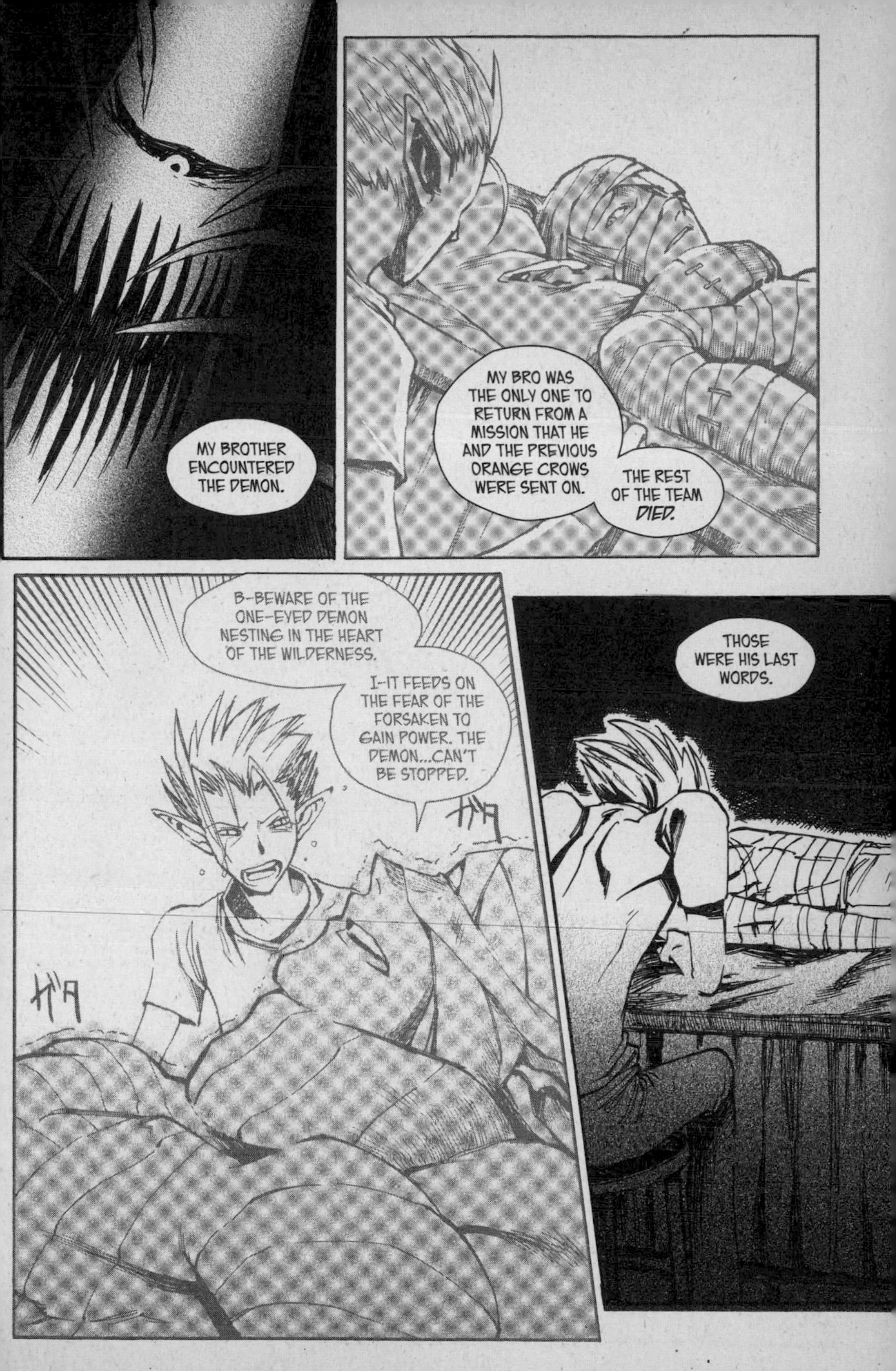
MY BROTHER ENCOUNTERED THE DEMON.
MY BRO WAS THE ONLY ONE TO RETURN FROM A MISSION THAT HE AND THE PREVIOUS ORANGE CROWS WERE SENT ON.
THE REST OF THE TEAM *DIED.*
B--BEWARE OF THE ONE-EYED DEMON NESTING IN THE HEART OF THE WILDERNESS.
I--IT FEEDS ON THE FEAR OF THE FORSAKEN TO GAIN POWER. THE DEMON...CAN'T BE STOPPED.
THOSE WERE HIS LAST WORDS.

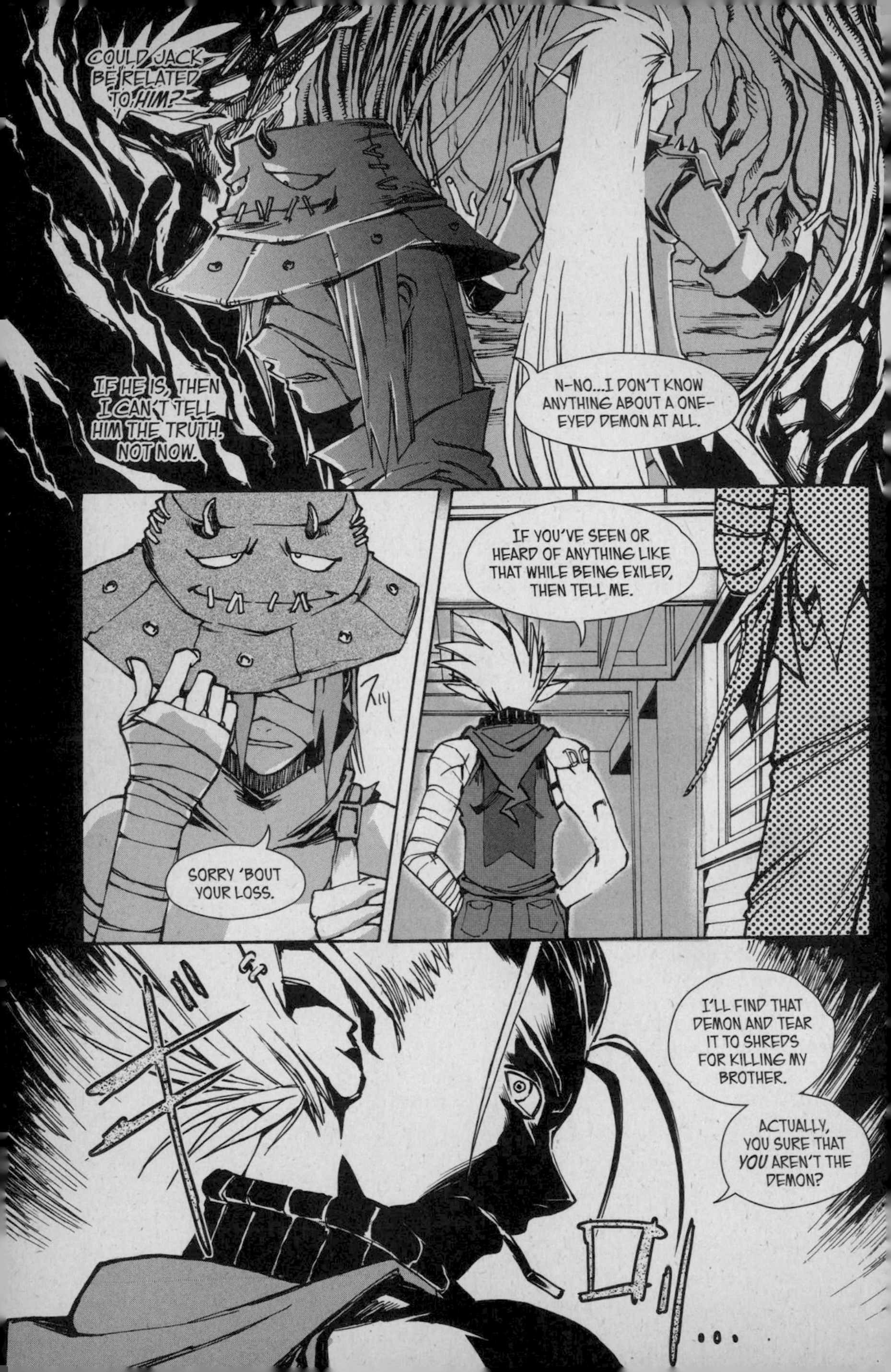
COULD JACK BE RELATED TO HIM?
IF HE IS, THEN I CAN'T TELL HIM THE TRUTH. NOT NOW.
N-NO...I DON'T KNOW ANYTHING ABOUT A ONE-EYED DEMON AT ALL.
SORRY 'BOUT YOUR LOSS.
IF YOU'VE SEEN OR HEARD OF ANYTHING LIKE THAT WHILE BEING EXILED, THEN TELL ME.
I'LL FIND THAT DEMON AND TEAR IT TO SHREDS FOR KILLING MY BROTHER.
ACTUALLY, YOU SURE THAT *YOU* AREN'T THE DEMON?
...

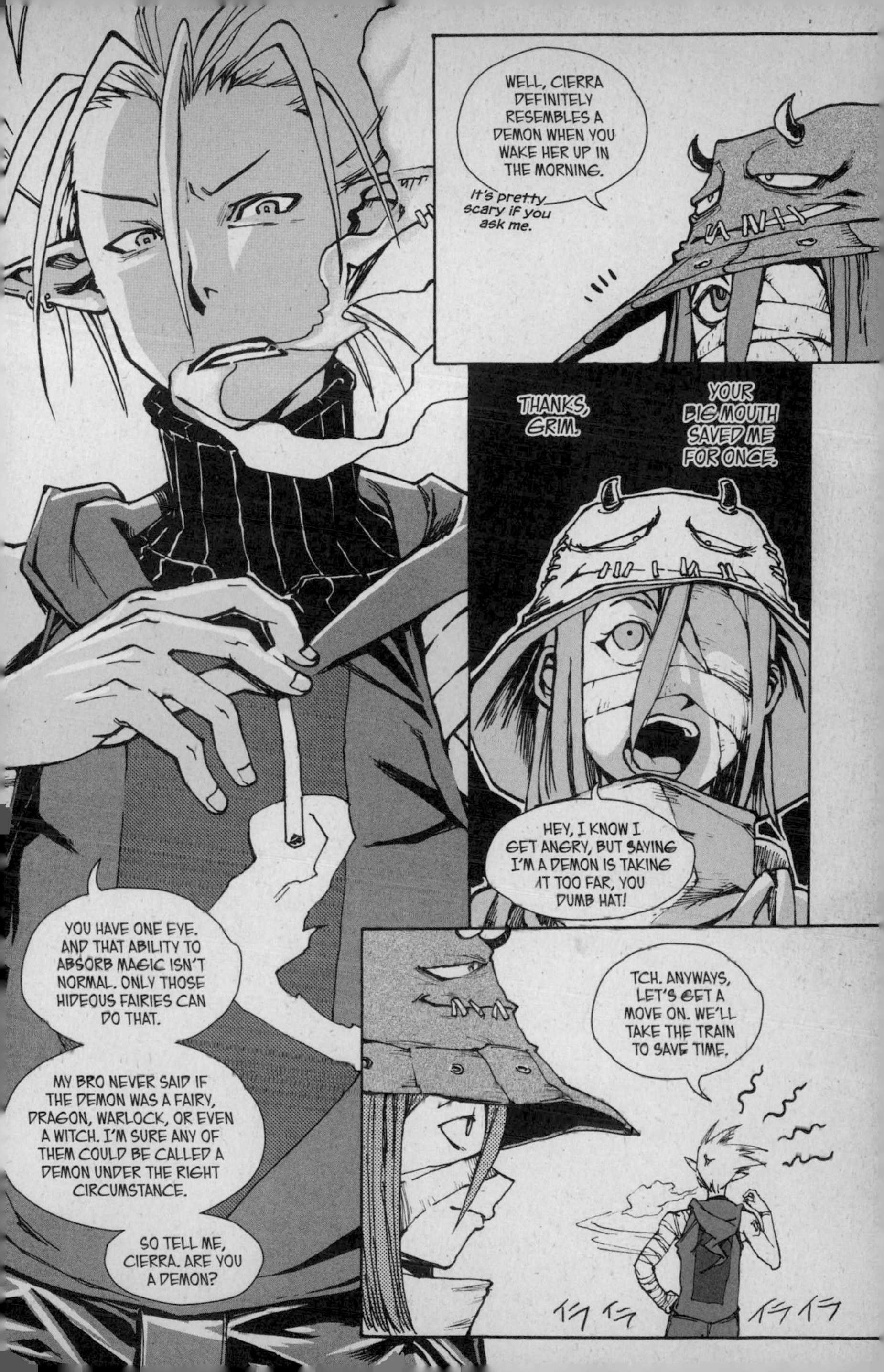
YOU HAVE ONE EYE. AND THAT ABILITY TO ABSORB MAGIC ISN'T NORMAL. ONLY THOSE HIDEOUS FAIRIES CAN DO THAT.
MY BRO NEVER SAID IF THE DEMON WAS A FAIRY, DRAGON, WARLOCK, OR EVEN A WITCH. I'M SURE ANY OF THEM COULD BE CALLED A DEMON UNDER THE RIGHT CIRCUMSTANCE.
SO TELL ME, CIERRA. ARE YOU A DEMON?
WELL, CIERRA DEFINITELY RESEMBLES A DEMON WHEN YOU WAKE HER UP IN THE MORNING.
It's pretty scary if you ask me.
THANKS, GRIM.
YOUR BIG MOUTH SAVED ME FOR ONCE.
HEY, I KNOW I GET ANGRY, BUT SAYING I'M A DEMON IS TAKING IT TOO FAR, YOU DUMB HAT!
TCH. ANYWAYS, LET'S GET A MOVE ON. WE'LL TAKE THE TRAIN TO SAVE TIME.
イラ イラ
イラ イラ

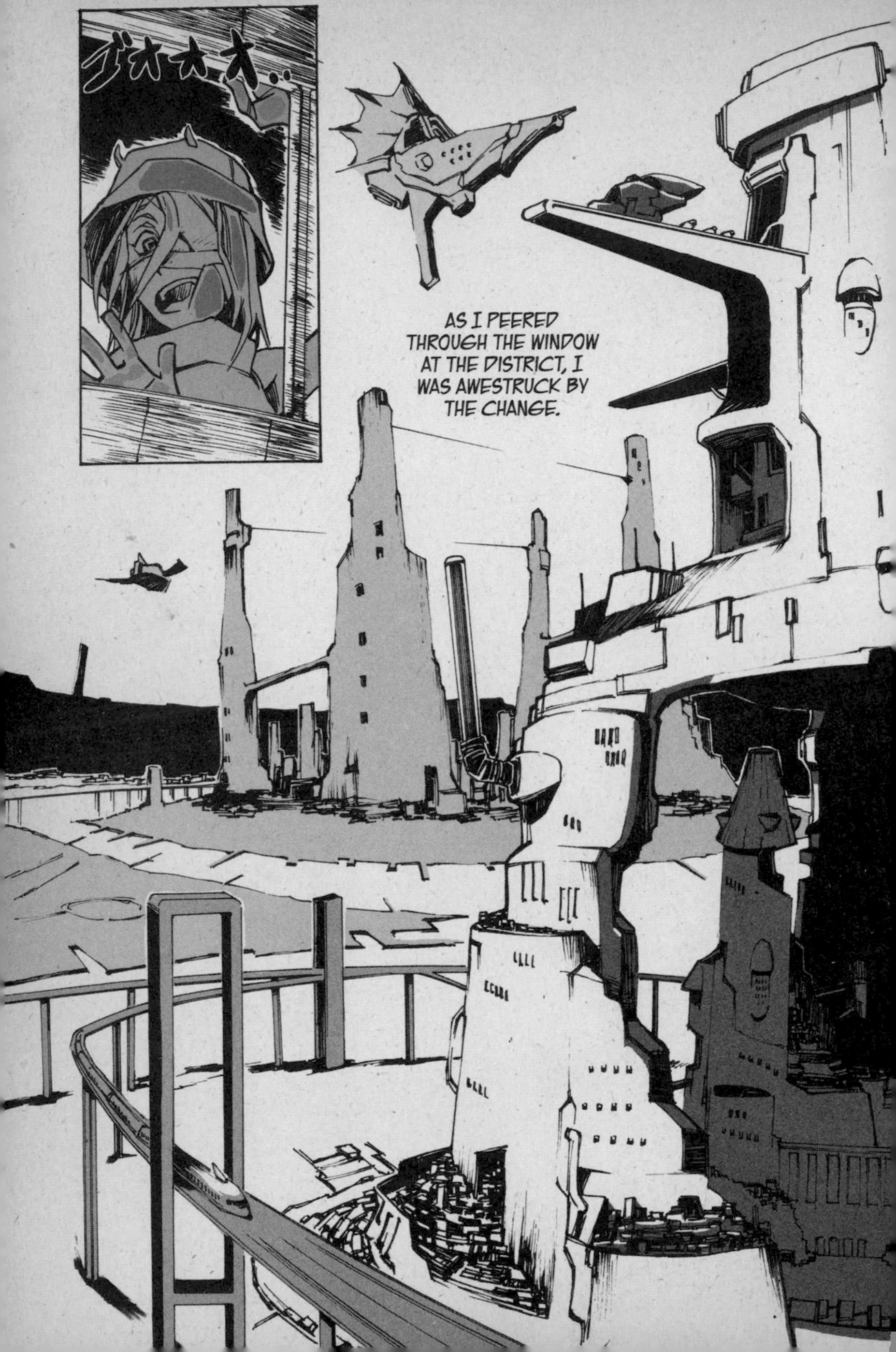
AS I PEERED THROUGH THE WINDOW AT THE DISTRICT, I WAS AWESTRUCK BY THE CHANGE.
ゴオオオ..

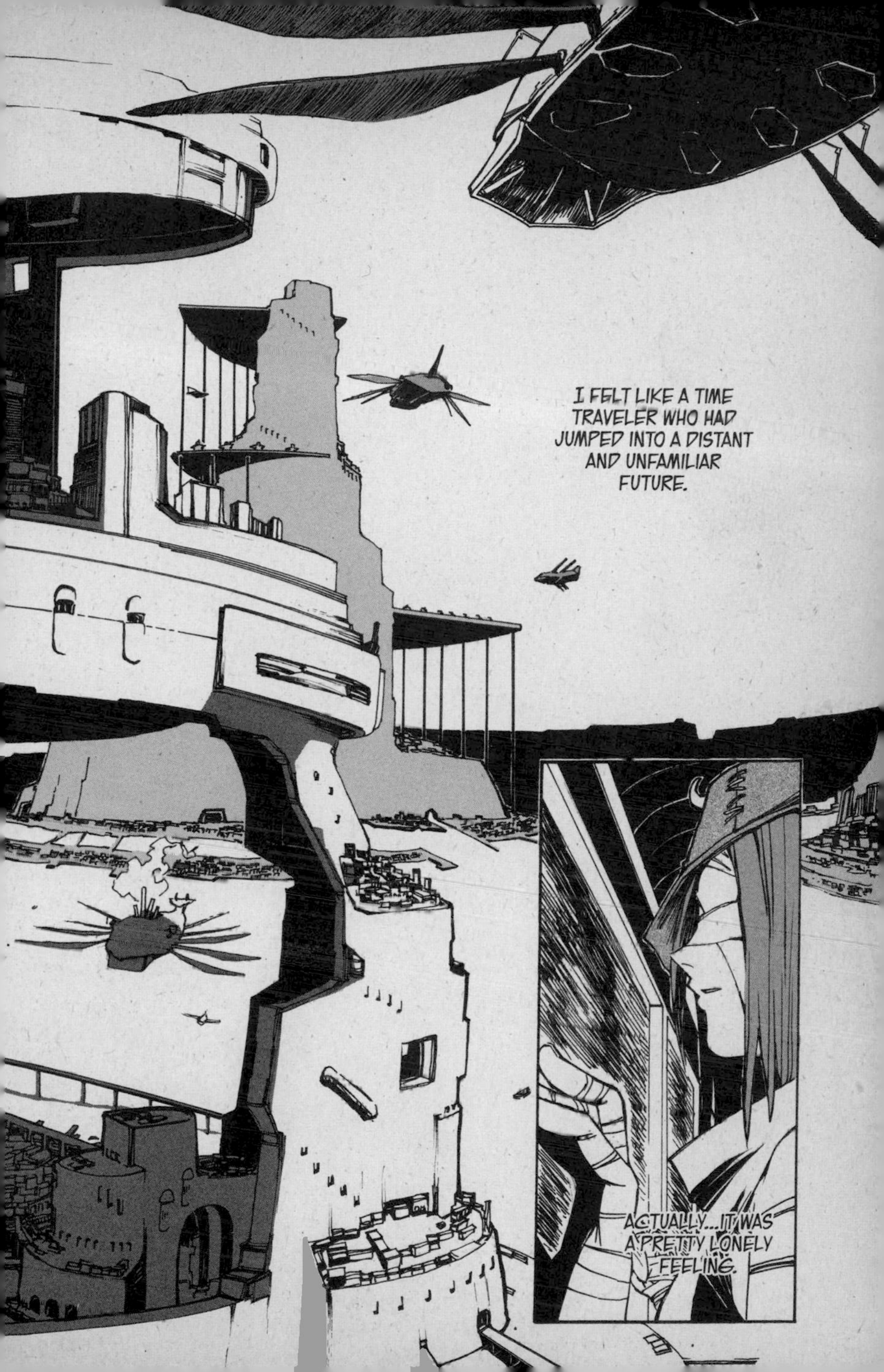
I FELT LIKE A TIME TRAVELER WHO HAD JUMPED INTO A DISTANT AND UNFAMILIAR FUTURE.
ACTUALLY... IT WAS A PRETTY LONELY FEELING.

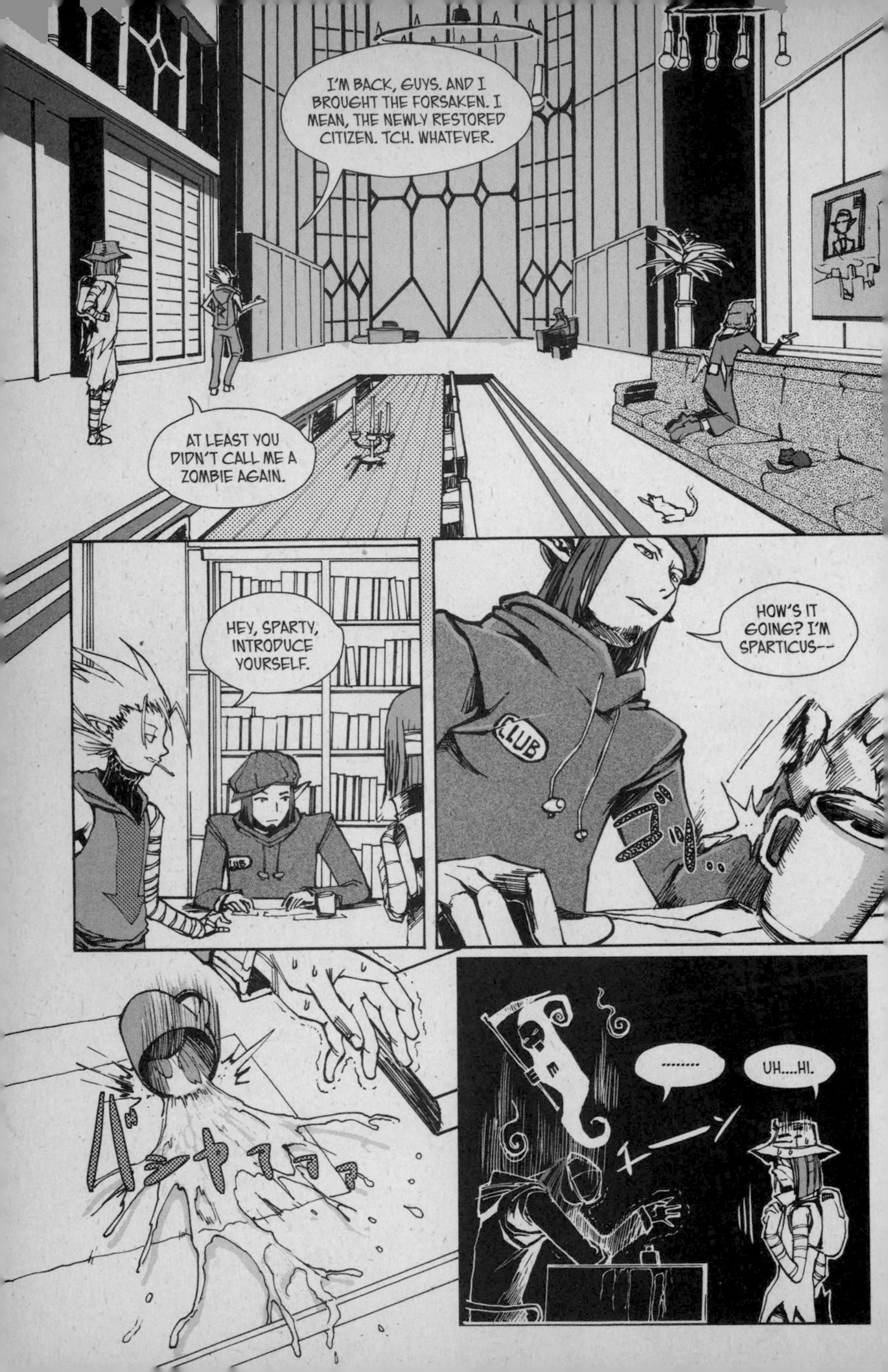
I'M BACK, GUYS. AND I BROUGHT THE FORSAKEN. I MEAN, THE NEWLY RESTORED CITIZEN. TCH. WHATEVER.
AT LEAST YOU DIDN'T CALL ME A ZOMBIE AGAIN.
HEY, SPARTY, INTRODUCE YOURSELF.
HOW'S IT GOING? I'M SPARTICUS--
CLUB
....
UH....HI.

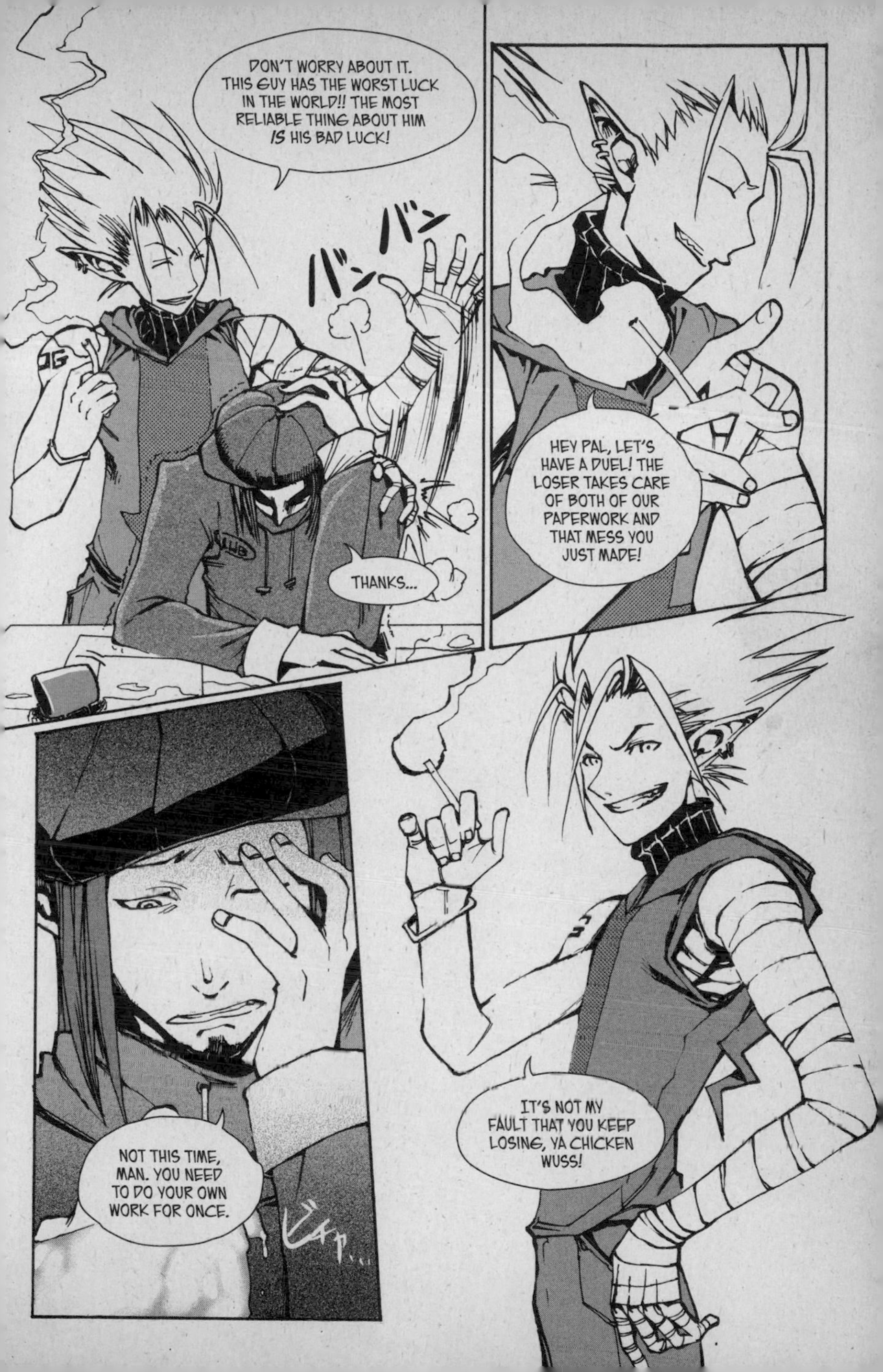
DON'T WORRY ABOUT IT. THIS GUY HAS THE WORST LUCK IN THE WORLD!! THE MOST RELIABLE THING ABOUT HIM *IS* HIS BAD LUCK!
バン
バン
THANKS...
HEY PAL, LET'S HAVE A DUEL! THE LOSER TAKES CARE OF BOTH OF OUR PAPERWORK AND THAT MESS YOU JUST MADE!
NOT THIS TIME, MAN. YOU NEED TO DO YOUR OWN WORK FOR ONCE.
IT'S NOT MY FAULT THAT YOU KEEP LOSING, YA CHICKEN WUSS!

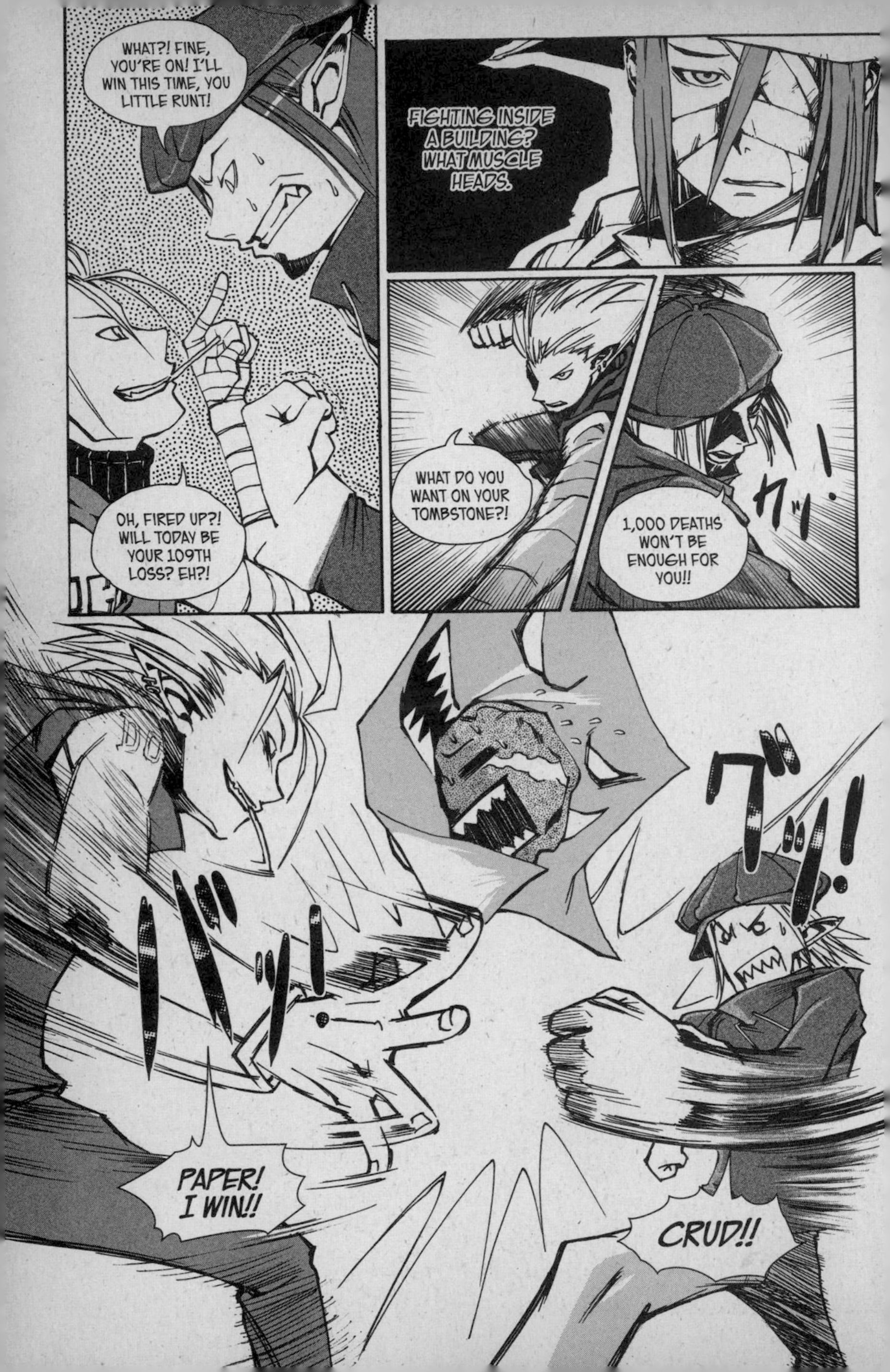
FIGHTING INSIDE A BUILDING? WHAT MUSCLE HEADS.
WHAT?! FINE, YOU'RE ON! I'LL WIN THIS TIME, YOU LITTLE RUNT!
OH, FIRED UP?! WILL TODAY BE YOUR 109TH LOSS? EH?!
1,000 DEATHS WON'T BE ENOUGH FOR YOU!!
WHAT DO YOU WANT ON YOUR TOMBSTONE?!
PAPER! I WIN!!
CRUD!!

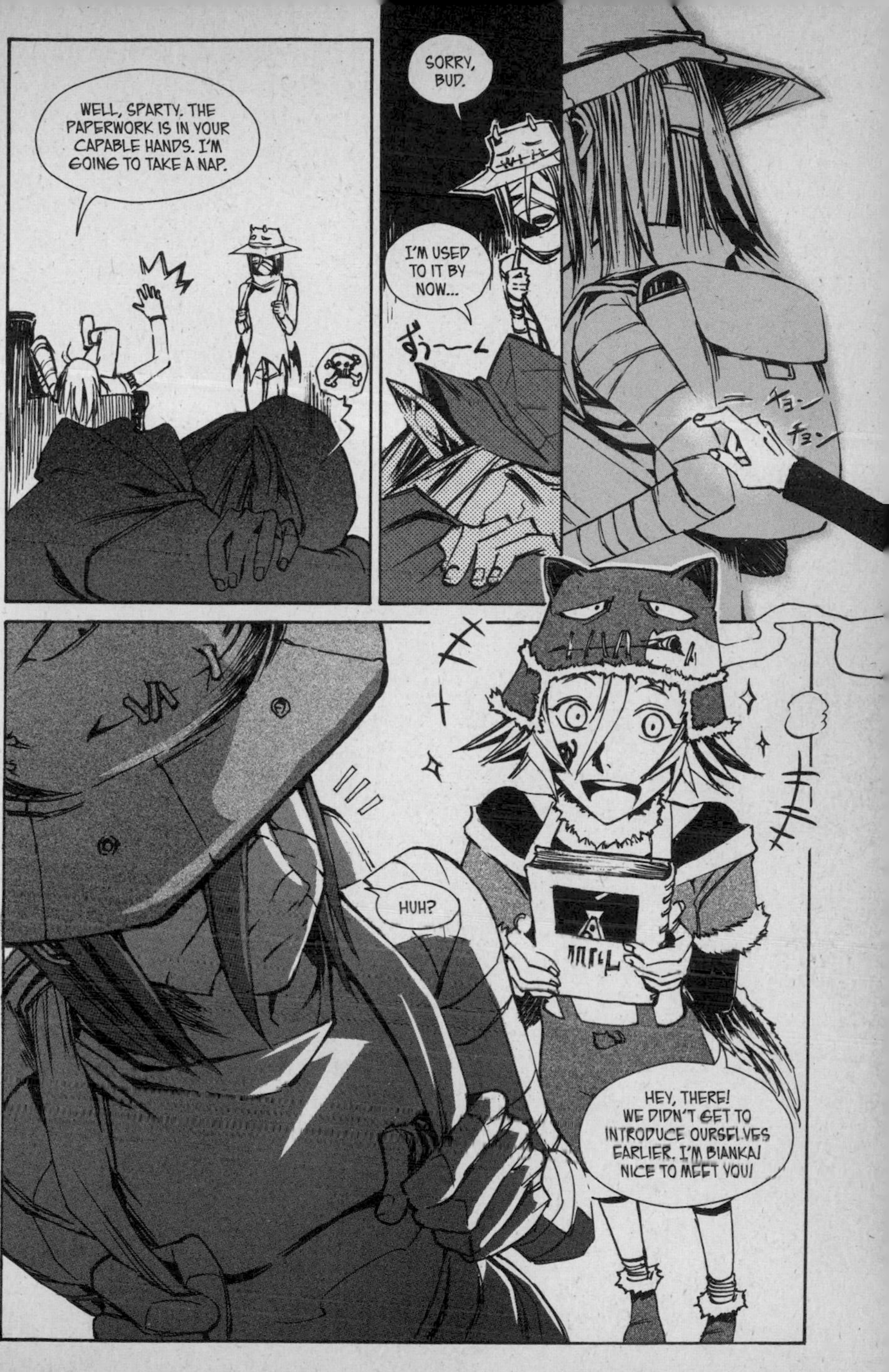
WELL, SPARTY. THE PAPERWORK IS IN YOUR CAPABLE HANDS. I'M GOING TO TAKE A NAP.
SORRY, BUD.
I'M USED TO IT BY NOW...
ずぅ～～ん
チョン
チョン
HUH?
HEY, THERE! WE DIDN'T GET TO INTRODUCE OURSELVES EARLIER. I'M BIANKA! NICE TO MEET YOU!

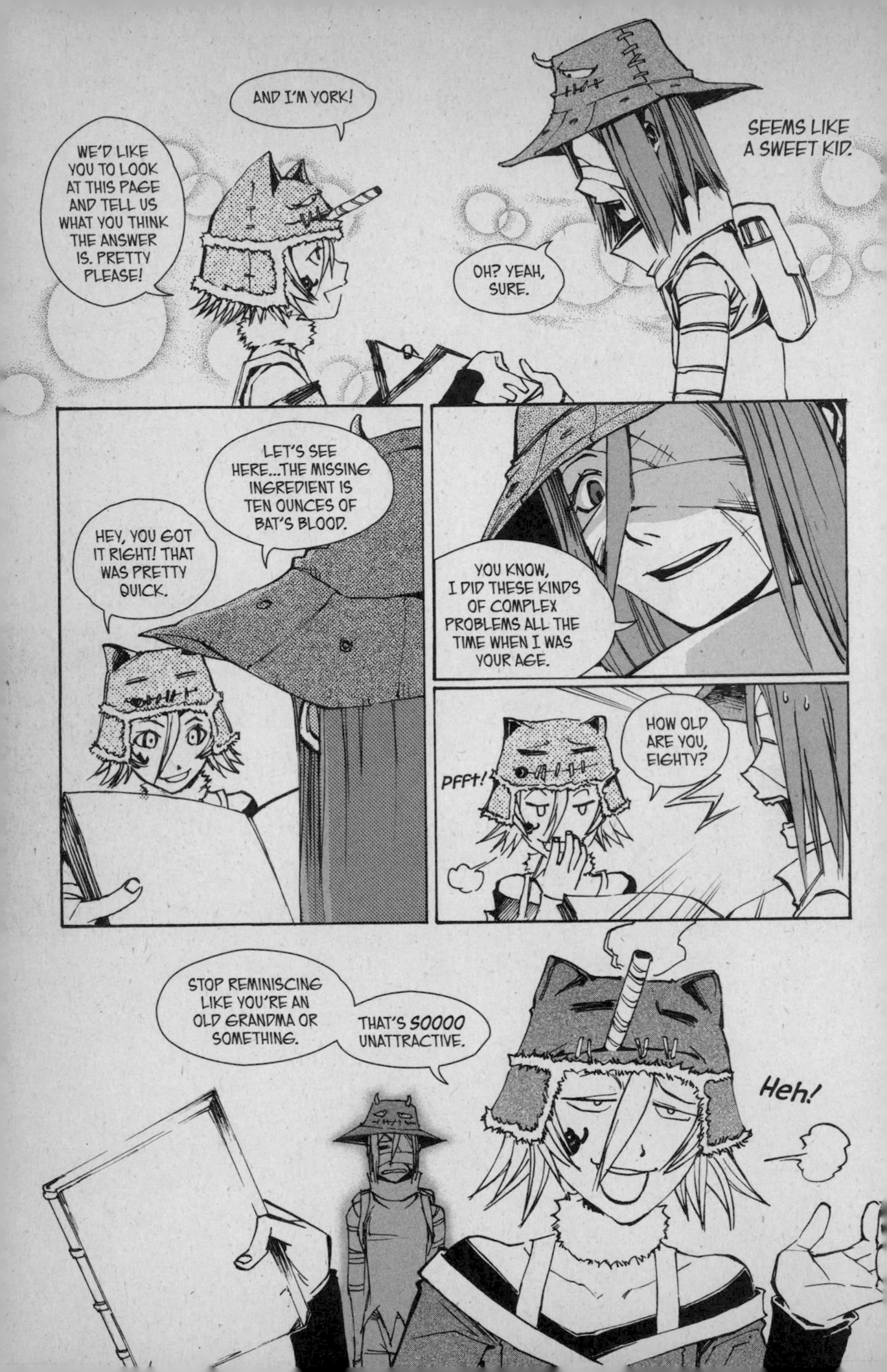
AND I'M YORK!
WE'D LIKE YOU TO LOOK AT THIS PAGE AND TELL US WHAT YOU THINK THE ANSWER IS. PRETTY PLEASE!
OH? YEAH, SURE.
SEEMS LIKE A SWEET KID.
LET'S SEE HERE...THE MISSING INGREDIENT IS TEN OUNCES OF BAT'S BLOOD.
HEY, YOU GOT IT RIGHT! THAT WAS PRETTY QUICK.
YOU KNOW, I DID THESE KINDS OF COMPLEX PROBLEMS ALL THE TIME WHEN I WAS YOUR AGE.
HOW OLD ARE YOU, EIGHTY?
PFFt!
STOP REMINISCING LIKE YOU'RE AN OLD GRANDMA OR SOMETHING.
THAT'S SOOOO UNATTRACTIVE.
Heh!

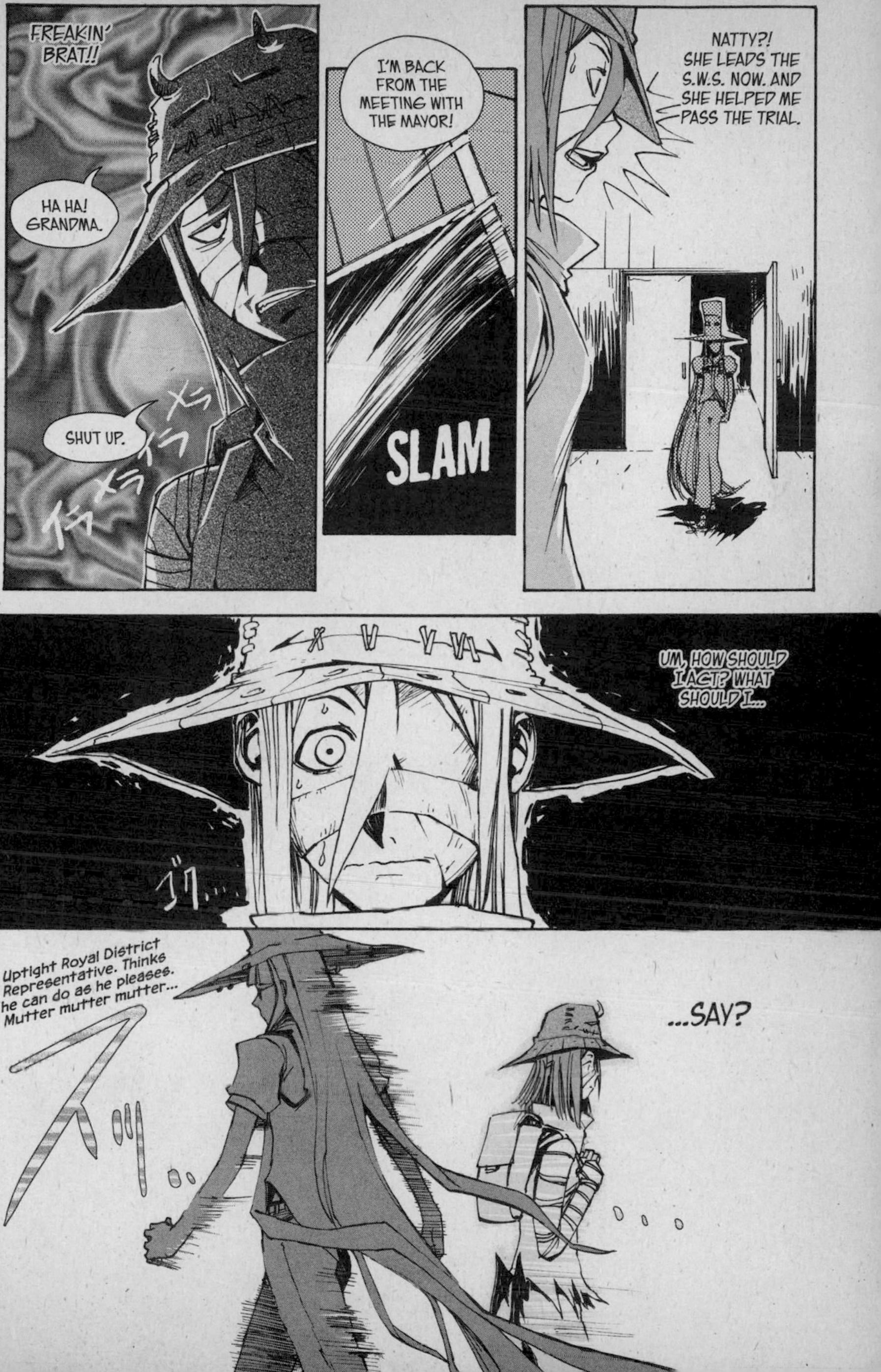
NATTY?! SHE LEADS THE S.W.S. NOW. AND SHE HELPED ME PASS THE TRIAL.
I'M BACK FROM THE MEETING WITH THE MAYOR!
SLAM
FREAKIN' BRAT!!
HA HA! GRANDMA.
SHUT UP.
UM, HOW SHOULD I ACT? WHAT SHOULD I...
...SAY?
Uptight Royal District Representative. Thinks he can do as he pleases. Mutter mutter mutter...

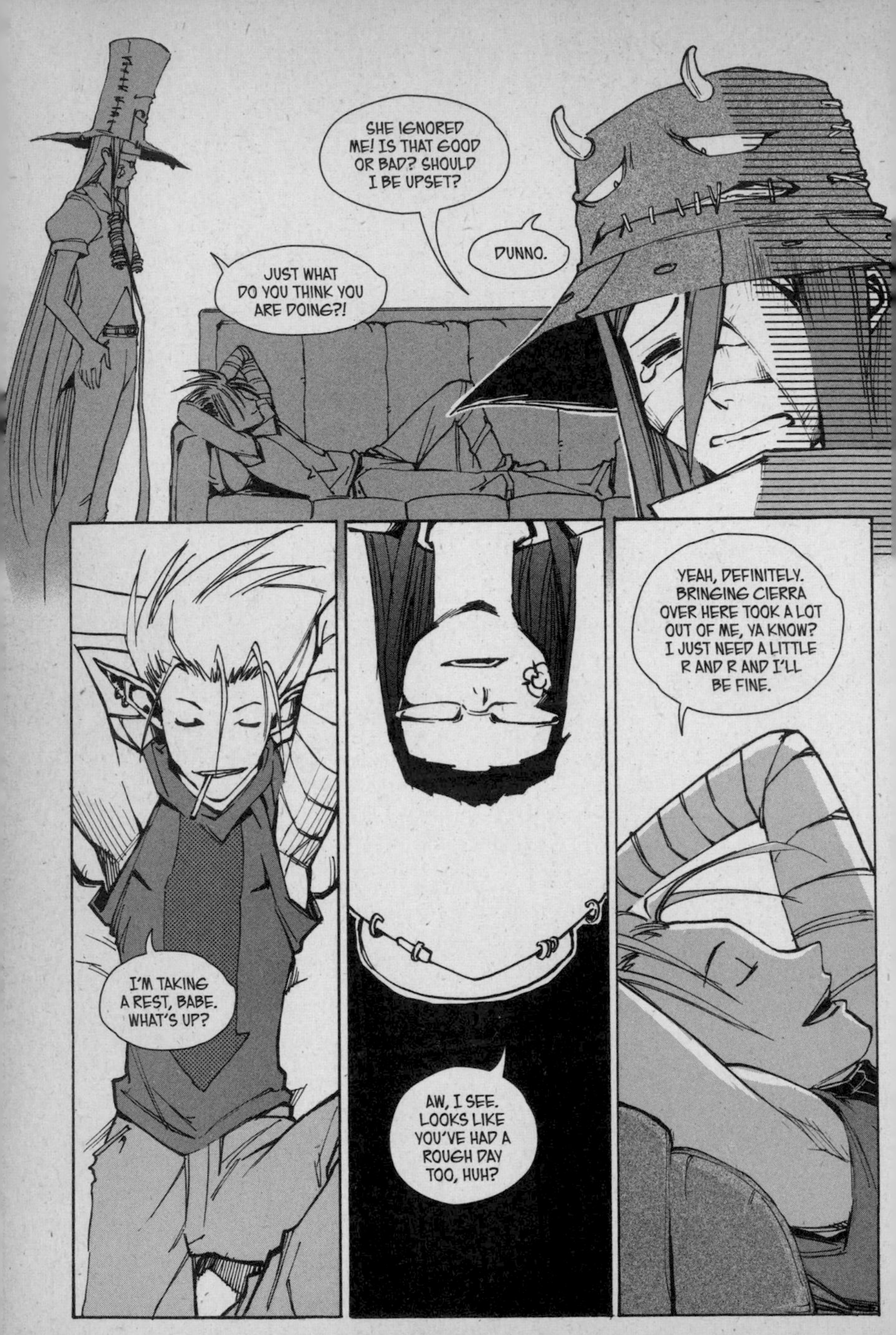
JUST WHAT DO YOU THINK YOU ARE DOING?!
SHE IGNORED ME! IS THAT GOOD OR BAD? SHOULD I BE UPSET?
DUNNO.
I'M TAKING A REST, BABE. WHAT'S UP?
AW, I SEE. LOOKS LIKE YOU'VE HAD A ROUGH DAY TOO, HUH?
YEAH, DEFINITELY. BRINGING CIERRA OVER HERE TOOK A LOT OUT OF ME, YA KNOW? I JUST NEED A LITTLE R AND R AND I'LL BE FINE.

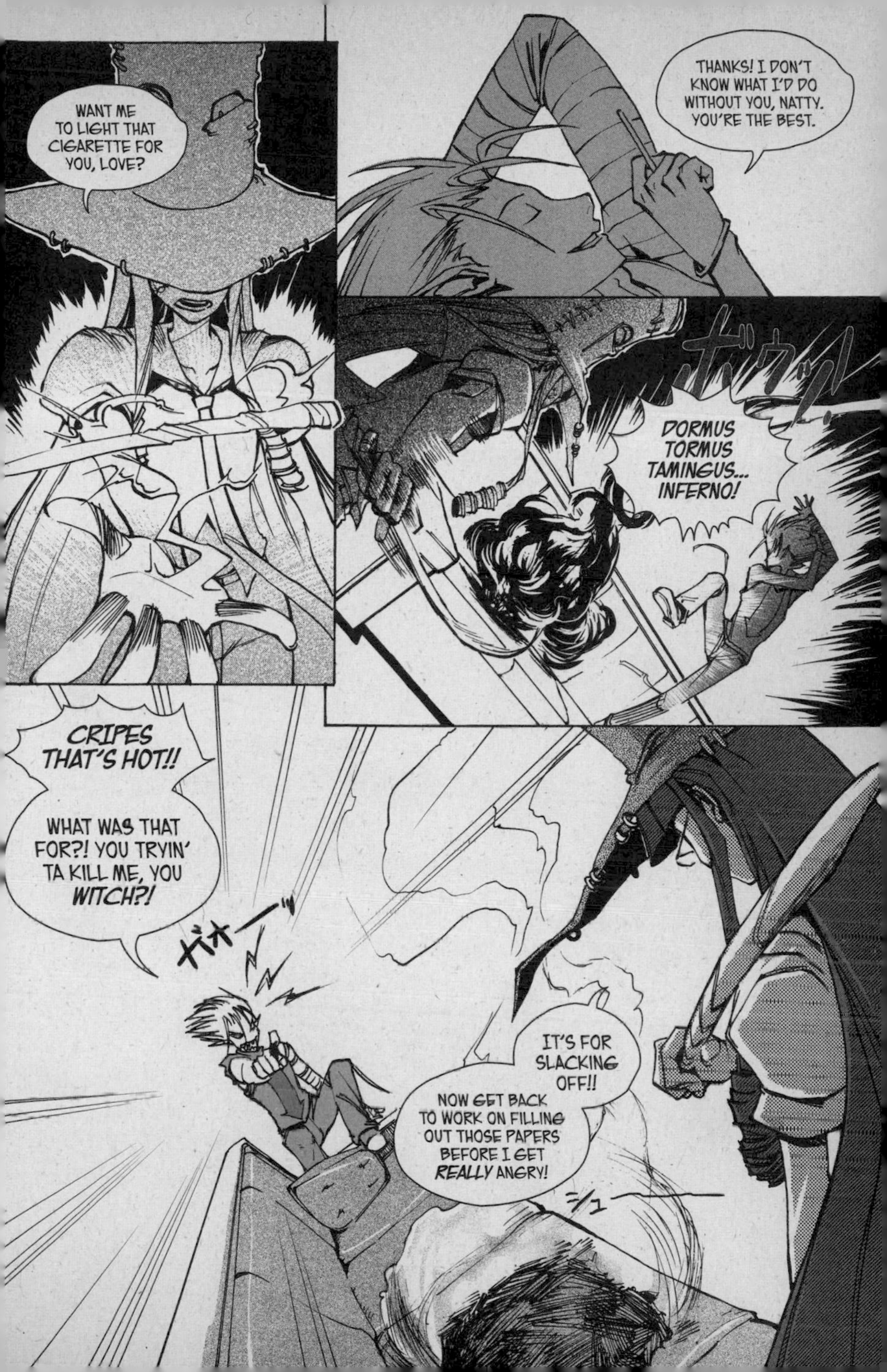
WANT ME TO LIGHT THAT CIGARETTE FOR YOU, LOVE?
THANKS! I DON'T KNOW WHAT I'D DO WITHOUT YOU, NATTY. YOU'RE THE BEST.
DORMUS TORMUS TAMINGUS... INFERNO!
CRIPES THAT'S HOT!!
WHAT WAS THAT FOR?! YOU TRYIN' TA KILL ME, YOU WITCH?!
IT'S FOR SLACKING OFF!!
NOW GET BACK TO WORK ON FILLING OUT THOSE PAPERS BEFORE I GET REALLY ANGRY!

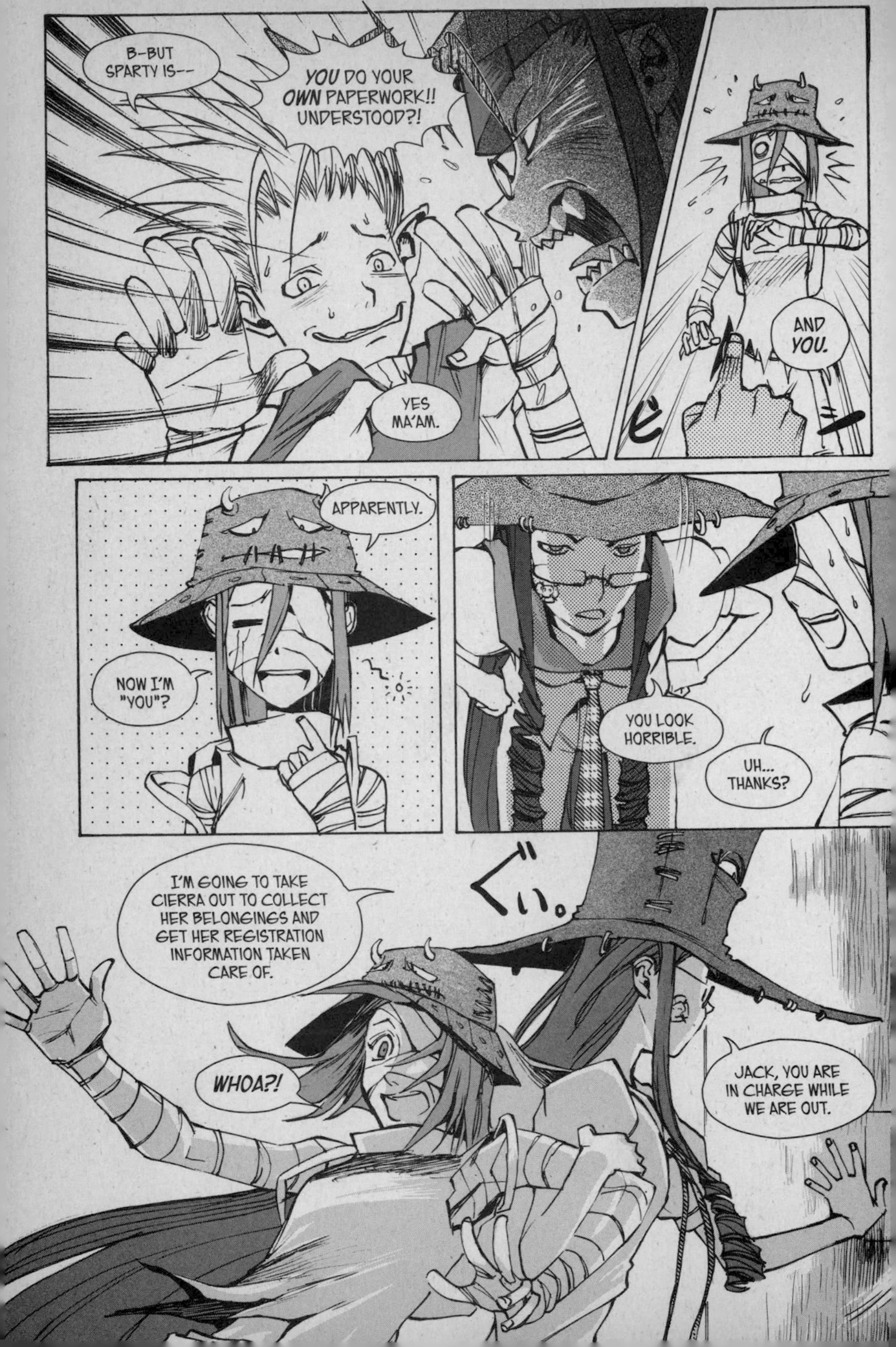
B-BUT SPARTY IS--
YOU DO YOUR *OWN* PAPERWORK!! UNDERSTOOD?!
YES MA'AM.
AND *YOU*.
APPARENTLY.
NOW I'M "YOU"?
YOU LOOK HORRIBLE.
UH... THANKS?
I'M GOING TO TAKE CIERRA OUT TO COLLECT HER BELONGINGS AND GET HER REGISTRATION INFORMATION TAKEN CARE OF.
WHOA?!
JACK, YOU ARE IN CHARGE WHILE WE ARE OUT.

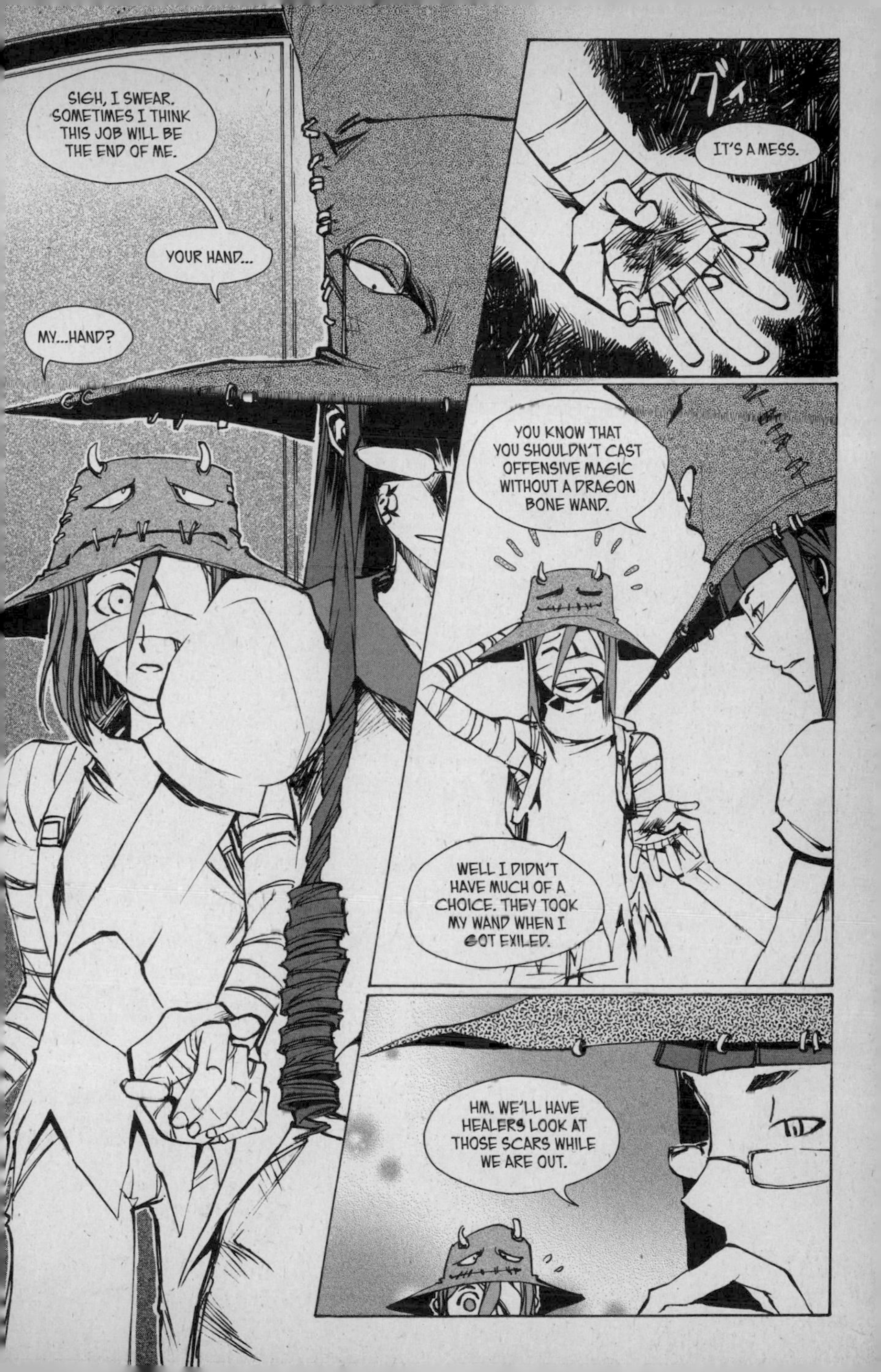
SIGH, I SWEAR. SOMETIMES I THINK THIS JOB WILL BE THE END OF ME.
YOUR HAND...
MY...HAND?
グィ
IT'S A MESS.
YOU KNOW THAT YOU SHOULDN'T CAST OFFENSIVE MAGIC WITHOUT A DRAGON BONE WAND.
WELL I DIDN'T HAVE MUCH OF A CHOICE. THEY TOOK MY WAND WHEN I GOT EXILED.
HM. WE'LL HAVE HEALERS LOOK AT THOSE SCARS WHILE WE ARE OUT.

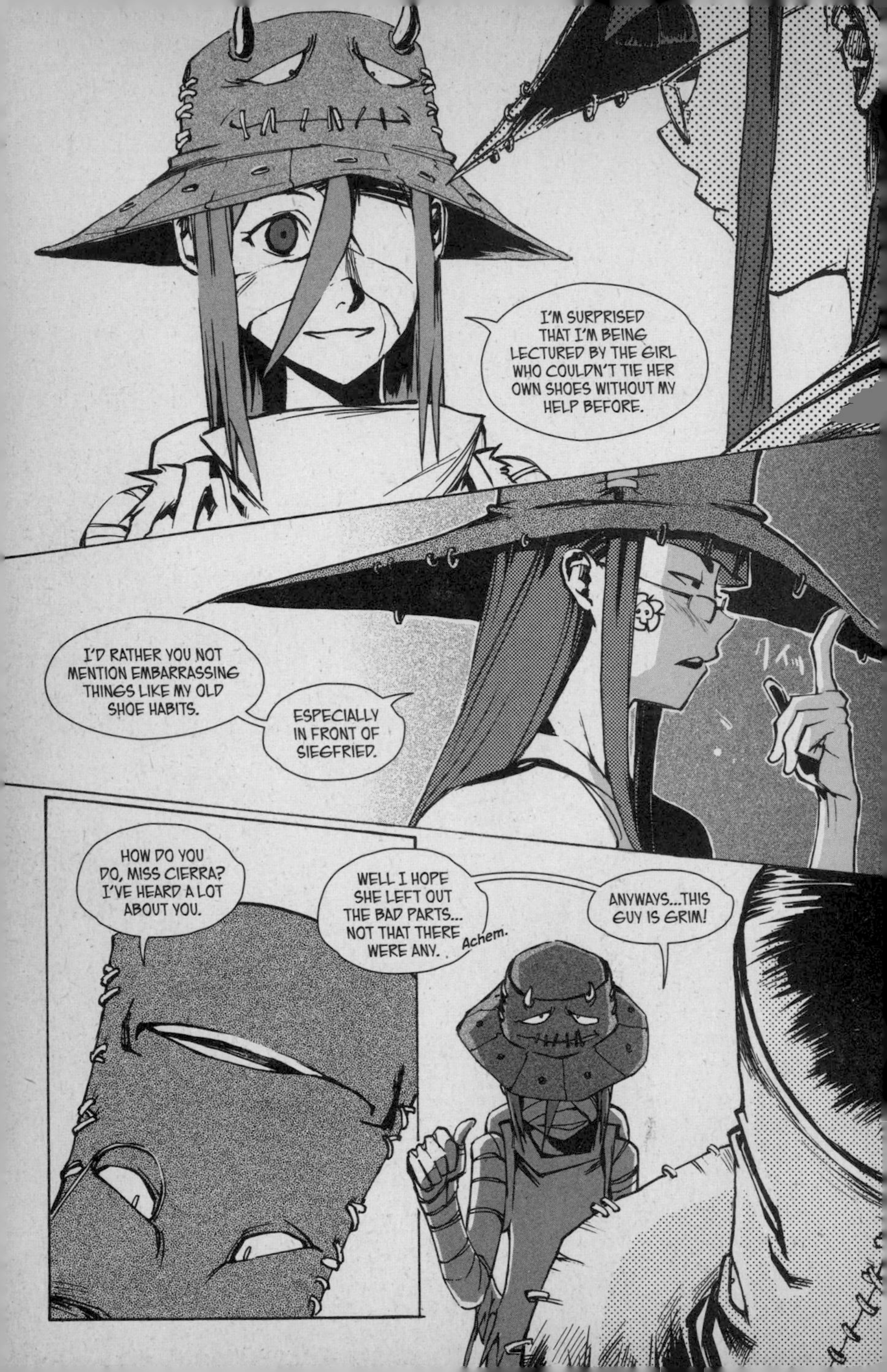
I'M SURPRISED THAT I'M BEING LECTURED BY THE GIRL WHO COULDN'T TIE HER OWN SHOES WITHOUT MY HELP BEFORE.
I'D RATHER YOU NOT MENTION EMBARRASSING THINGS LIKE MY OLD SHOE HABITS.
ESPECIALLY IN FRONT OF SIEGFRIED.
HOW DO YOU DO, MISS CIERRA? I'VE HEARD A LOT ABOUT YOU.
WELL I HOPE SHE LEFT OUT THE BAD PARTS... NOT THAT THERE WERE ANY.
Achem.
ANYWAYS...THIS GUY IS GRIM!

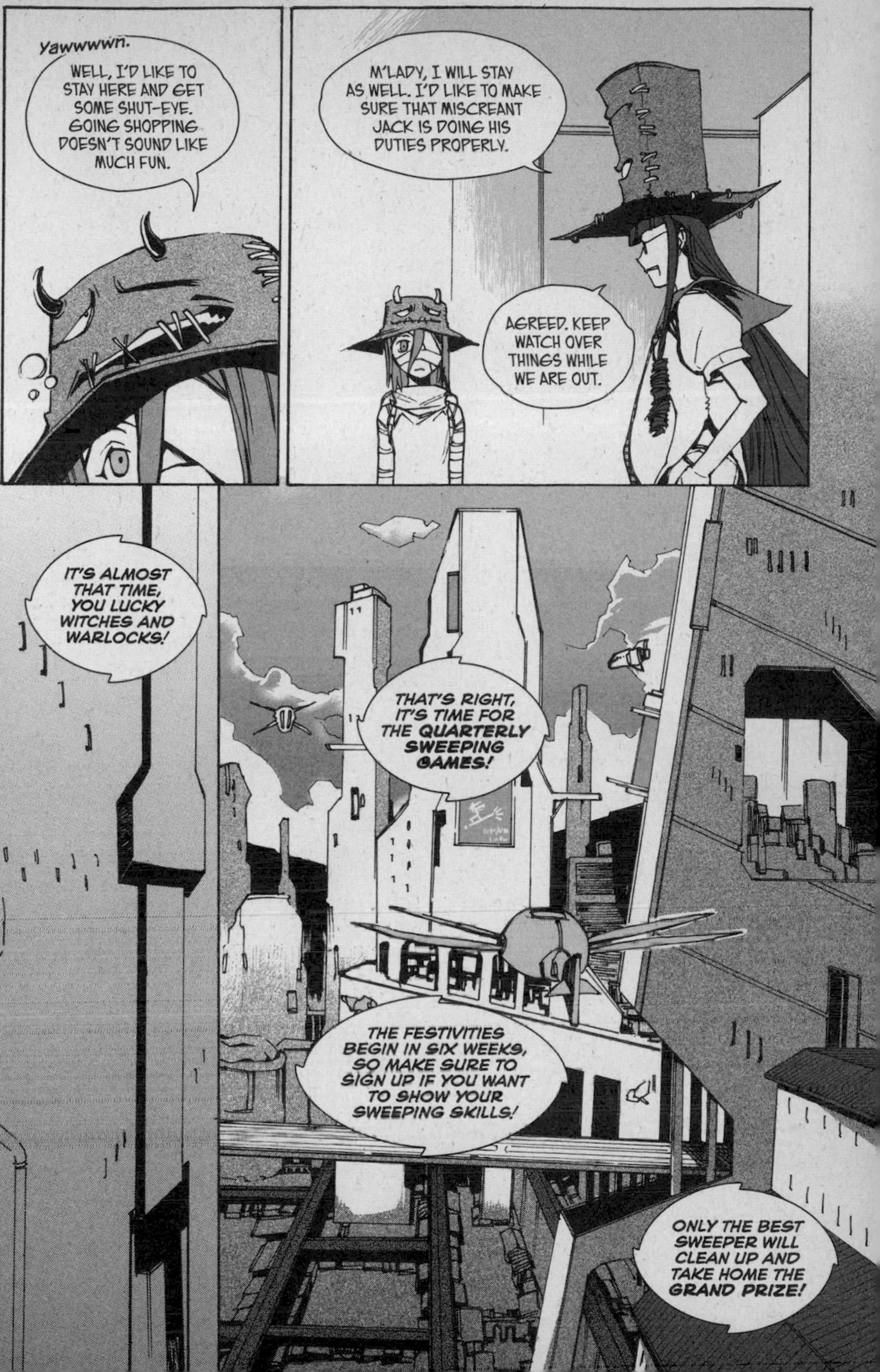
yawwwwn.
WELL, I'D LIKE TO STAY HERE AND GET SOME SHUT-EYE. GOING SHOPPING DOESN'T SOUND LIKE MUCH FUN.
M'LADY, I WILL STAY AS WELL. I'D LIKE TO MAKE SURE THAT MISCREANT JACK IS DOING HIS DUTIES PROPERLY.
AGREED. KEEP WATCH OVER THINGS WHILE WE ARE OUT.
IT'S ALMOST THAT TIME, YOU LUCKY WITCHES AND WARLOCKS!
THAT'S RIGHT, IT'S TIME FOR THE QUARTERLY SWEEPING GAMES!
THE FESTIVITIES BEGIN IN SIX WEEKS, SO MAKE SURE TO SIGN UP IF YOU WANT TO SHOW YOUR SWEEPING SKILLS!
ONLY THE BEST SWEEPER WILL CLEAN UP AND TAKE HOME THE GRAND PRIZE!

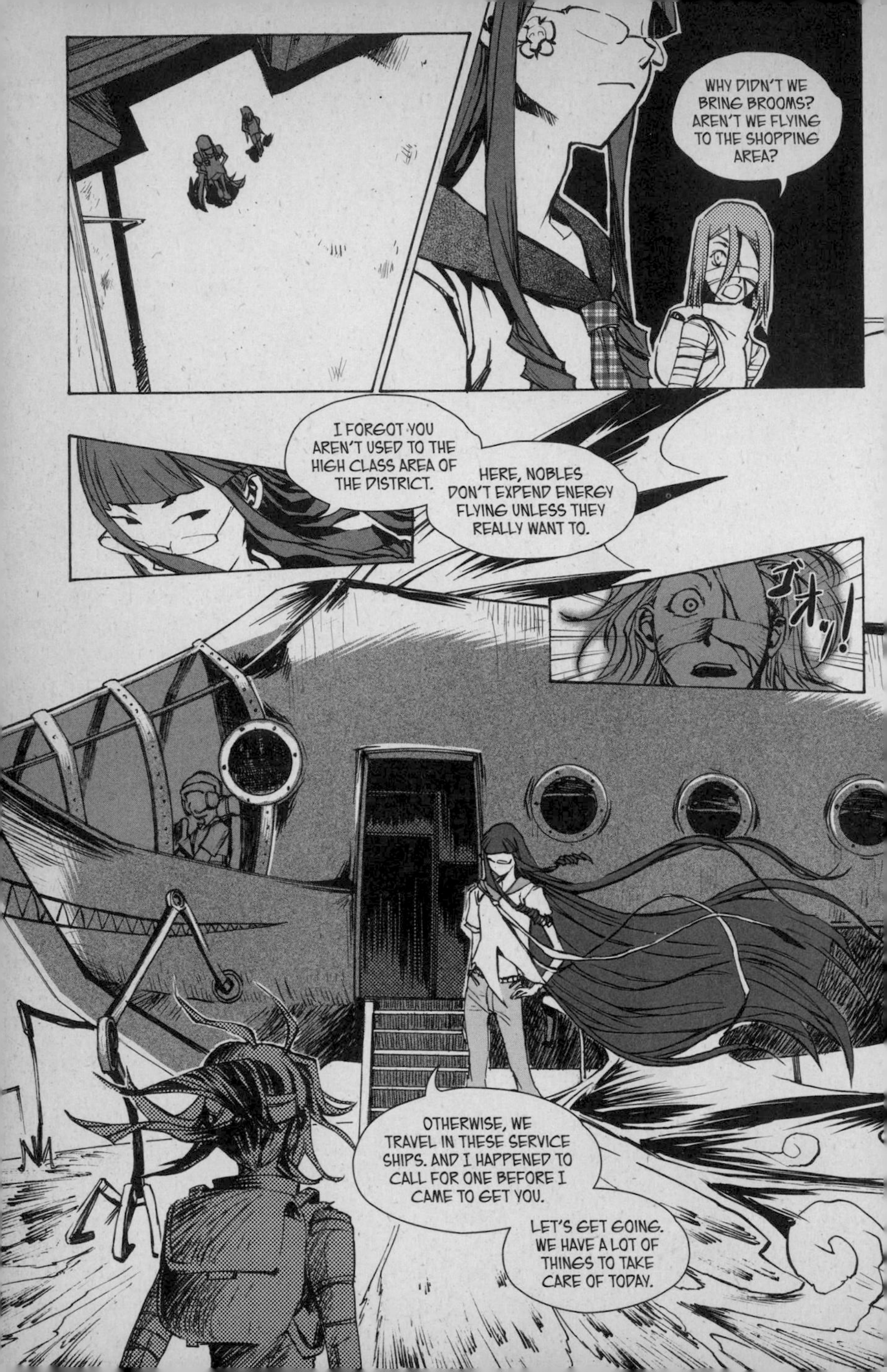
WHY DIDN'T WE BRING BROOMS? AREN'T WE FLYING TO THE SHOPPING AREA?
I FORGOT YOU AREN'T USED TO THE HIGH CLASS AREA OF THE DISTRICT.
HERE, NOBLES DON'T EXPEND ENERGY FLYING UNLESS THEY REALLY WANT TO.
ゴオッ!
OTHERWISE, WE TRAVEL IN THESE SERVICE SHIPS. AND I HAPPENED TO CALL FOR ONE BEFORE I CAME TO GET YOU.
LET'S GET GOING. WE HAVE A LOT OF THINGS TO TAKE CARE OF TODAY.

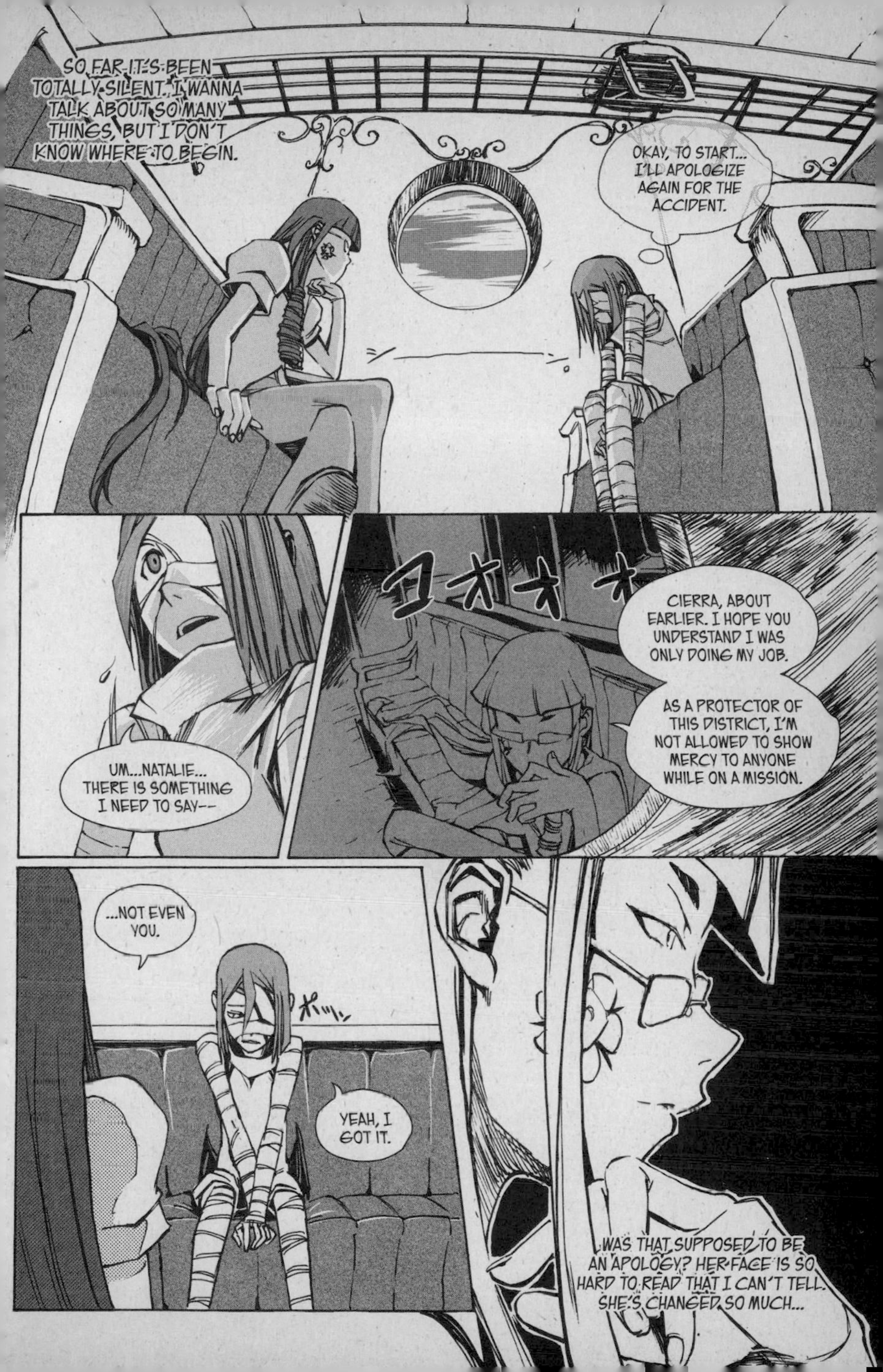
SO FAR IT'S BEEN TOTALLY SILENT. I WANNA TALK ABOUT SO MANY THINGS, BUT I DON'T KNOW WHERE TO BEGIN.
OKAY, TO START... I'LL APOLOGIZE AGAIN FOR THE ACCIDENT.
UM...NATALIE... THERE IS SOMETHING I NEED TO SAY--
CIERRA, ABOUT EARLIER. I HOPE YOU UNDERSTAND I WAS ONLY DOING MY JOB.
AS A PROTECTOR OF THIS DISTRICT, I'M NOT ALLOWED TO SHOW MERCY TO ANYONE WHILE ON A MISSION.
...NOT EVEN YOU.
YEAH, I GOT IT.
WAS THAT SUPPOSED TO BE AN APOLOGY? HER FACE IS SO HARD TO READ THAT I CAN'T TELL. SHE'S CHANGED SO MUCH...

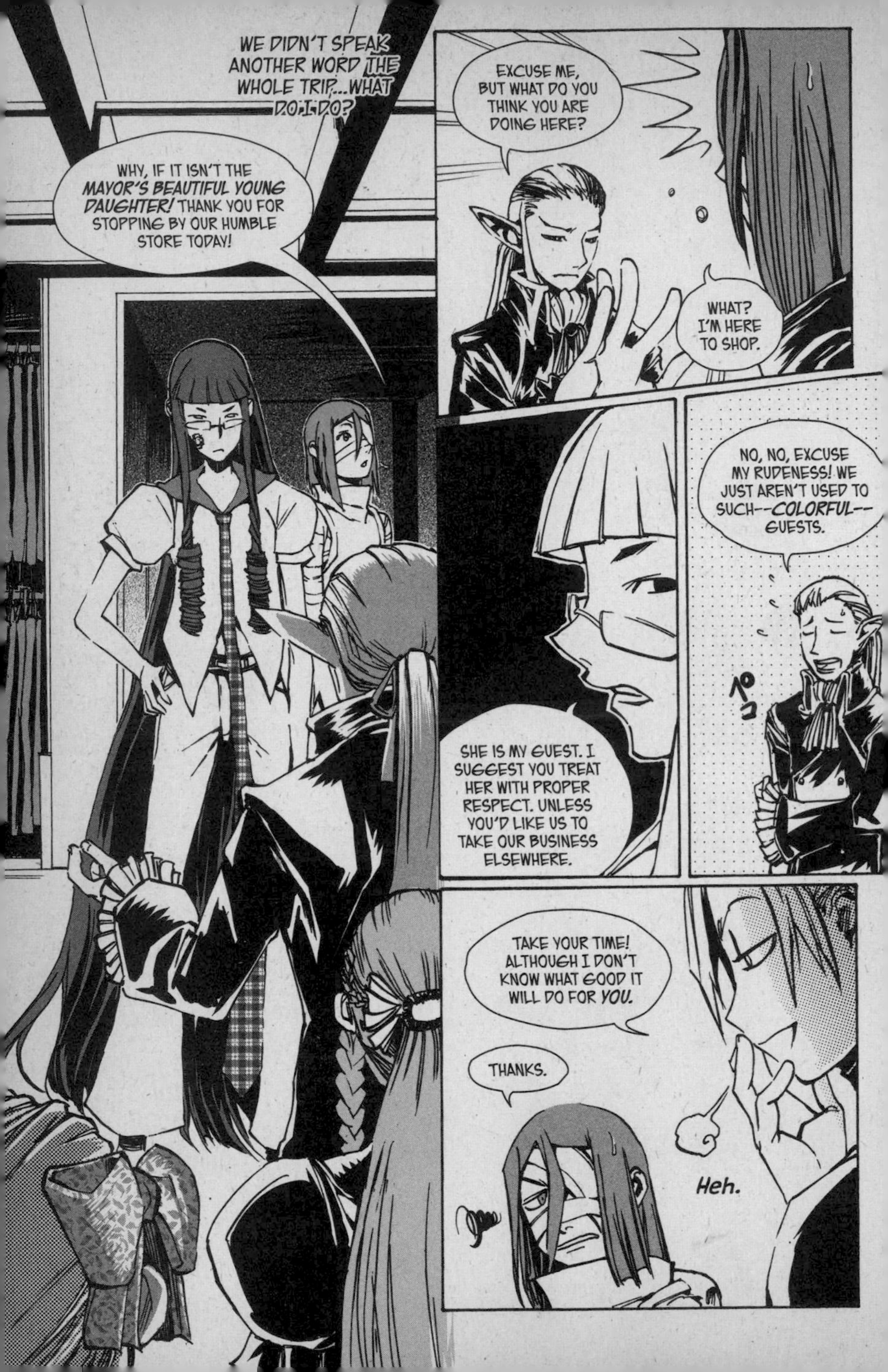
WE DIDN'T SPEAK ANOTHER WORD THE WHOLE TRIP...WHAT DO I DO?
WHY, IF IT ISN'T THE MAYOR'S BEAUTIFUL YOUNG DAUGHTER! THANK YOU FOR STOPPING BY OUR HUMBLE STORE TODAY!
EXCUSE ME, BUT WHAT DO YOU THINK YOU ARE DOING HERE?
WHAT? I'M HERE TO SHOP.
SHE IS MY GUEST. I SUGGEST YOU TREAT HER WITH PROPER RESPECT. UNLESS YOU'D LIKE US TO TAKE OUR BUSINESS ELSEWHERE.
NO, NO, EXCUSE MY RUDENESS! WE JUST AREN'T USED TO SUCH--COLORFUL--GUESTS.
ペコ
TAKE YOUR TIME! ALTHOUGH I DON'T KNOW WHAT GOOD IT WILL DO FOR YOU.
THANKS.
Heh.

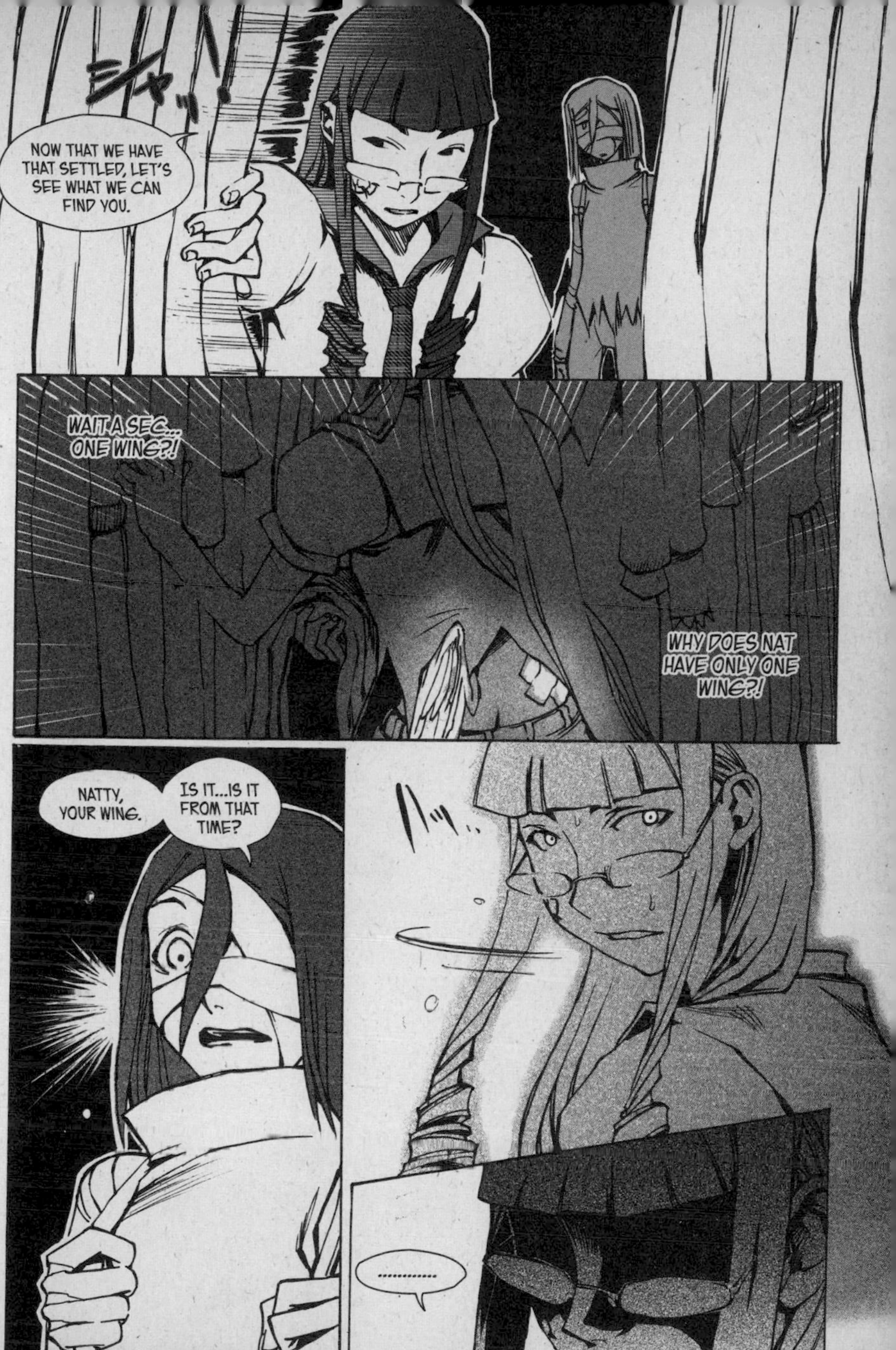
シャッ
NOW THAT WE HAVE THAT SETTLED, LET'S SEE WHAT WE CAN FIND YOU.
WAIT A SEC... ONE WING?!
WHY DOES NAT HAVE ONLY ONE WING?!
NATTY, YOUR WING.
IS IT...IS IT FROM THAT TIME?
....

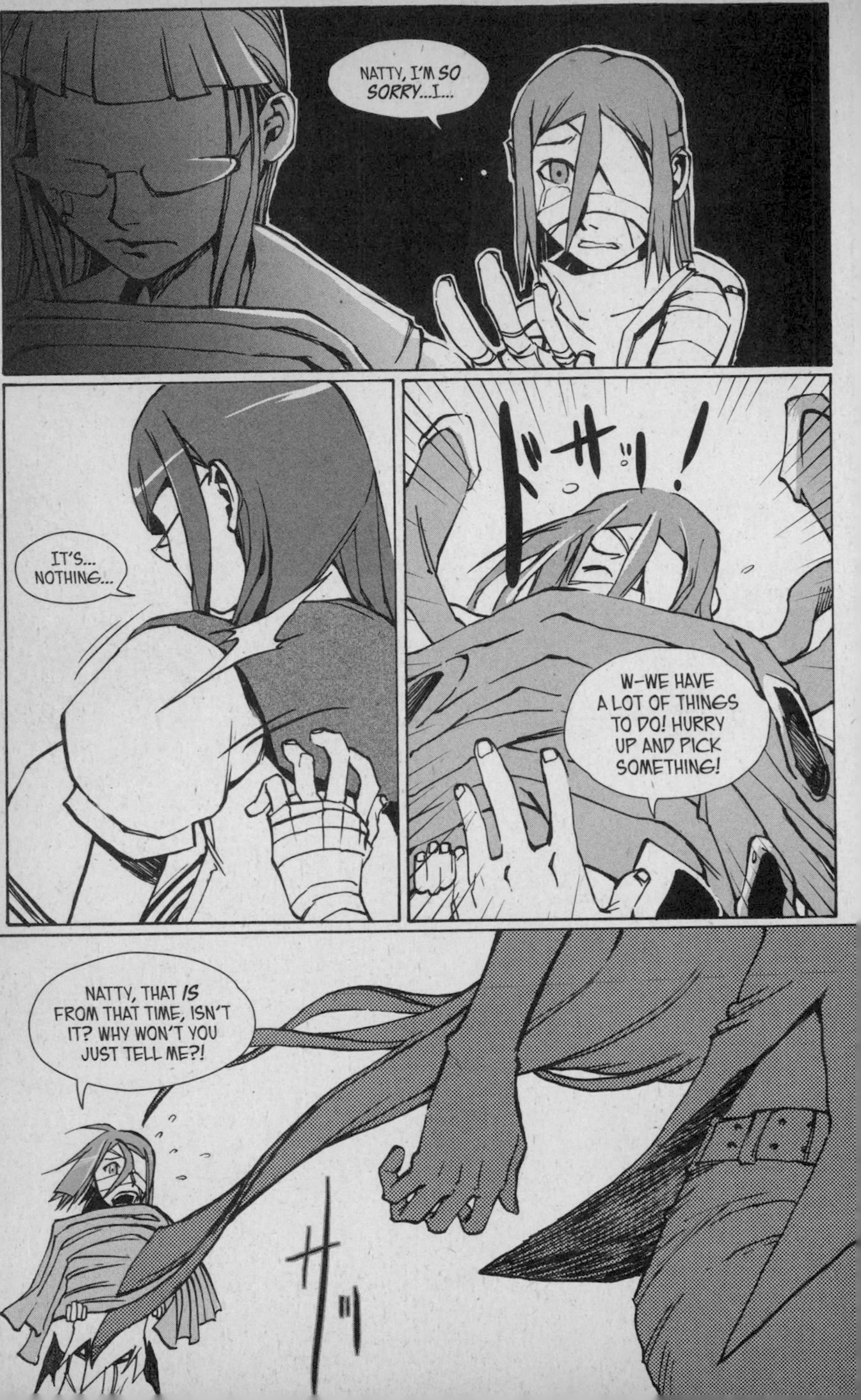
NATTY, I'M SO SORRY...I...
ドサッ!!
W-WE HAVE A LOT OF THINGS TO DO! HURRY UP AND PICK SOMETHING!
IT'S... NOTHING...
NATTY, THAT IS FROM THAT TIME, ISN'T IT? WHY WON'T YOU JUST TELL ME?!
ザッ

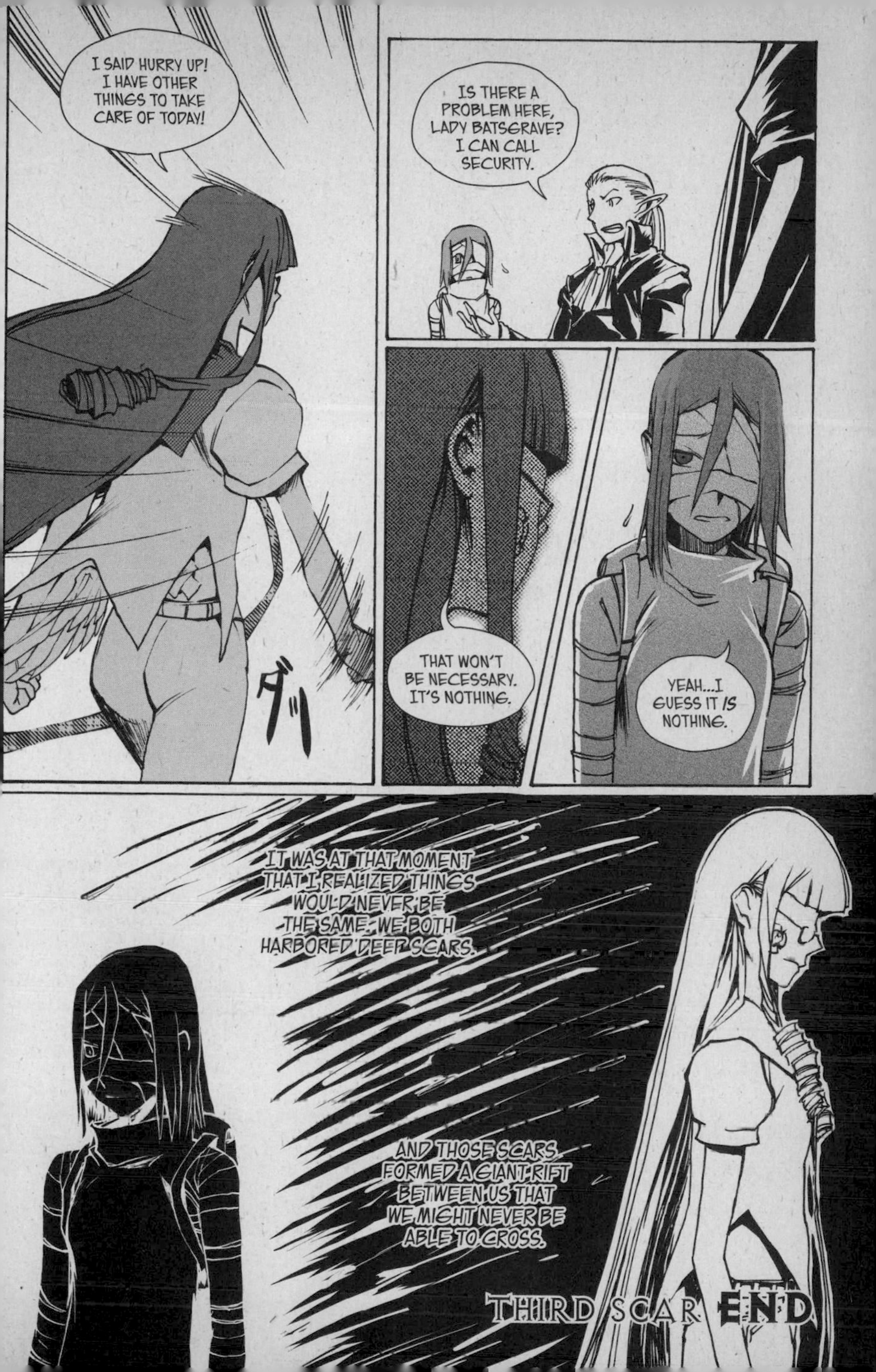
I SAID HURRY UP! I HAVE OTHER THINGS TO TAKE CARE OF TODAY!
ダッ
IS THERE A PROBLEM HERE, LADY BATSGRAVE? I CAN CALL SECURITY.
THAT WON'T BE NECESSARY. IT'S NOTHING.
YEAH...I GUESS IT *IS* NOTHING.
IT WAS AT THAT MOMENT THAT I REALIZED THINGS WOULD NEVER BE THE SAME. WE BOTH HARBORED DEEP SCARS.
AND THOSE SCARS FORMED A GIANT RIFT BETWEEN US THAT WE MIGHT NEVER BE ABLE TO CROSS.
THIRD SCAR END

QUEEN BIANKA'S CRASH COURSE

CHAPTER THREE: SWEEPING

NOT ONLY IS SWEEPING THE FASTEST WAY TA TRAVEL, BUT IT'S ALSO A MAJOR SPORT THAT'S FAME SPREADS ACROSS ALL OF THE DISTRICTS. EACH DISTRICT HOLDS ITS OWN QUARTERLY EVENTS, AND EACH YEAR THE BEST SWEEPERS FROM EVERY DISTRICT ARE NOMINATED TA COMPETE AGAINST EACH OTHER IN THE GRAND WITCH SWEEP!

SWEEP EVENTS LIST

1. TRICK EVENTS
2. RACES
3. TEAM SNARTER BALL
4. MANY MORE!

OUR STUCK UP...ER, I MEAN... "HONORABLE" LEADER NATALIE WON 2ND PLACE IN THE GRAND WITCH SWEEP LAST YEAR. I COULD BEAT HER EASY, BUT I'VE GOT MORE IMPORTANT THINGS TA TAKE CARE OF. ALL OF WITCH-KIND IS DEPENDING ON ME TA SAVE THE WORLD BY BECOMING THEIR RIGHTFUL RULER!

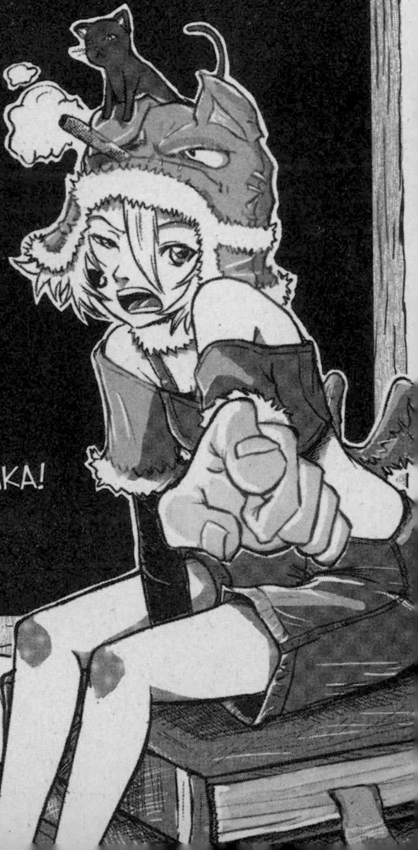

ALL HAIL THE CAT QUEEN BIANKA!

IF YA LIKE SPORTS, LISTEN TA THIS!

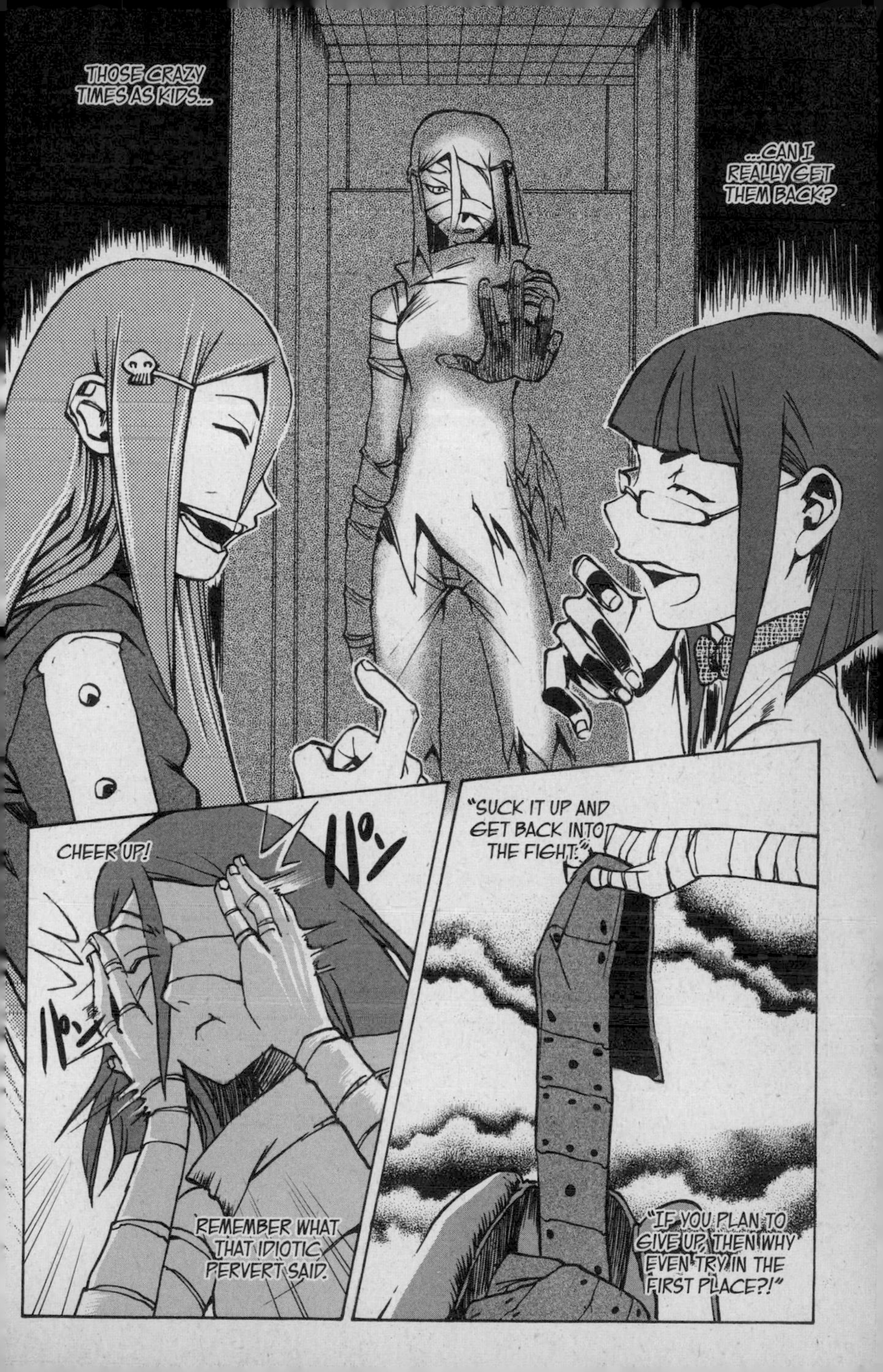
THOSE CRAZY TIMES AS KIDS...
...CAN I REALLY GET THEM BACK?
CHEER UP!
REMEMBER WHAT THAT IDIOTIC PERVERT SAID.
"SUCK IT UP AND GET BACK INTO THE FIGHT."
"IF YOU PLAN TO GIVE UP, THEN WHY EVEN TRY IN THE FIRST PLACE?!"

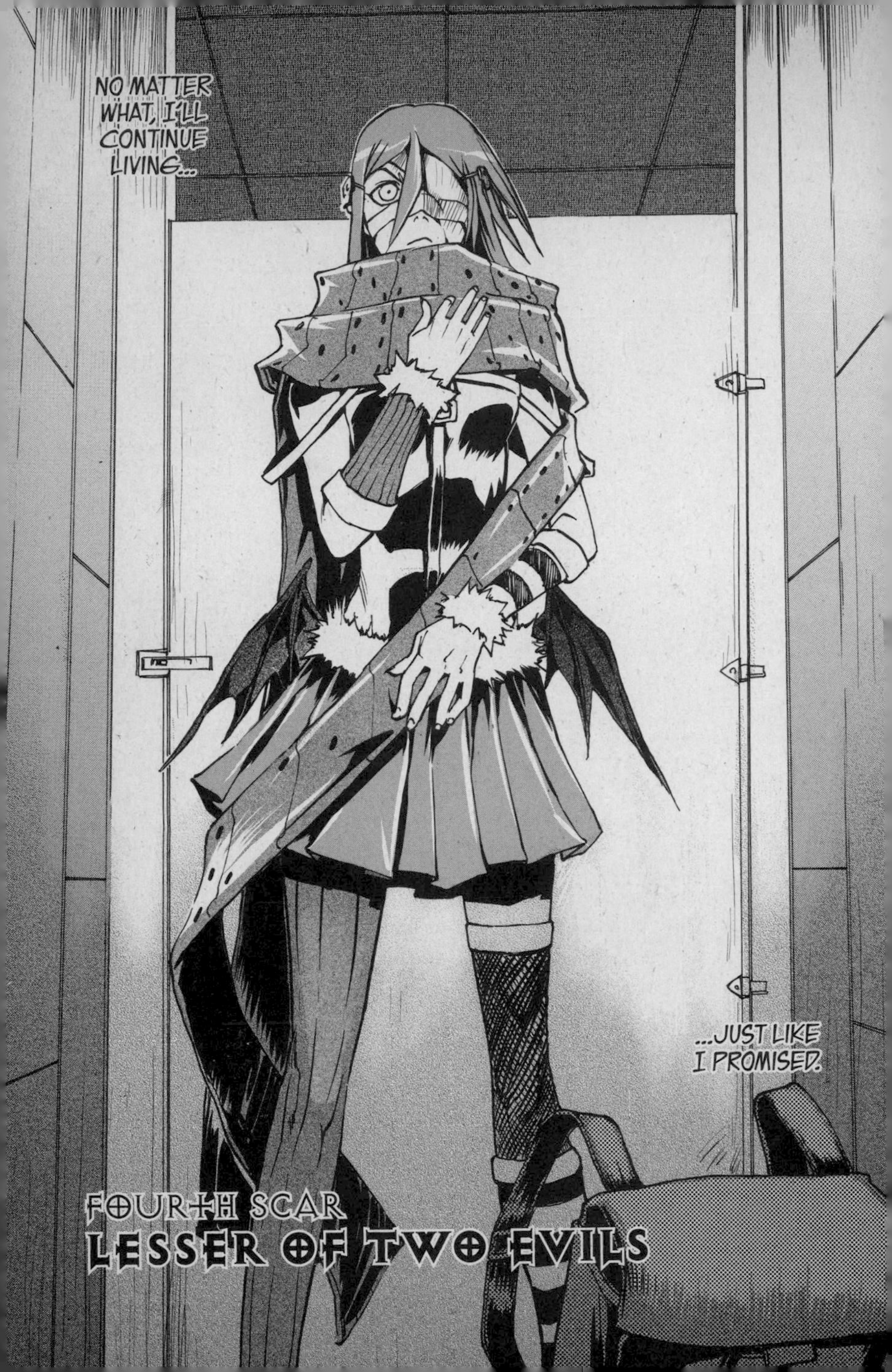
NO MATTER WHAT, I'LL CONTINUE LIVING...
...JUST LIKE I PROMISED.
FOURTH SCAR
LESSER OF TWO EVILS

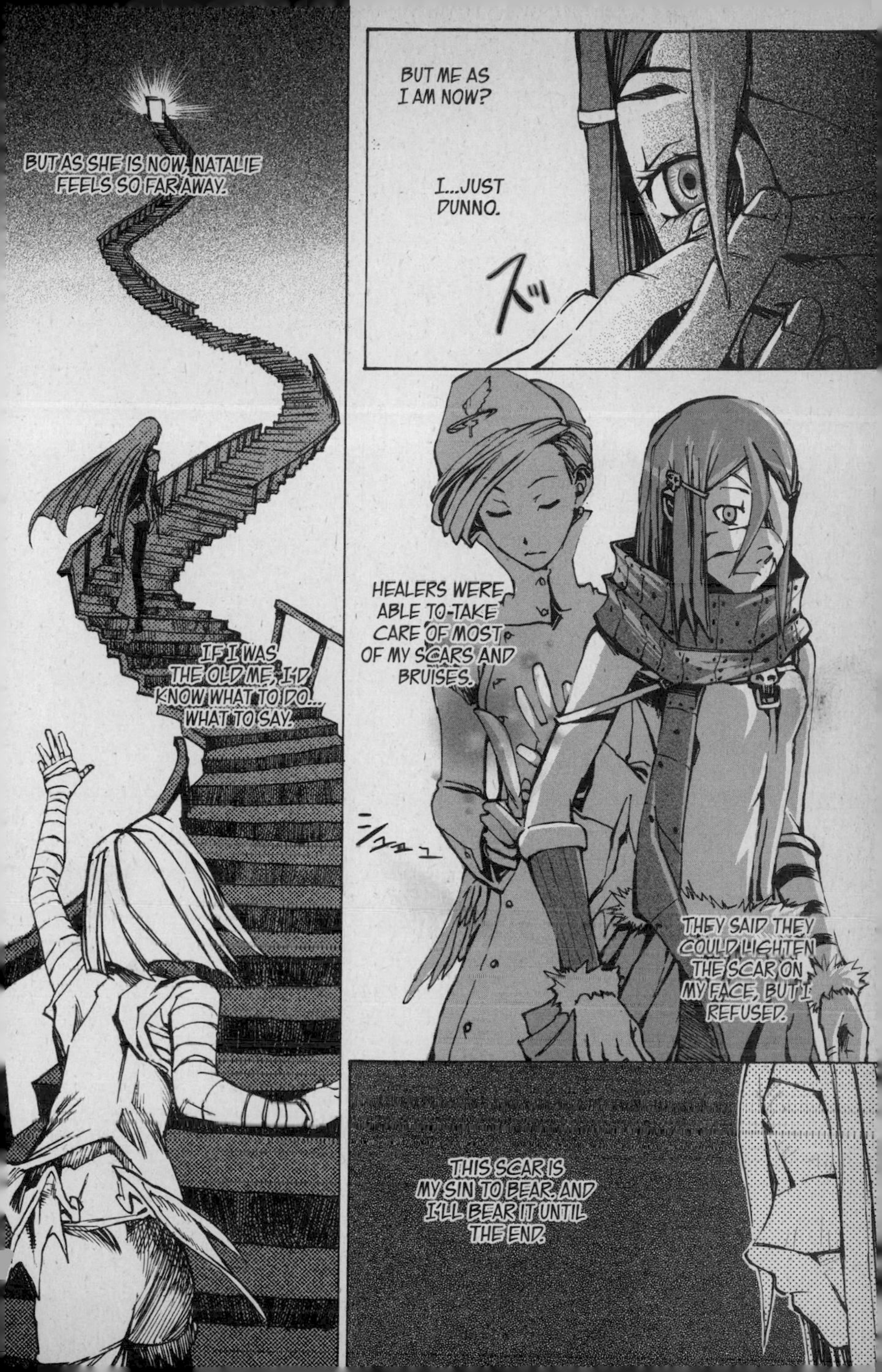
BUT AS SHE IS NOW, NATALIE FEELS SO FAR AWAY.
IF I WAS THE OLD ME, I'D KNOW WHAT TO DO... WHAT TO SAY.
BUT ME AS I AM NOW?
I...JUST DUNNO.
HEALERS WERE ABLE TO TAKE CARE OF MOST OF MY SCARS AND BRUISES.
THEY SAID THEY COULD LIGHTEN THE SCAR ON MY FACE, BUT I REFUSED.
THIS SCAR IS MY SIN TO BEAR. AND I'LL BEAR IT UNTIL THE END.

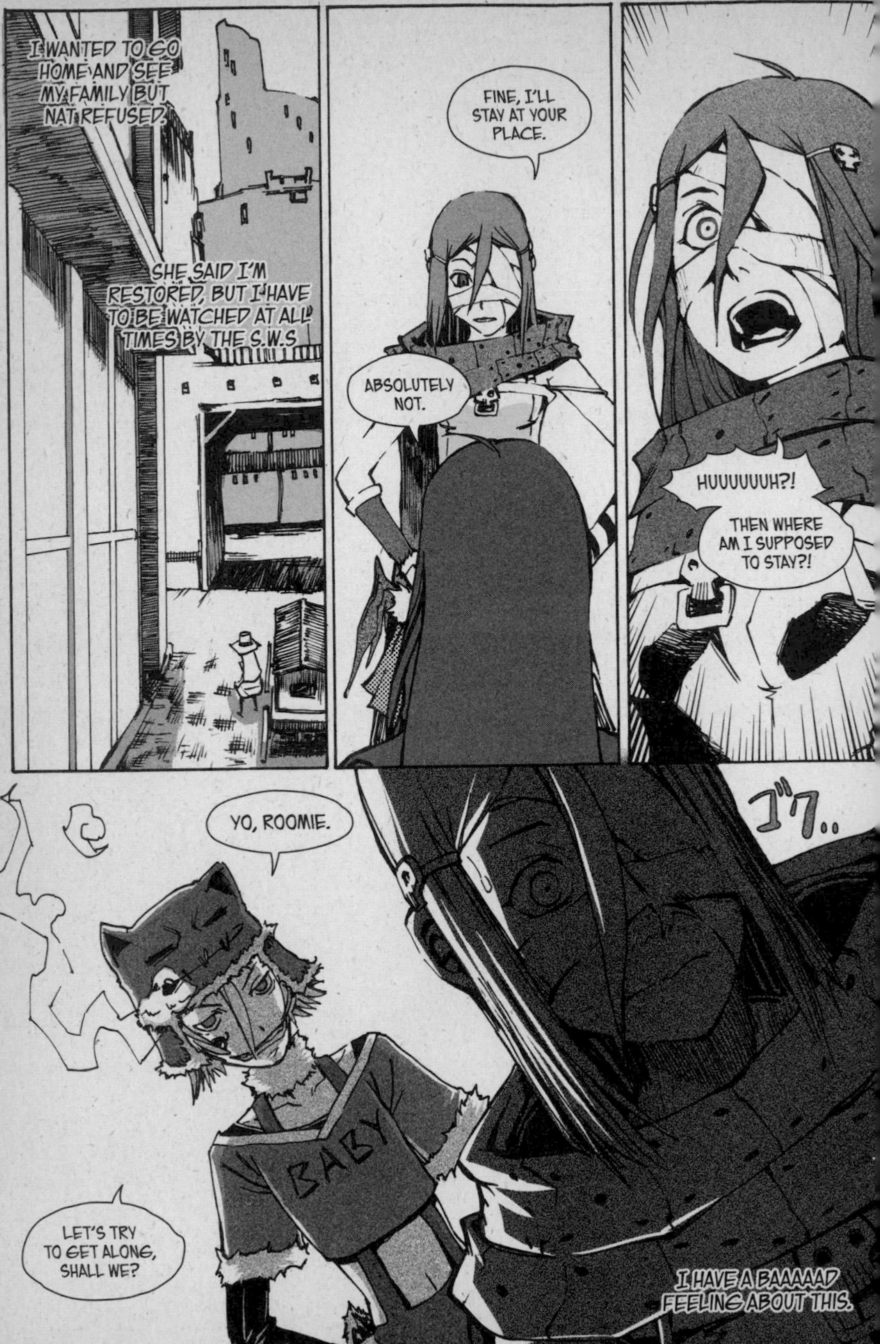
I WANTED TO GO HOME AND SEE MY FAMILY BUT NAT REFUSED.
SHE SAID I'M RESTORED, BUT I HAVE TO BE WATCHED AT ALL TIMES BY THE S.W.S
FINE, I'LL STAY AT YOUR PLACE.
ABSOLUTELY NOT.
HUUUUUUH?!
THEN WHERE AM I SUPPOSED TO STAY?!
YO, ROOMIE.
LET'S TRY TO GET ALONG, SHALL WE?
BABY
I HAVE A BAAAAAD FEELING ABOUT THIS.

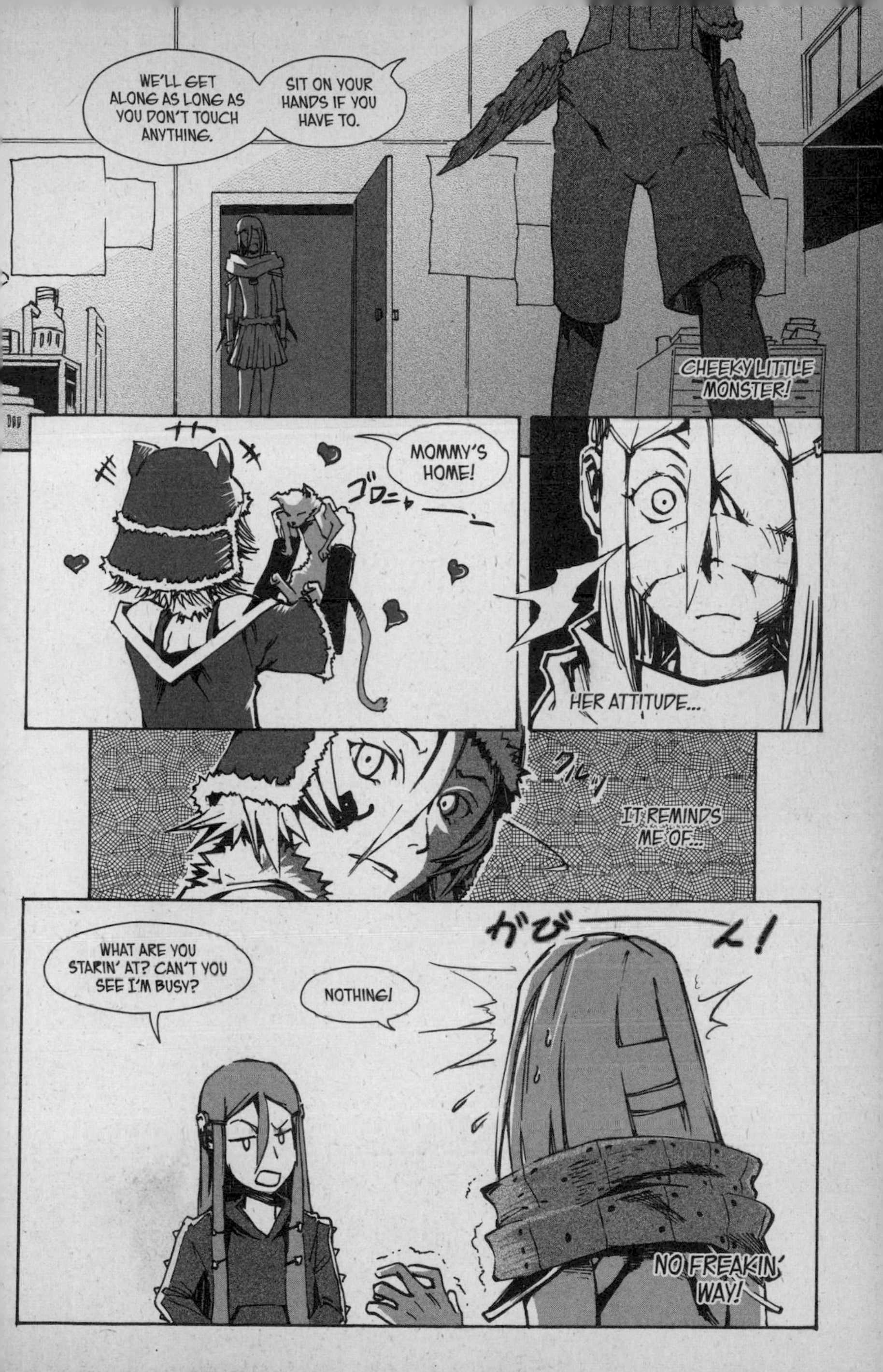
WE'LL GET ALONG AS LONG AS YOU DON'T TOUCH ANYTHING.
SIT ON YOUR HANDS IF YOU HAVE TO.
CHEEKY LITTLE MONSTER!
MOMMY'S HOME!
HER ATTITUDE...
IT REMINDS ME OF...
WHAT ARE YOU STARIN' AT? CAN'T YOU SEE I'M BUSY?
NOTHING!
がびーん!
NO FREAKIN' WAY!

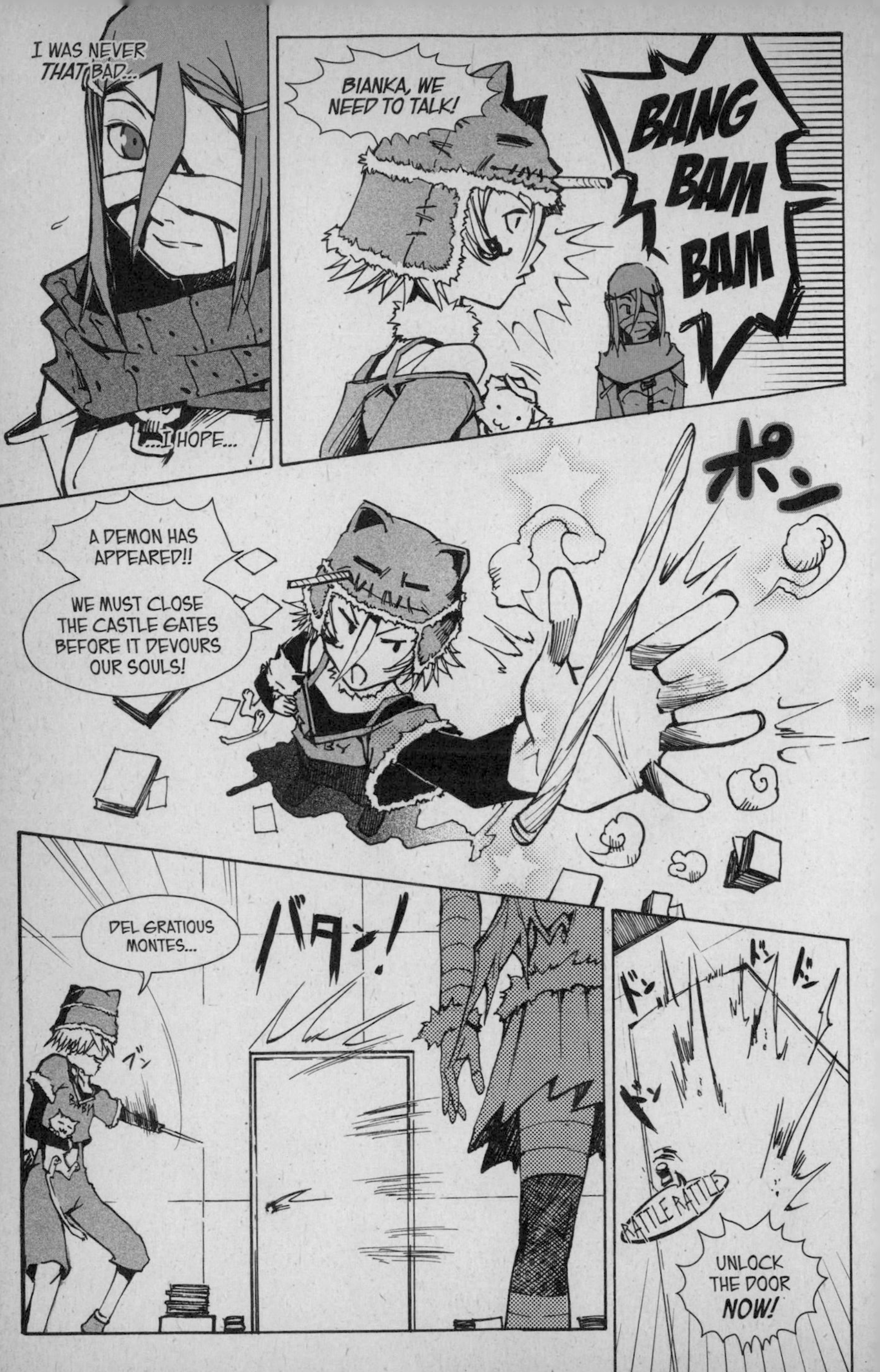
I WAS NEVER THAT BAD...
...I HOPE...
BIANKA, WE NEED TO TALK!
BANG BAM BAM
A DEMON HAS APPEARED!!
WE MUST CLOSE THE CASTLE GATES BEFORE IT DEVOURS OUR SOULS!
ポン
DEL GRATIOUS MONTES...
ブン
バタン!
ドン ドン ドン ドン
RATTLE RATTLE
UNLOCK THE DOOR NOW!

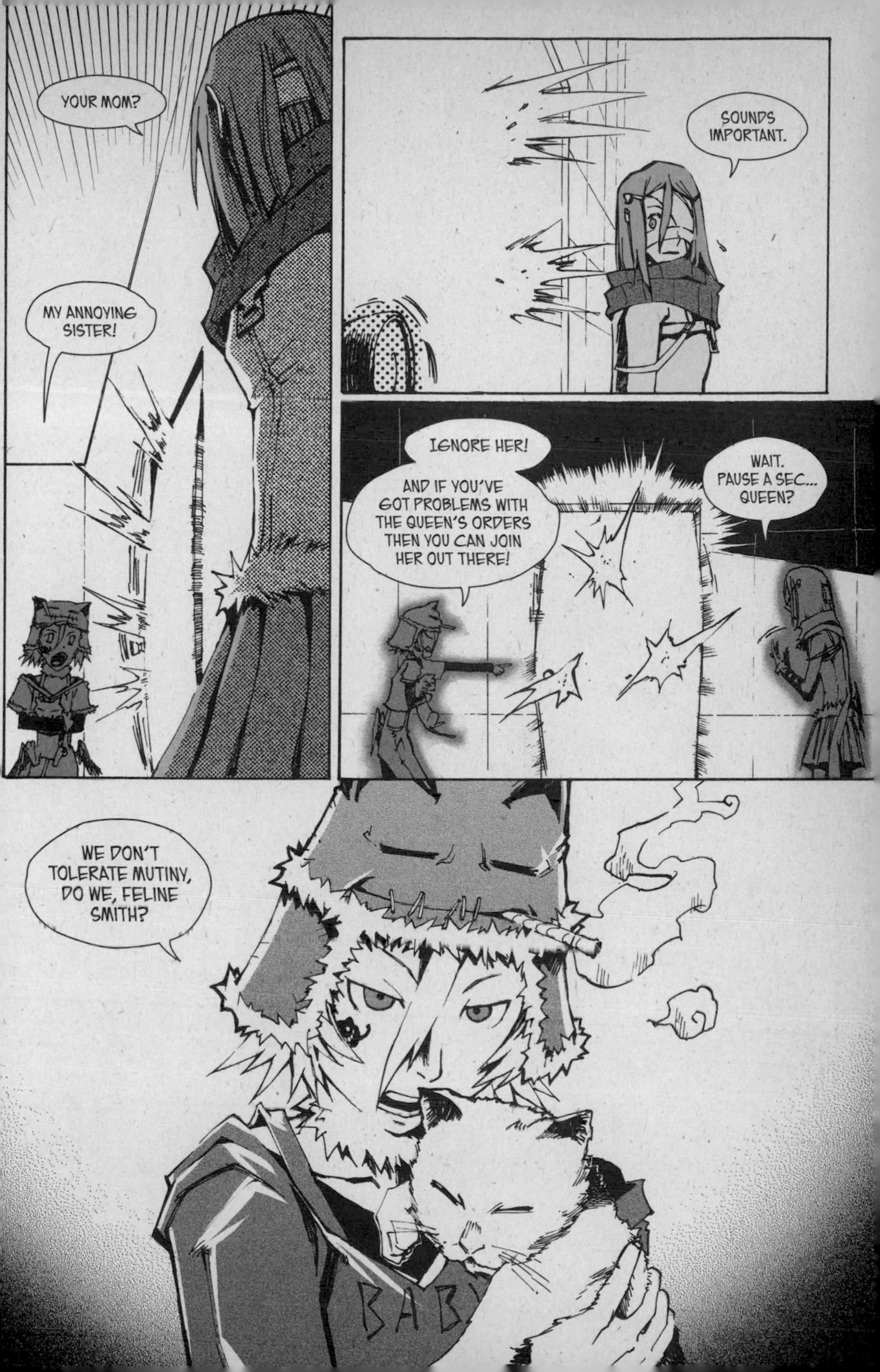
YOUR MOM?
MY ANNOYING SISTER!
SOUNDS IMPORTANT.
IGNORE HER!
AND IF YOU'VE GOT PROBLEMS WITH THE QUEEN'S ORDERS THEN YOU CAN JOIN HER OUT THERE!
WAIT. PAUSE A SEC... QUEEN?
WE DON'T TOLERATE MUTINY, DO WE, FELINE SMITH?
BAB

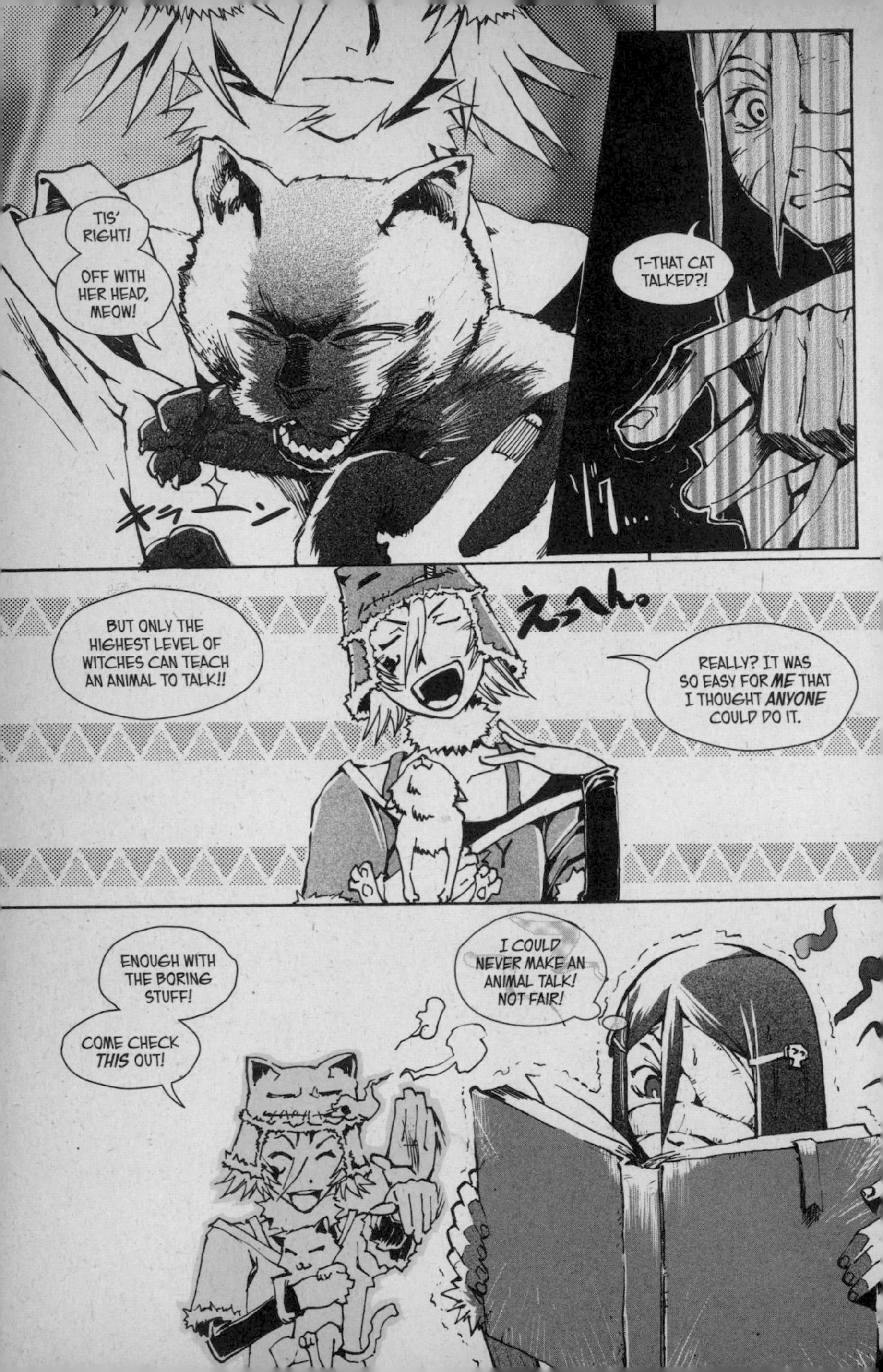
TIS' RIGHT!
OFF WITH HER HEAD, MEOW!
キラーン
T-THAT CAT TALKED?!
ゾク...
BUT ONLY THE HIGHEST LEVEL OF WITCHES CAN TEACH AN ANIMAL TO TALK!!
えっへん。
REALLY? IT WAS SO EASY FOR *ME* THAT I THOUGHT *ANYONE* COULD DO IT.
ENOUGH WITH THE BORING STUFF!
COME CHECK *THIS* OUT!
I COULD NEVER MAKE AN ANIMAL TALK! NOT FAIR!

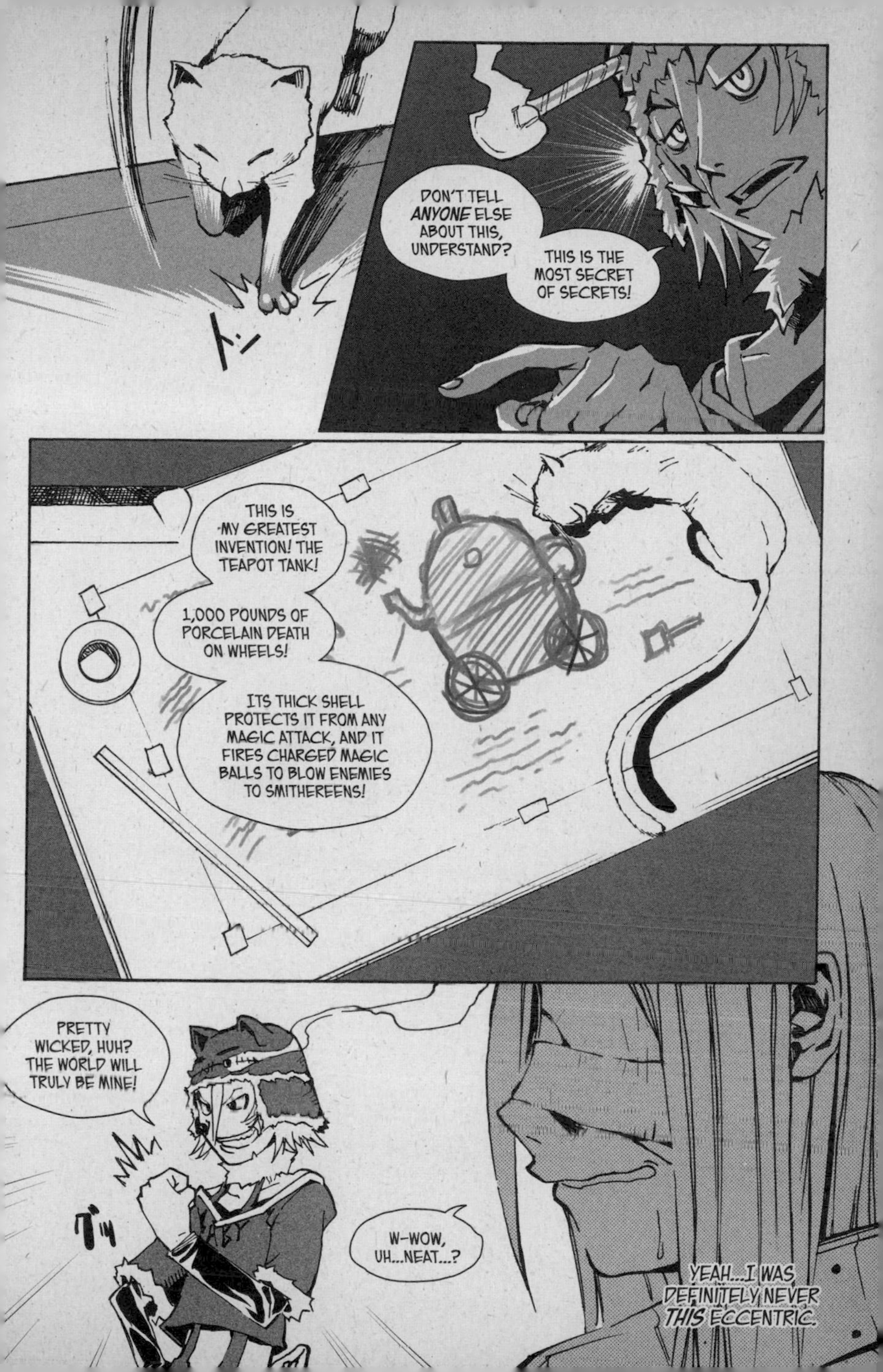
ドン
DON'T TELL ANYONE ELSE ABOUT THIS, UNDERSTAND?
THIS IS THE MOST SECRET OF SECRETS!
THIS IS MY GREATEST INVENTION! THE TEAPOT TANK!
1,000 POUNDS OF PORCELAIN DEATH ON WHEELS!
ITS THICK SHELL PROTECTS IT FROM ANY MAGIC ATTACK, AND IT FIRES CHARGED MAGIC BALLS TO BLOW ENEMIES TO SMITHEREENS!
PRETTY WICKED, HUH? THE WORLD WILL TRULY BE MINE!
グッ
W-WOW, UH...NEAT...?
YEAH...I WAS DEFINITELY NEVER THIS ECCENTRIC.

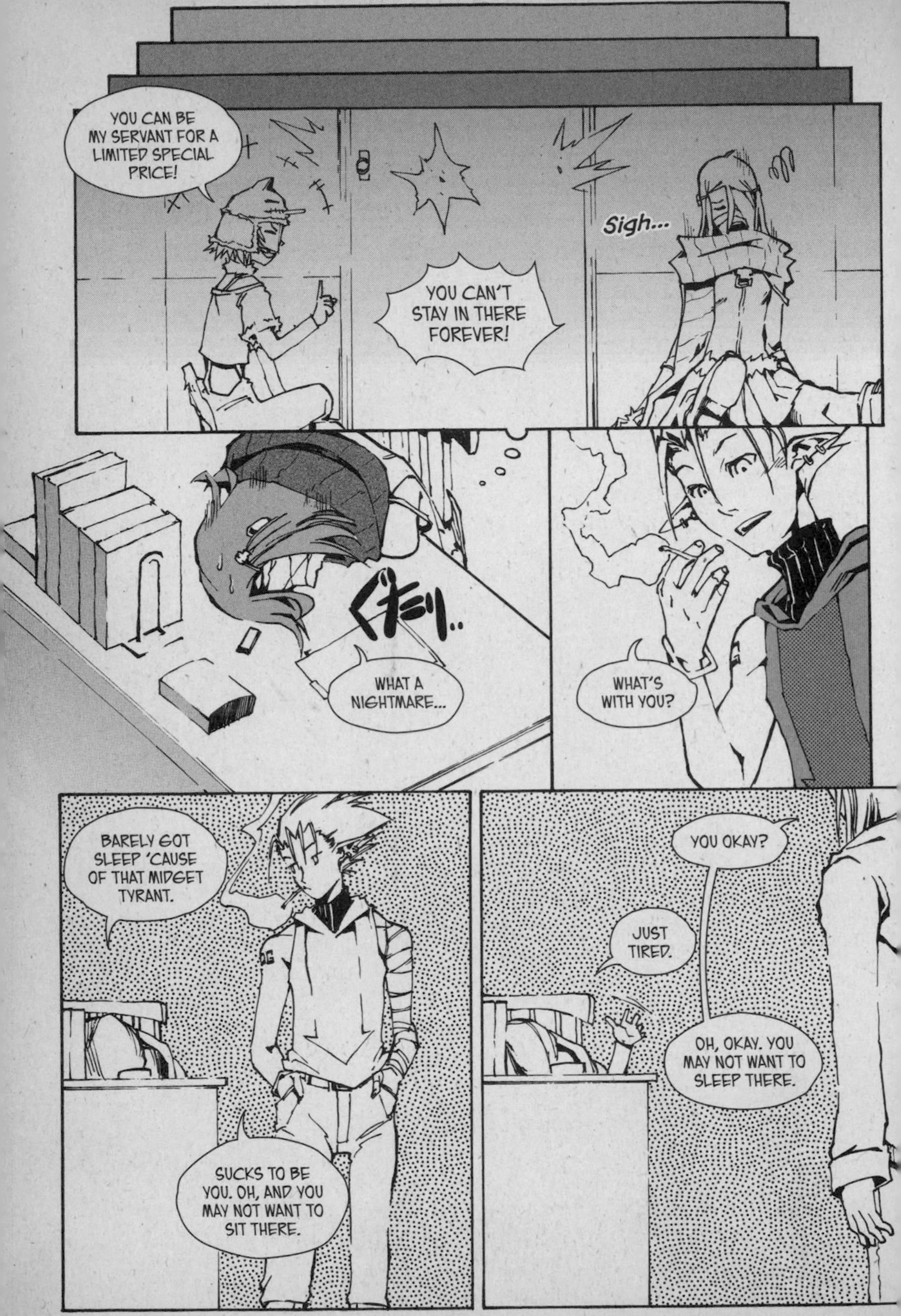
YOU CAN BE MY SERVANT FOR A LIMITED SPECIAL PRICE!
YOU CAN'T STAY IN THERE FOREVER!
Sigh...
WHAT A NIGHTMARE...
WHAT'S WITH YOU?
BARELY GOT SLEEP 'CAUSE OF THAT MIDGET TYRANT.
SUCKS TO BE YOU. OH, AND YOU MAY NOT WANT TO SIT THERE.
YOU OKAY?
JUST TIRED.
OH, OKAY. YOU MAY NOT WANT TO SLEEP THERE.

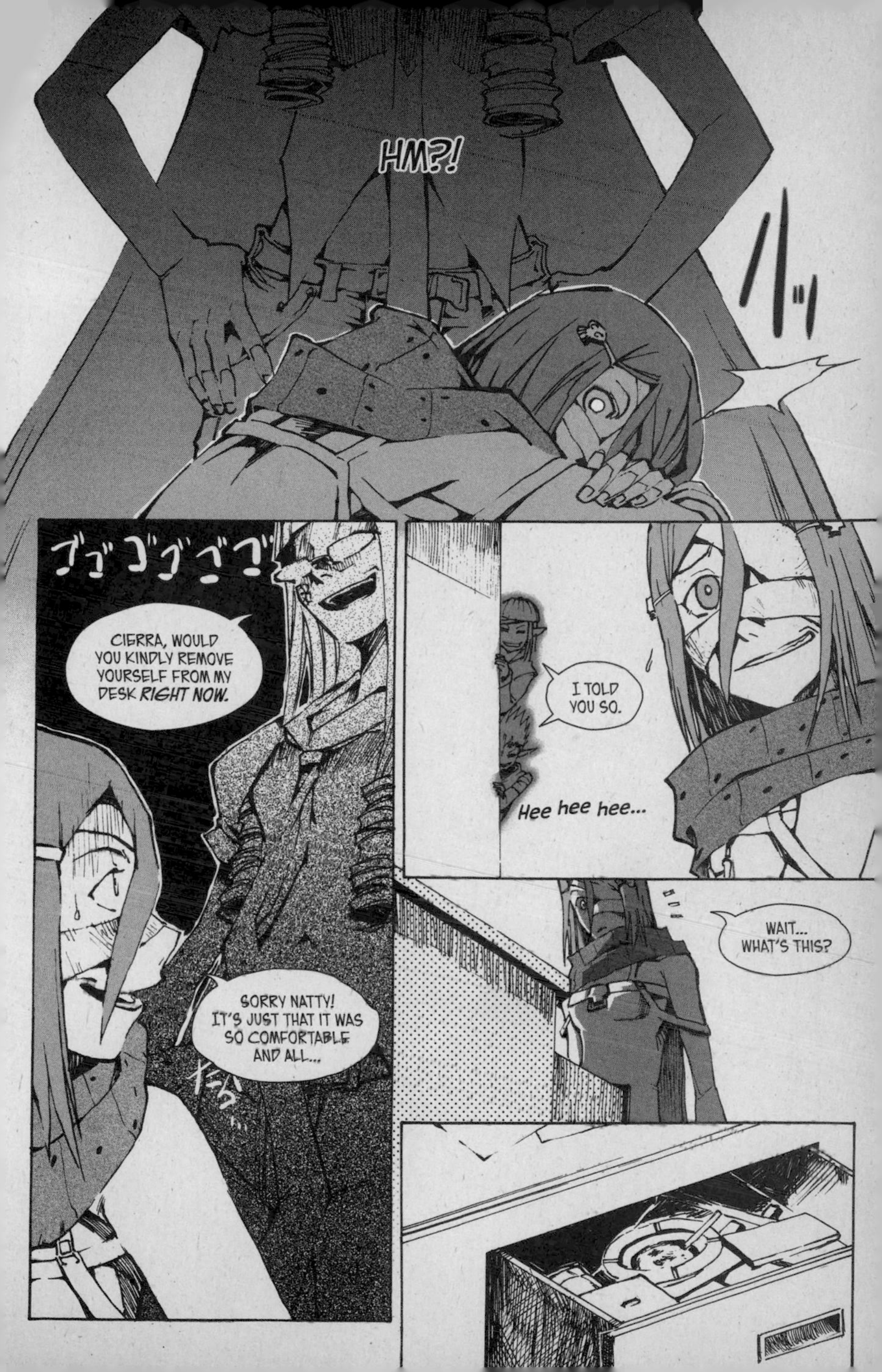
HM?!
ハッ
I TOLD YOU SO.
Hee hee hee...
WAIT... WHAT'S THIS?
ゴゴゴゴゴゴ
CIERRA, WOULD YOU KINDLY REMOVE YOURSELF FROM MY DESK *RIGHT NOW.*
SORRY NATTY! IT'S JUST THAT IT WAS SO COMFORTABLE AND ALL...

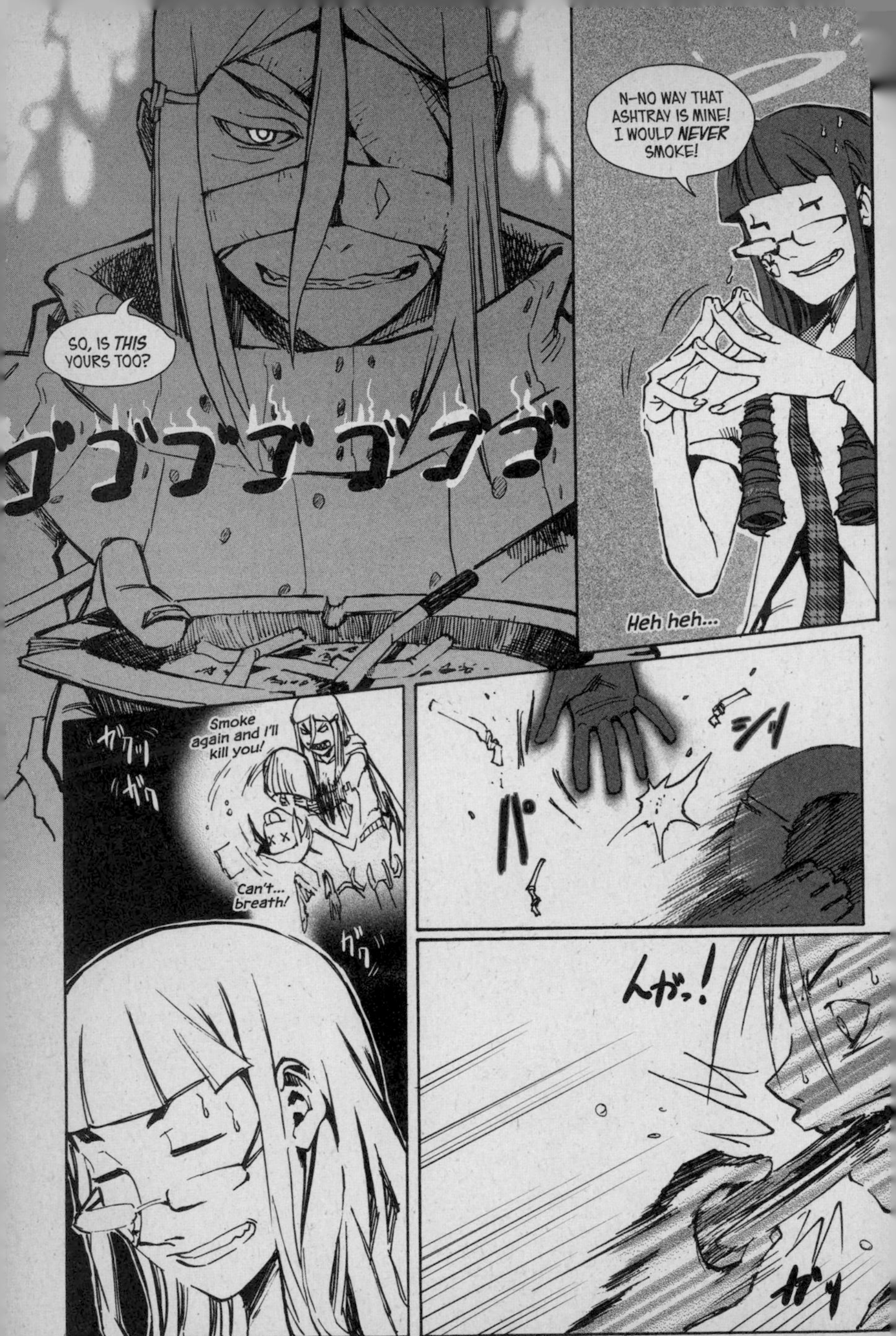
N-NO WAY THAT ASHTRAY IS MINE! I WOULD NEVER SMOKE!
Heh heh...
SO, IS THIS YOURS TOO?
ゴゴゴゴゴゴ
シッ
パ
Smoke again and I'll kill you!
ガクッ
ガク
Can't... breath!
ガク
んがっ!
ガッ

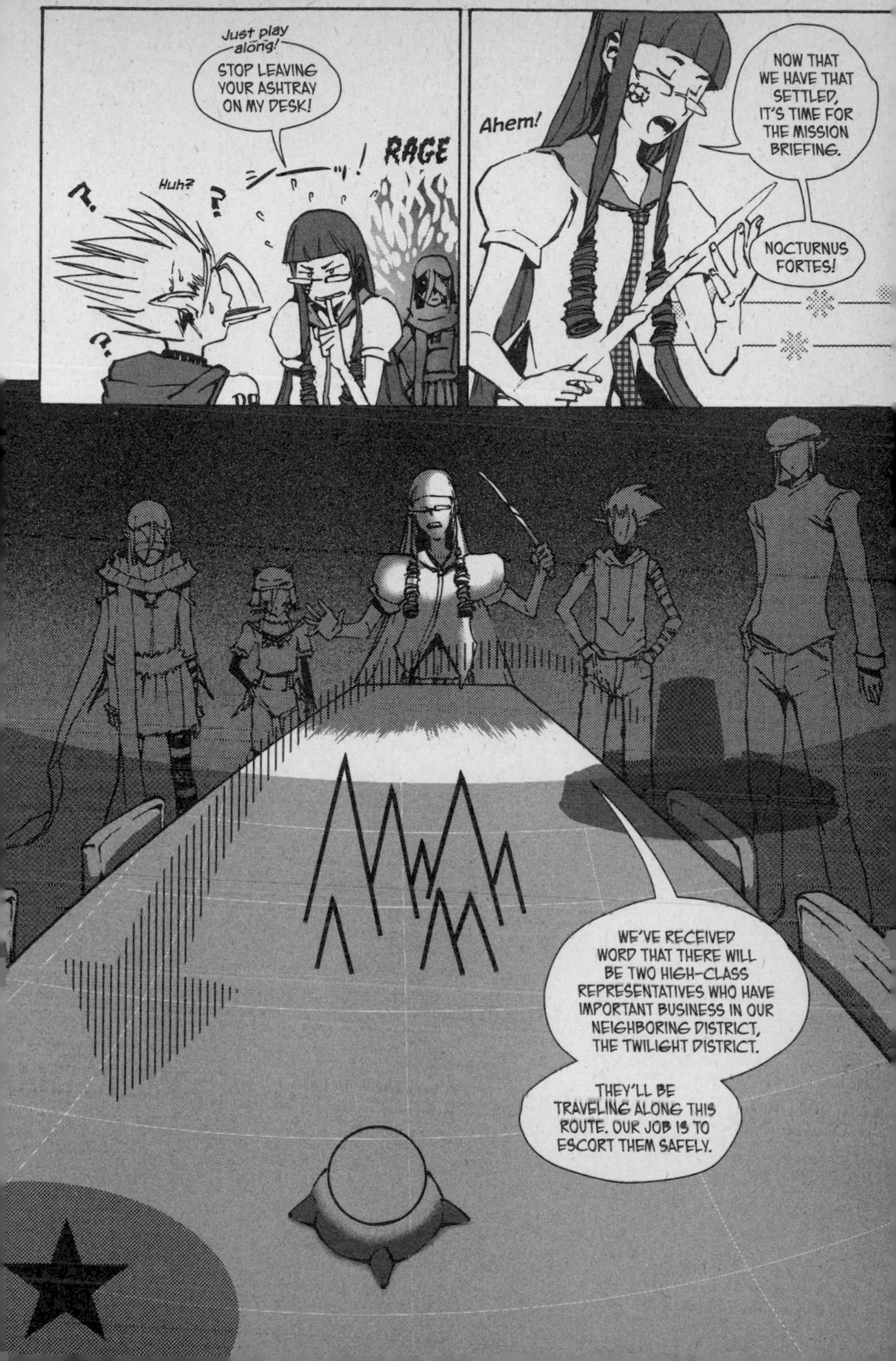
Just play along!
STOP LEAVING YOUR ASHTRAY ON MY DESK!
Huh?
RAGE
Ahem!
NOW THAT WE HAVE THAT SETTLED, IT'S TIME FOR THE MISSION BRIEFING.
NOCTURNUS FORTES!
WE'VE RECEIVED WORD THAT THERE WILL BE TWO HIGH-CLASS REPRESENTATIVES WHO HAVE IMPORTANT BUSINESS IN OUR NEIGHBORING DISTRICT, THE TWILIGHT DISTRICT.
THEY'LL BE TRAVELING ALONG THIS ROUTE. OUR JOB IS TO ESCORT THEM SAFELY.

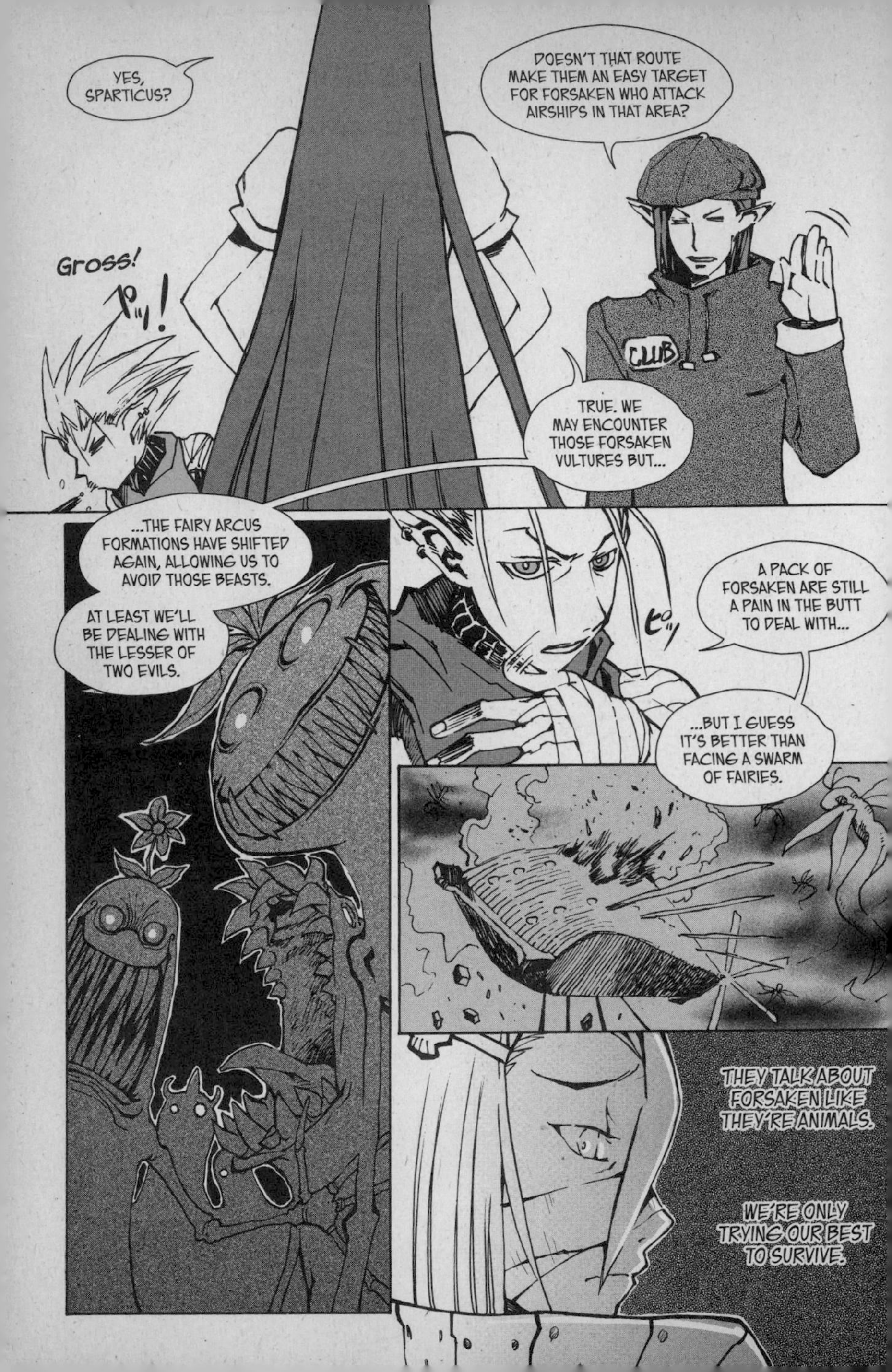
YES, SPARTICUS?
DOESN'T THAT ROUTE MAKE THEM AN EASY TARGET FOR FORSAKEN WHO ATTACK AIRSHIPS IN THAT AREA?
Gross!
TRUE. WE MAY ENCOUNTER THOSE FORSAKEN VULTURES BUT...
...THE FAIRY ARCUS FORMATIONS HAVE SHIFTED AGAIN, ALLOWING US TO AVOID THOSE BEASTS.
AT LEAST WE'LL BE DEALING WITH THE LESSER OF TWO EVILS.
A PACK OF FORSAKEN ARE STILL A PAIN IN THE BUTT TO DEAL WITH...
...BUT I GUESS IT'S BETTER THAN FACING A SWARM OF FAIRIES.
THEY TALK ABOUT FORSAKEN LIKE THEY'RE ANIMALS.
WE'RE ONLY TRYING OUR BEST TO SURVIVE.

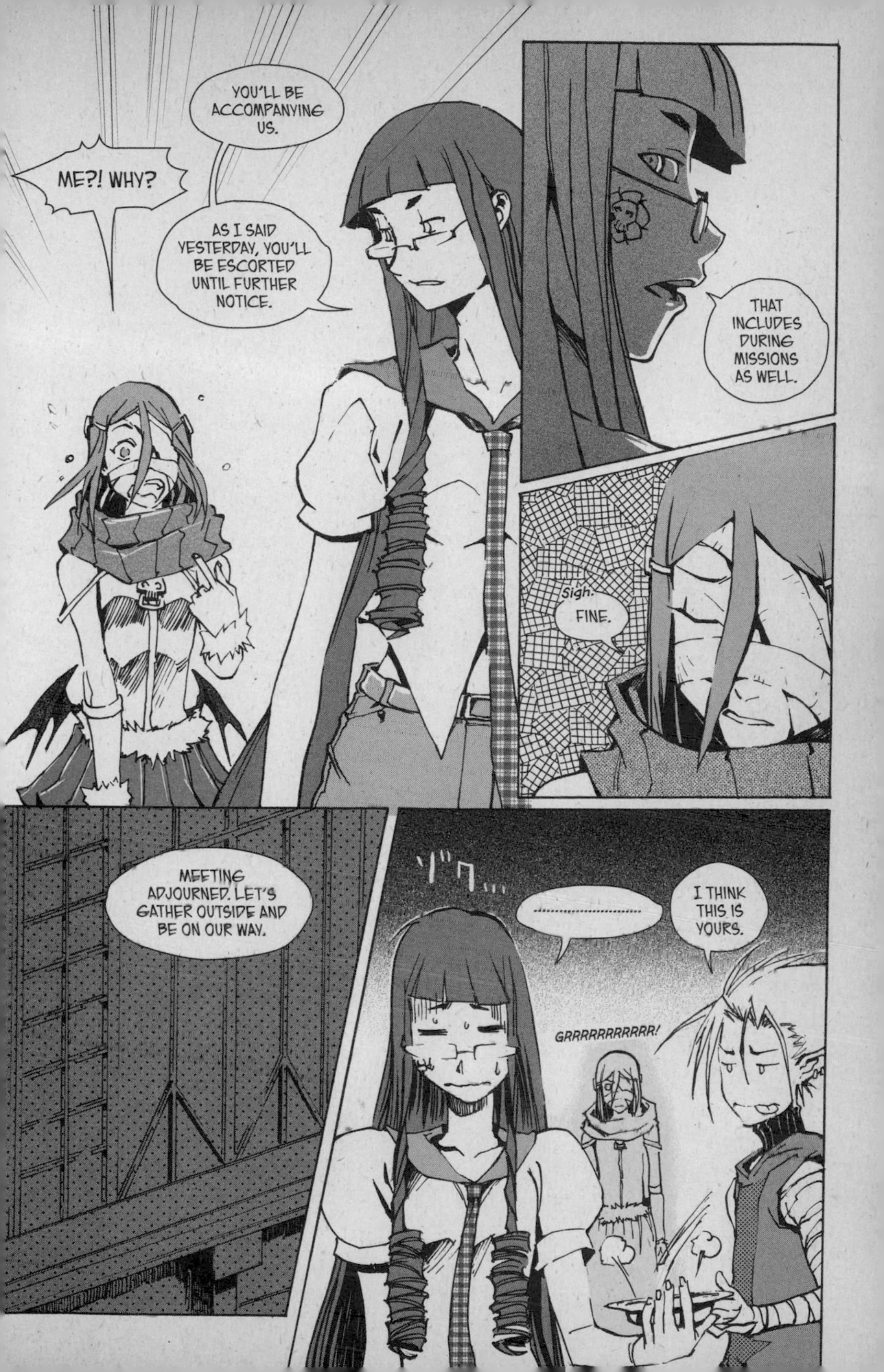
YOU'LL BE ACCOMPANYING US.
ME?! WHY?
AS I SAID YESTERDAY, YOU'LL BE ESCORTED UNTIL FURTHER NOTICE.
THAT INCLUDES DURING MISSIONS AS WELL.
Sigh.
FINE.
MEETING ADJOURNED. LET'S GATHER OUTSIDE AND BE ON OUR WAY.
....
I THINK THIS IS YOURS.
GRRRRRRRRRRR!

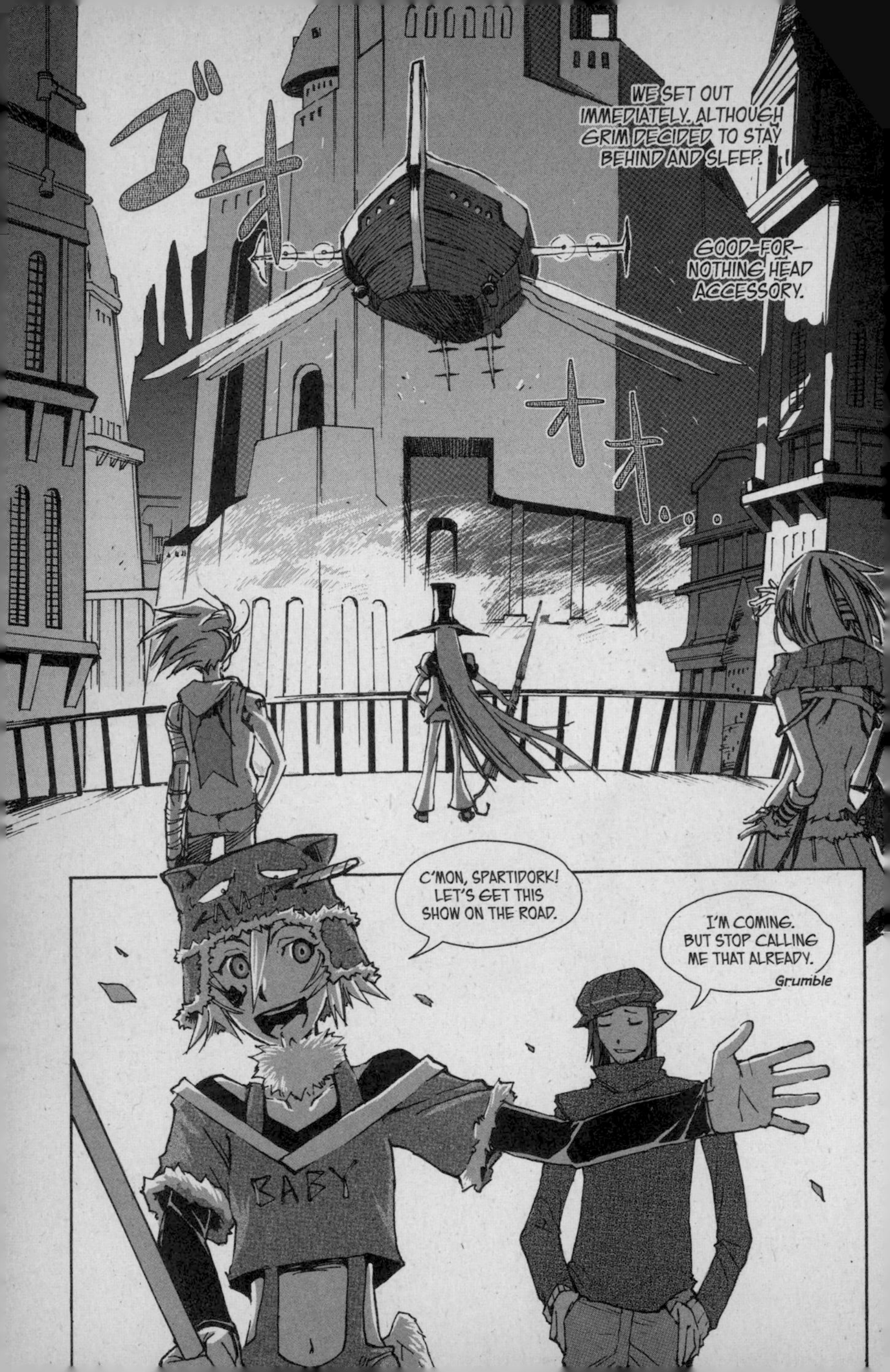
WE SET OUT IMMEDIATELY. ALTHOUGH GRIM DECIDED TO STAY BEHIND AND SLEEP.
GOOD-FOR-NOTHING HEAD ACCESSORY.
ゴオ
オオ...
C'MON, SPARTIDORK! LET'S GET THIS SHOW ON THE ROAD.
I'M COMING. BUT STOP CALLING ME THAT ALREADY.
Grumble
BABY

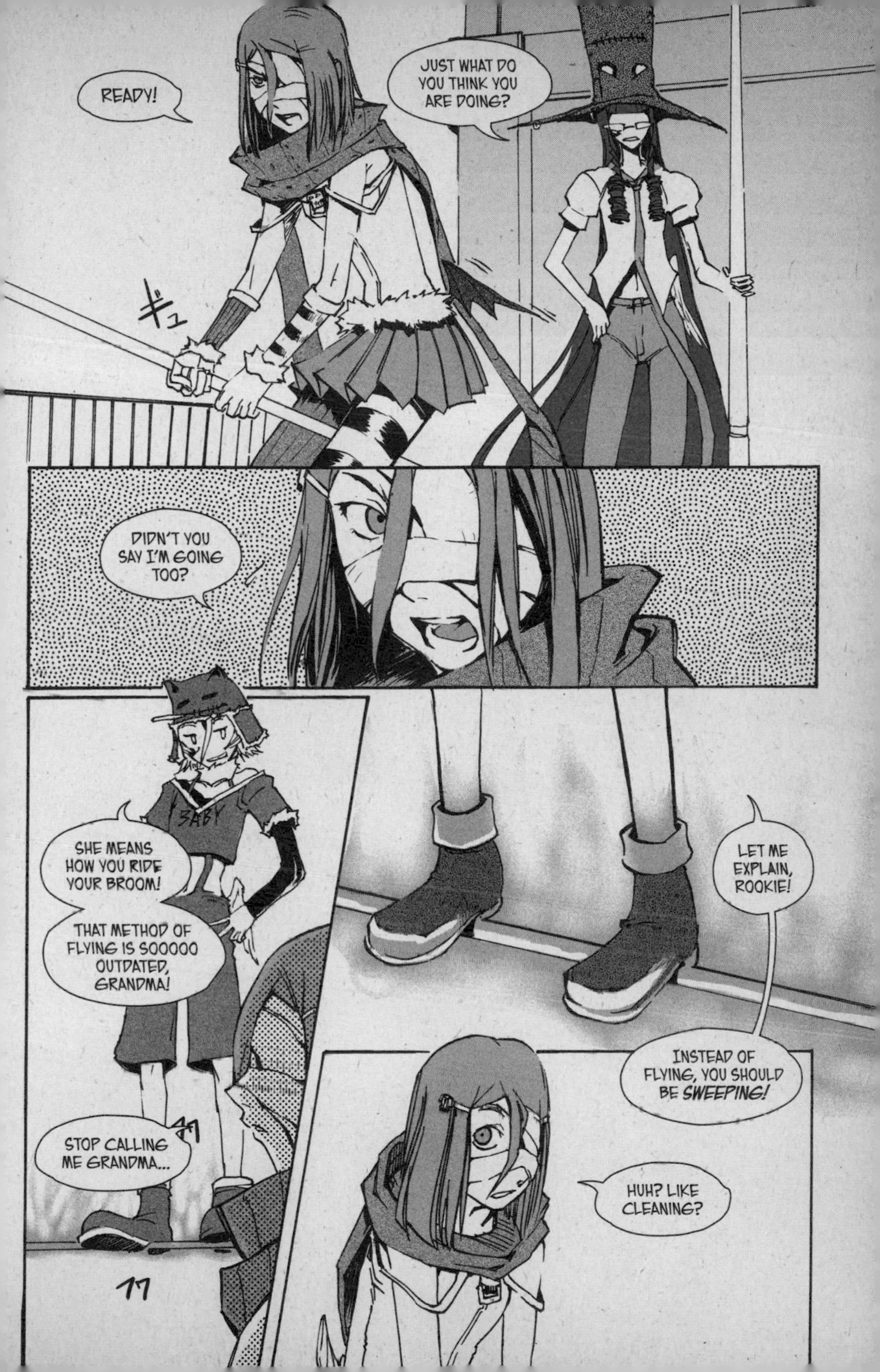
READY!
JUST WHAT DO YOU THINK YOU ARE DOING?
ギュ
DIDN'T YOU SAY I'M GOING TOO?
SHE MEANS HOW YOU RIDE YOUR BROOM!
THAT METHOD OF FLYING IS SOOOOO OUTDATED, GRANDMA!
STOP CALLING ME GRANDMA...
LET ME EXPLAIN, ROOKIE!
INSTEAD OF FLYING, YOU SHOULD BE *SWEEPING!*
HUH? LIKE CLEANING?

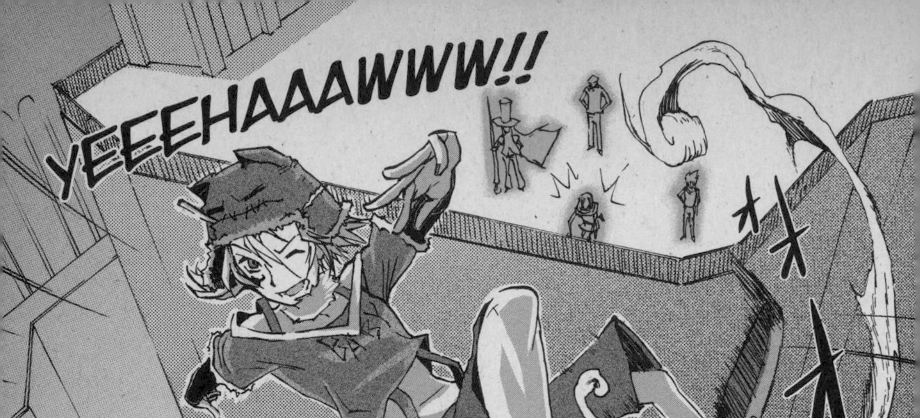
YEEEHAAAWWW!!
SWEEPING IS A NEW STYLE OF FLYING DISCOVERED A FEW YEARS BACK.
IT BECAME SO POPULAR THAT IT'S BEEN APPLIED TO SPORTS AS WELL. THERE ARE RACES, TRICK CONTESTS, AND OTHER EVENTS HELD ACROSS THE DISTRICTS.
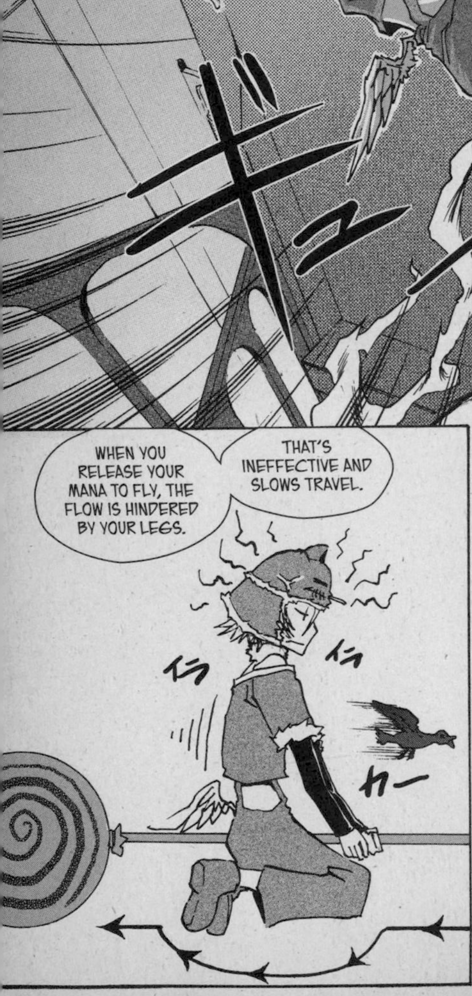
WHEN YOU RELEASE YOUR MANA TO FLY, THE FLOW IS HINDERED BY YOUR LEGS.
THAT'S INEFFECTIVE AND SLOWS TRAVEL.
イラ
イラ
カー
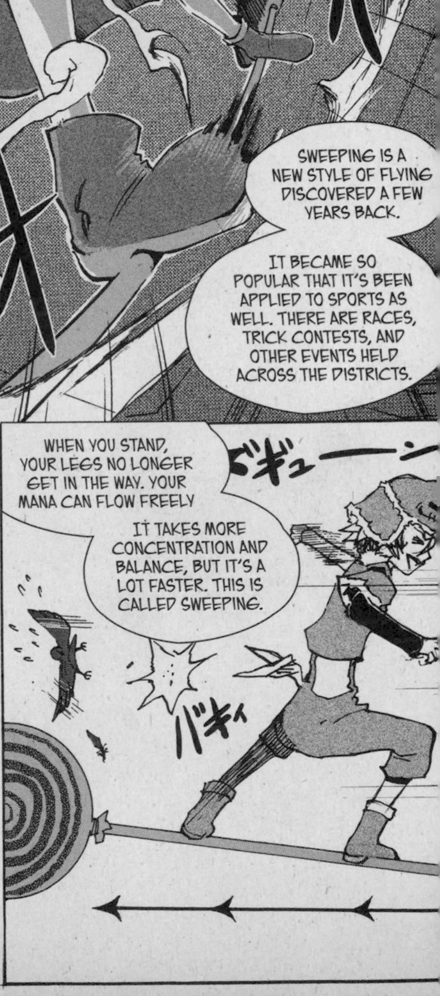
WHEN YOU STAND, YOUR LEGS NO LONGER GET IN THE WAY. YOUR MANA CAN FLOW FREELY
IT TAKES MORE CONCENTRATION AND BALANCE, BUT IT'S A LOT FASTER. THIS IS CALLED SWEEPING.
バキィ

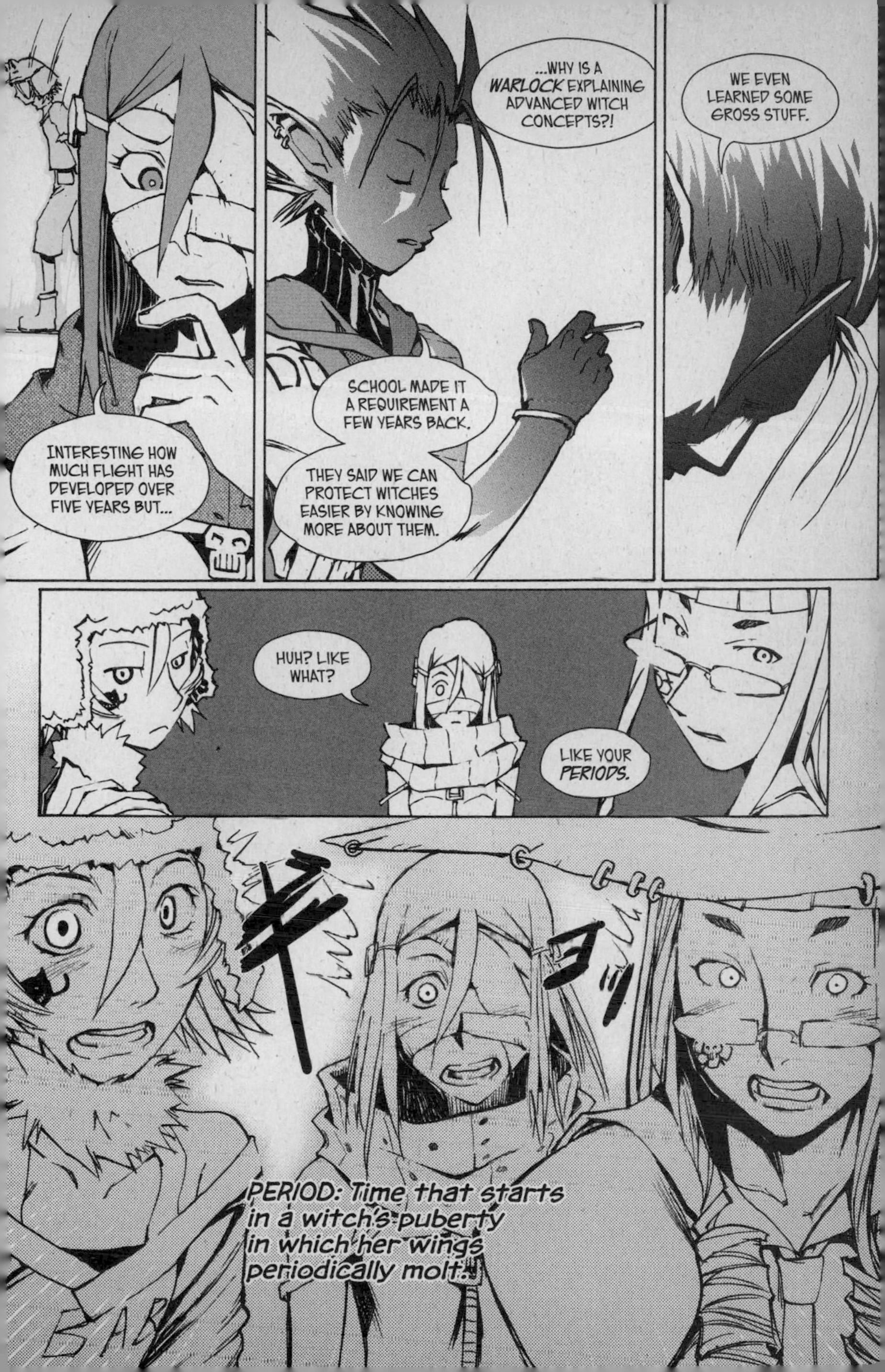
INTERESTING HOW MUCH FLIGHT HAS DEVELOPED OVER FIVE YEARS BUT...
...WHY IS A WARLOCK EXPLAINING ADVANCED WITCH CONCEPTS?!
SCHOOL MADE IT A REQUIREMENT A FEW YEARS BACK.
THEY SAID WE CAN PROTECT WITCHES EASIER BY KNOWING MORE ABOUT THEM.
WE EVEN LEARNED SOME GROSS STUFF.
HUH? LIKE WHAT?
LIKE YOUR PERIODS.
PERIOD: Time that starts in a witch's puberty in which her wings periodically molt.

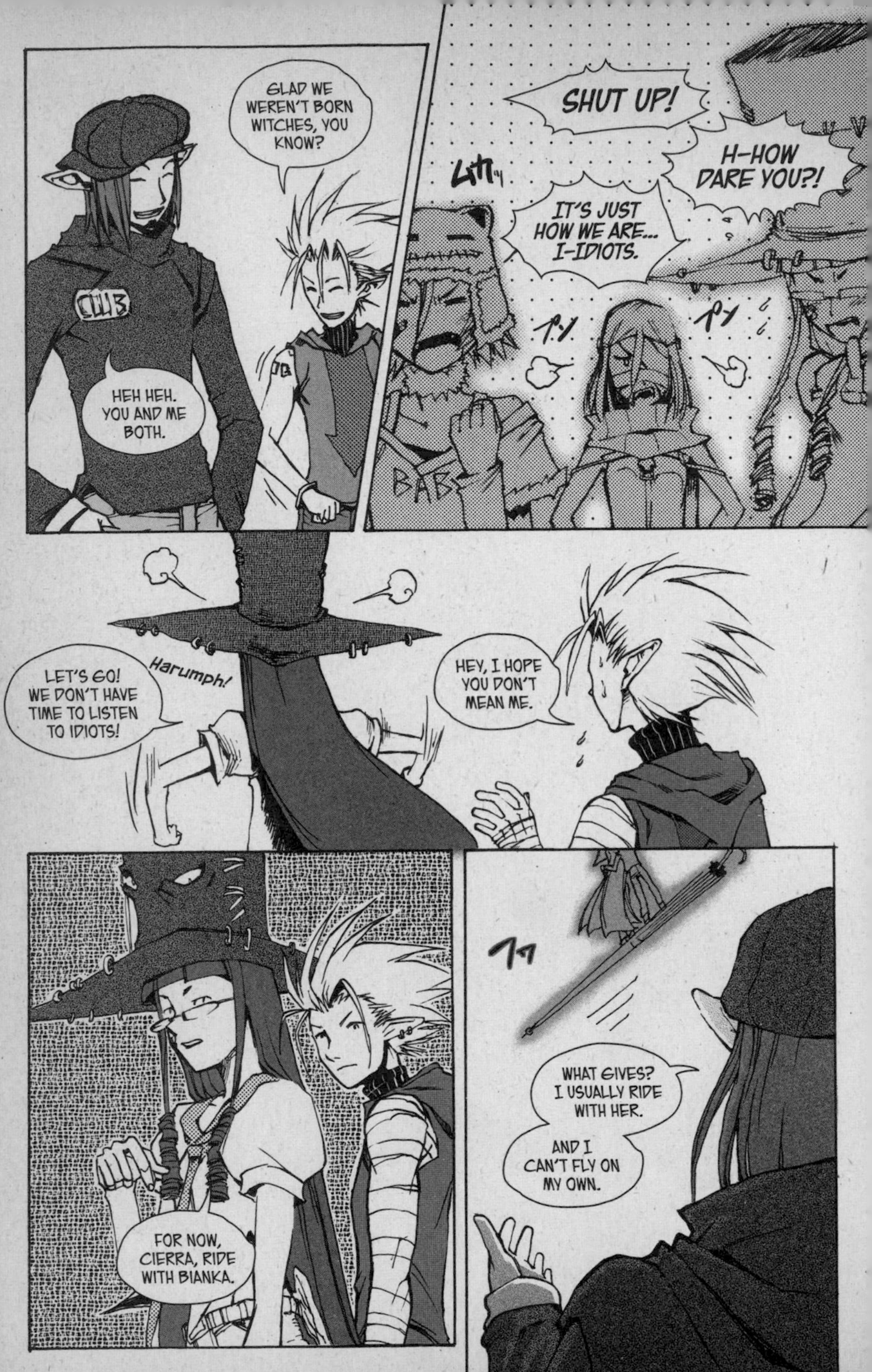
GLAD WE WEREN'T BORN WITCHES, YOU KNOW?
HEH HEH. YOU AND ME BOTH.
SHUT UP!
H-HOW DARE YOU?!
IT'S JUST HOW WE ARE... I-IDIOTS.
LET'S GO! WE DON'T HAVE TIME TO LISTEN TO IDIOTS!
Harumph!
HEY, I HOPE YOU DON'T MEAN ME.
FOR NOW, CIERRA, RIDE WITH BIANKA.
WHAT GIVES? I USUALLY RIDE WITH HER.
AND I CAN'T FLY ON MY OWN.

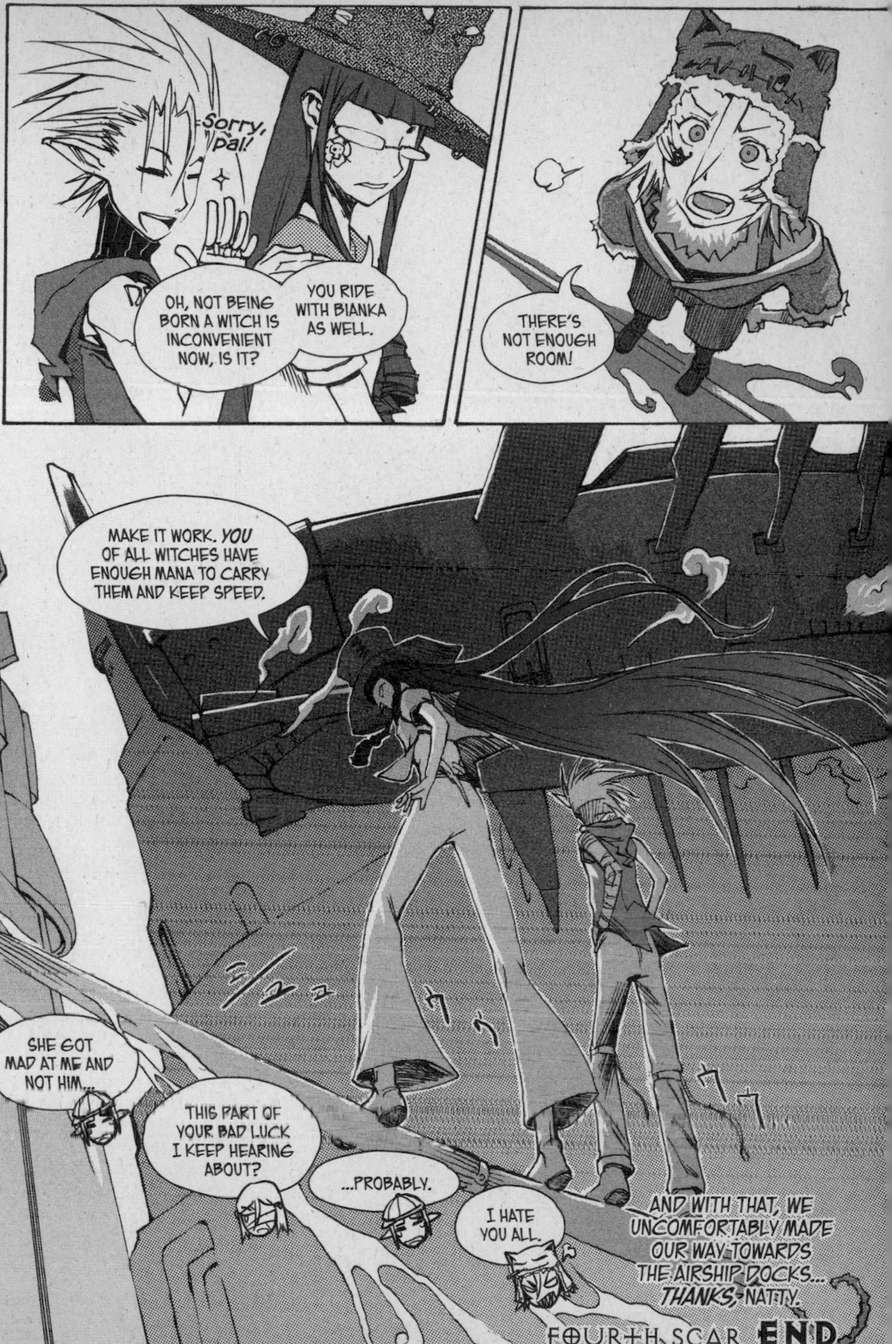
THERE'S NOT ENOUGH ROOM!
YOU RIDE WITH BIANKA AS WELL.
Sorry, pal!
OH, NOT BEING BORN A WITCH IS INCONVENIENT NOW, IS IT?
MAKE IT WORK. *YOU* OF ALL WITCHES HAVE ENOUGH MANA TO CARRY THEM AND KEEP SPEED.
SHE GOT MAD AT ME AND NOT HIM...
THIS PART OF YOUR BAD LUCK I KEEP HEARING ABOUT?
...PROBABLY.
I HATE YOU ALL.
AND WITH THAT, WE UNCOMFORTABLY MADE OUR WAY TOWARDS THE AIRSHIP DOCKS... *THANKS,* NATTY.
FOURTH SCAR END

QUEEN BIANKA'S CRASH COURSE

CHAPTER FOUR: FAIRIES

FAIRIES...I HATE THE DISGUSTING THINGS. THEY EAT WITCHES TA FEED ON OUR MAGICAL ENERGY AND SATISFY THEIR HUNGER. THE THINGS COME IN LOTS OF DIFFERENT SHAPES AND SIZES DEPENDING ON HOW MUCH MAGIC THEY ABSORB. ONLY WARLOCKS HAVE A REAL CHANCE AGAINST THEM BECAUSE THEY CAN'T USE MAGIC LIKE US WITCHES. BUT FAIRIES ARE AGGRESSIVE AND'LL STILL TEAR A WARLOCK TA PIECES, EVEN IF THEY DON'T EAT THEM. HERE ARE SOME THINGS TA REMEMBER ABOUT FAIRIES...

FAIRY FACTS

1. ABSORBS ANY MAGIC ATTACK
2. EATS WITCHES
3. CAN EXTEND THEIR ARMS
4. CAN'T FLY
5. FAIRY ARCUS NEGATES FACT 4

HERE'S THE DEAL ABOUT THE FAIRY ARCUS. IT'S A THICK, DARK MIST THAT SURROUNDS SOME AREAS OF THE WILDERNESS. FAIRIES CAN TRAVEL ANYWHERE WITHIN THE MIST. USING THIS, THEY CAN REACH THE AIR AND "FLY" FOR LACK OF BETTER WORDS. IT'S BEST FOR AIRSHIPS TA STEER CLEAR.

WITCHES...***RUN IF YOU SEE A FAIRY!***

WARLOCKS BETTER DO THE SAME!

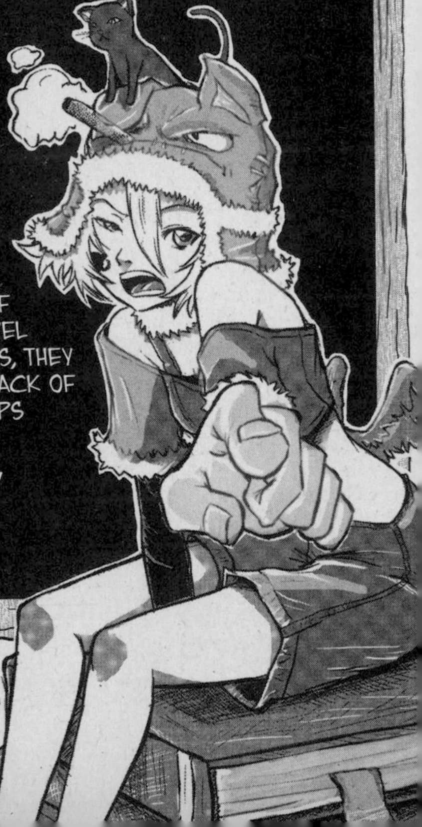
WHAT, YA WANT TO KNOW ABOUT FAIRIES?! OKAY, BUT YA WON'T LIKE WHAT YA HEAR...

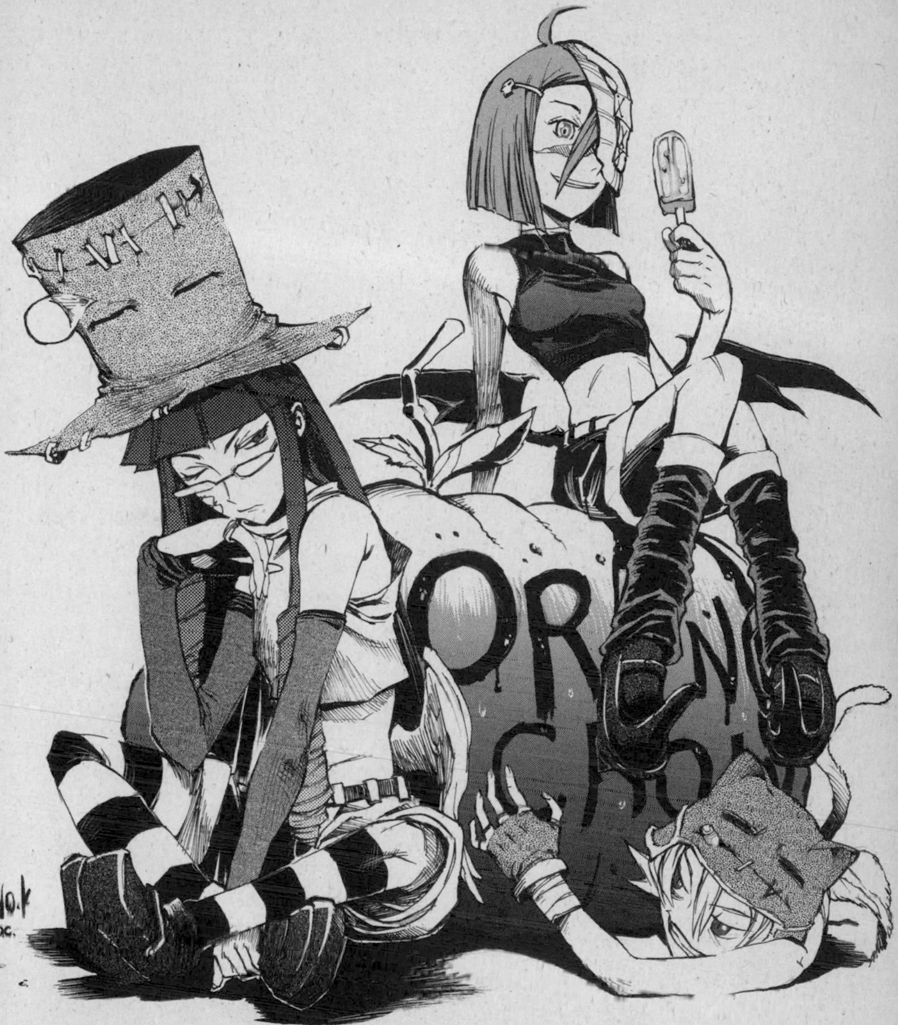

FIFTH SCAR

WELCOME HOME

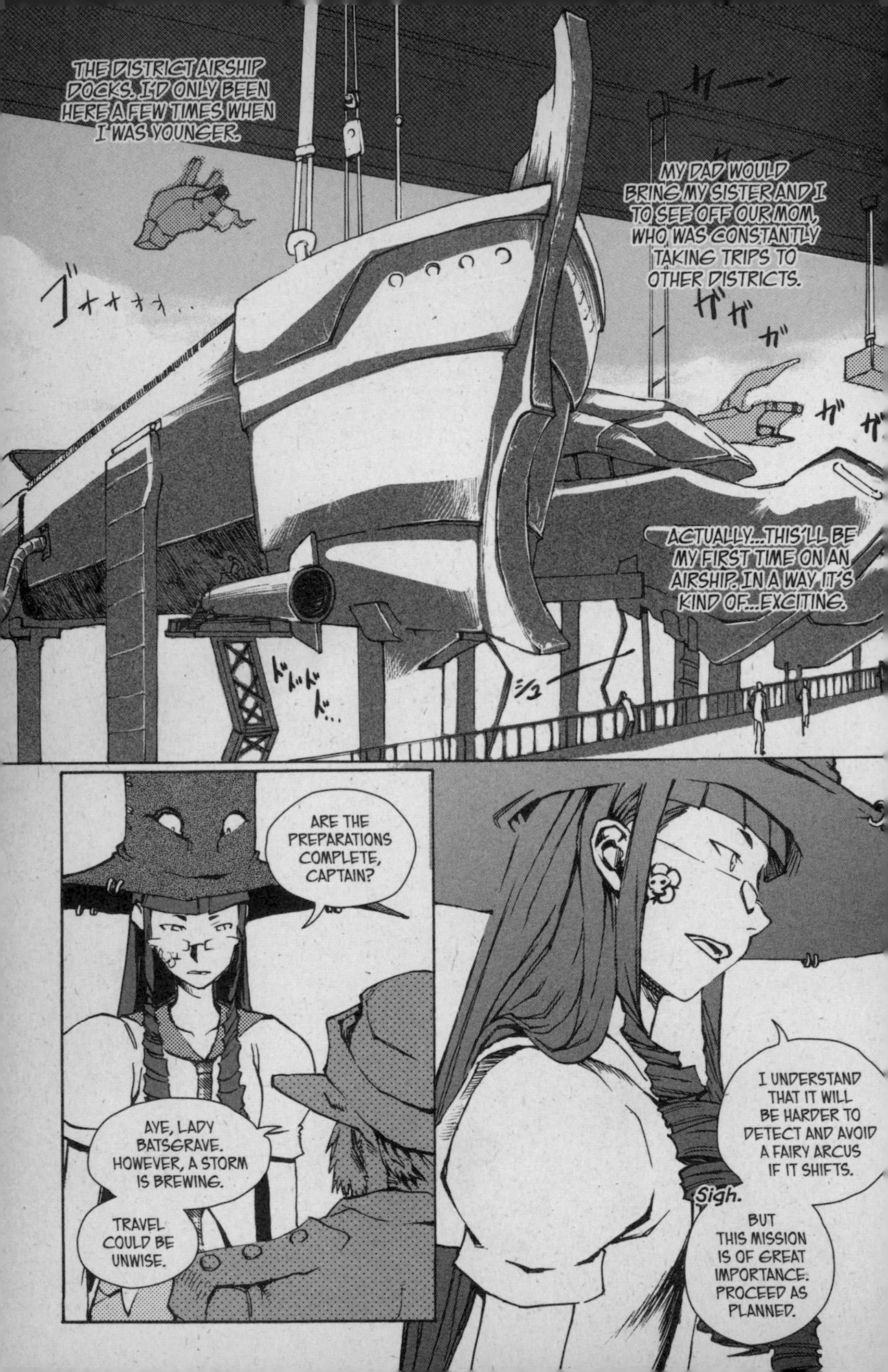
THE DISTRICT AIRSHIP DOCKS. I'D ONLY BEEN HERE A FEW TIMES WHEN I WAS YOUNGER.
MY DAD WOULD BRING MY SISTER AND I TO SEE OFF OUR MOM, WHO WAS CONSTANTLY TAKING TRIPS TO OTHER DISTRICTS.
ACTUALLY...THIS'LL BE MY FIRST TIME ON AN AIRSHIP. IN A WAY IT'S KIND OF...EXCITING.
ARE THE PREPARATIONS COMPLETE, CAPTAIN?
AYE, LADY BATSGRAVE. HOWEVER, A STORM IS BREWING.
TRAVEL COULD BE UNWISE.
I UNDERSTAND THAT IT WILL BE HARDER TO DETECT AND AVOID A FAIRY ARCUS IF IT SHIFTS.
Sigh.
BUT THIS MISSION IS OF GREAT IMPORTANCE. PROCEED AS PLANNED.

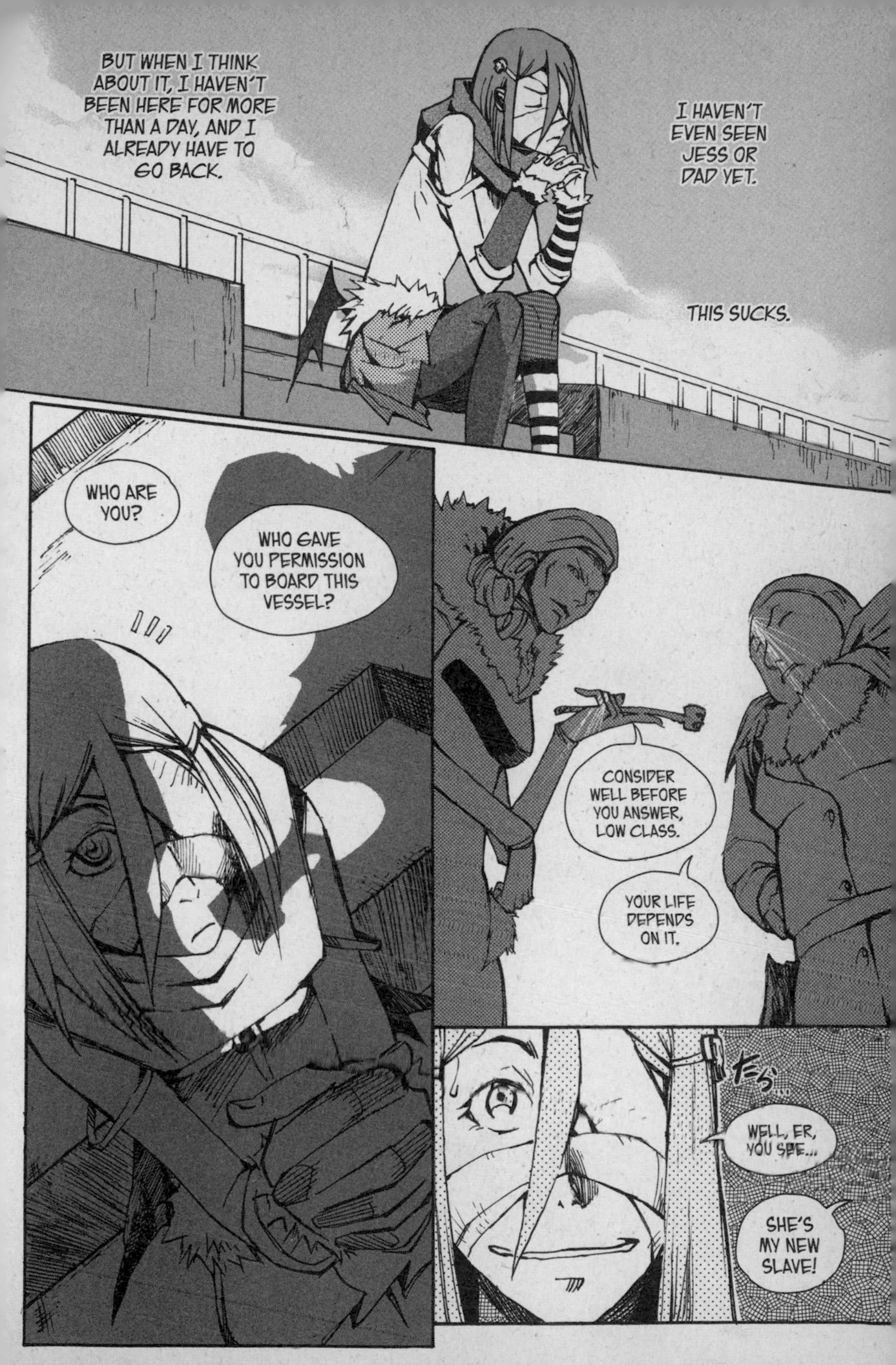
BUT WHEN I THINK ABOUT IT, I HAVEN'T BEEN HERE FOR MORE THAN A DAY, AND I ALREADY HAVE TO GO BACK.
I HAVEN'T EVEN SEEN JESS OR DAD YET.
THIS SUCKS.
WHO ARE YOU?
WHO GAVE YOU PERMISSION TO BOARD THIS VESSEL?
CONSIDER WELL BEFORE YOU ANSWER, LOW CLASS.
YOUR LIFE DEPENDS ON IT.
WELL, ER, YOU SEE...
SHE'S MY NEW SLAVE!

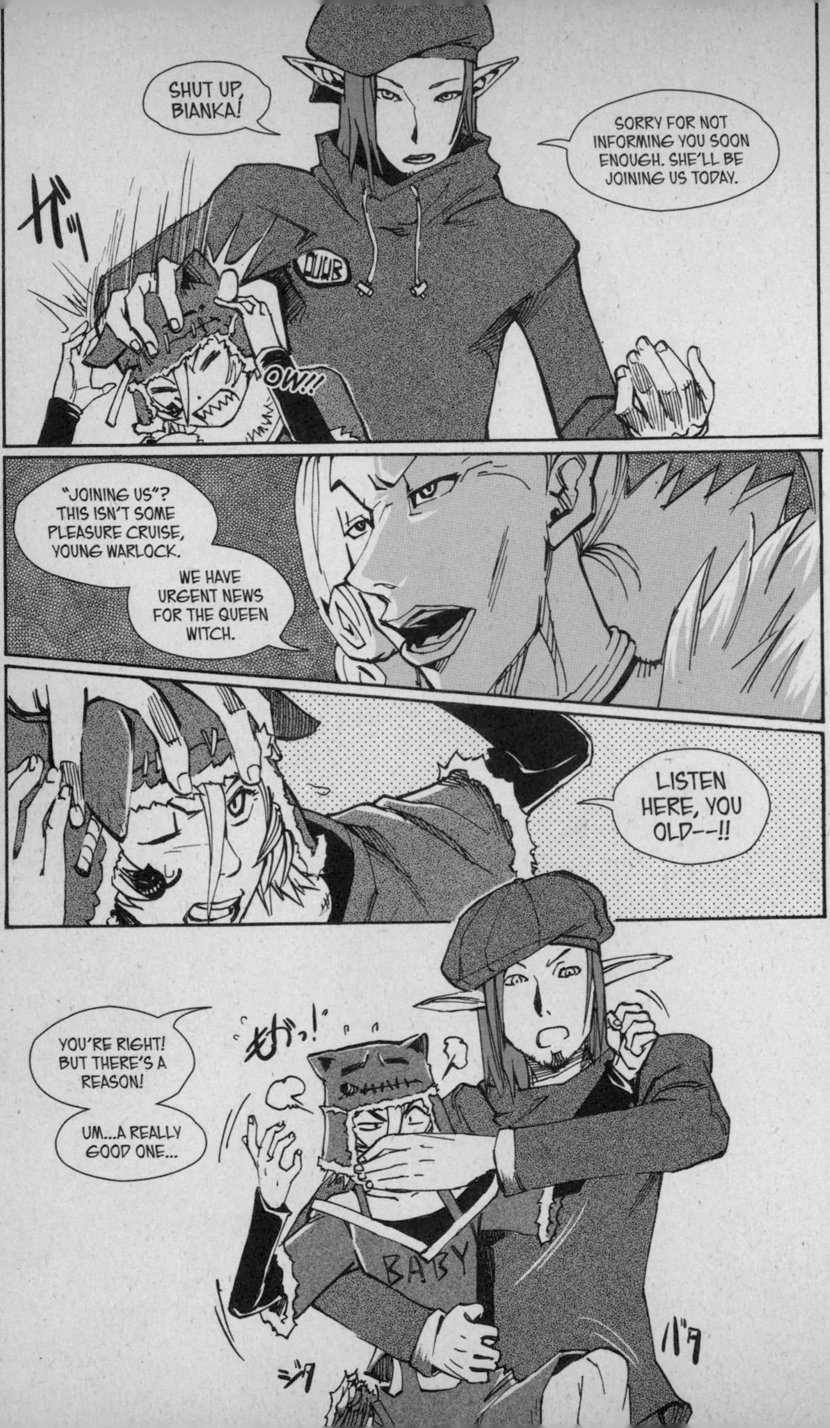
SHUT UP, BIANKA!
SORRY FOR NOT INFORMING YOU SOON ENOUGH. SHE'LL BE JOINING US TODAY.
ガッ
OW!!
"JOINING US"? THIS ISN'T SOME PLEASURE CRUISE, YOUNG WARLOCK.
WE HAVE URGENT NEWS FOR THE QUEEN WITCH.
LISTEN HERE, YOU OLD--!!
もがっ!
YOU'RE RIGHT! BUT THERE'S A REASON!
UM...A REALLY GOOD ONE...
BABY
バタ
ジタ

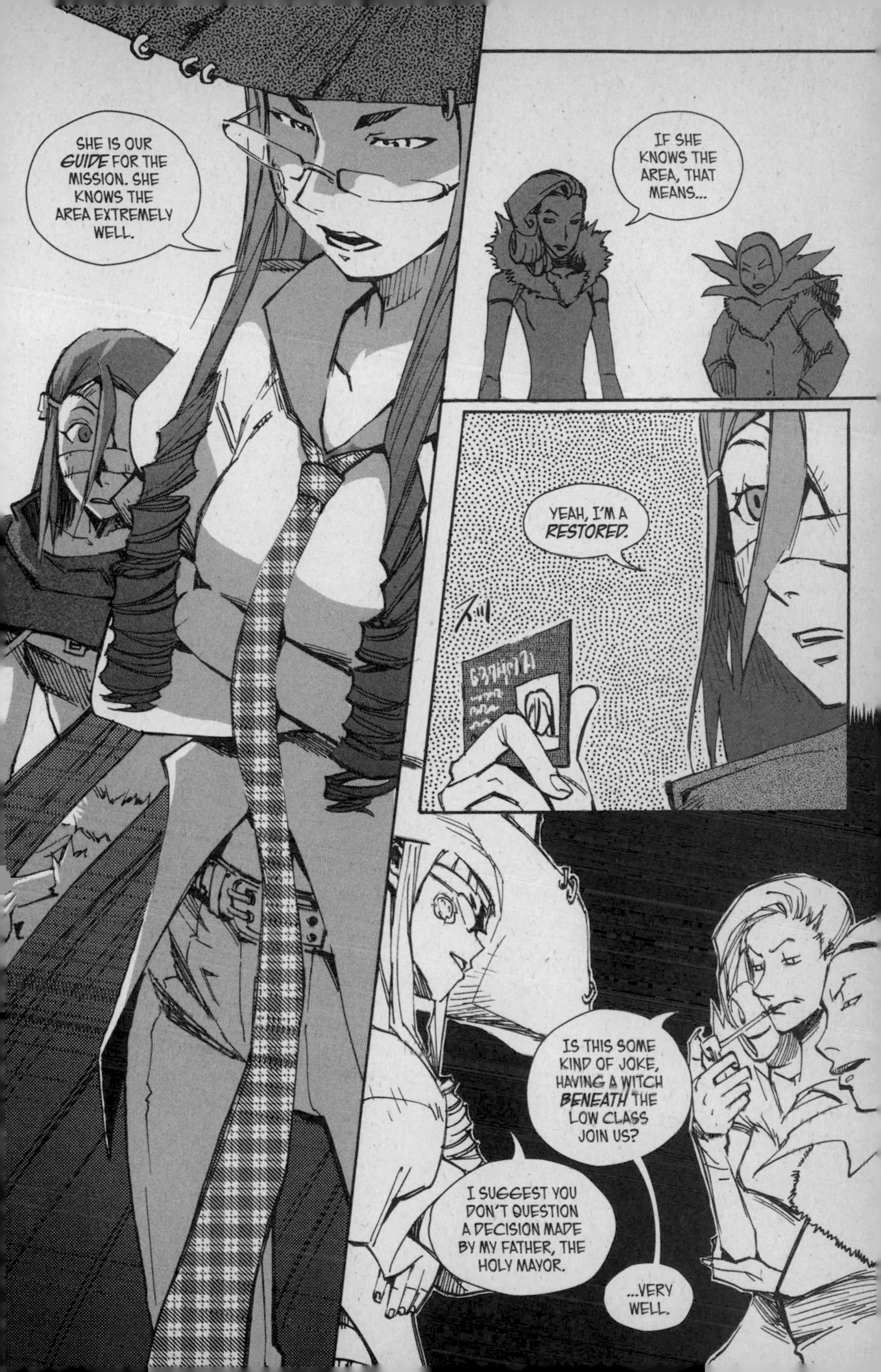
SHE IS OUR *GUIDE* FOR THE MISSION. SHE KNOWS THE AREA EXTREMELY WELL.
IF SHE KNOWS THE AREA, THAT MEANS...
YEAH, I'M A *RESTORED*.
IS THIS SOME KIND OF JOKE, HAVING A WITCH *BENEATH* THE LOW CLASS JOIN US?
I SUGGEST YOU DON'T QUESTION A DECISION MADE BY MY FATHER, THE HOLY MAYOR.
...VERY WELL.

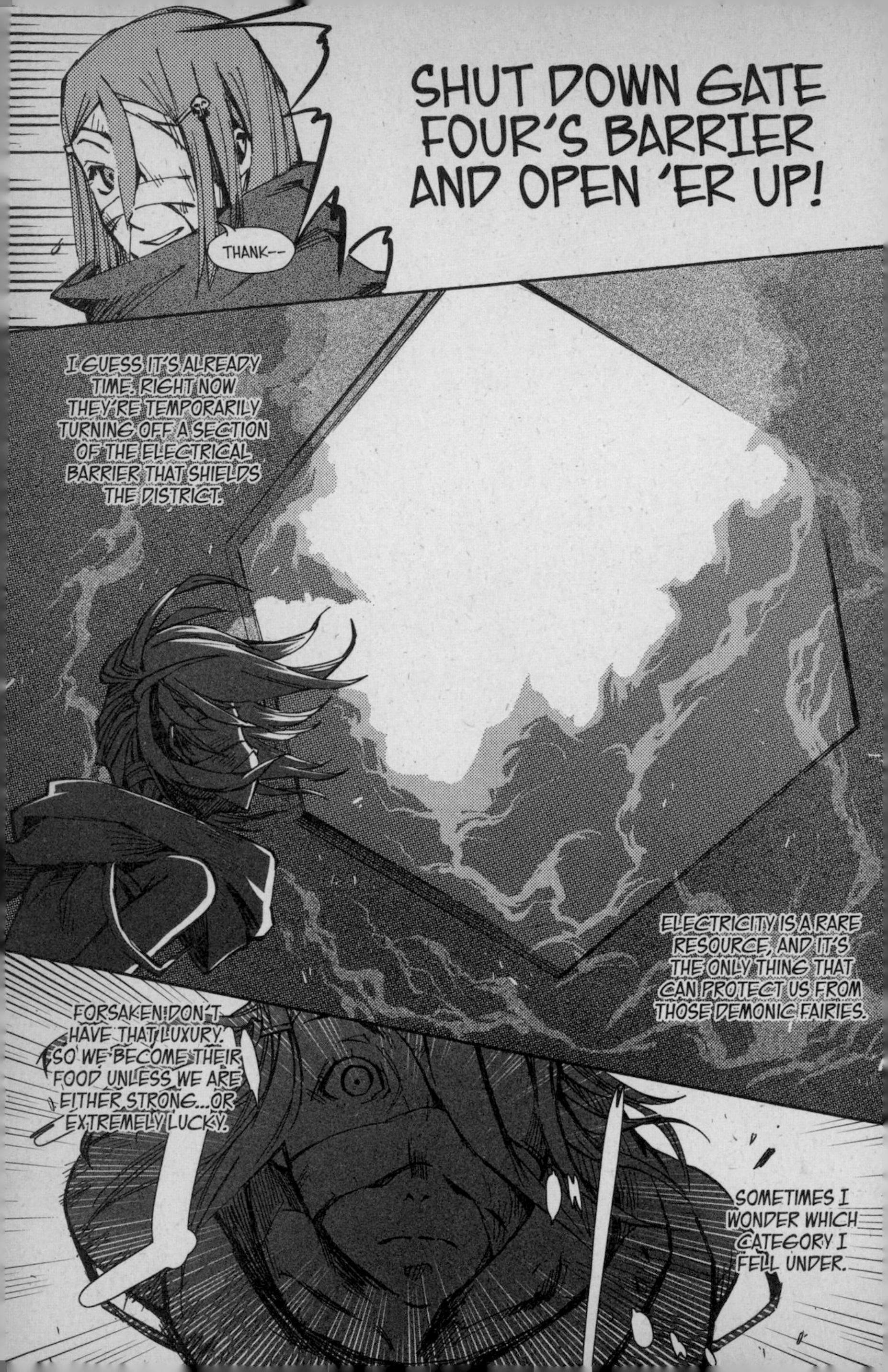
SHUT DOWN GATE FOUR'S BARRIER AND OPEN 'ER UP!
THANK--
I GUESS IT'S ALREADY TIME. RIGHT NOW THEY'RE TEMPORARILY TURNING OFF A SECTION OF THE ELECTRICAL BARRIER THAT SHIELDS THE DISTRICT.
ELECTRICITY IS A RARE RESOURCE, AND IT'S THE ONLY THING THAT CAN PROTECT US FROM THOSE DEMONIC FAIRIES.
FORSAKEN DON'T HAVE THAT LUXURY. SO WE BECOME THEIR FOOD UNLESS WE ARE EITHER STRONG...OR EXTREMELY LUCKY.
SOMETIMES I WONDER WHICH CATEGORY I FELL UNDER.

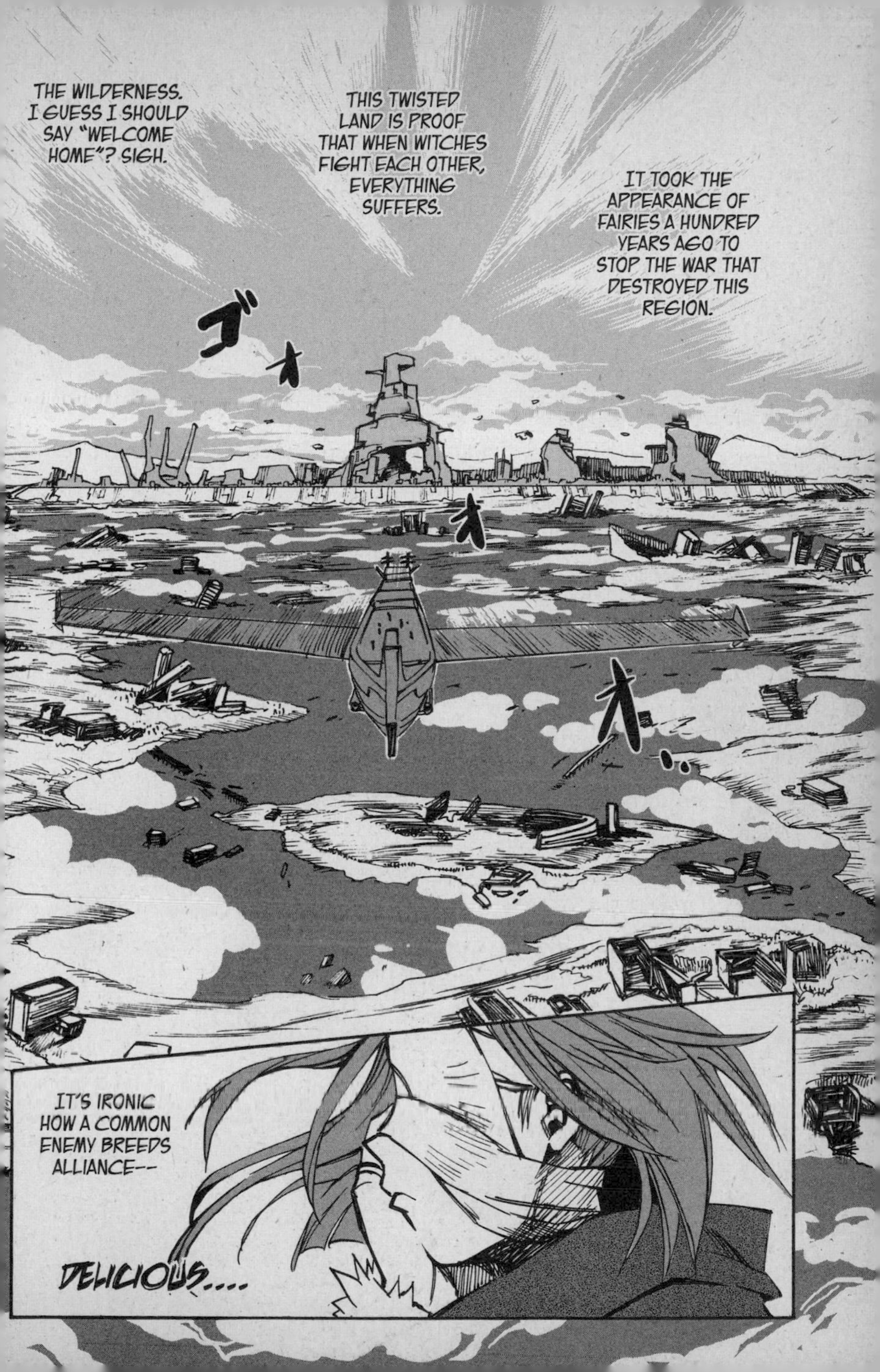
THE WILDERNESS. I GUESS I SHOULD SAY "WELCOME HOME"? SIGH.
THIS TWISTED LAND IS PROOF THAT WHEN WITCHES FIGHT EACH OTHER, EVERYTHING SUFFERS.
IT TOOK THE APPEARANCE OF FAIRIES A HUNDRED YEARS AGO TO STOP THE WAR THAT DESTROYED THIS REGION.
ゴオオオ..
IT'S IRONIC HOW A COMMON ENEMY BREEDS ALLIANCE--
DELICIOUS....

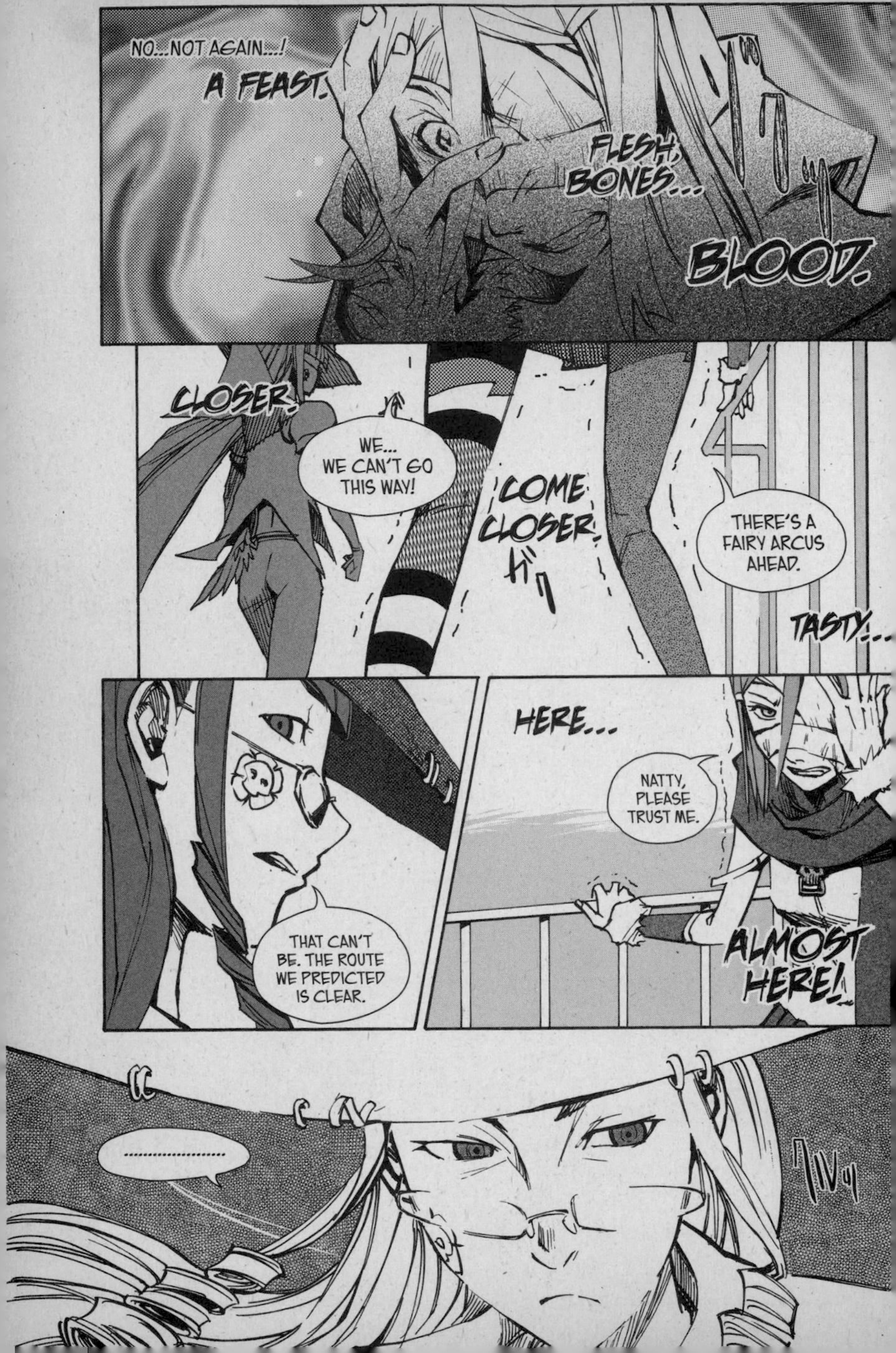
NO...NOT AGAIN...!
A FEAST.
FLESH, BONES...
BLOOD.
THERE'S A FAIRY ARCUS AHEAD.
TASTY...
COME CLOSER.
WE... WE CAN'T GO THIS WAY!
CLOSER.
HERE...
NATTY, PLEASE TRUST ME.
ALMOST HERE!
THAT CAN'T BE. THE ROUTE WE PREDICTED IS CLEAR.
....

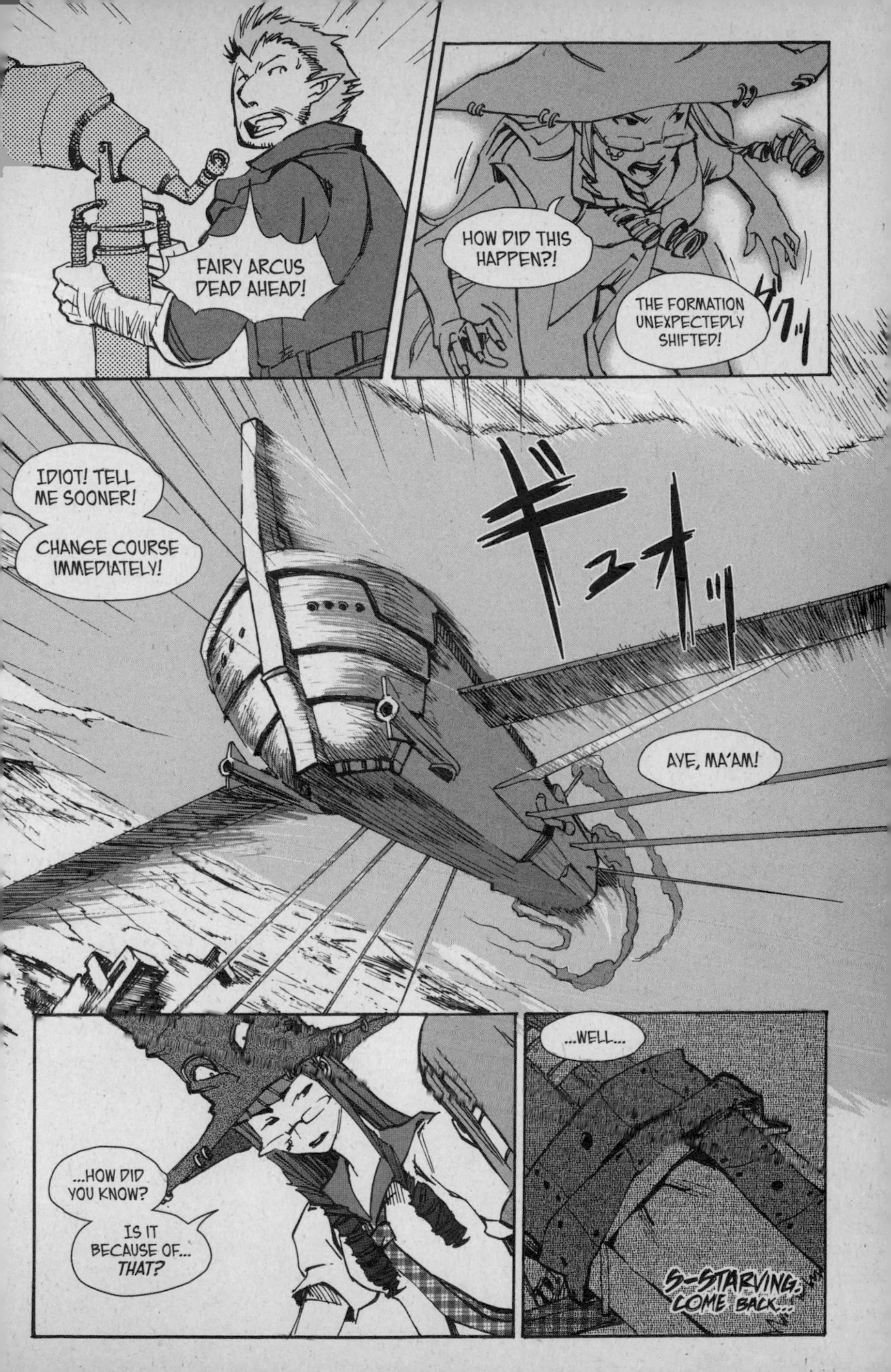
HOW DID THIS HAPPEN?!
THE FORMATION UNEXPECTEDLY SHIFTED!
FAIRY ARCUS DEAD AHEAD!
IDIOT! TELL ME SOONER!
CHANGE COURSE IMMEDIATELY!
ギュオッ
AYE, MA'AM!
...WELL...
S-STARVING. COME BACK...
...HOW DID YOU KNOW?
IS IT BECAUSE OF... *THAT?*

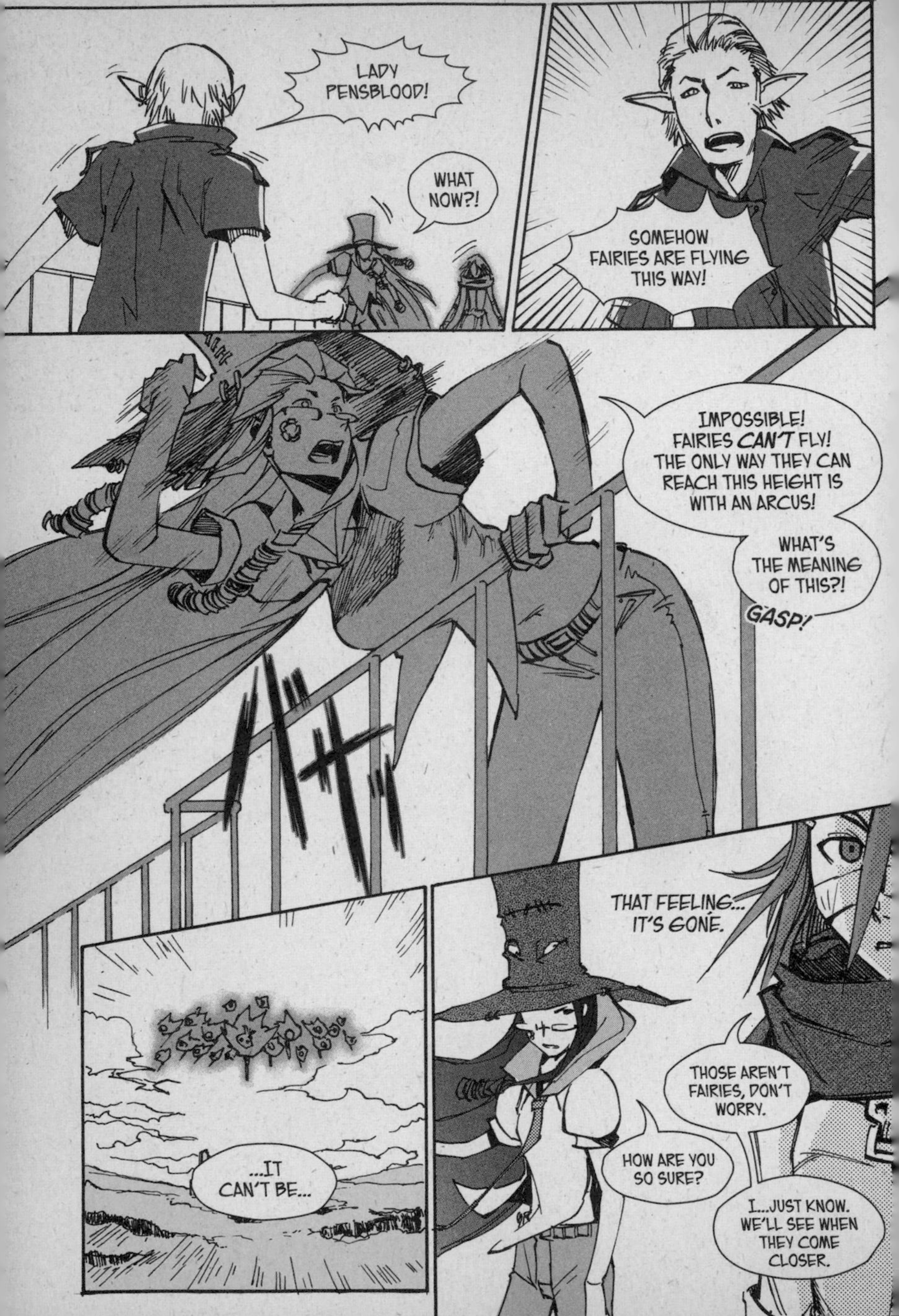
LADY PENSBLOOD!
WHAT NOW?!
SOMEHOW FAIRIES ARE FLYING THIS WAY!
IMPOSSIBLE! FAIRIES CAN'T FLY! THE ONLY WAY THEY CAN REACH THIS HEIGHT IS WITH AN ARCUS!
WHAT'S THE MEANING OF THIS?!
GASP!
...IT CAN'T BE...
THAT FEELING... IT'S GONE.
THOSE AREN'T FAIRIES, DON'T WORRY.
HOW ARE YOU SO SURE?
I...JUST KNOW. WE'LL SEE WHEN THEY COME CLOSER.

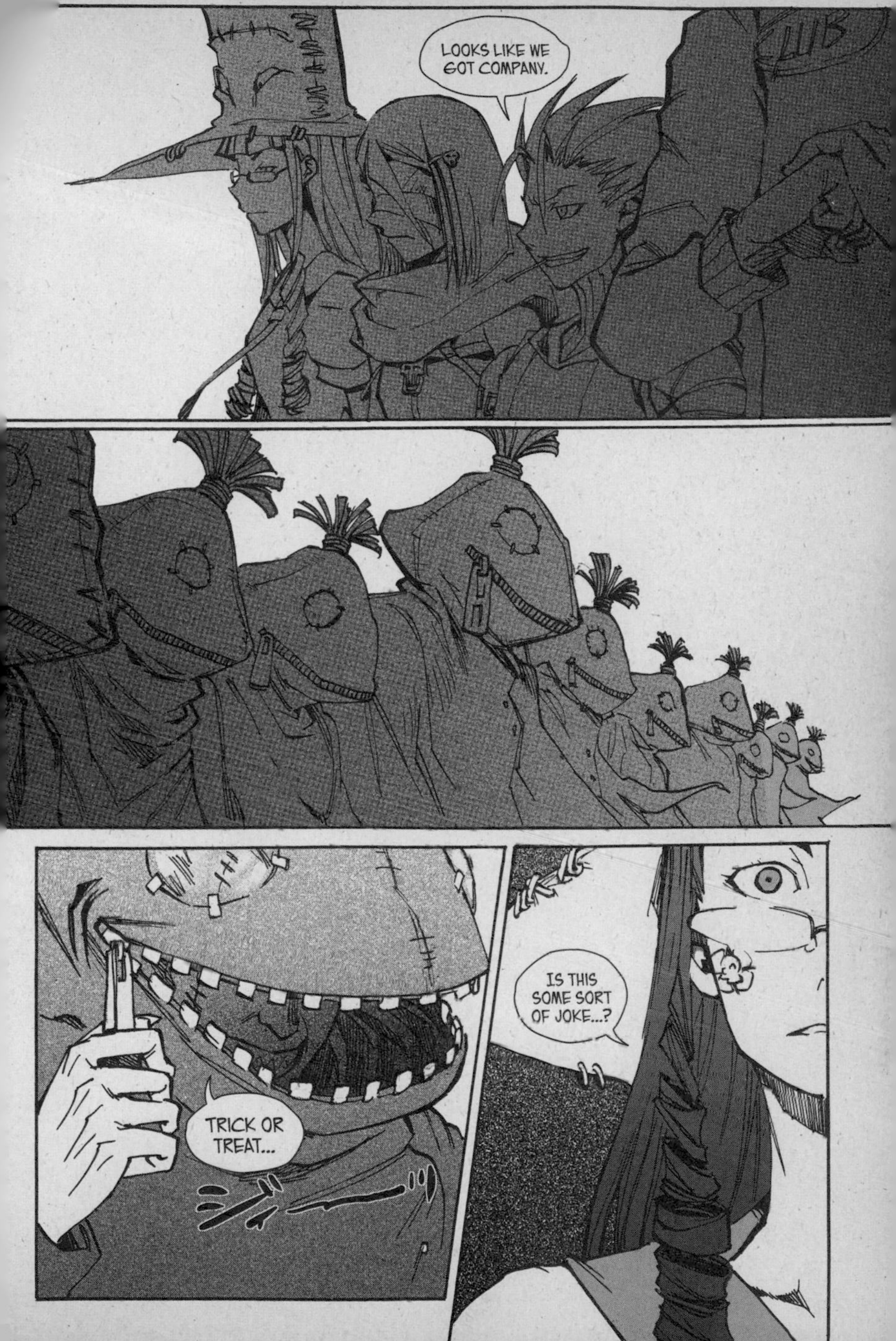
LOOKS LIKE WE GOT COMPANY.
IS THIS SOME SORT OF JOKE...?
TRICK OR TREAT...

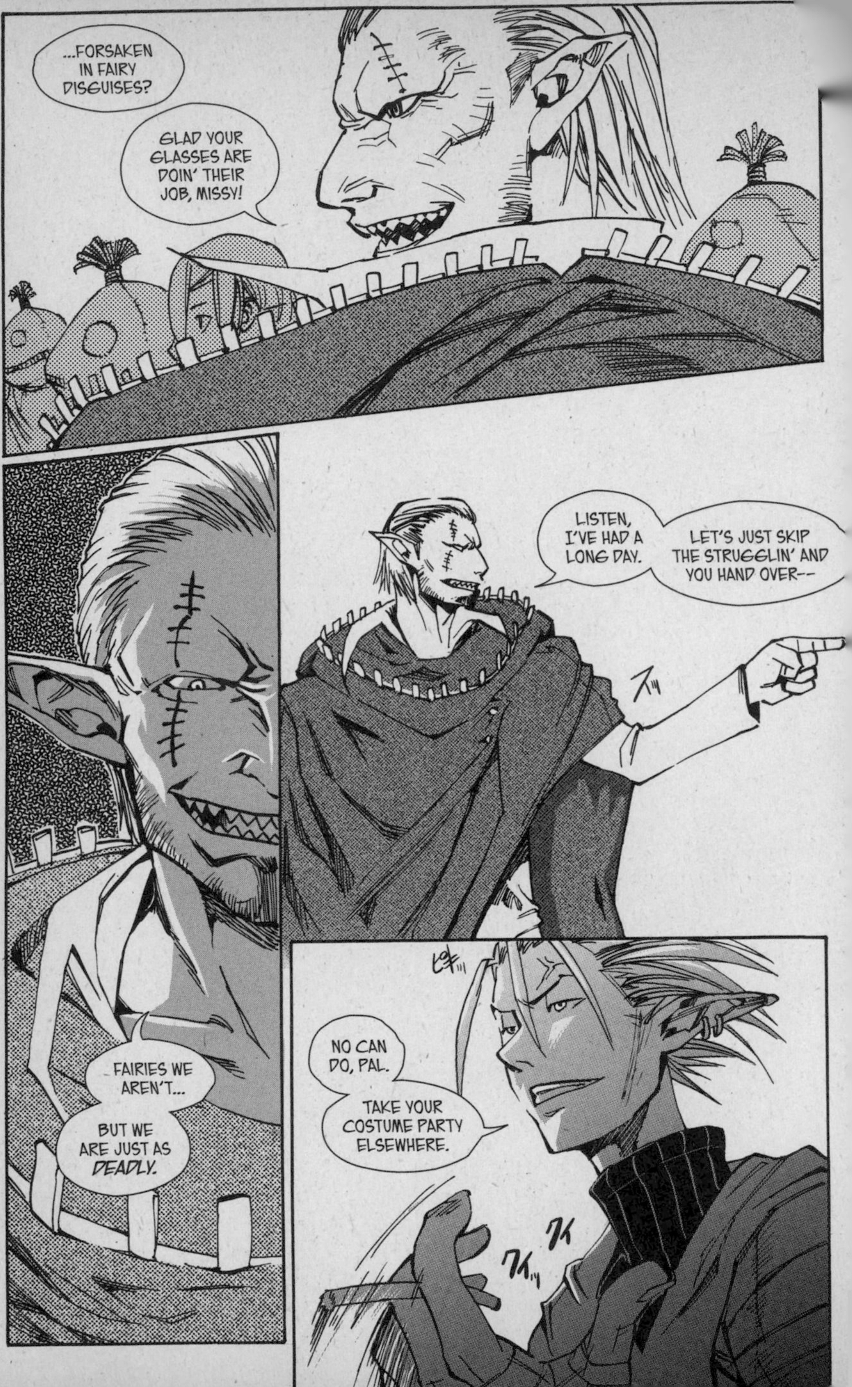
...FORSAKEN IN FAIRY DISGUISES?
GLAD YOUR GLASSES ARE DOIN' THEIR JOB, MISSY!
FAIRIES WE AREN'T...
BUT WE ARE JUST AS *DEADLY*.
LISTEN, I'VE HAD A LONG DAY.
LET'S JUST SKIP THE STRUGGLIN' AND YOU HAND OVER--
NO CAN DO, PAL.
TAKE YOUR COSTUME PARTY ELSEWHERE.

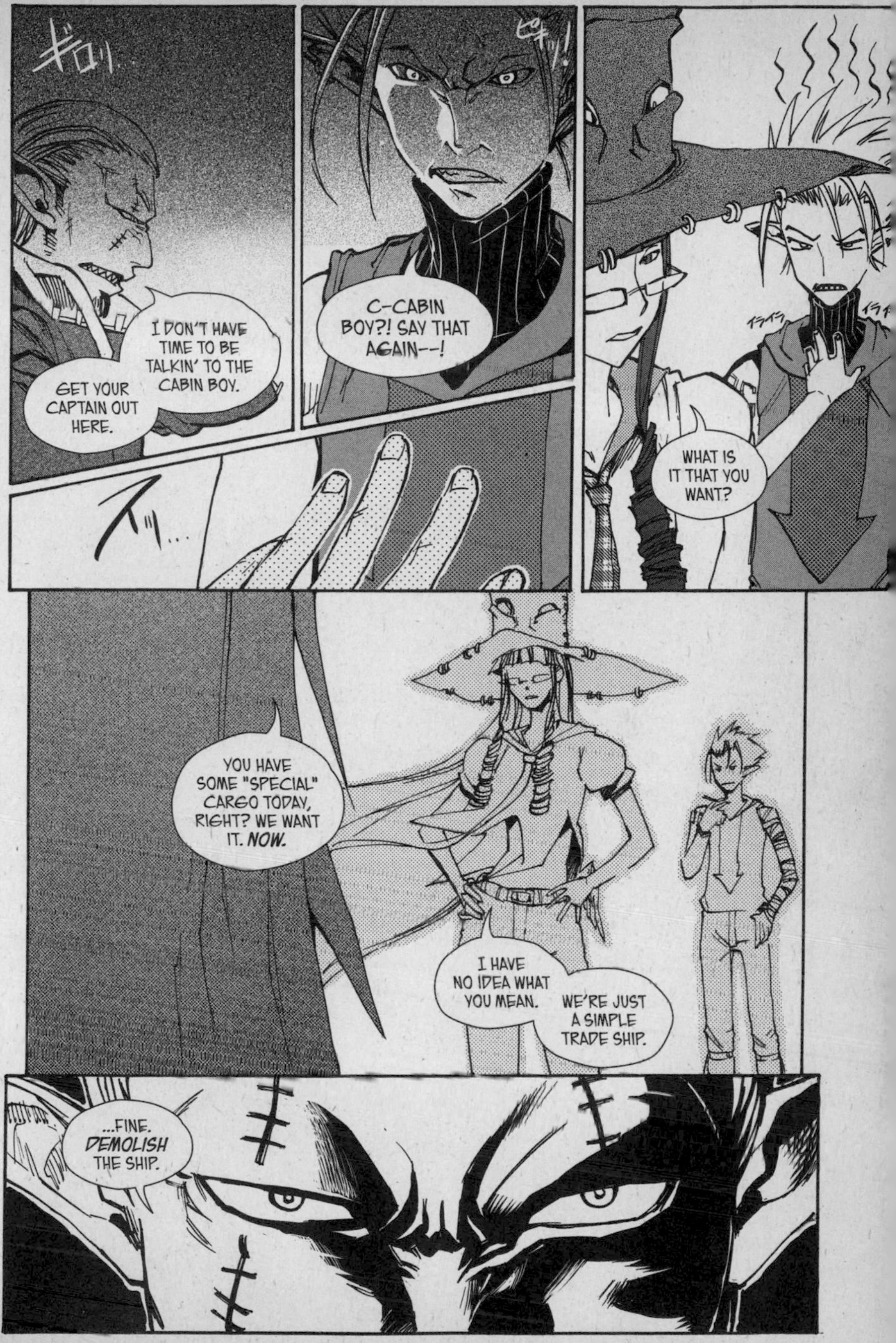
I DON'T HAVE TIME TO BE TALKIN' TO THE CABIN BOY.
GET YOUR CAPTAIN OUT HERE.
C-CABIN BOY?! SAY THAT AGAIN--!
スッ…
イライラ
WHAT IS IT THAT YOU WANT?
YOU HAVE SOME "SPECIAL" CARGO TODAY, RIGHT? WE WANT IT. *NOW.*
I HAVE NO IDEA WHAT YOU MEAN.
WE'RE JUST A SIMPLE TRADE SHIP.
...FINE. *DEMOLISH* THE SHIP.

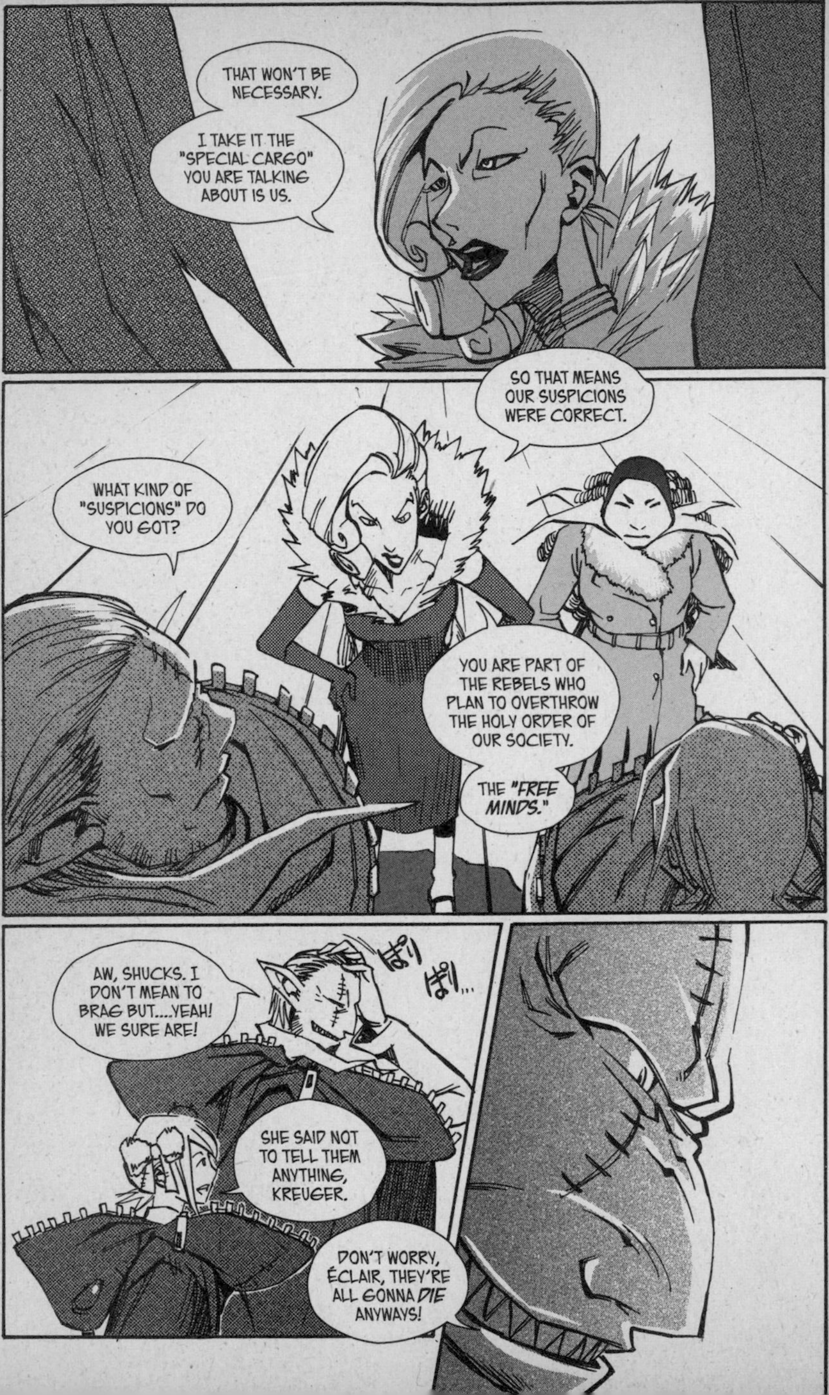
THAT WON'T BE NECESSARY.
I TAKE IT THE "SPECIAL CARGO" YOU ARE TALKING ABOUT IS US.
SO THAT MEANS OUR SUSPICIONS WERE CORRECT.
WHAT KIND OF "SUSPICIONS" DO YOU GOT?
YOU ARE PART OF THE REBELS WHO PLAN TO OVERTHROW THE HOLY ORDER OF OUR SOCIETY.
THE "*FREE MINDS.*"
AW, SHUCKS. I DON'T MEAN TO BRAG BUT....YEAH! WE SURE ARE!
ぽり ぽり...
SHE SAID NOT TO TELL THEM ANYTHING, KREUGER.
DON'T WORRY, ÉCLAIR, THEY'RE ALL GONNA *DIE* ANYWAYS!

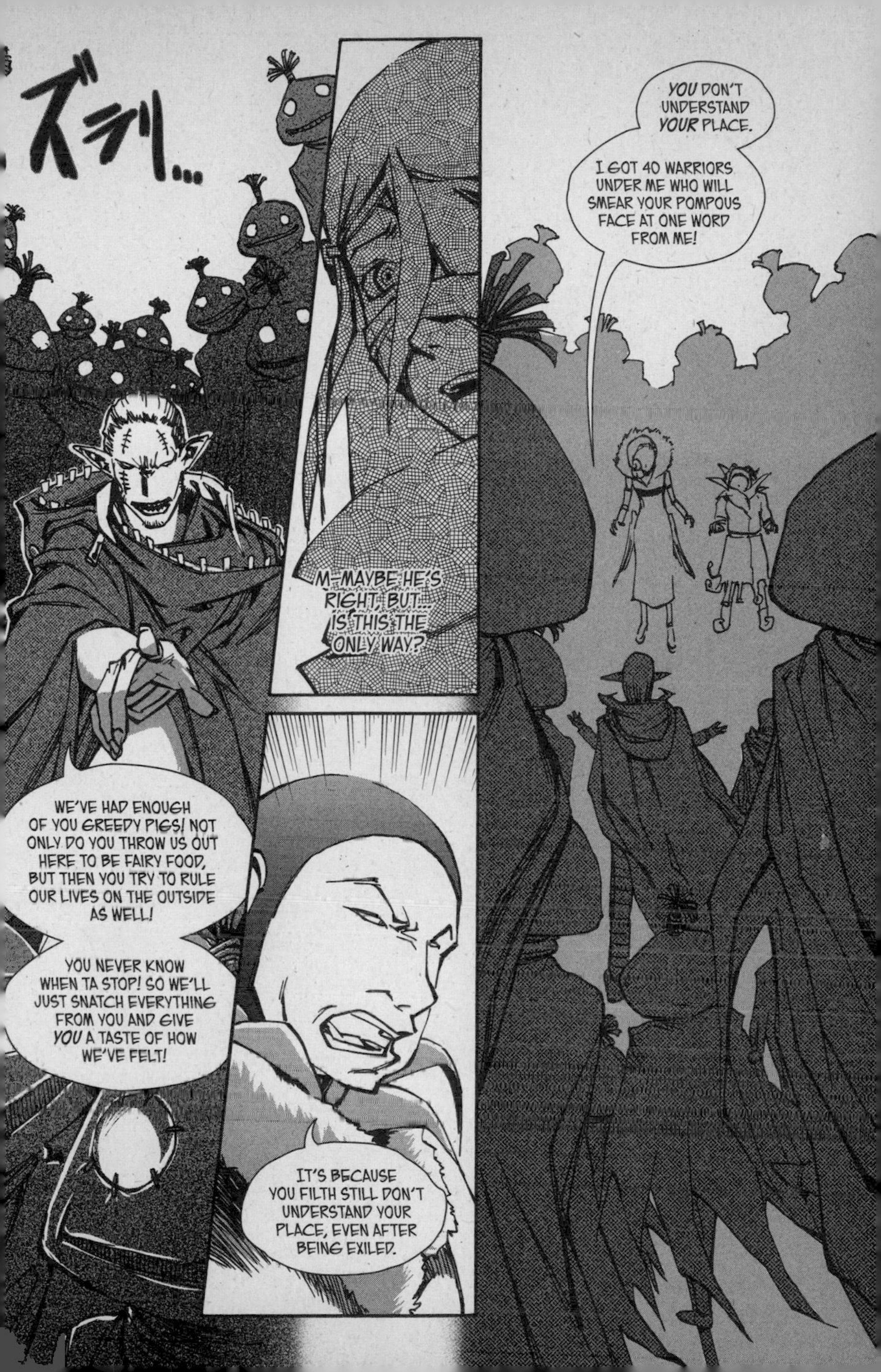
ズラリ...
WE'VE HAD ENOUGH OF YOU GREEDY PIGS! NOT ONLY DO YOU THROW US OUT HERE TO BE FAIRY FOOD, BUT THEN YOU TRY TO RULE OUR LIVES ON THE OUTSIDE AS WELL!
YOU NEVER KNOW WHEN TA STOP! SO WE'LL JUST SNATCH EVERYTHING FROM YOU AND GIVE *YOU* A TASTE OF HOW WE'VE FELT!
M-MAYBE HE'S RIGHT, BUT... IS THIS THE ONLY WAY?
IT'S BECAUSE YOU FILTH STILL DON'T UNDERSTAND YOUR PLACE, EVEN AFTER BEING EXILED.
YOU DON'T UNDERSTAND *YOUR* PLACE.
I GOT 40 WARRIORS UNDER ME WHO WILL SMEAR YOUR POMPOUS FACE AT ONE WORD FROM ME!

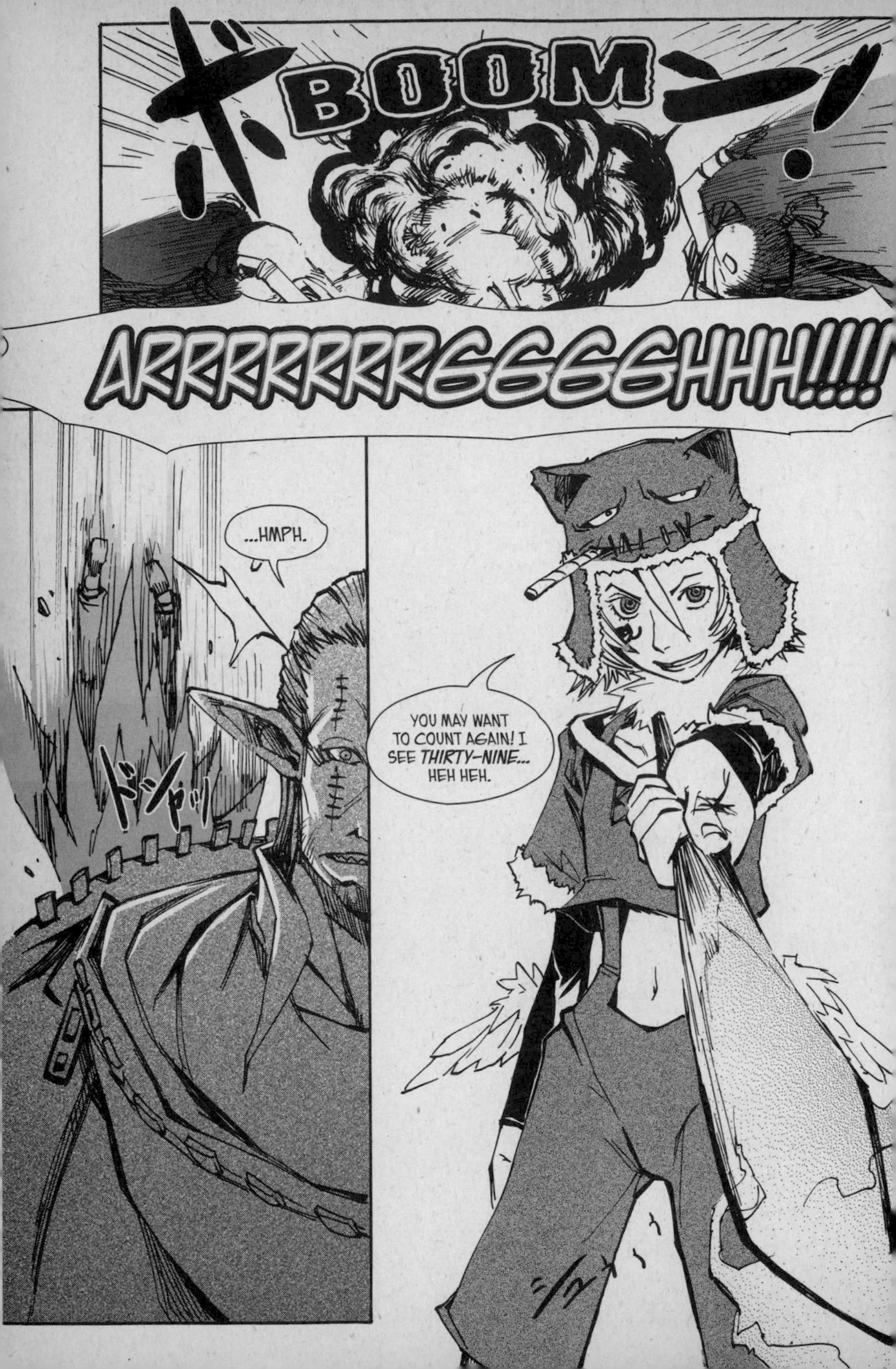
BOOM
ARRRRRRRRGGGGHHH!!!!
YOU MAY WANT TO COUNT AGAIN! I SEE *THIRTY-NINE*... HEH HEH.
...HMPH.

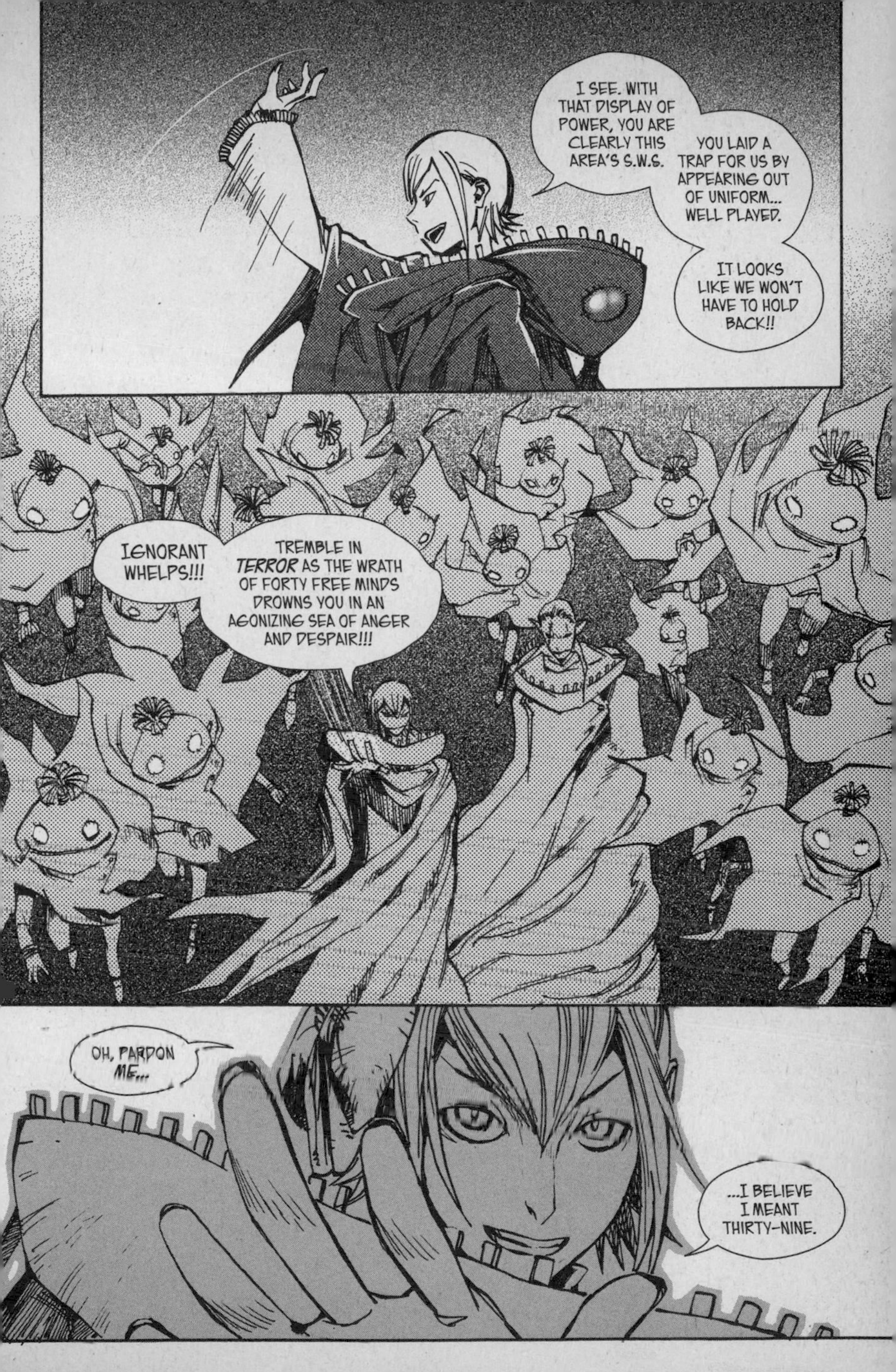
I SEE. WITH THAT DISPLAY OF POWER, YOU ARE CLEARLY THIS AREA'S S.W.S.
YOU LAID A TRAP FOR US BY APPEARING OUT OF UNIFORM... WELL PLAYED.
IT LOOKS LIKE WE WON'T HAVE TO HOLD BACK!!
IGNORANT WHELPS!!!
TREMBLE IN *TERROR* AS THE WRATH OF FORTY FREE MINDS DROWNS YOU IN AN AGONIZING SEA OF ANGER AND DESPAIR!!!
OH, PARDON *ME...*
...I BELIEVE I MEANT THIRTY-NINE.

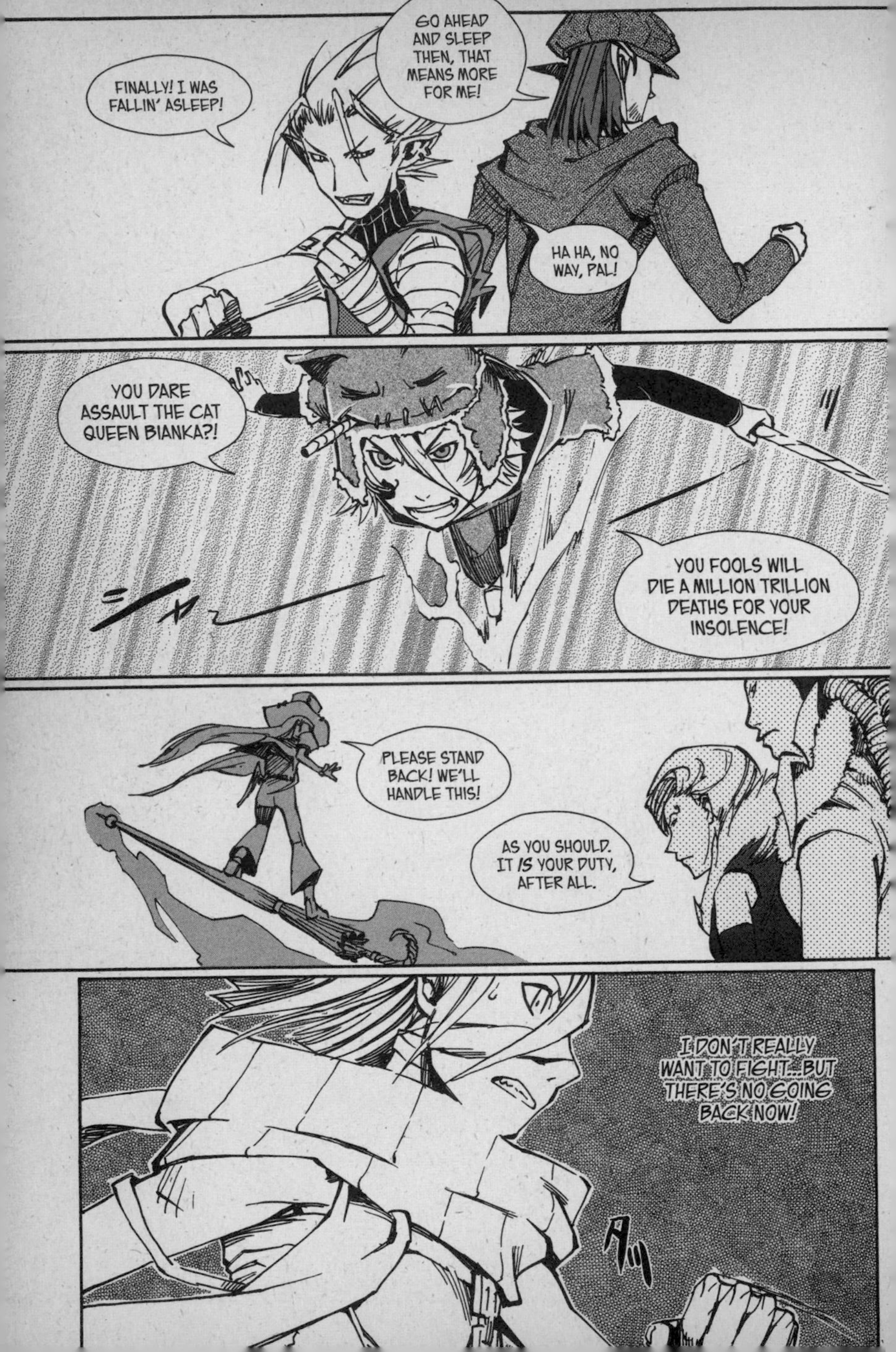
FINALLY! I WAS FALLIN' ASLEEP!
GO AHEAD AND SLEEP THEN, THAT MEANS MORE FOR ME!
HA HA, NO WAY, PAL!
YOU DARE ASSAULT THE CAT QUEEN BIANKA?!
YOU FOOLS WILL DIE A MILLION TRILLION DEATHS FOR YOUR INSOLENCE!
PLEASE STAND BACK! WE'LL HANDLE THIS!
AS YOU SHOULD. IT IS YOUR DUTY, AFTER ALL.
I DON'T REALLY WANT TO FIGHT...BUT THERE'S NO GOING BACK NOW!

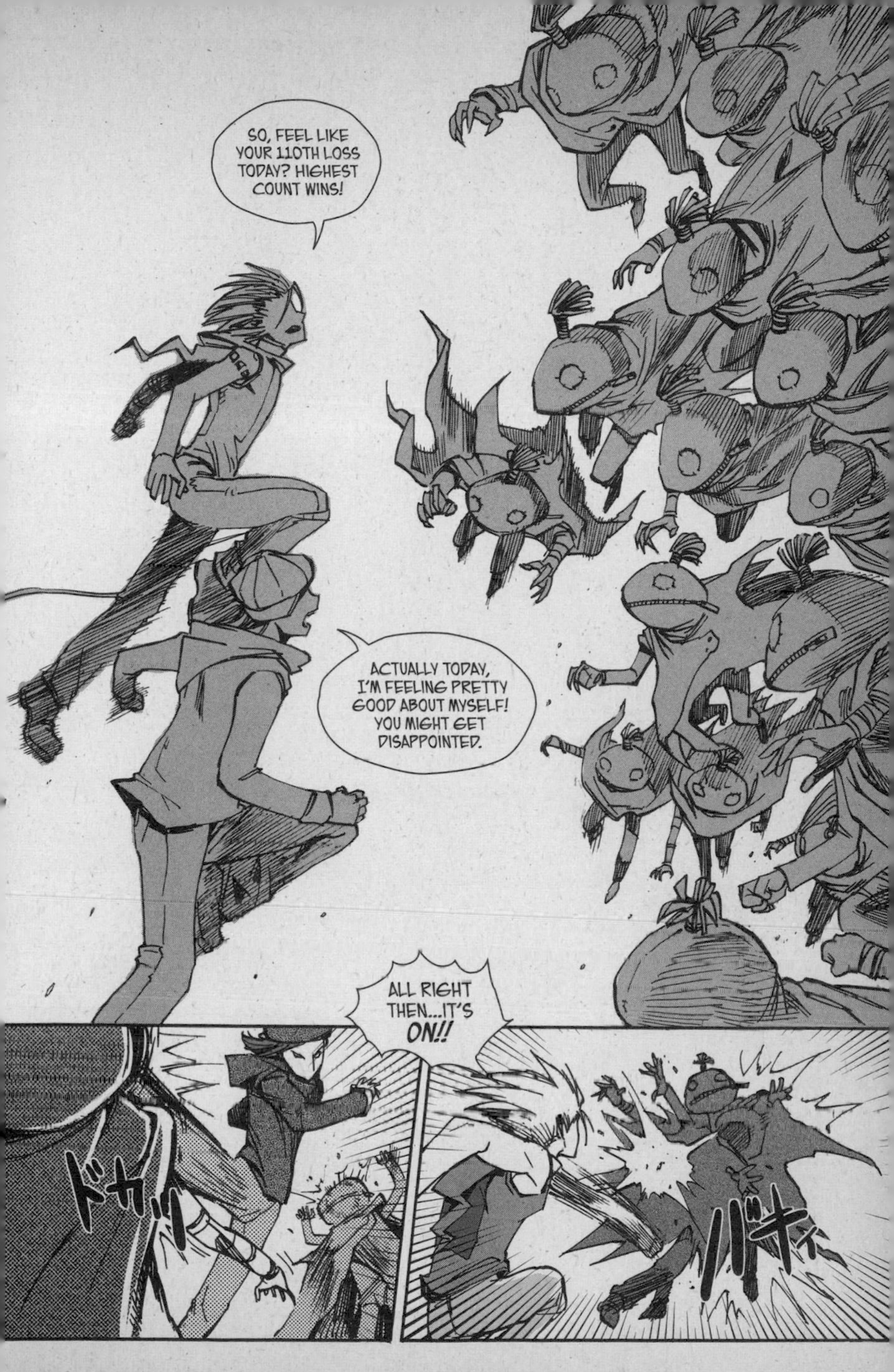
SO, FEEL LIKE YOUR 110TH LOSS TODAY? HIGHEST COUNT WINS!
ACTUALLY TODAY, I'M FEELING PRETTY GOOD ABOUT MYSELF! YOU MIGHT GET DISAPPOINTED.
ALL RIGHT THEN...IT'S ON!!
バキィ
ドカッ

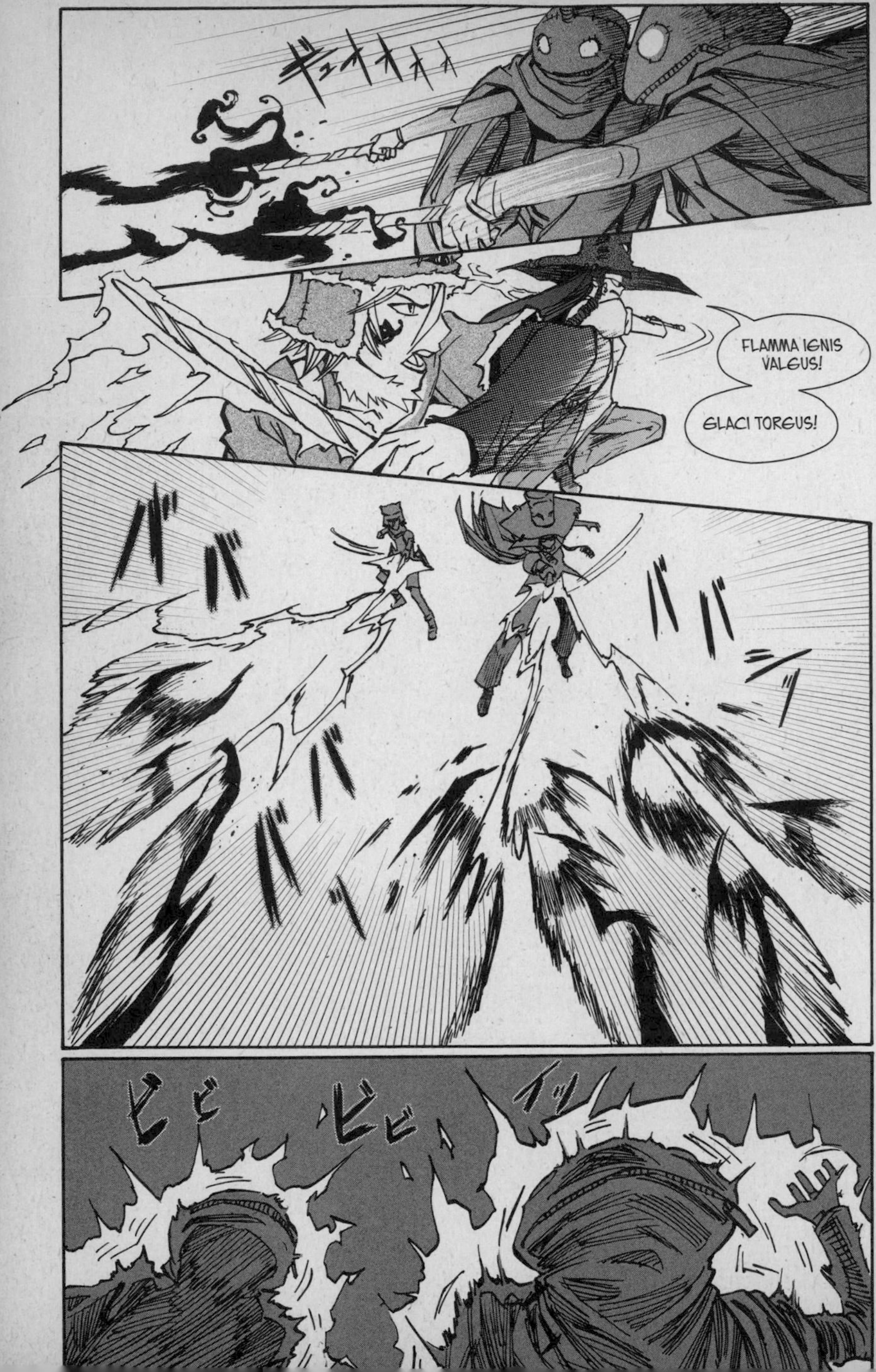
FLAMMA IGNIS VALGUS!
GLACI TORGUS!

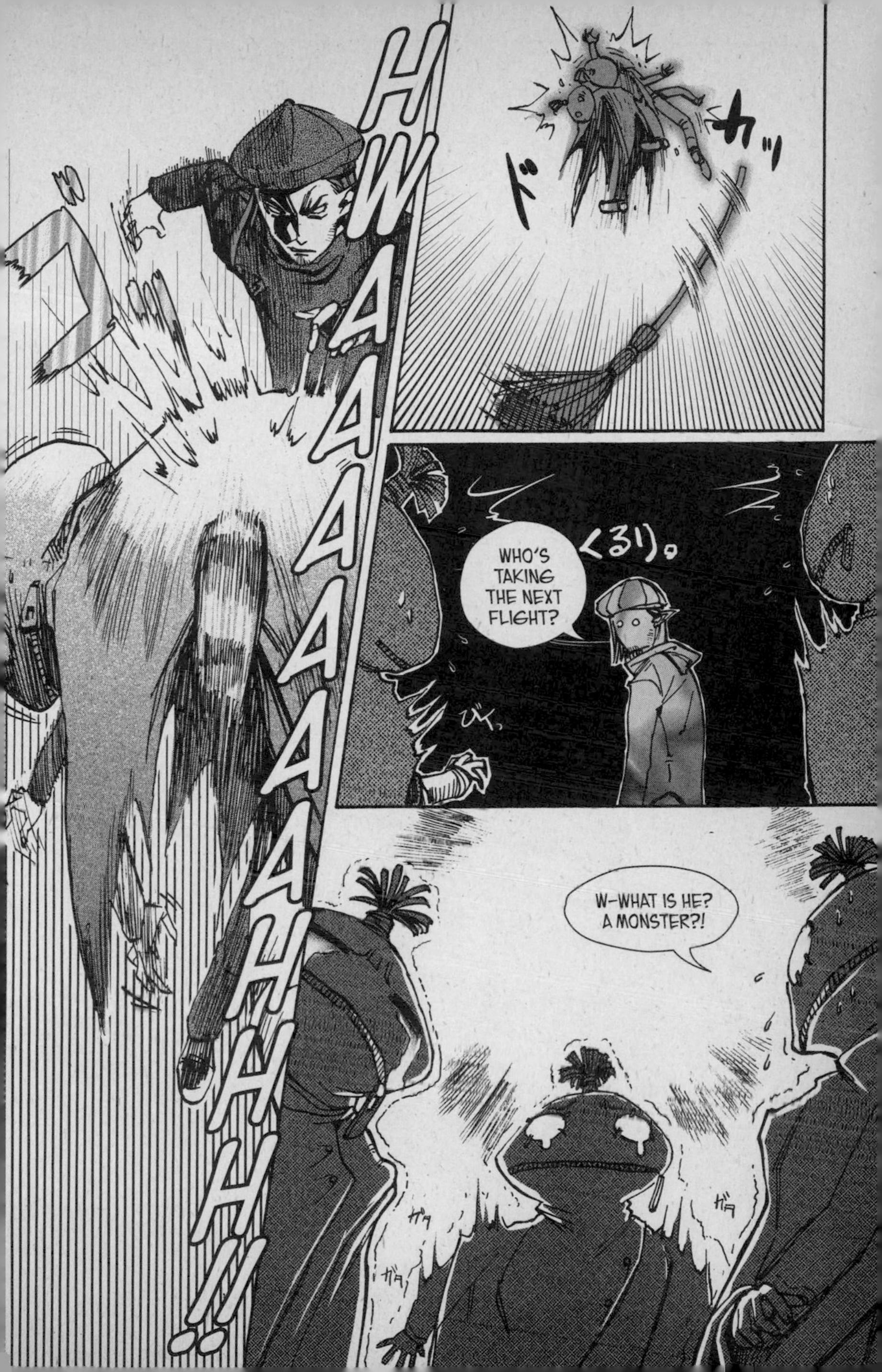
ドカッ
くるり。
WHO'S TAKING THE NEXT FLIGHT?
HWAAAAAAAAAHHHHH!!
W-WHAT IS HE? A MONSTER?!

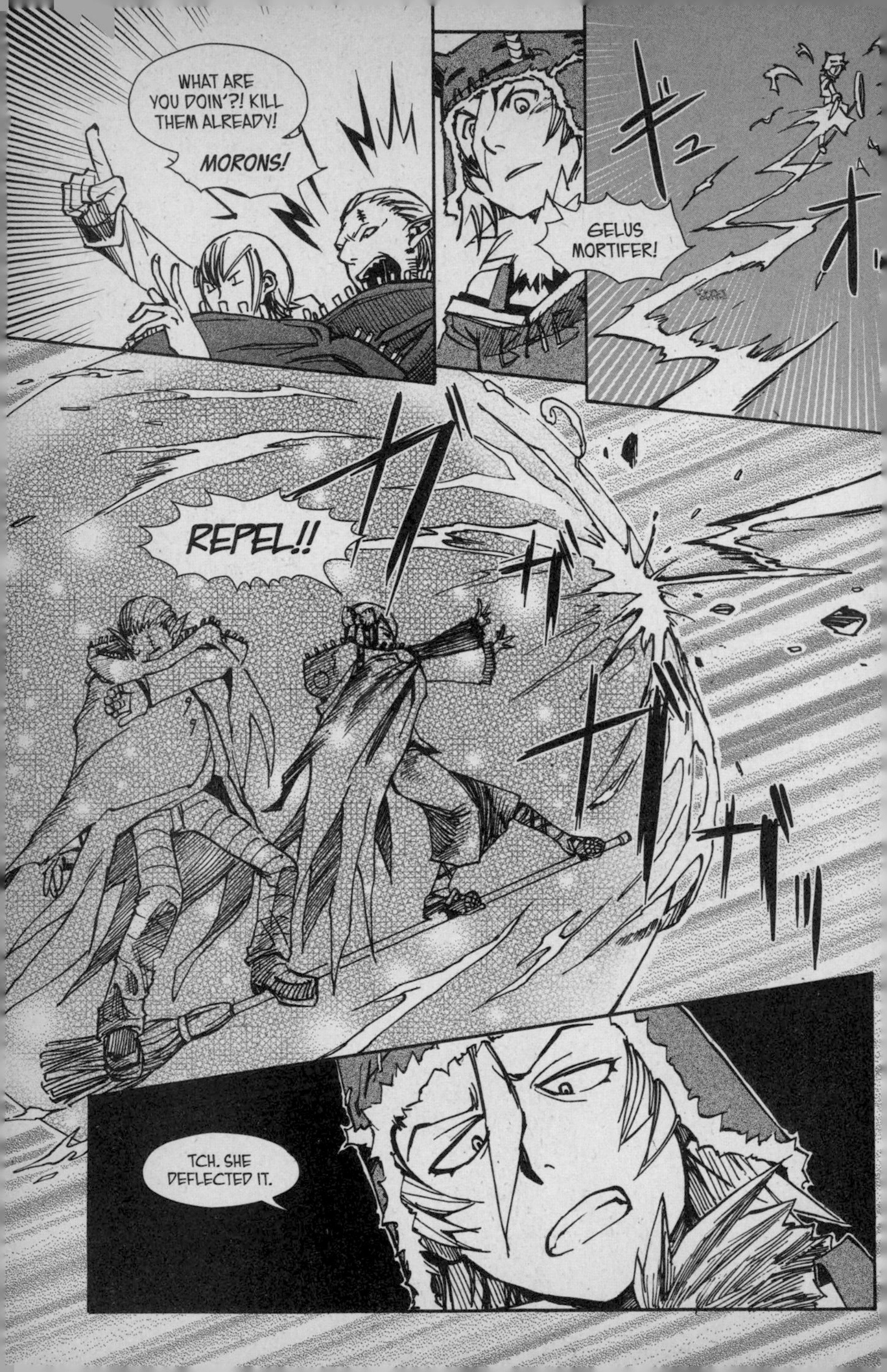
WHAT ARE YOU DOIN'?! KILL THEM ALREADY!
MORONS!
GELUS MORTIFER!
REPEL!!
TCH. SHE DEFLECTED IT.

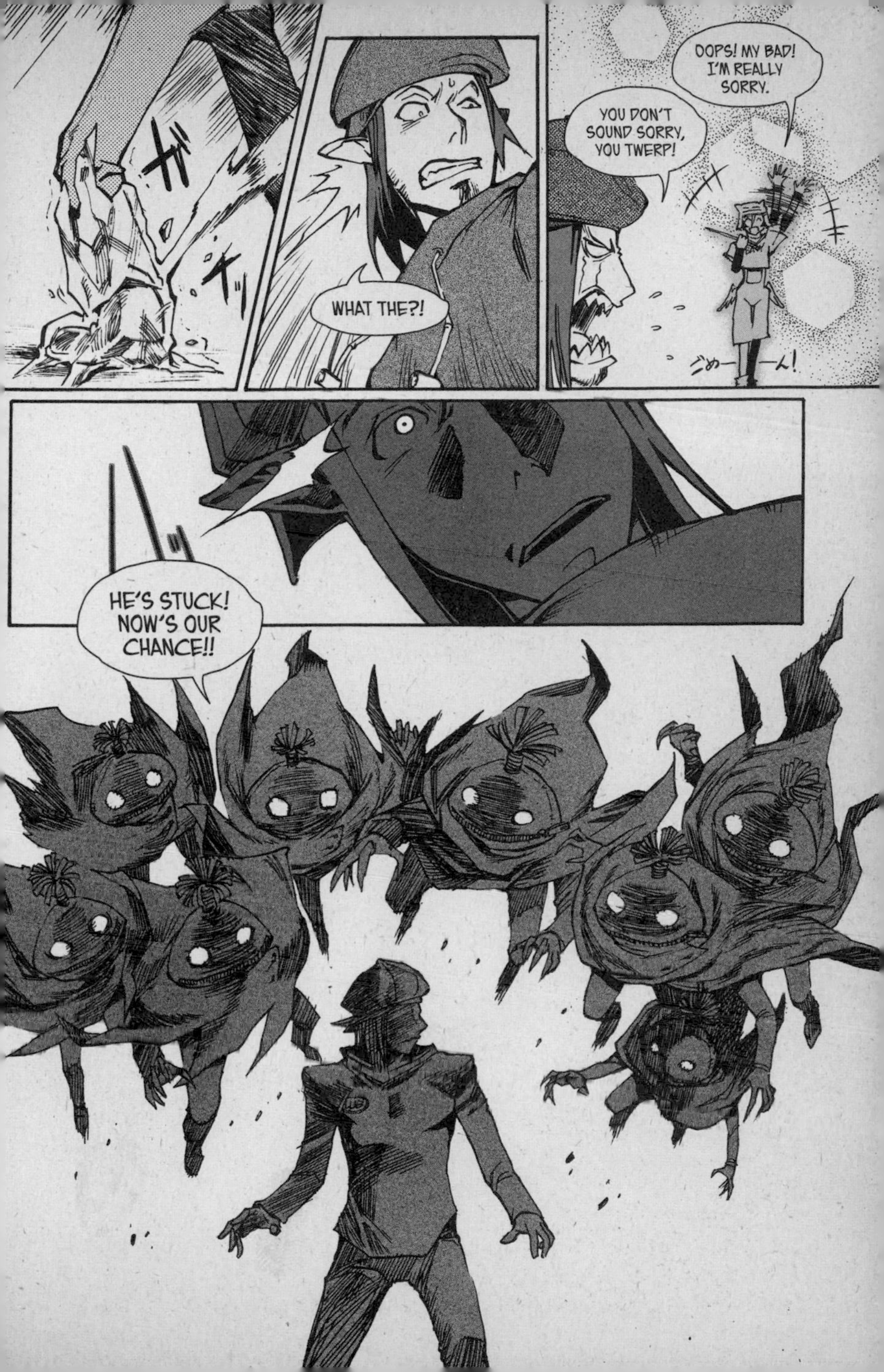
WHAT THE?!
OOPS! MY BAD! I'M REALLY SORRY.
YOU DON'T SOUND SORRY, YOU TWERP!
ごめーーん!
HE'S STUCK! NOW'S OUR CHANCE!!

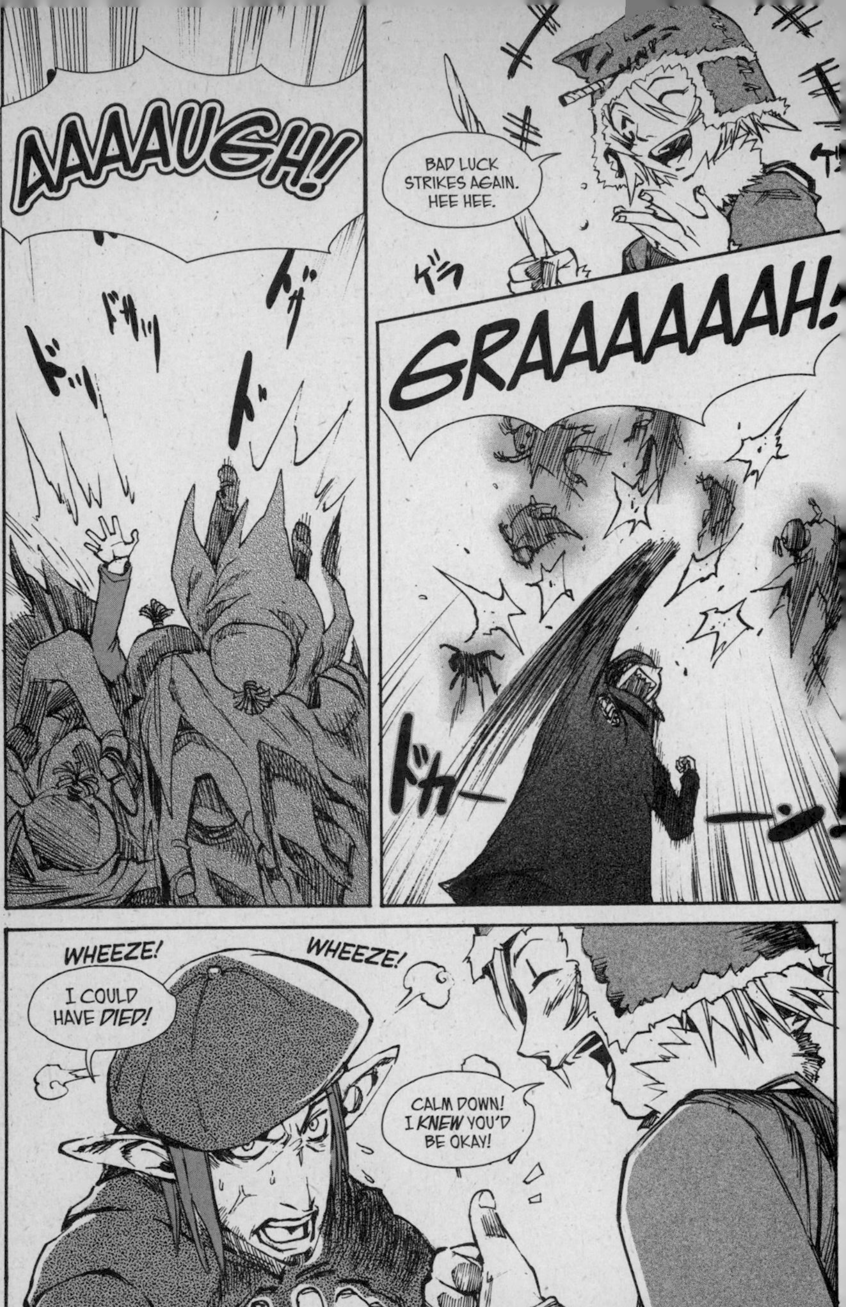
BAD LUCK STRIKES AGAIN. HEE HEE.
GRAAAAAAH!
AAAAUGH!
WHEEZE!
WHEEZE!
I COULD HAVE DIED!
CALM DOWN! I KNEW YOU'D BE OKAY!

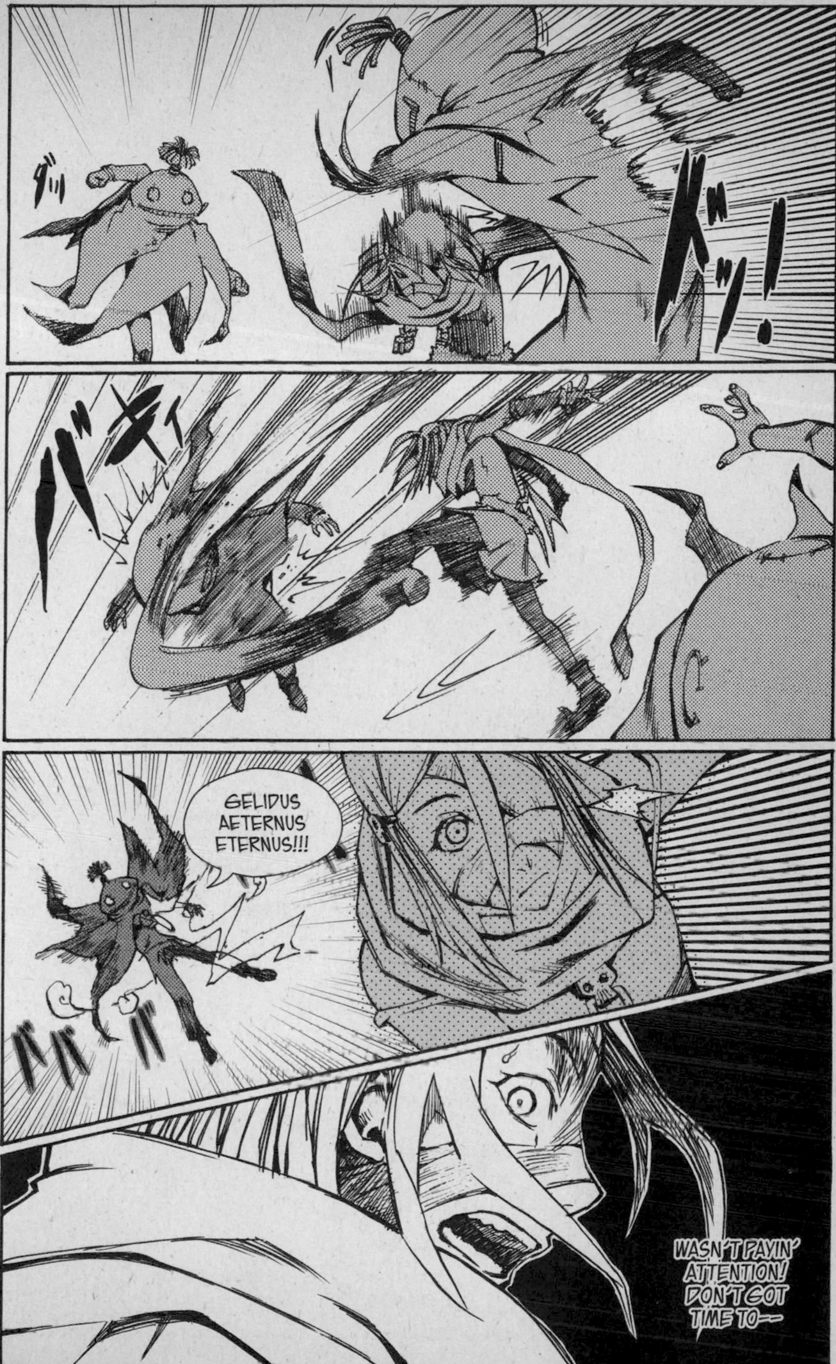
GELIDUS AETERNUS ETERNUS!!!
WASN'T PAYIN' ATTENTION! DON'T GOT TIME TO—

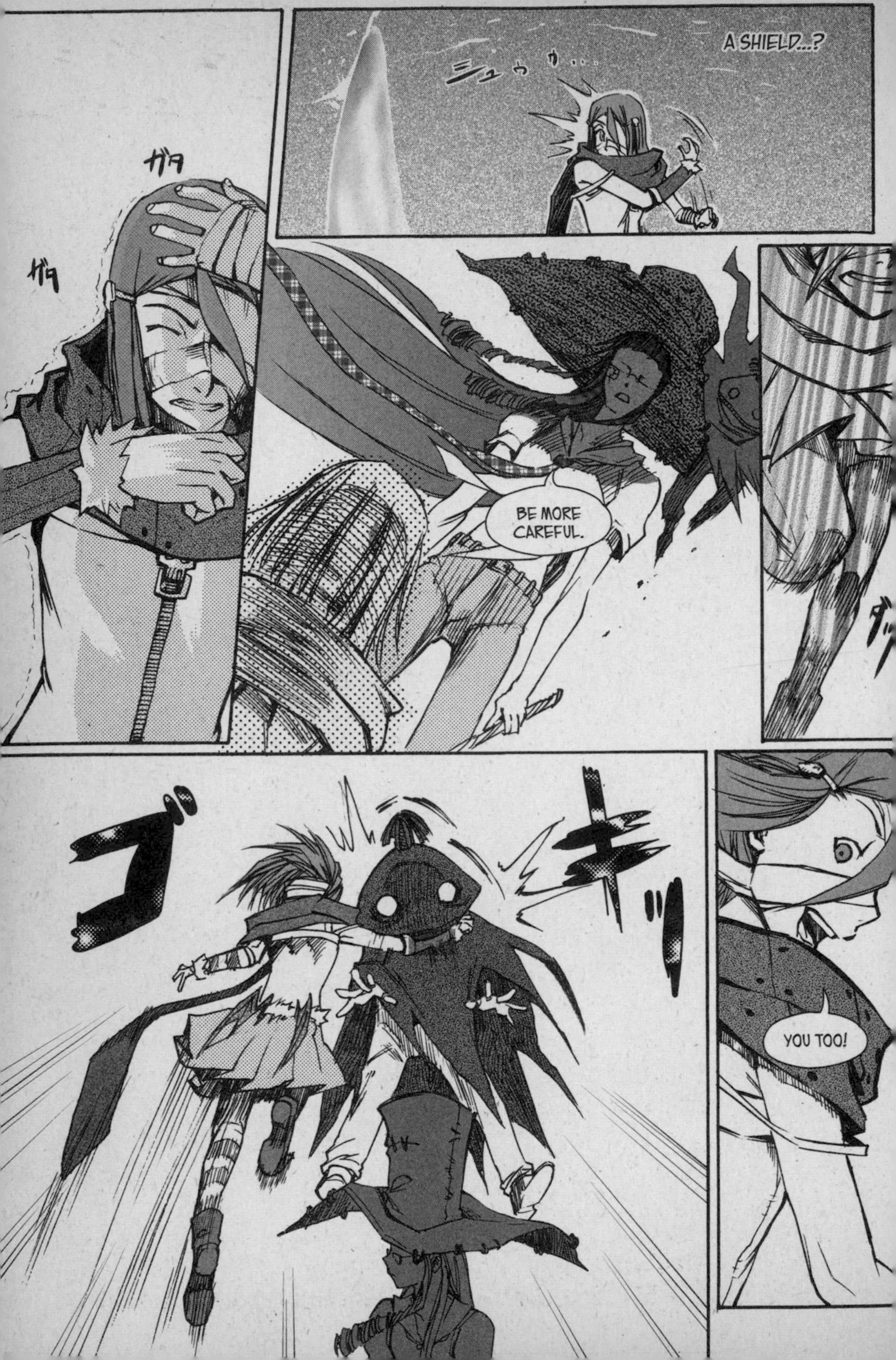
A SHIELD...?
ガタ
ガタ
BE MORE CAREFUL.
YOU TOO!

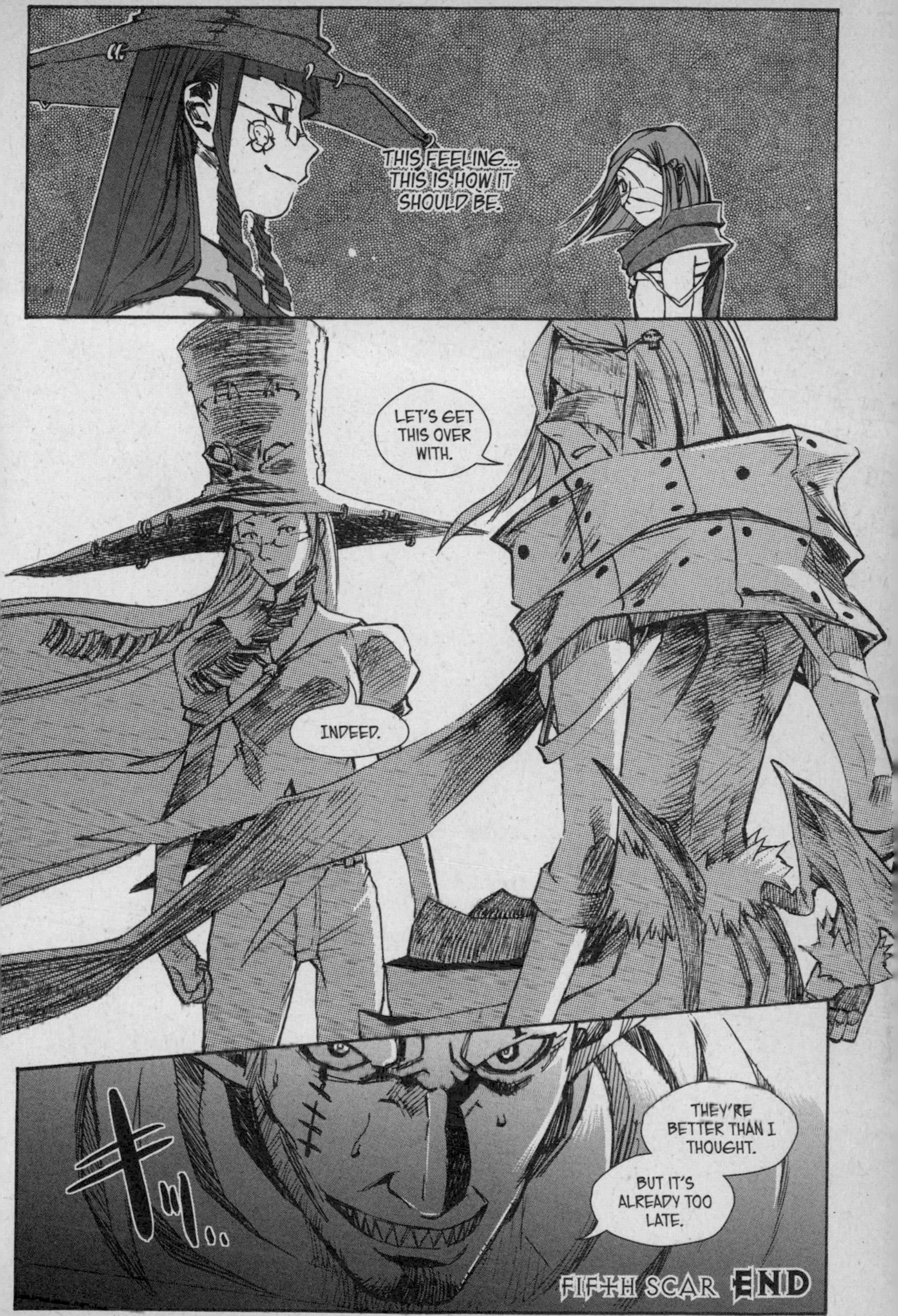
THIS FEELING... THIS IS HOW IT SHOULD BE.
LET'S GET THIS OVER WITH.
INDEED.
THEY'RE BETTER THAN I THOUGHT.
BUT IT'S ALREADY TOO LATE.
FIFTH SCAR END

QUEEN BIANKA'S CRASH COURSE

CHAPTER FIVE: DISTRICTS

A DISTRICT IS A CITY. TOGETHER THERE ARE 8 DISTRICTS AROUND THE WORLD. THEY ARE SURROUNDED BY ELECTRICAL SHIELDS THAT PROTECT THEM FROM FAIRIES. I AIN'T NEVER SEEN THE SHIELDS GO DOWN BEFORE IN MY LIFE TIME. BUT I IMAGINE IF THEY DID GO DOWN, IT'D BE A BLOODY NIGHTMARE AND WE'D BE OVERRUN BY A HORDE OF STARVING FAIRIES.

TA BE HONEST, MOST WITCHES NEVER SEE ANY DISTRICT OUTSIDE OF THE ONE THAT THEY WERE BORN IN. WHY? WELL...TAKE THE ORANGE DISTRICT FER EXAMPLE. WE GOT EVERYTHING YA NEED RIGHT HERE!

DISTRICT LIST

1. RESTAURANTS
2. RESIDENTIAL AREAS
3. SPORTS STADIUMS
4. SHOPPING AREAS
5. LOADS MORE!

BECAUSE THE AVERAGE WITCH/ WARLOCK NEVER LEAVES, EACH DISTRICT IS LIKE ITS OWN UNIQUE WORLD, AND EACH ONE HAS SLIGHT CULTURAL AND RULE DIFFERENCES. I HEAR THAT THE EMERALD SKULL DISTRICT SACRIFICES CATS!

UNACCEPTABLE!

THAT PLACE'LL BE THE FIRST TA TASTE THE TERROR OF MY TEAPOT TANK!!

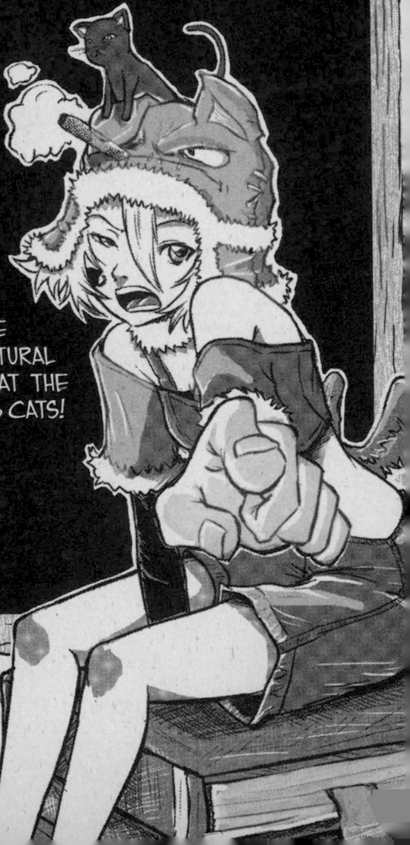
ALMOST DONE! I EXPECT A WRITTEN REPORT BEFORE CLASS ENDS... I AM *NOT* JOKIN'!

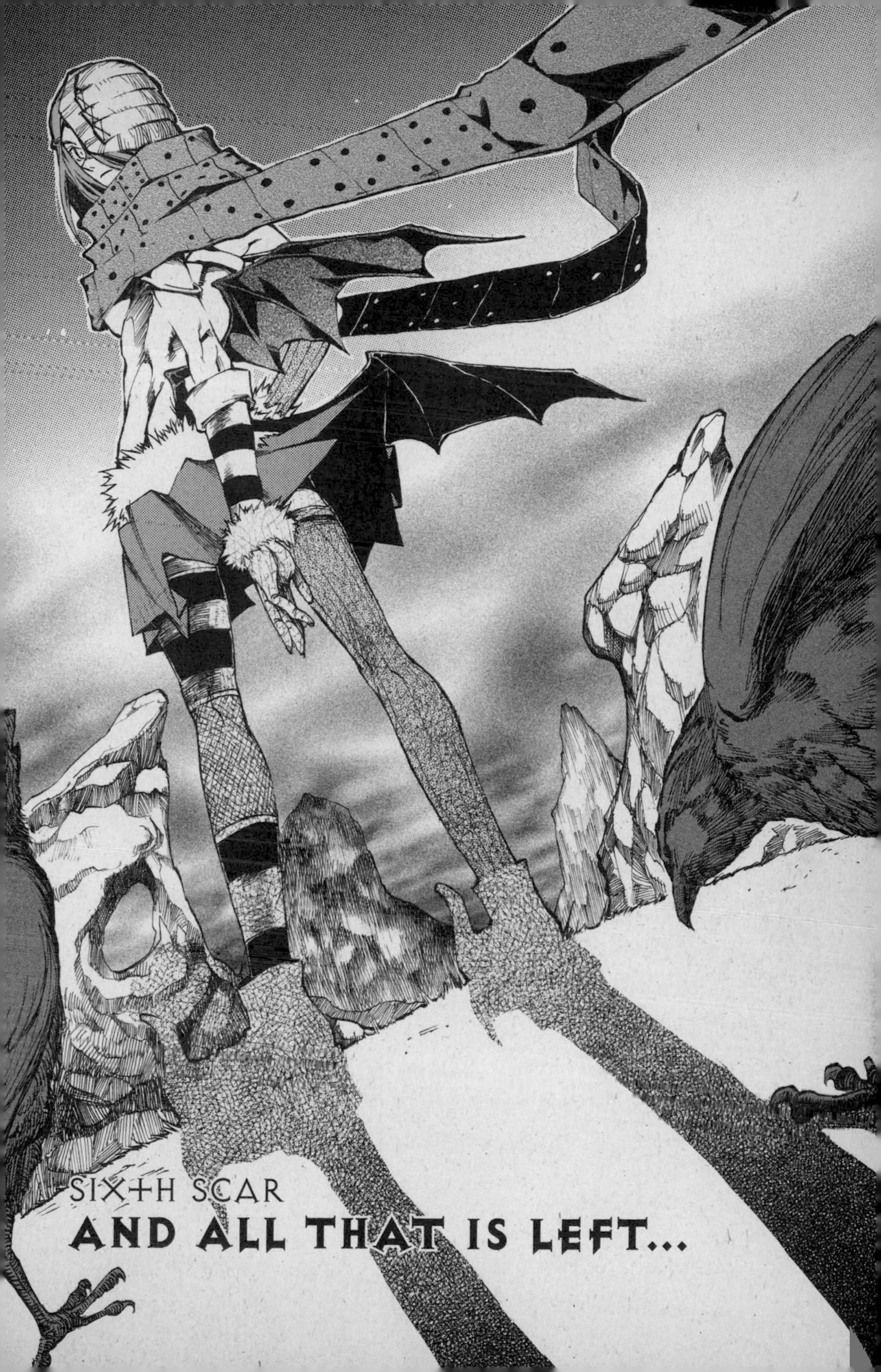
SIX+H SCAR
AND ALL THAT IS LEFT...

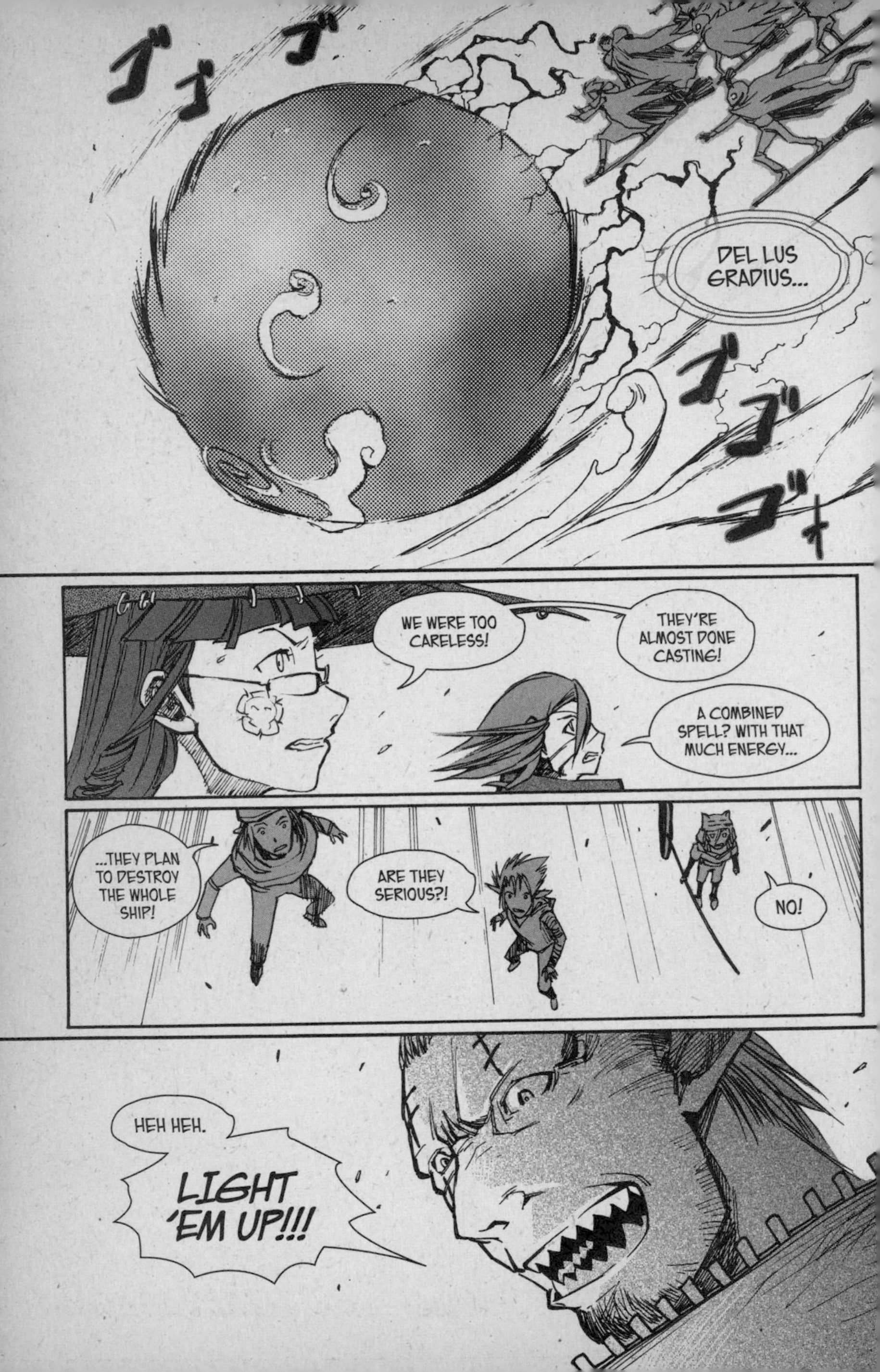
ゴゴ
DEL LUS GRADIUS...
ゴゴゴッ
THEY'RE ALMOST DONE CASTING!
WE WERE TOO CARELESS!
A COMBINED SPELL? WITH THAT MUCH ENERGY...
...THEY PLAN TO DESTROY THE WHOLE SHIP!
ARE THEY SERIOUS?!
NO!
HEH HEH.
LIGHT 'EM UP!!!

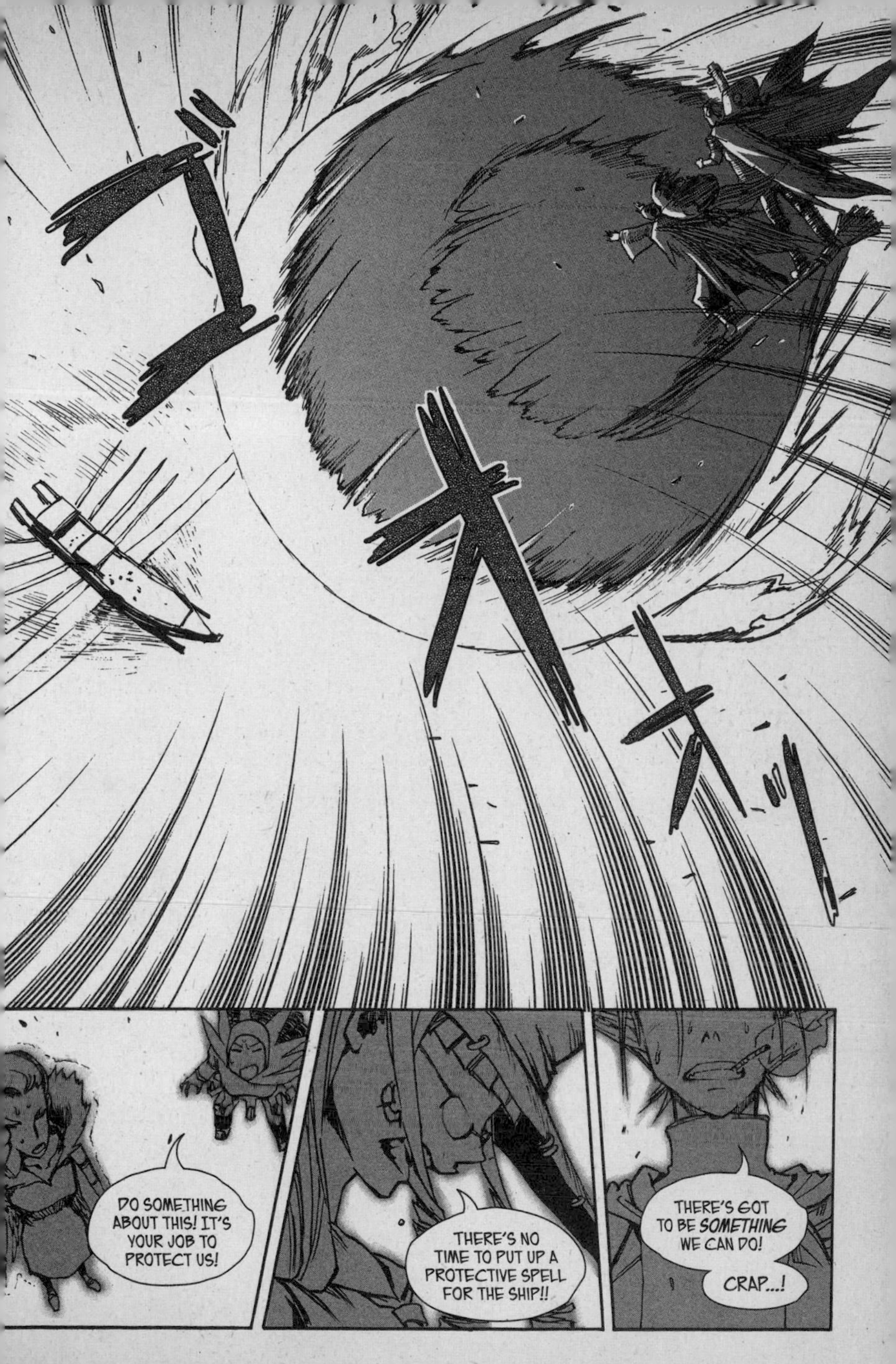
THERE'S GOT TO BE *SOMETHING* WE CAN DO!
CRAP...!
THERE'S NO TIME TO PUT UP A PROTECTIVE SPELL FOR THE SHIP!!
DO SOMETHING ABOUT THIS! IT'S YOUR JOB TO PROTECT US!

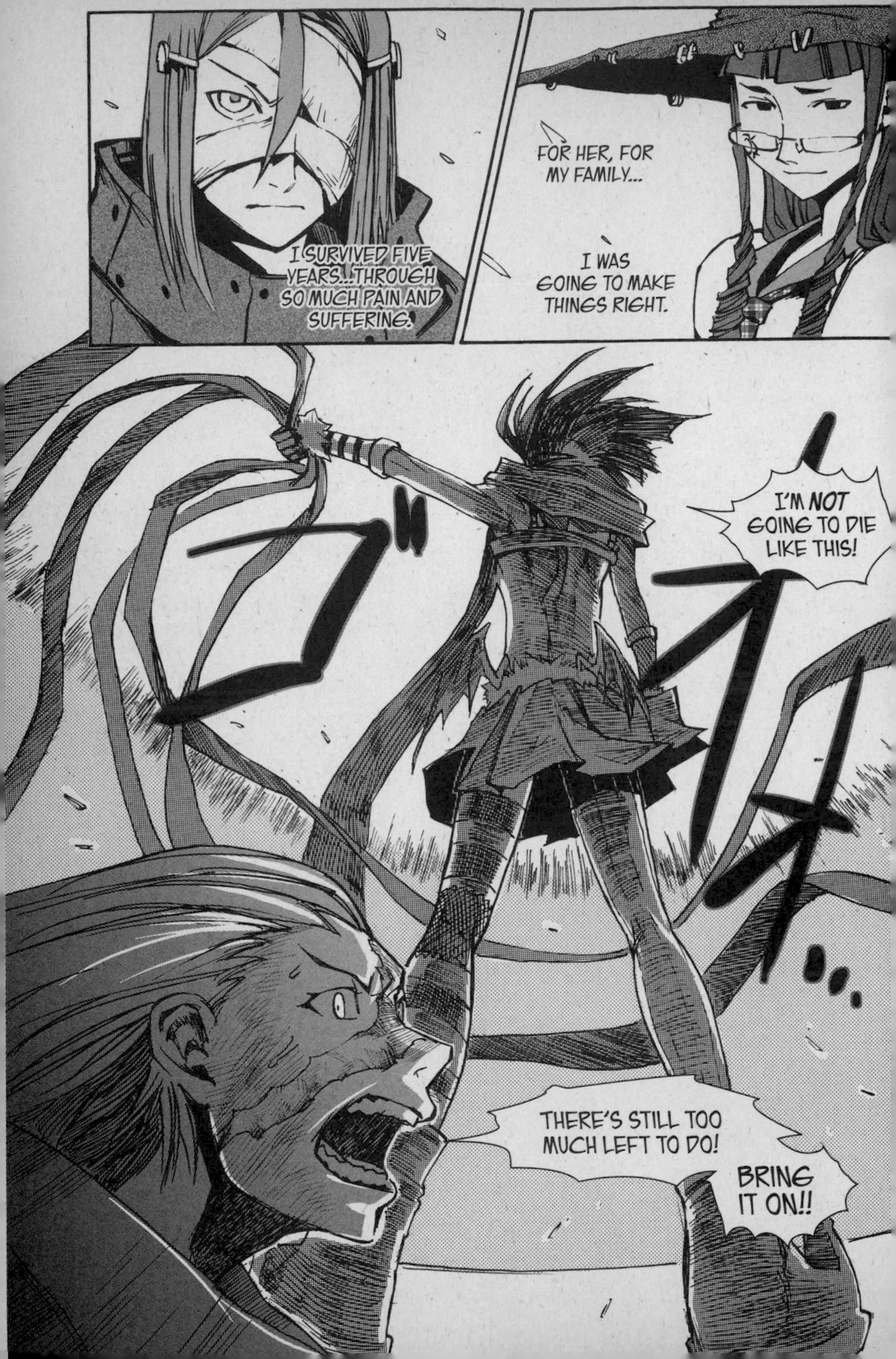
FOR HER, FOR MY FAMILY...
I WAS GOING TO MAKE THINGS RIGHT.
I SURVIVED FIVE YEARS...THROUGH SO MUCH PAIN AND SUFFERING.
I'M ***NOT*** GOING TO DIE LIKE THIS!
THERE'S STILL TOO MUCH LEFT TO DO!
BRING IT ON!!

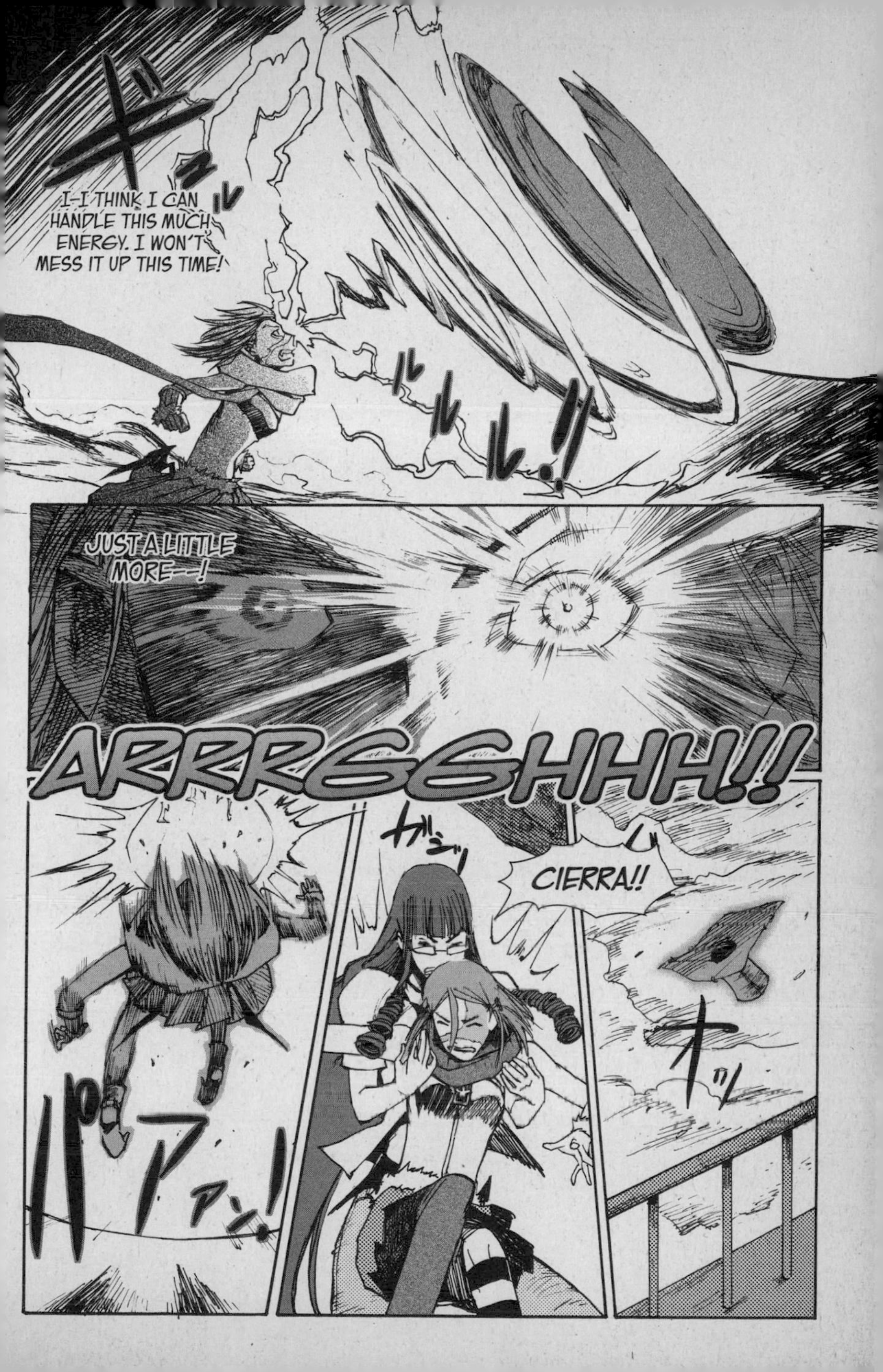
I-I THINK I CAN HANDLE THIS MUCH ENERGY. I WON'T MESS IT UP THIS TIME!
JUST A LITTLE MORE--!
ARRRGGHHH!!
CIERRA!!

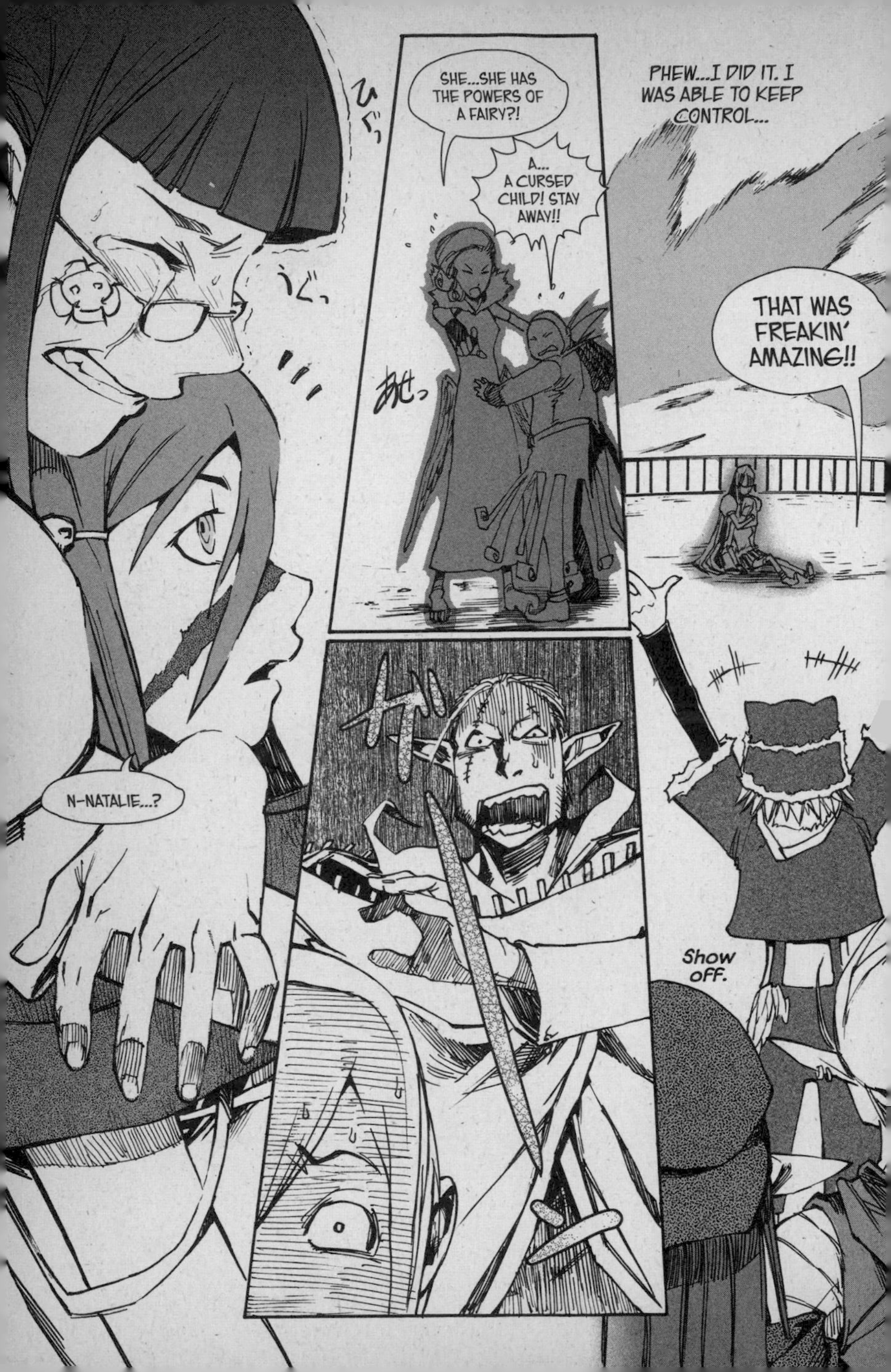
PHEW...I DID IT. I WAS ABLE TO KEEP CONTROL...
THAT WAS FREAKIN' AMAZING!!
Show off.
SHE...SHE HAS THE POWERS OF A FAIRY?!
A... A CURSED CHILD! STAY AWAY!!
N-NATALIE...?

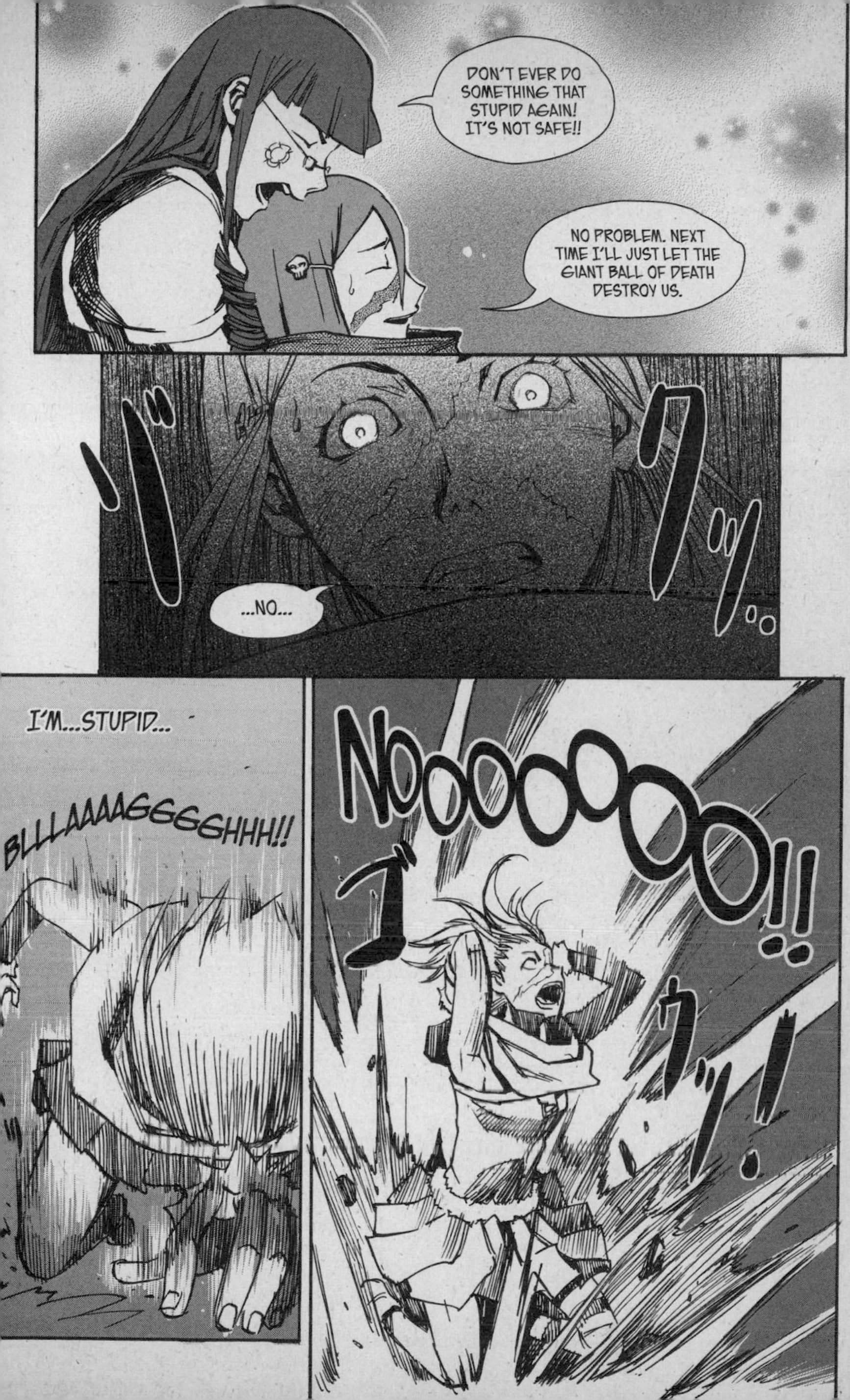
DON'T EVER DO SOMETHING THAT STUPID AGAIN! IT'S NOT SAFE!!
NO PROBLEM. NEXT TIME I'LL JUST LET THE GIANT BALL OF DEATH DESTROY US.
...NO...
NOOOOOOO!!
I'M...STUPID...
BLLLAAAAGGGGHHH!!

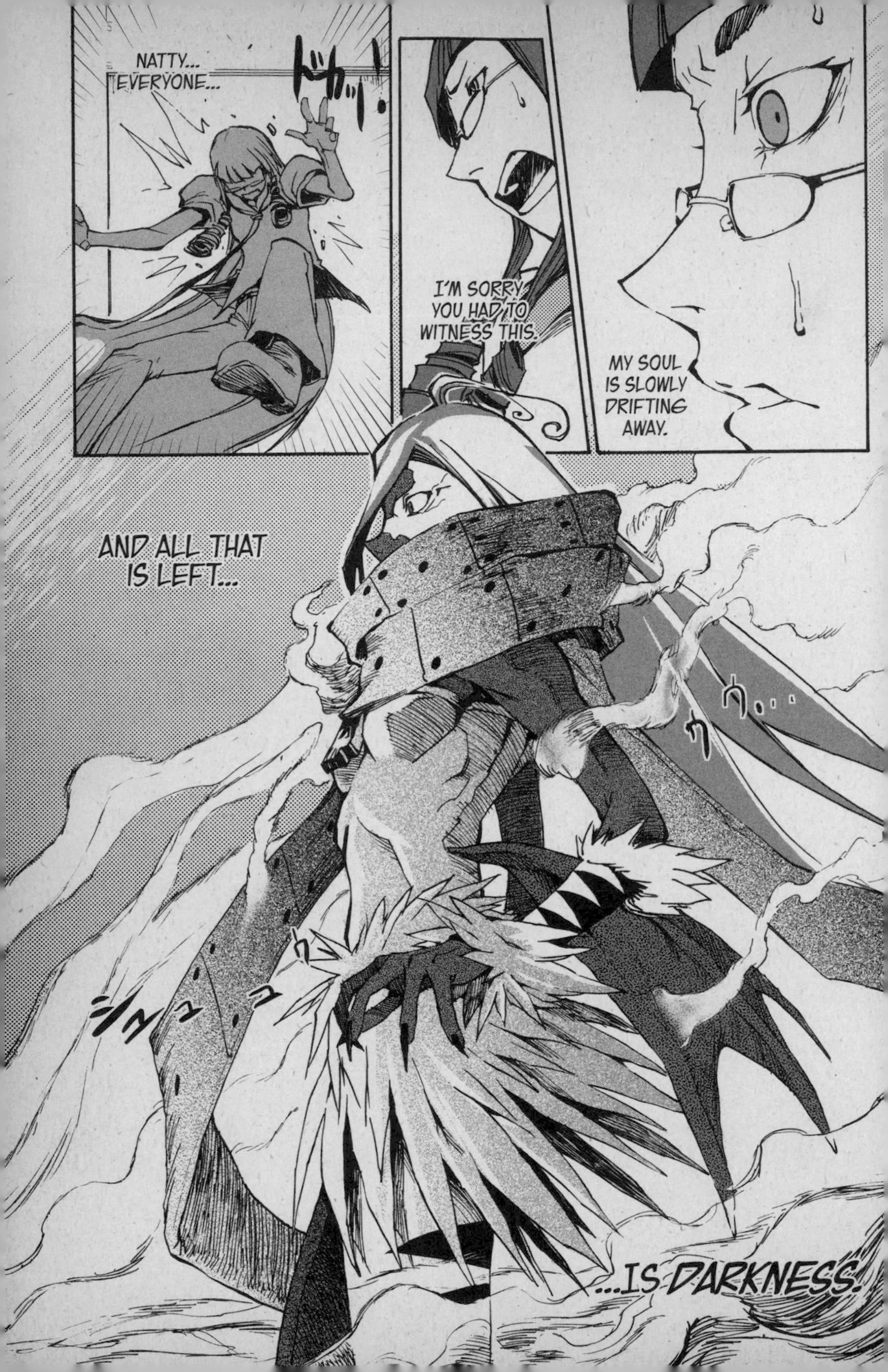
MY SOUL IS SLOWLY DRIFTING AWAY.
I'M SORRY YOU HAD TO WITNESS THIS.
ドカッ!
NATTY... EVERYONE...
AND ALL THAT IS LEFT...
...IS DARKNESS.

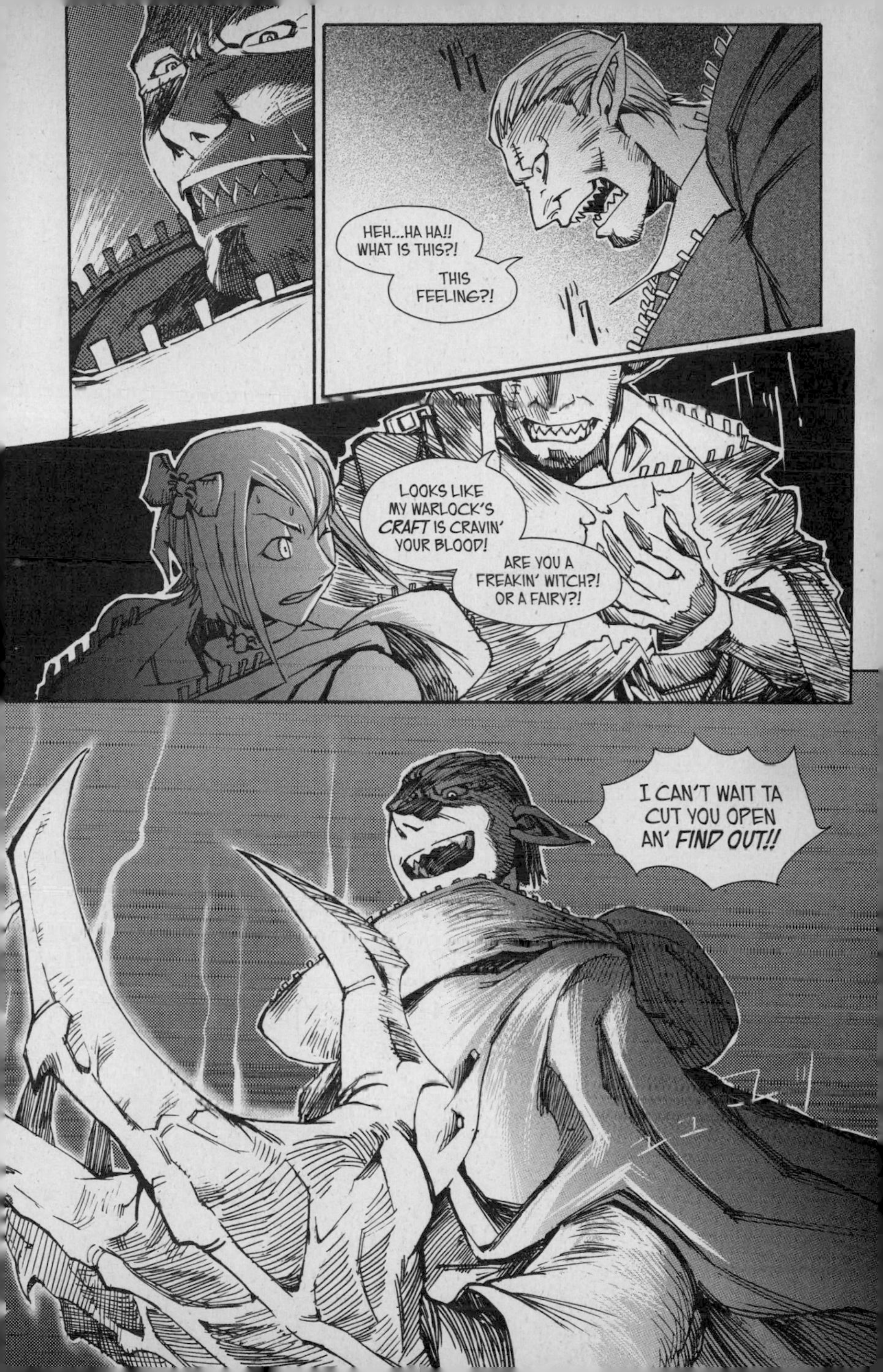
HEH...HA HA!! WHAT IS THIS?!
THIS FEELING?!
LOOKS LIKE MY WARLOCK'S *CRAFT* IS CRAVIN' YOUR BLOOD!
ARE YOU A FREAKIN' WITCH?! OR A FAIRY?!
I CAN'T WAIT TA CUT YOU OPEN AN' ***FIND OUT!!***

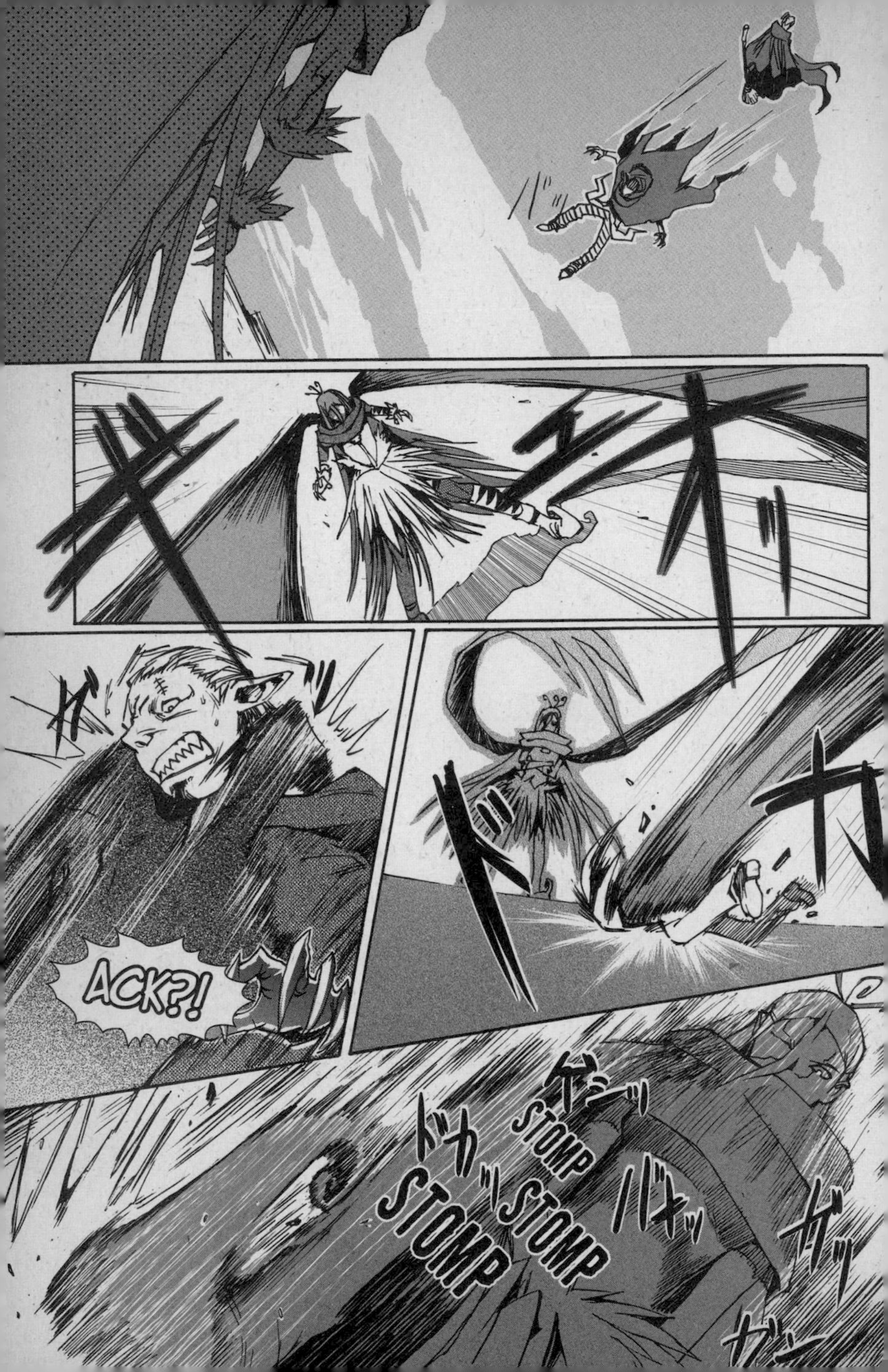
ACK?!
STOMP
STOMP
STOMP

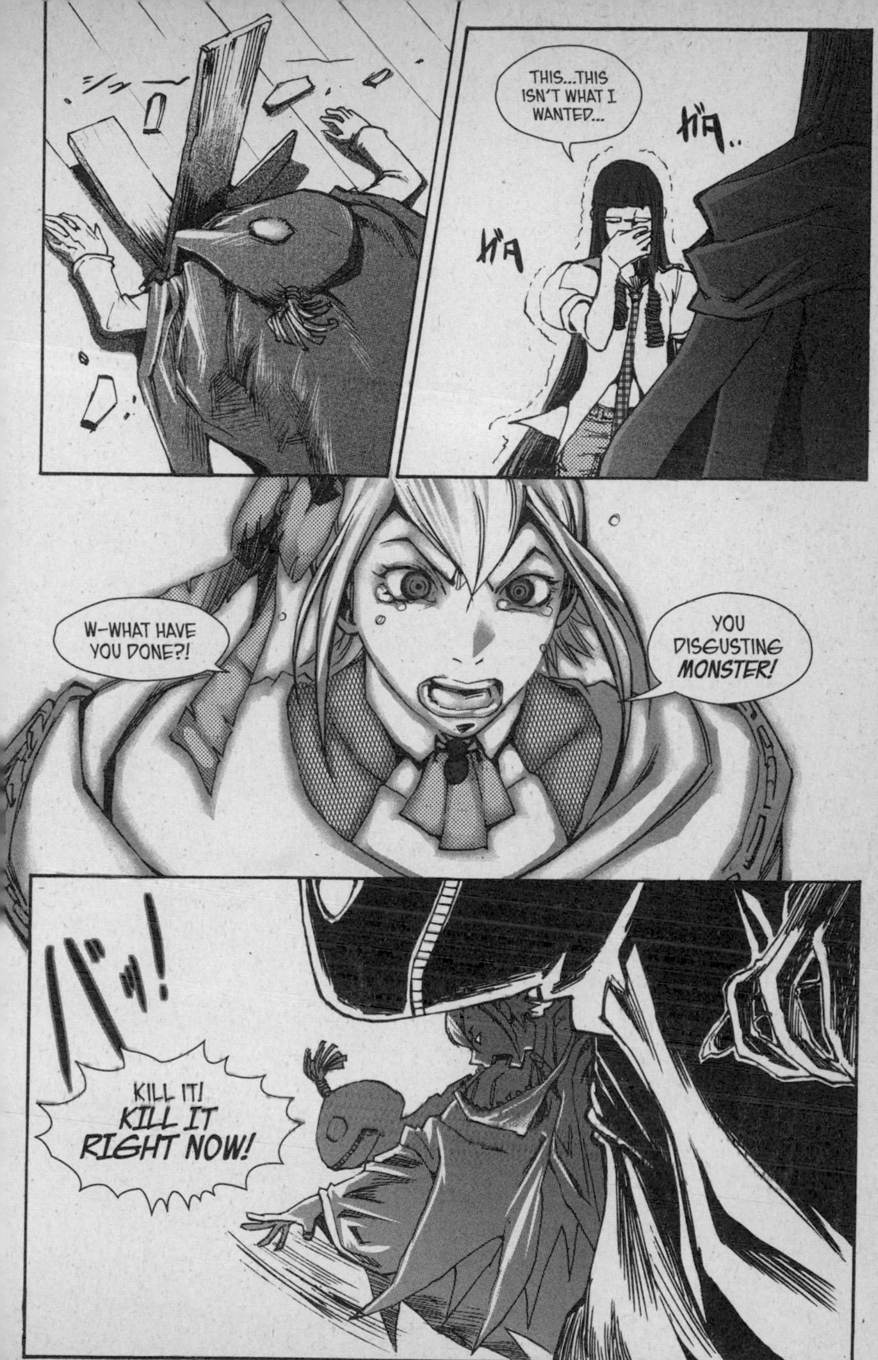
THIS...THIS ISN'T WHAT I WANTED...
ガタ..
ガタ
W-WHAT HAVE YOU DONE?!
YOU DISGUSTING MONSTER!
バッ!
KILL IT! KILL IT RIGHT NOW!

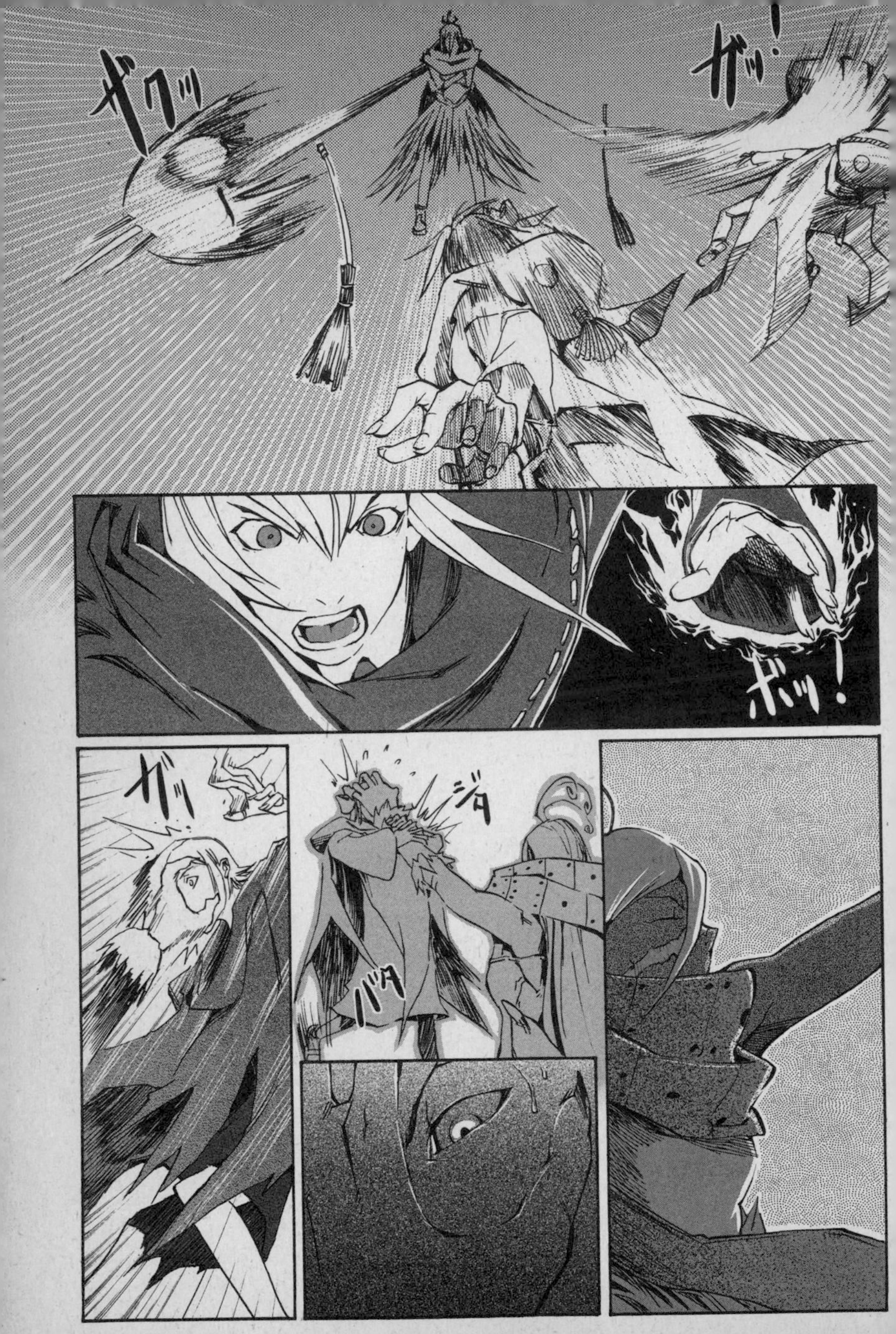
ガッ!
ギクッ
ボッ!
ジタ
バタ
ガッ

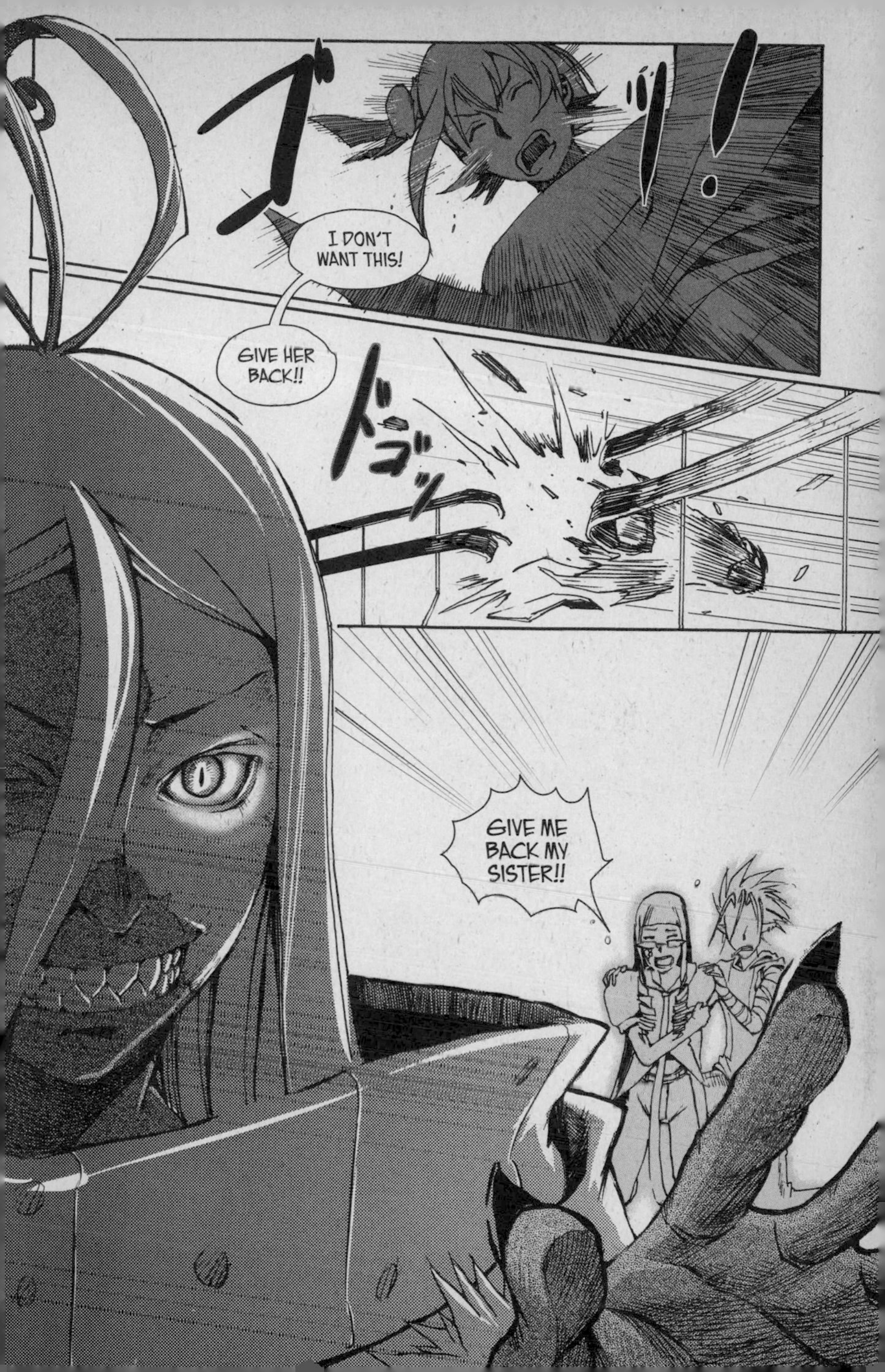
I DON'T WANT THIS!
GIVE HER BACK!!
GIVE ME BACK MY SISTER!!

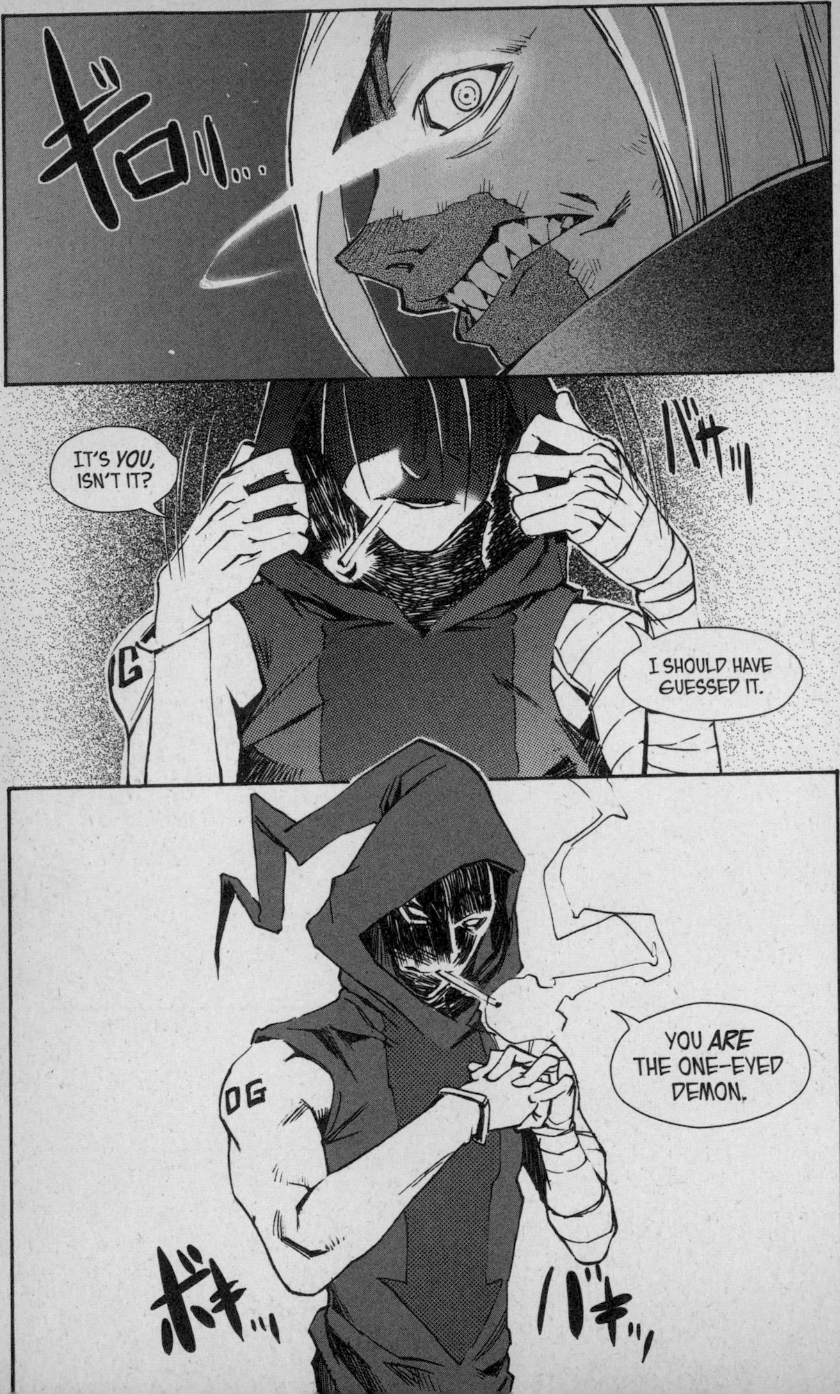

ギロッ…
バサッ
IT'S *YOU*, ISN'T IT?
I SHOULD HAVE GUESSED IT.
YOU *ARE* THE ONE-EYED DEMON.
バキッ
ボキッ

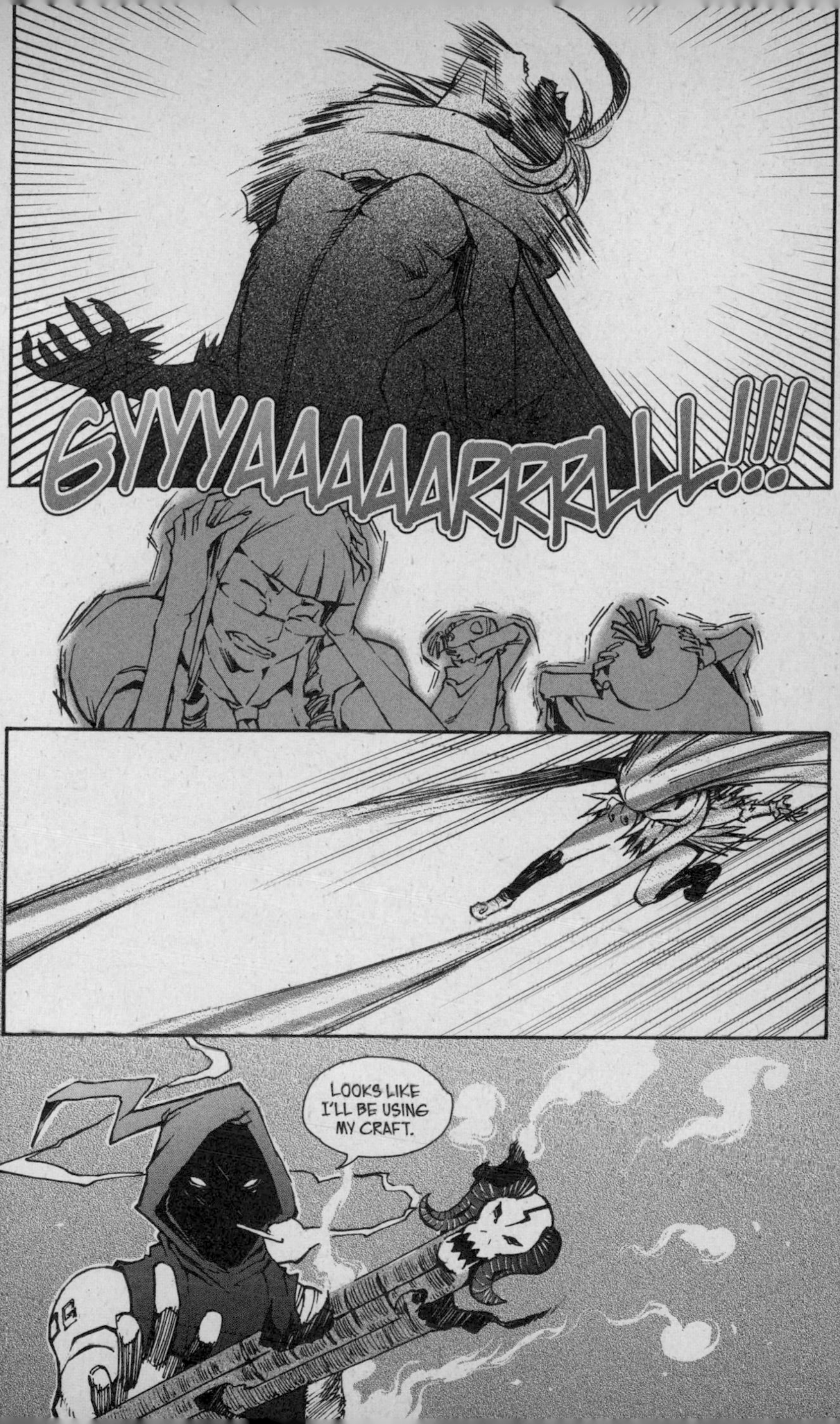
GYYYAAAAAARRRLLL!!!
LOOKS LIKE I'LL BE USING MY CRAFT.

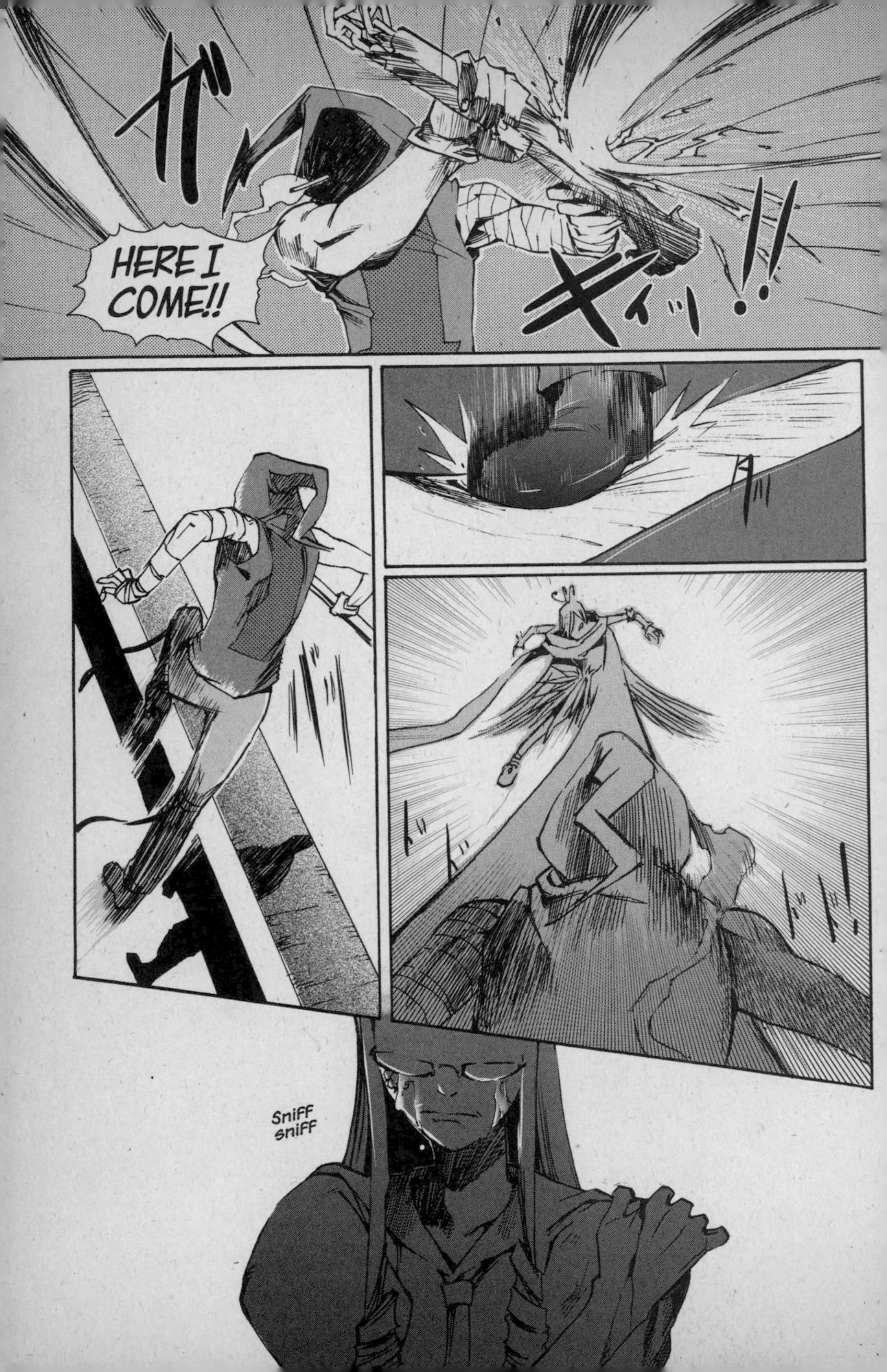
HERE I COME!!
Sniff sniff

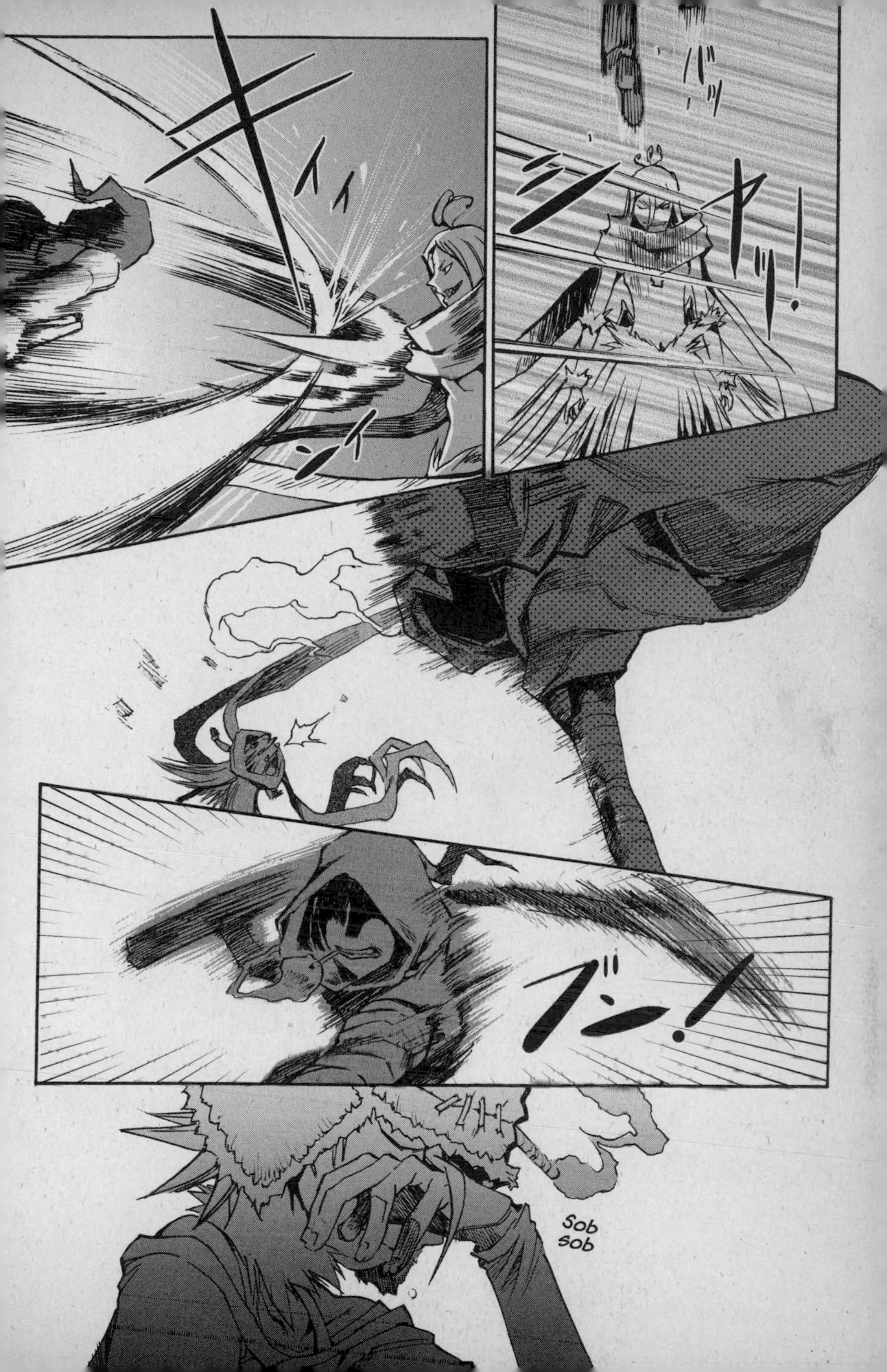
バッ
シャッ!
キィィン
ブン!
Sob
sob

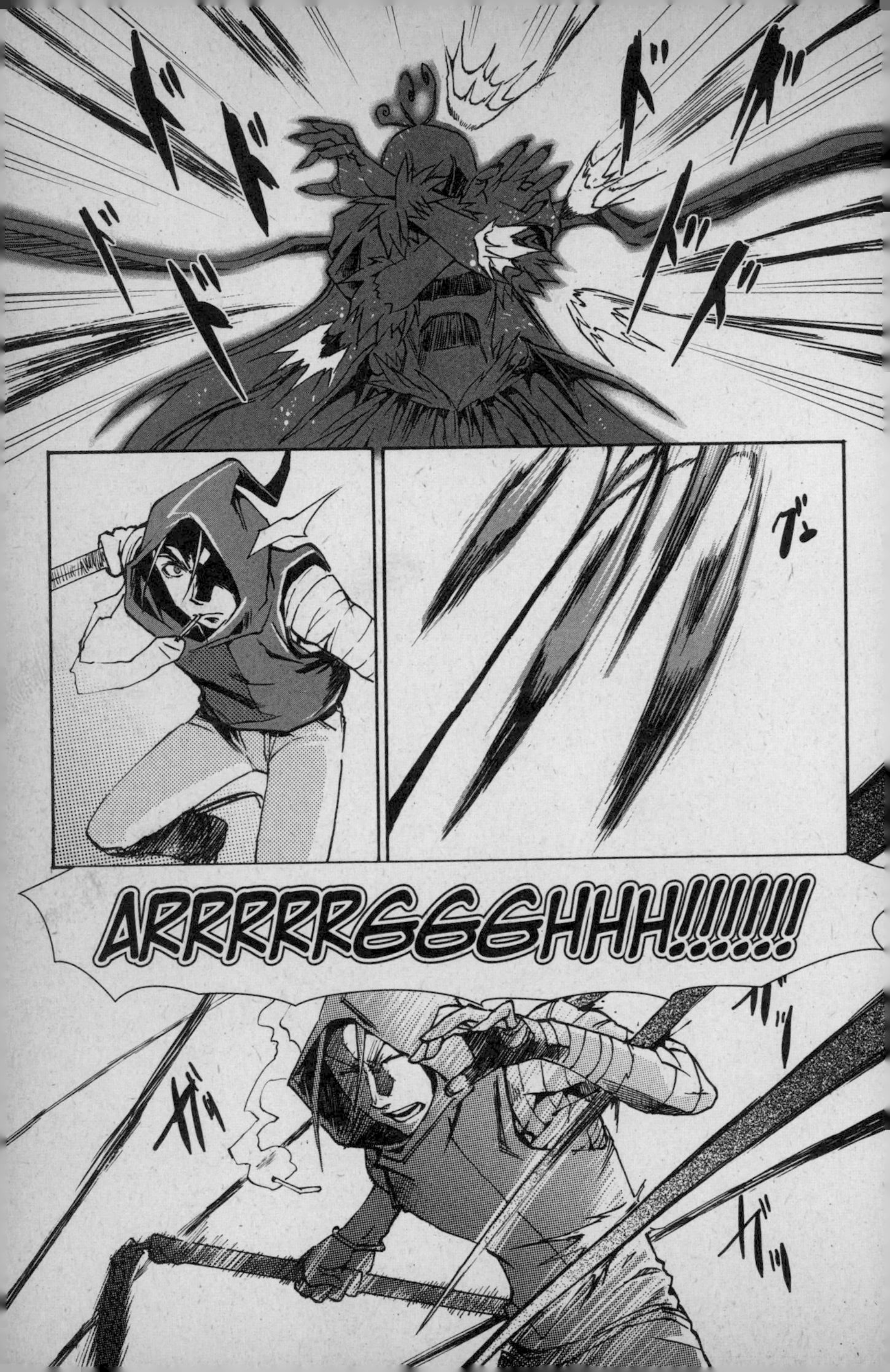
ARRRRRGGGHHH!!!!!!!

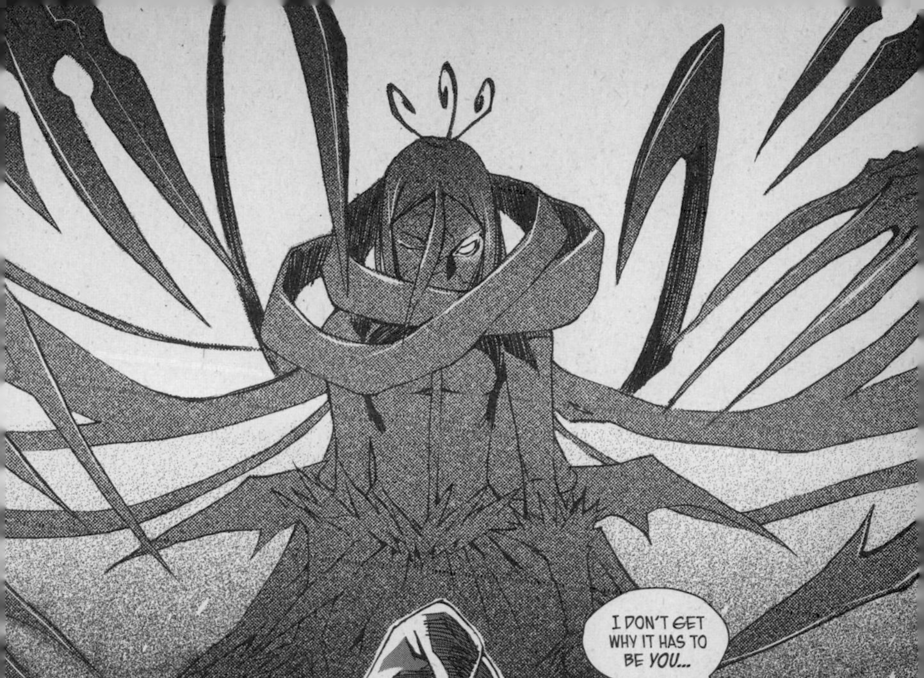
I DON'T GET WHY IT HAS TO BE *YOU*...
...FINE! KILL ME IF YOU CAN.... *CIERRA!!*
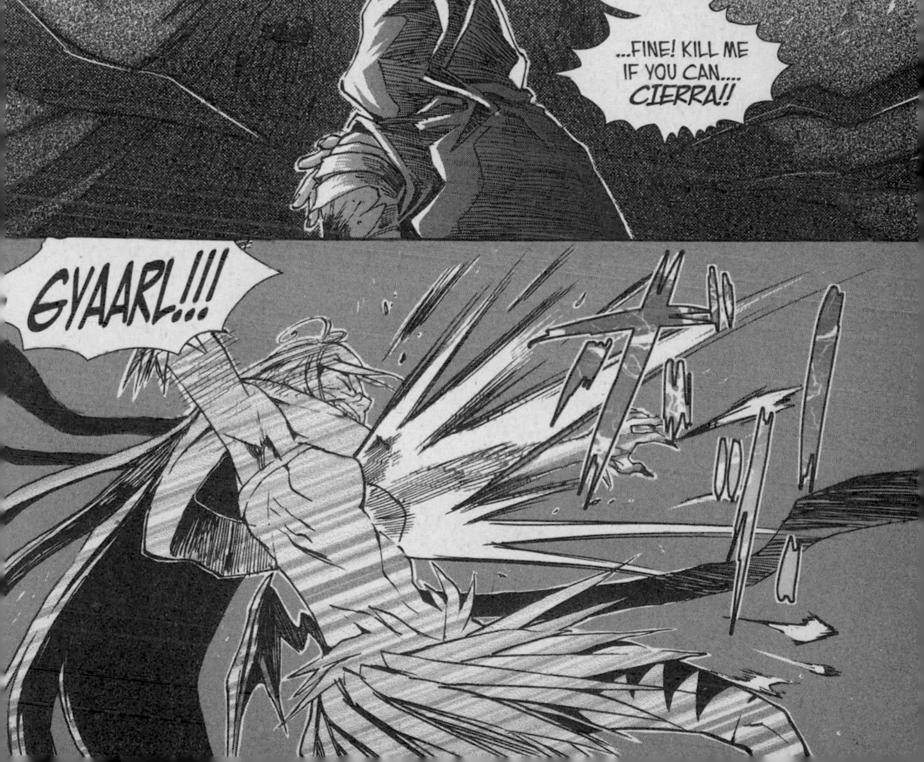
GYAARL!!!

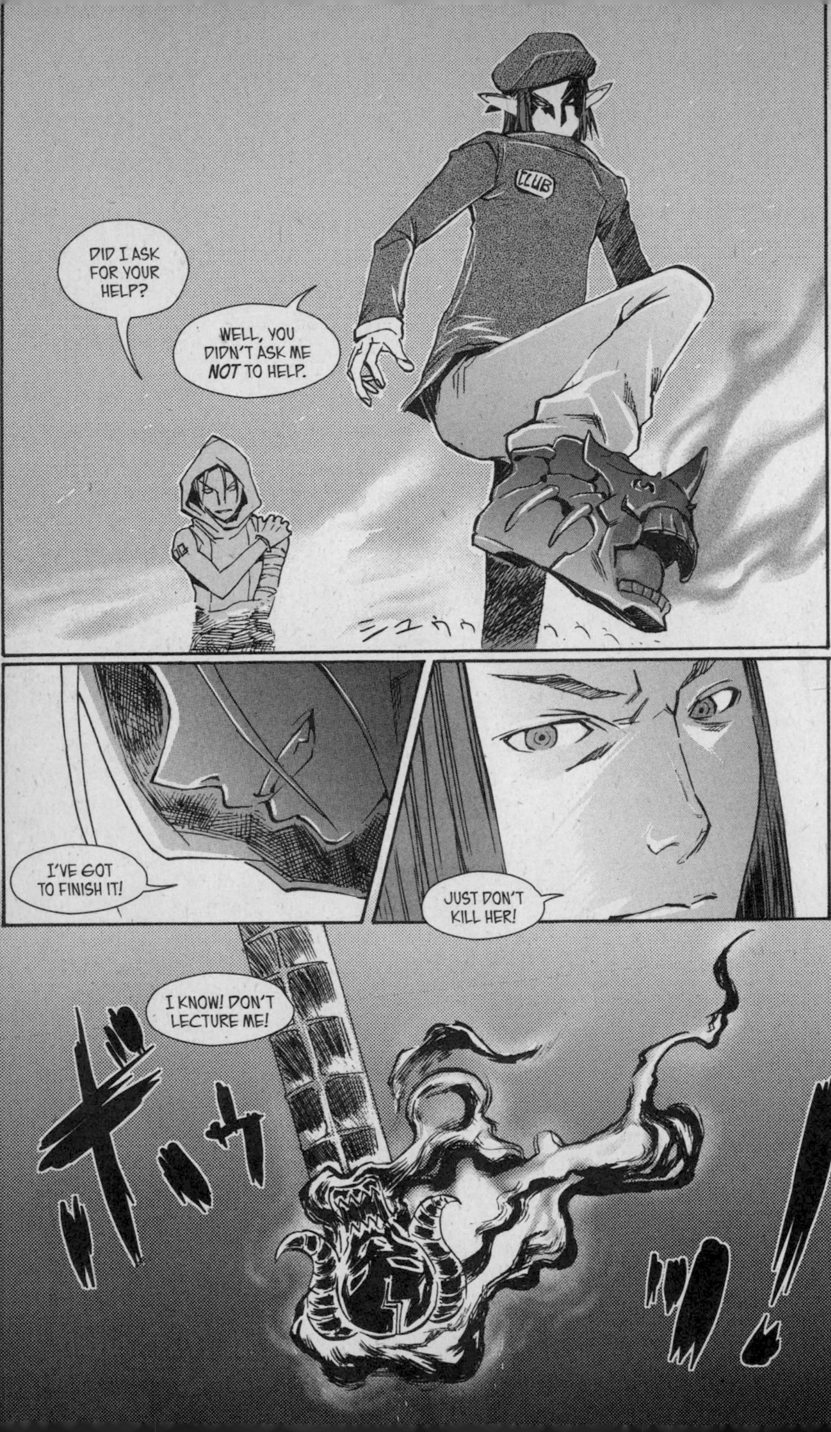
DID I ASK FOR YOUR HELP?
WELL, YOU DIDN'T ASK ME *NOT* TO HELP.
I'VE GOT TO FINISH IT!
JUST DON'T KILL HER!
I KNOW! DON'T LECTURE ME!

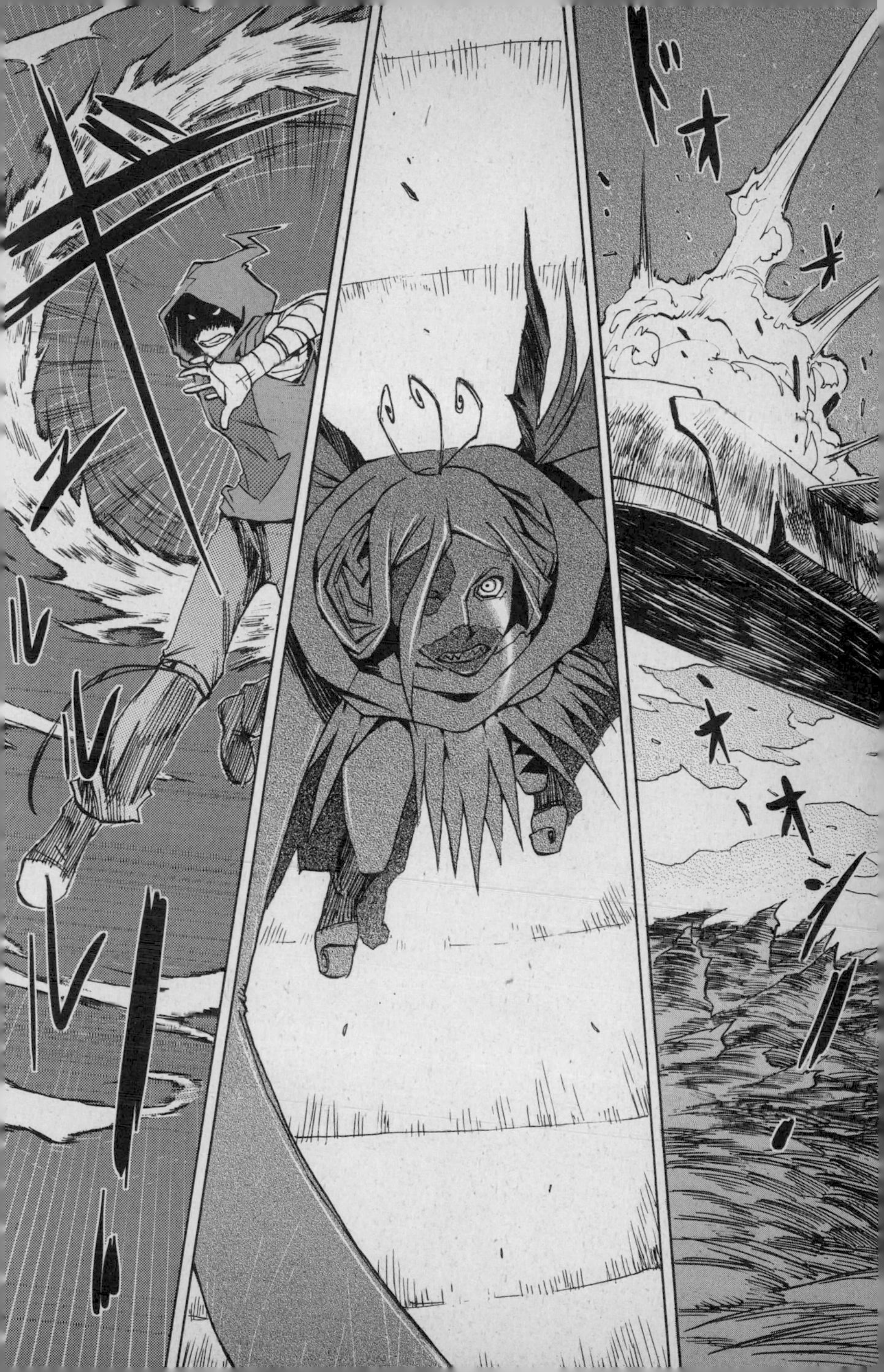
ドォォォ
ギュルルル

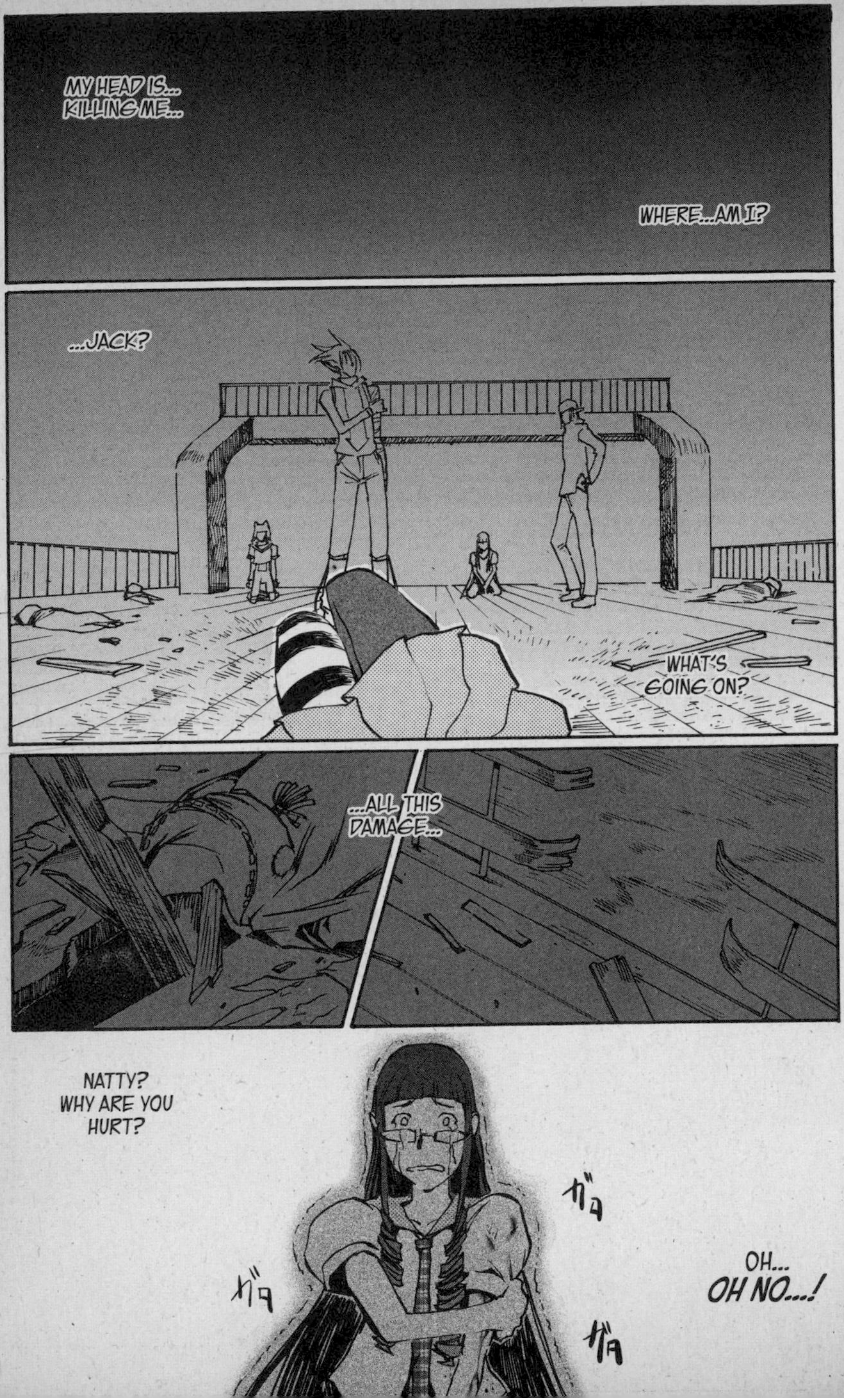
MY HEAD IS... KILLING ME...
WHERE...AM I?
...JACK?
WHAT'S GOING ON?
...ALL THIS DAMAGE...
NATTY? WHY ARE YOU HURT?
ガタ
OH... OH NO...!
ガタ
ガタ

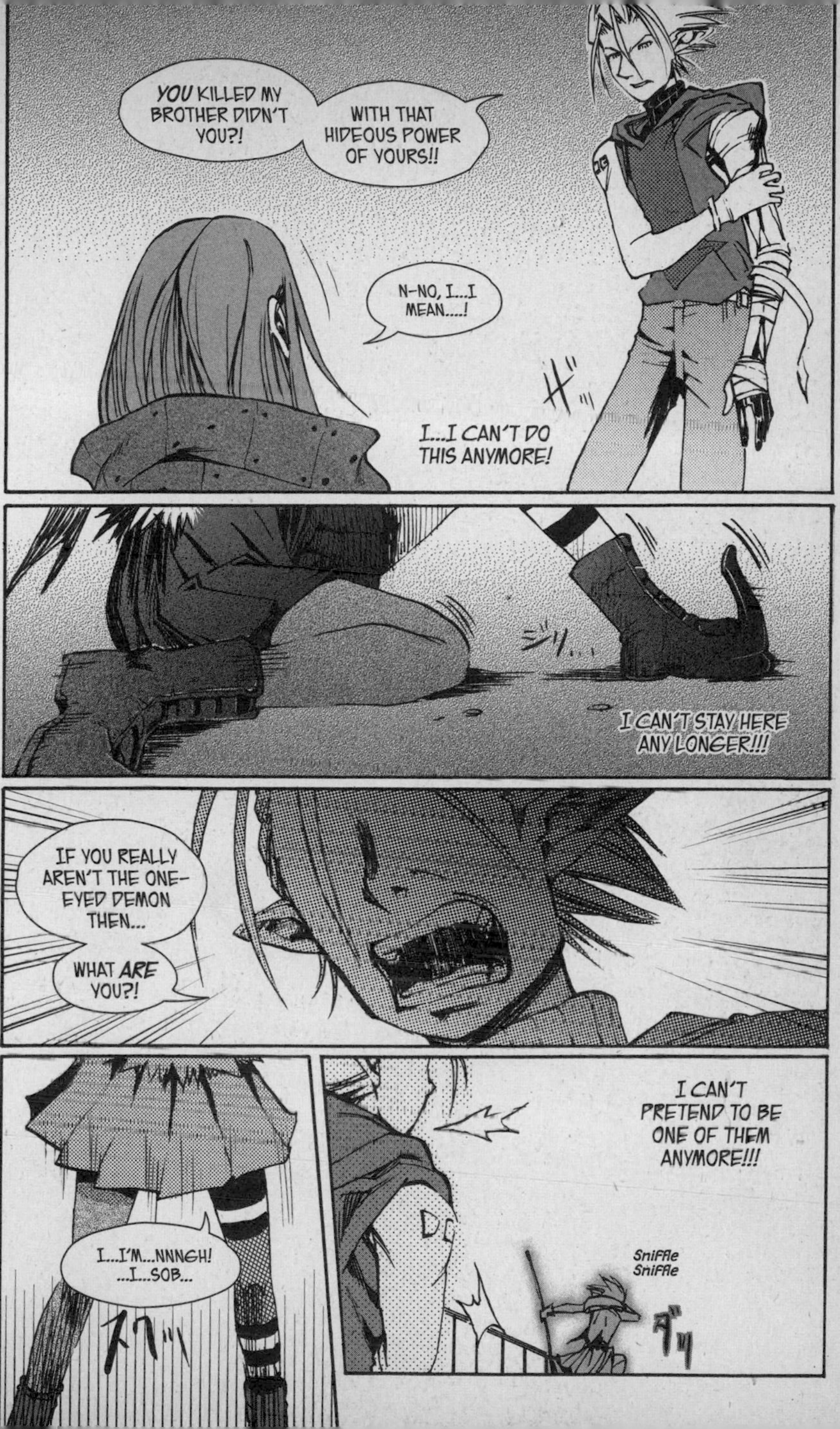
YOU KILLED MY BROTHER DIDN'T YOU?!
WITH THAT HIDEOUS POWER OF YOURS!!
N-NO, I...I MEAN....!
I...I CAN'T DO THIS ANYMORE!
I CAN'T STAY HERE ANY LONGER!!!
IF YOU REALLY AREN'T THE ONE-EYED DEMON THEN...
WHAT ARE YOU?!
I...I'M...NNNGH! ...I...SOB...
I CAN'T PRETEND TO BE ONE OF THEM ANYMORE!!!
Sniffle Sniffle

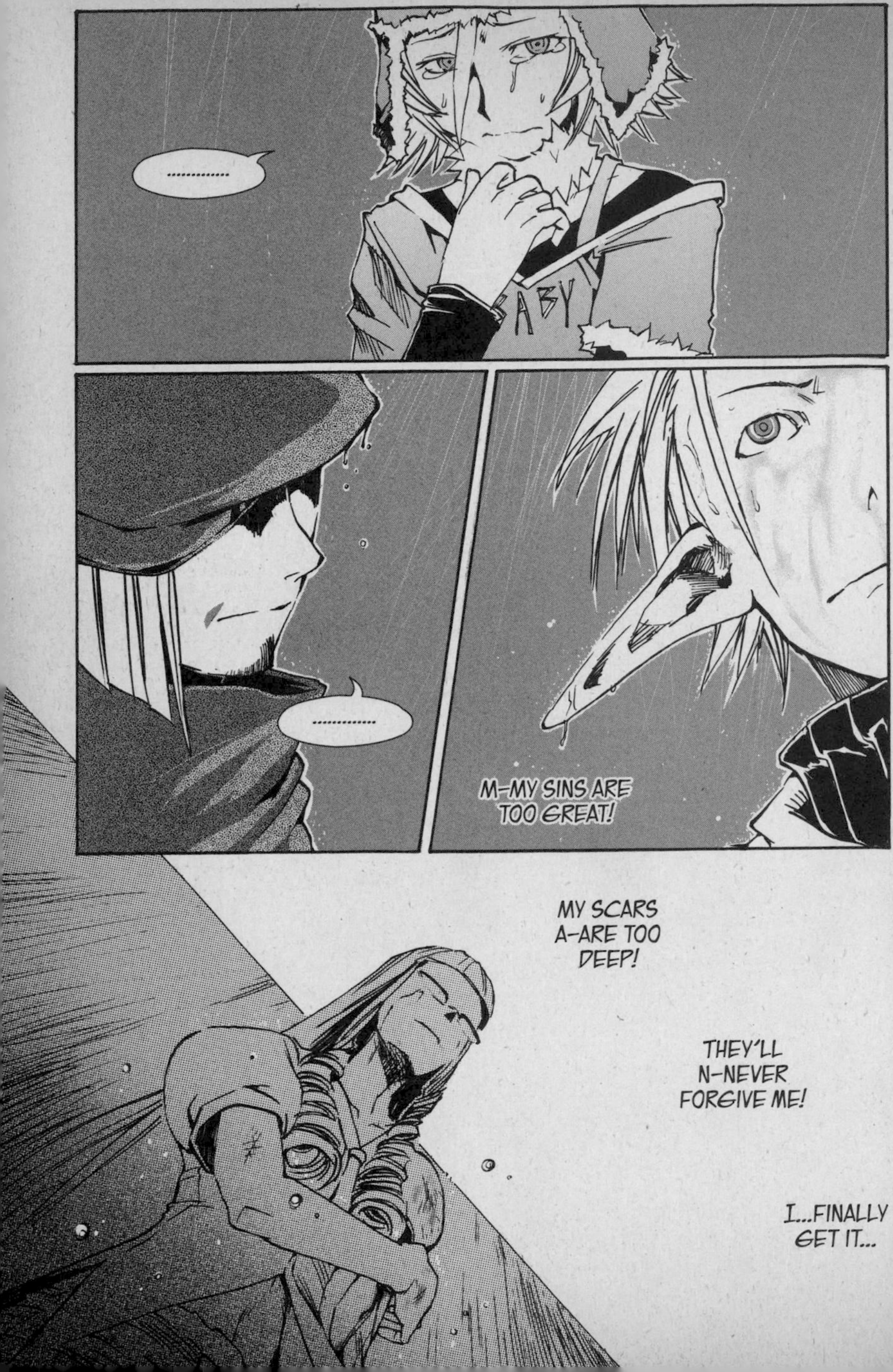
....
M-MY SINS ARE TOO GREAT!
....
MY SCARS A-ARE TOO DEEP!
THEY'LL N-NEVER FORGIVE ME!
I...FINALLY GET IT...

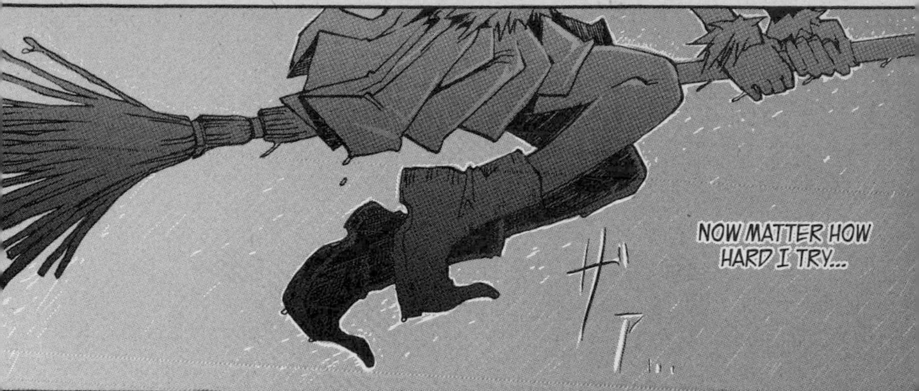
NOW MATTER HOW HARD I TRY...
ザァ...

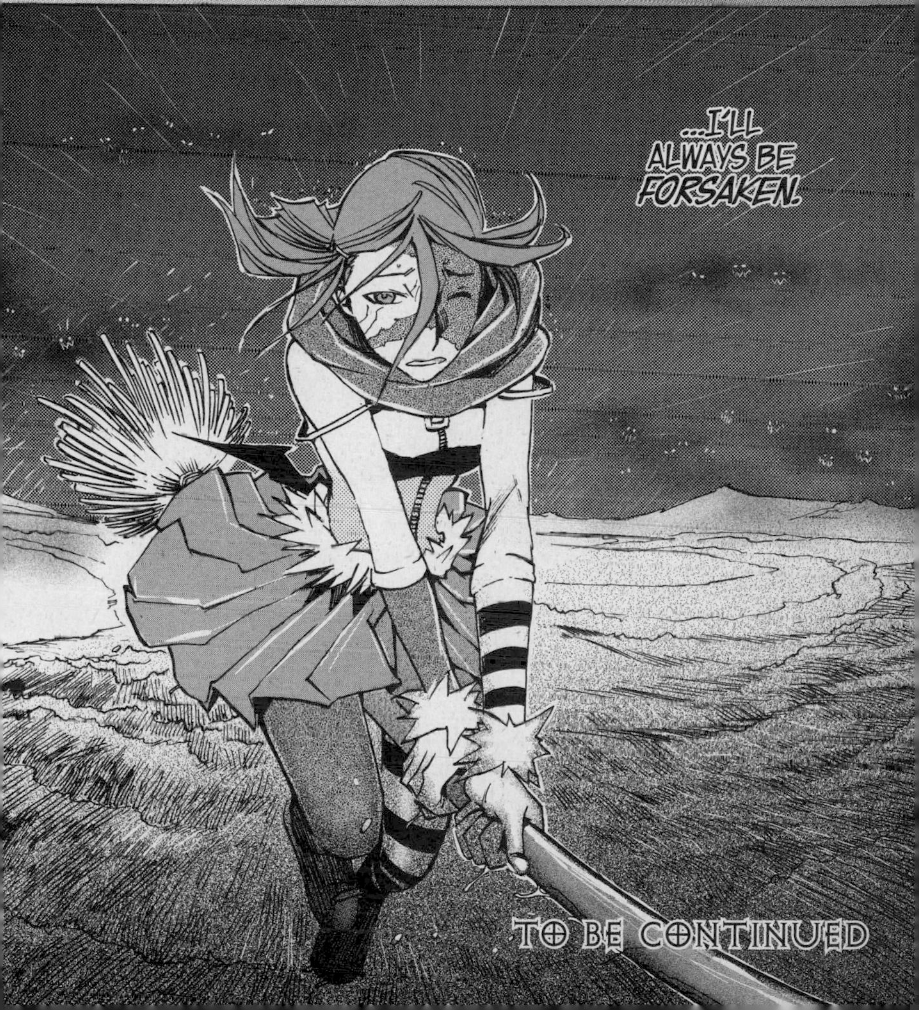
...I'LL ALWAYS BE FORSAKEN.
TO BE CONTINUED

QUEEN BIANKA'S CRASH COURSE

CHAPTER SIX: FREE MINDS

INSTEAD OF TRYING TA COME BACK TO SOCIETY AFTER PASSING THE EXILE, SOME WITCHES/WARLOCKS DECIDE TA STAY IN THE WILDERNESS. I HEAR IT'S EITHER BECAUSE THEY CAN'T HANDLE CIVILIZED CULTURE ANYMORE, OR THEY ARE SO OPPRESSED BY SOCIETY FOR BEING FORSAKEN THAT THEY TRY TA ESCAPE BACK TA THE 'FREEDOM' OF THE OUTSIDE. THERE ARE RUMORS THAT A LARGE GROUP HAS JOINED TOGETHER AND PLANS TO OVERTHROW THE CURRENT SOCIETY. RUMOR HAS IT THAT THEY HAVE SEVERAL REASONS....

REASONS TA REVOLT

1. ALL WITCHES AND WARLOCKS ARE NOT TREATED EQUALLY
2. LOW CLASS WITCHES ARE RESTRICTED FROM LEARNING HIGHER MAGICS
3. RESTORED FORSAKEN ARE BELOW THE LOW CLASS AND TREATED PRETTY BADLY

THERE ARE A LOT MORE REASONS THAT I HEARD, BUT BASICALLY THEY AREN'T HAPPY. I DUNNO WHAT TA THINK. I EASILY MADE HIGH CLASS, SO I DON'T KNOW WHAT IT'S LIKE AT THE BOTTOM! ANYWAYS, THERE'S NO WAY ENOUGH FORSAKEN COULD GATHER TOGETHER TA TAKE OVER! I GUARANTEE!

SEE YA NEXT TIME, LOYAL SERVANTS!

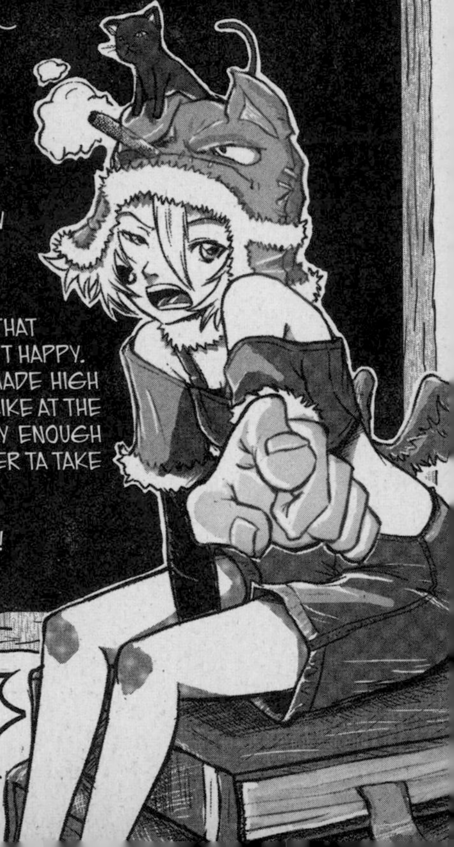

LOOKS LIKE YOU PASSED! I'M PRETTY IMPRESSED! WELL THEN, SEE YA NEXT VOLUME!

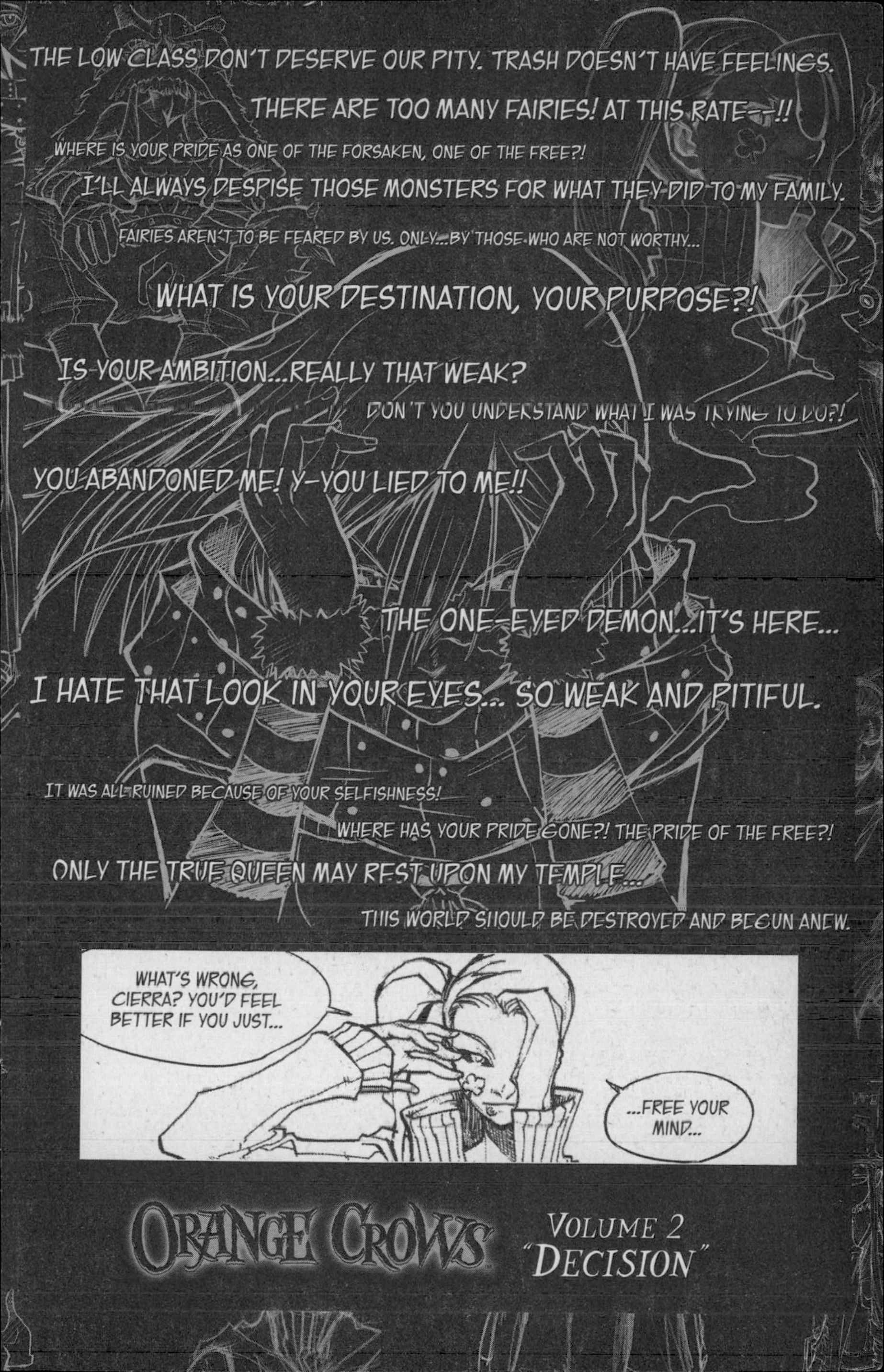
THE LOW CLASS DON'T DESERVE OUR PITY. TRASH DOESN'T HAVE FEELINGS.
THERE ARE TOO MANY FAIRIES! AT THIS RATE--!!
WHERE IS YOUR PRIDE AS ONE OF THE FORSAKEN, ONE OF THE FREE?!
I'LL ALWAYS DESPISE THOSE MONSTERS FOR WHAT THEY DID TO MY FAMILY.
FAIRIES AREN'T TO BE FEARED BY US. ONLY...BY THOSE WHO ARE NOT WORTHY...
WHAT IS YOUR DESTINATION, YOUR PURPOSE?!
IS YOUR AMBITION...REALLY THAT WEAK?
DON'T YOU UNDERSTAND WHAT I WAS TRYING TO DO?!
YOU ABANDONED ME! Y-YOU LIED TO ME!!
THE ONE-EYED DEMON...IT'S HERE...
I HATE THAT LOOK IN YOUR EYES... SO WEAK AND PITIFUL.
IT WAS ALL RUINED BECAUSE OF YOUR SELFISHNESS!
WHERE HAS YOUR PRIDE GONE?! THE PRIDE OF THE FREE?!
ONLY THE TRUE QUEEN MAY REST UPON MY TEMPLE...
THIS WORLD SHOULD BE DESTROYED AND BEGUN ANEW.
WHAT'S WRONG, CIERRA? YOU'D FEEL BETTER IF YOU JUST...
...FREE YOUR MIND...
ORANGE CROWS
VOLUME 2
"DECISION"

Overboard

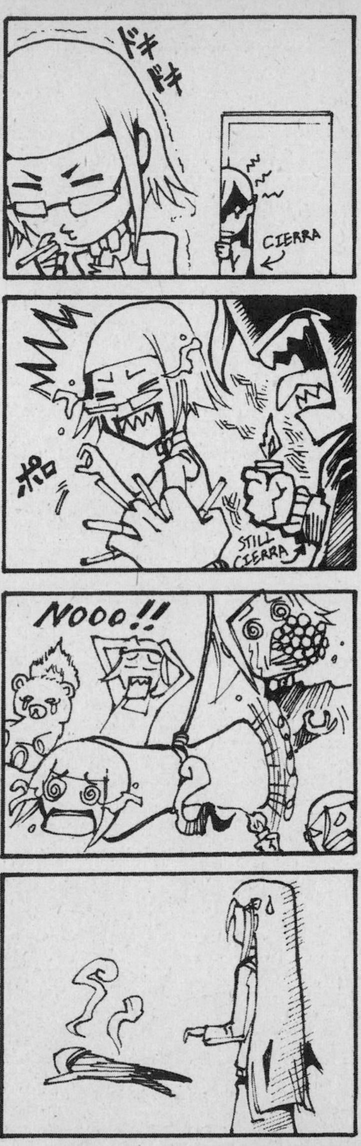
ドキ
ドキ
CIERRA
ポロ
STILL CIERRA
NOOO!!

Animals Shouldn't Talk

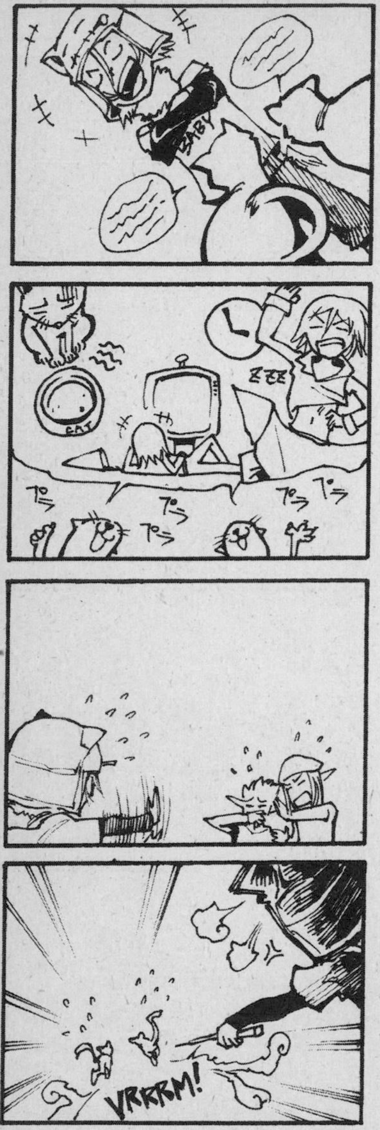
BABY
CAT
ZZZ
VRRRM!

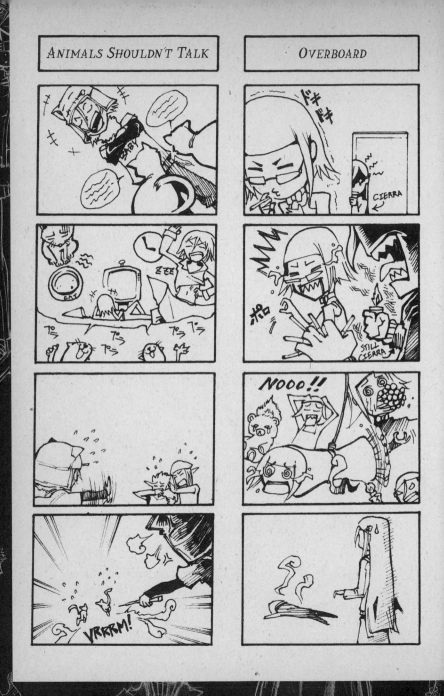

I WANT TO PLAY, TOO!

ギロ
チラ
ギロ
チラ
CRAFT BOX

BFF

TO MY BFF -JACK
ドキ
ドキ
REPORT

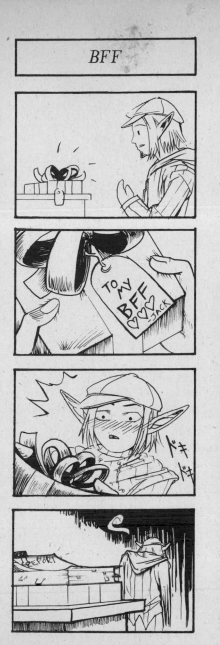

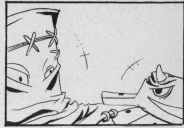

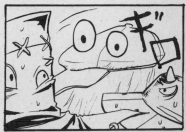

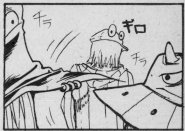

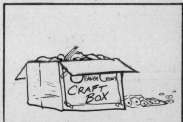

MISUNDERSTANDING! OC BONUS COMIC!!

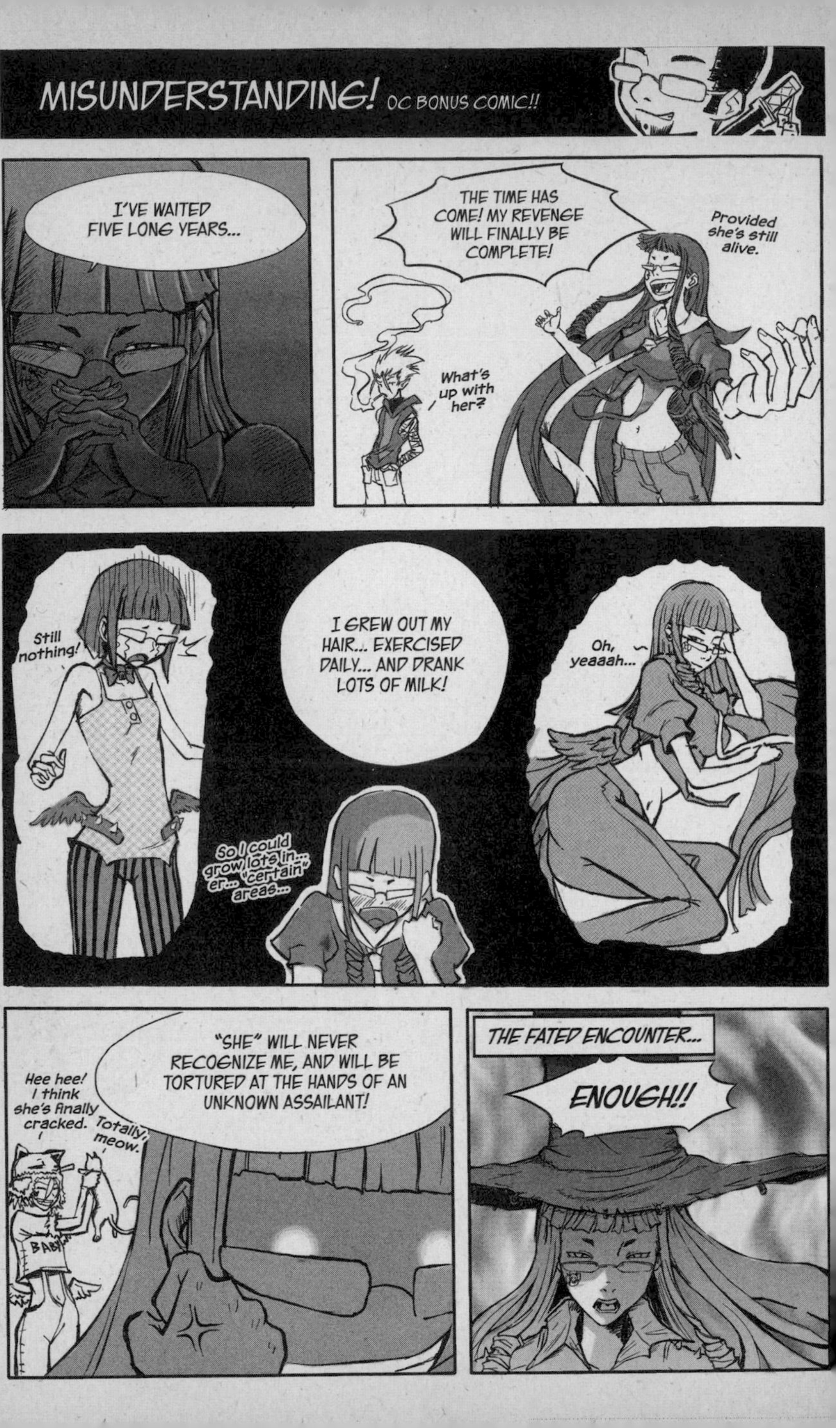
I'VE WAITED FIVE LONG YEARS...
THE TIME HAS COME! MY REVENGE WILL FINALLY BE COMPLETE!
What's up with her?
Provided she's still alive.
Still nothing!
I GREW OUT MY HAIR... EXERCISED DAILY... AND DRANK LOTS OF MILK!
So I could grow lots in... er... "certain" areas...
Oh, yeaaah...
"SHE" WILL NEVER RECOGNIZE ME, AND WILL BE TORTURED AT THE HANDS OF AN UNKNOWN ASSAILANT!
Hee hee! I think she's finally cracked.
Totally, meow.
BABY
THE FATED ENCOUNTER...
ENOUGH!!

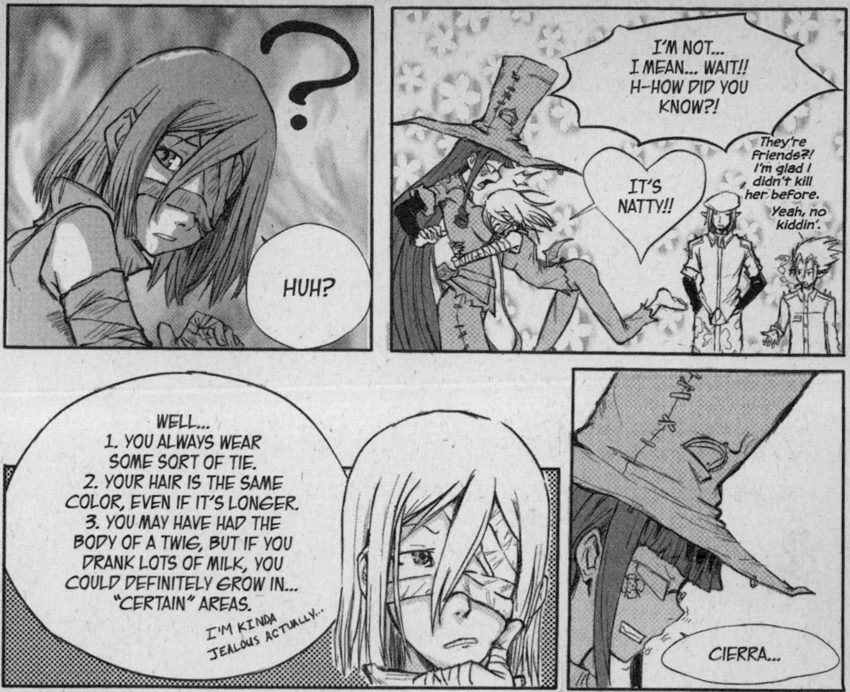
HUH?
I'M NOT... I MEAN... WAIT!! H-HOW DID YOU KNOW?!
IT'S NATTY!!
They're friends?! I'm glad I didn't kill her before.
Yeah, no kiddin'.
WELL... 1. YOU ALWAYS WEAR SOME SORT OF TIE. 2. YOUR HAIR IS THE SAME COLOR, EVEN IF IT'S LONGER. 3. YOU MAY HAVE HAD THE BODY OF A TWIG, BUT IF YOU DRANK LOTS OF MILK, YOU COULD DEFINITELY GROW IN... "CERTAIN" AREAS.
I'M KINDA JEALOUS ACTUALLY...
CIERRA...

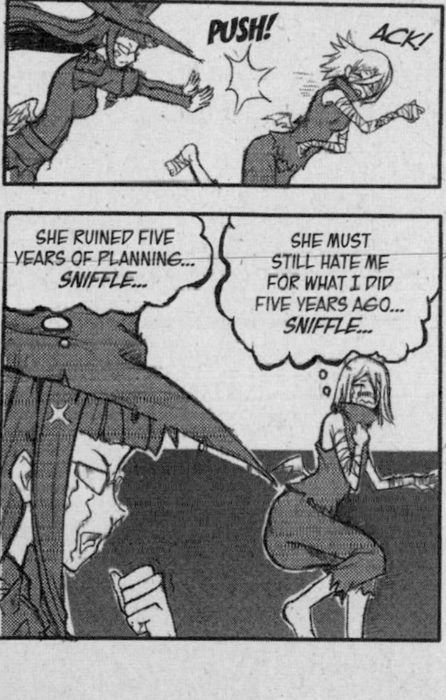
PUSH!
ACK!
SHE RUINED FIVE YEARS OF PLANNING... SNIFFLE...
SHE MUST STILL HATE ME FOR WHAT I DID FIVE YEARS AGO... SNIFFLE...

I WANT TO GIVE A SPECIAL THANKS TO HOPE DONOVAN, WHO NOTICED ME, GAVE ME A CHANCE, AND HELPED SHAPE MY STORY. EVEN THOUGH I'M AN ARTIST, I WASN'T GOOD ENOUGH BACK THEN TO DRAW THE MANGA FOR MYSELF, AND I WAS INTRODUCED TO RYO. HE'S AWESOME, AND REALLY HELPED BREATHE LIFE INTO THE O.C. CAST.

I THINK MY ONLY REGRET FOR VOLUME 1 IS THERE ISN'T EVEN HALF AS MUCH ACTION AS I WANTED, BUT HEY, ALL STORIES GOTTA START SOMEWHERE, RIGHT?

STAY TUNED FOR A LOT MORE ACTION NEXT VOLUME, AND PLENTY OF FUN! THANKS FOR READING!

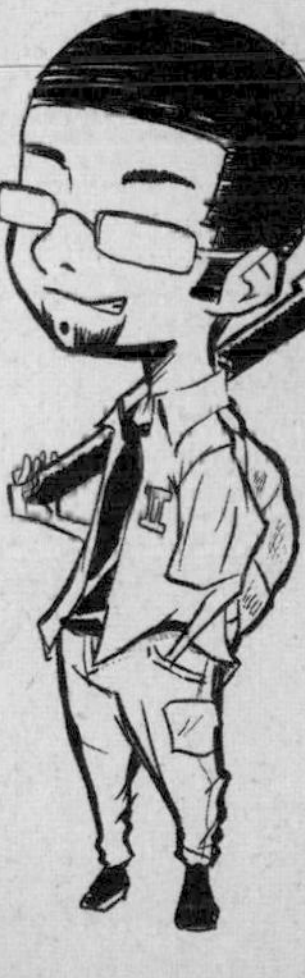

"Which Way do I Go"

By Karen Perry

Tonight I looked up at the clear night sky,
Up towards God and all the stars he placed high.
Although the sky may be clear, cloudy or rain,
The placement of his stars never change.
For each and every soul, God has a big plan,
But he will not tell his intent to any man.
We are his children and must find our own way
And take our earthly lives slowly day by day.
Although we're oblivious to what the future holds,
We keep on chasing our pot of gold.
Sometimes we get lost at a fork in the road.
Stressed, we wonder, "Which way do I go?"
At times we all wish our lives were like stars—
Beautiful, constant, and predictable in course.
But if your lives were like the stars in the sky
Our lives and future would hold no surprise.
So keep traveling along life's road,
But if you get lost, ask God, "Which way do I go?"

In honor of my dear friend, Karen Perry
~Ryo Kawakami 10.08

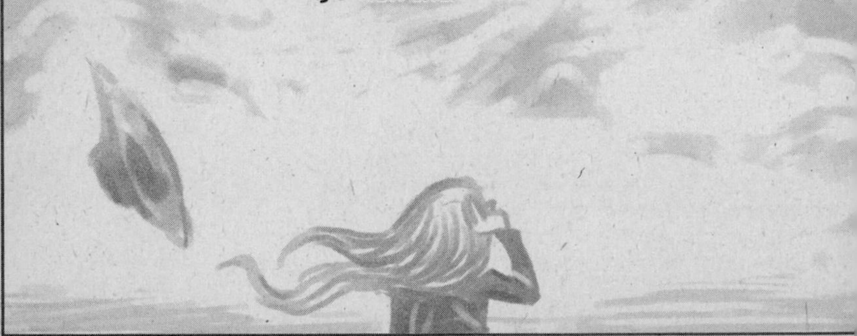

Special thanks: By Ryo K.

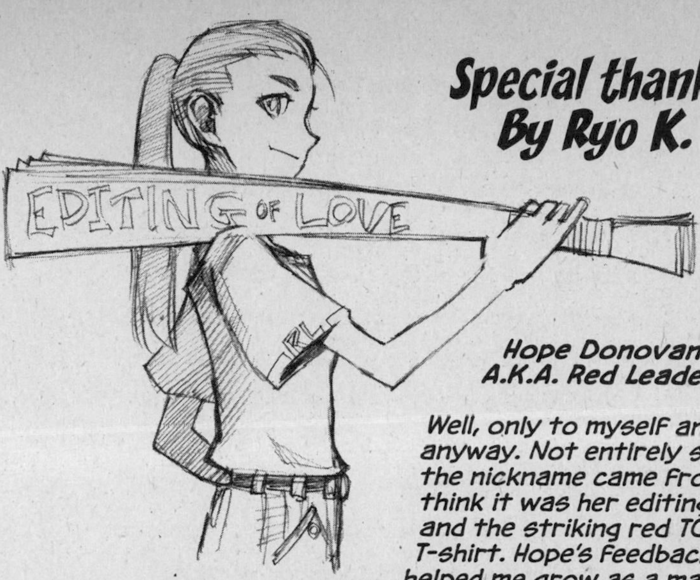
EDITING OF LOVE

Hope Donovan– A.K.A. Red Leader

Well, only to myself and James, anyway. Not entirely sure where the nickname came from, but I think it was her editing charisma and the striking red TOKYOPOP T-shirt. Hope's feedback had helped me grow as a manga artist who had just placed in RSOM 6, still came as an amateur, barely understood much direction & guidance that I needed. Although my work has a long, long way to go, there are drastic differences between my RSOM 6 entry (Little Miss Witch Hater) and Orange Crows.

Amy Reeder Hadley– A.K.A Tentopet

Tento's multi-talented skills are always inspiring. One of the early OGM artists of TOKYOPOP, she's also a singer, designer and a fine artist. Currently an artist for a major publisher. I've met a lot of people who do one of those things in their lifetime...but not all at once! Tento had encouraged me from the beginning, and really noticed my work. Her encouragement helped me push forward to where I stand now.

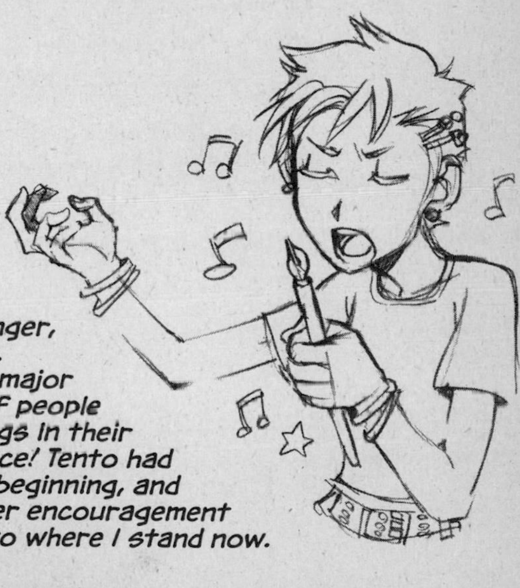

THE SPELL OF ORANGE CROWS

Caster (s): 1 writer, 1 artist, 1 editor
Prep time: 2 years
Results: 1 enchanting manga

1. To begin, send one editor crawling through a pile of unsolicited submissions to find one from hundreds with "something special."

2. Hammer eager writer's script into a pleasing shape.

3. Mix with an artist to adapt writer's designs and breathe life into the world.

Serves: Many contented readers

Concoctions:

SPARTICUS

Here is the big guy as I originally drew him.

I used James' designs for the characters, but added my own touch.

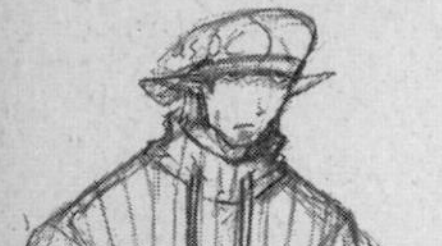

James

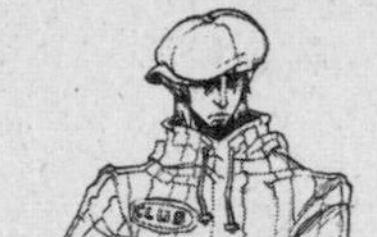

Ryo

FINAL PAGE

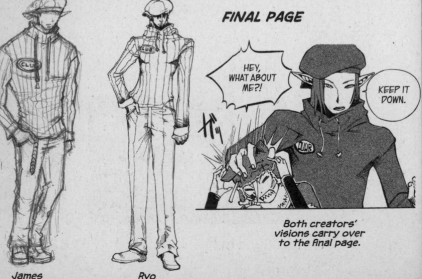

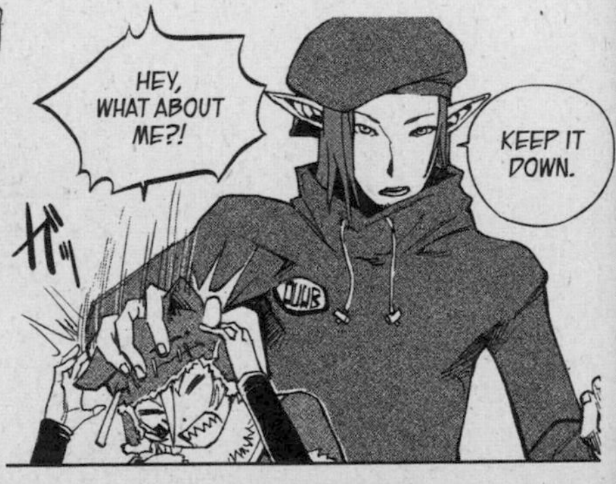
HEY, WHAT ABOUT ME?!
KEEP IT DOWN.
ガッ

Both creators' visions carry over to the final page.

James

KREUGER

Ryo

Kreuger was designed later than the central cast.

After Ryo drew his version of James' design, Hope stepped in and suggested we try a different approach.

I love what Ryo did with Kreuger. I wish he could have gotten more screen time at the end of the book, but there wasn't enough space. I'd like to do more with him in the future.

NO EYE BROWS

For the revision, I decided to toughen him up and give him more of a Yakuza, or thug feel.

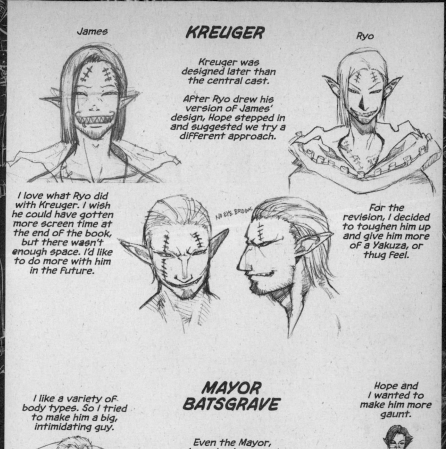

MAYOR BATSGRAVE

I like a variety of body types. So I tried to make him a big, intimidating guy.

Hope and I wanted to make him more gaunt.

Even the Mayor, who only shows up in a few frames, gets the design treatment.

HOPE AND RYO HAVE WON THIS BATTLE.

HOWEVER, THE WAR *NEVER* ENDS...

James

Ryo

FAN ART

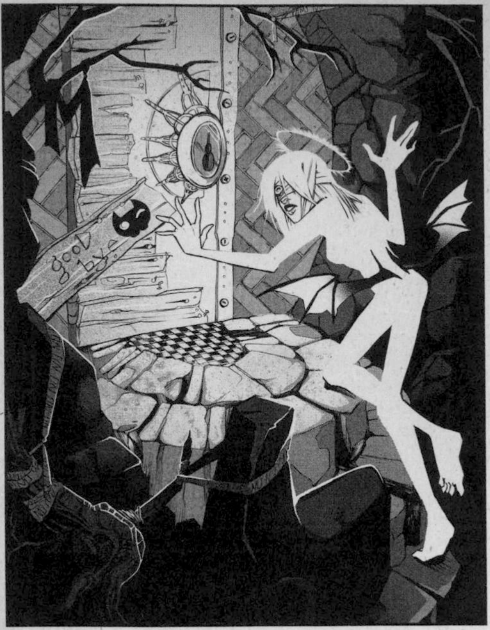
good bye

By Cari Corene

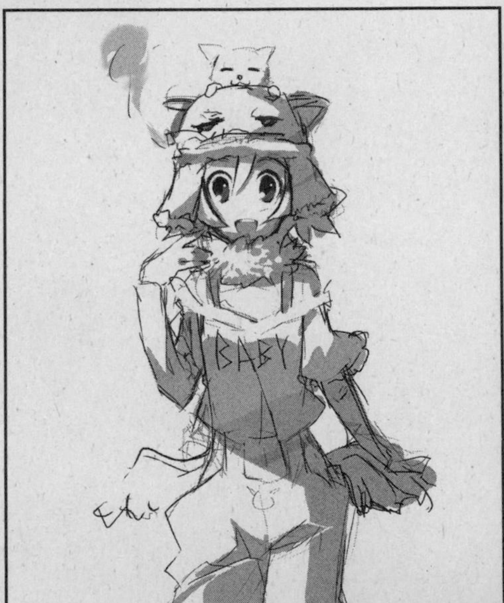
BABY

By Mop

By Mike Laster

By Kao

TOKYOPOP®.com
WHERE MANGA LIVES!
JOIN the TOKYOPOP community:
www.TOKYOPOP.com
COME AND PREVIEW THE HOTTEST MANGA AROUND!
CREATE...
UPLOAD...
DOWNLOAD...
BLOG...
CHAT...
VOTE...
LIVE!!!!
WWW.TOKYOPOP.COM HAS:
• Exclusives
• Manga Pilot Program
• Contests
• Games
• Rising Stars of Manga
• iManga
• and more...
TOKYOPOP :: Leading the Manga Revolution for 10 Years and Beyond
http://www.TOKYOPOP.com/
SHANALOGIC.COM
ONLINE MANGA
TOKYOPOP®
STARS
ART
LIFE
MOBILE
SHOP
HOT
Are you featured this week?
click here for a new POP-Cast
MOST RECENT
MOST POPPED
TOKYOPOP.COM NOW LIVE!
THE MANGA REVOLUTION · LEADING
漫画革命
© Svetlana Chmakova and TOKYOPOP Inc.

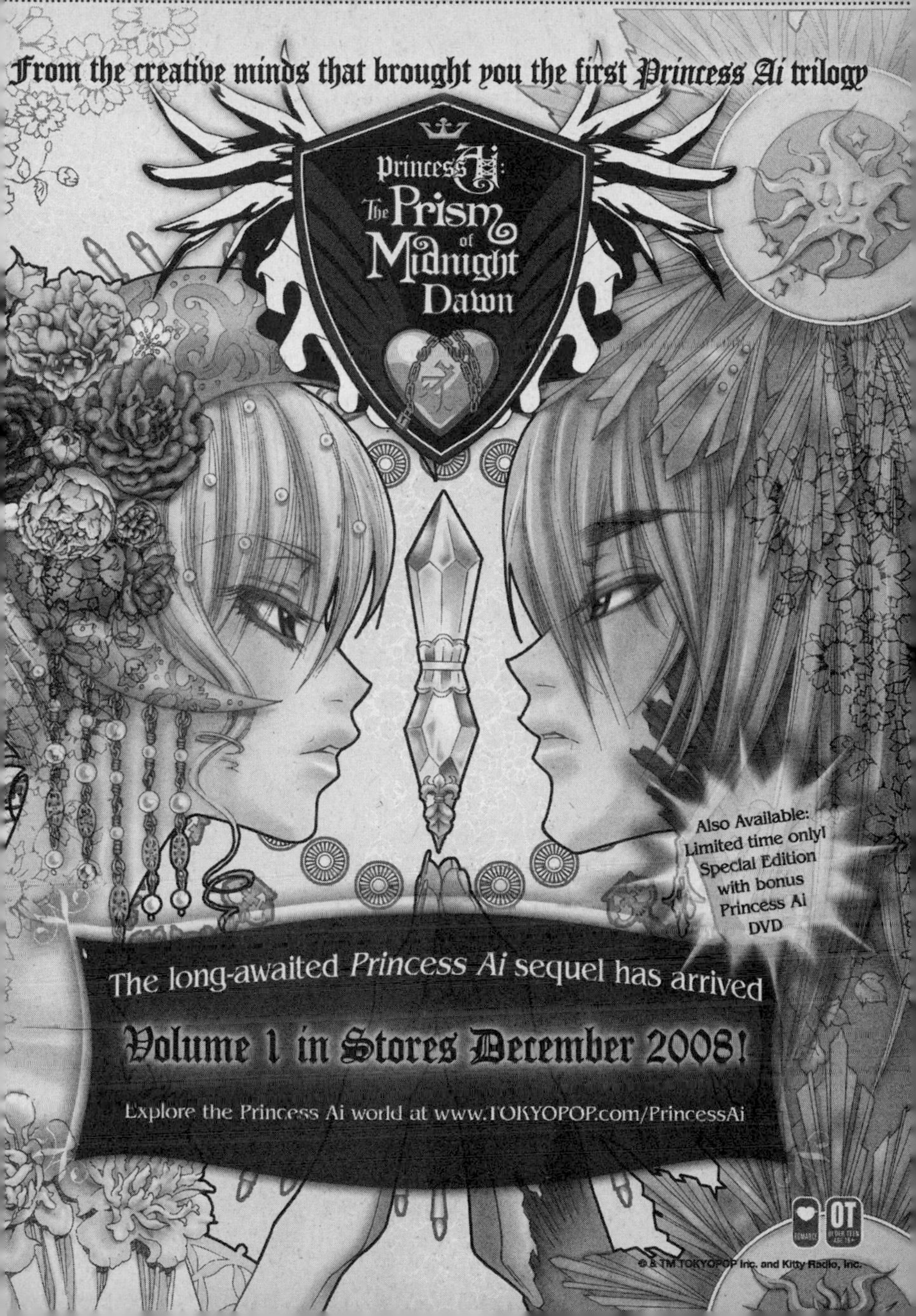
From the creative minds that brought you the first Princess Ai trilogy
Princess Ai: The Prism of Midnight Dawn
Also Available: Limited time only! Special Edition with bonus Princess Ai DVD
The long-awaited Princess Ai sequel has arrived
Volume 1 in Stores December 2008!
Explore the Princess Ai world at www.TOKYOPOP.com/PrincessAi
© & TM TOKYOPOP Inc. and Kitty Radio, Inc.

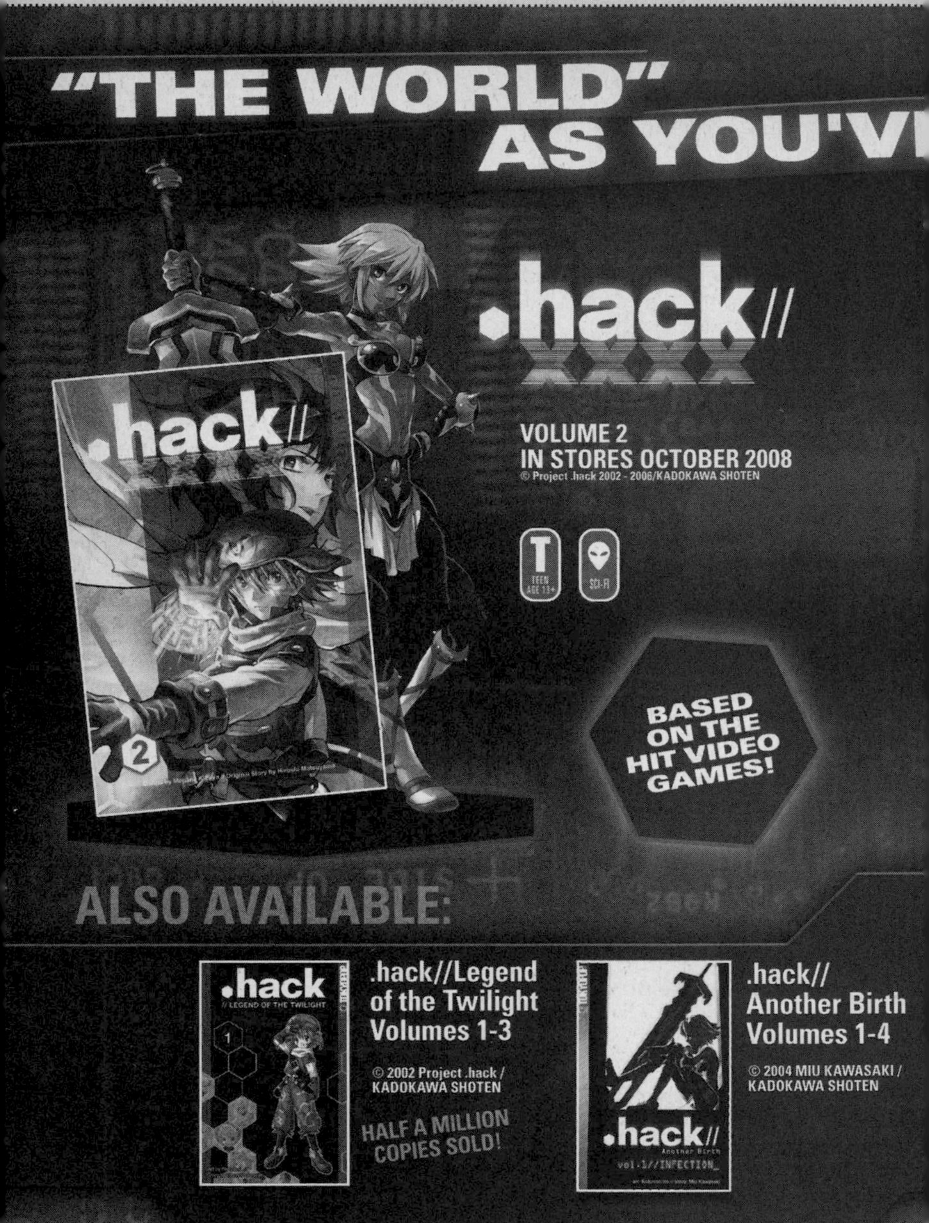
"THE WORLD"
AS YOU'VE
.hack//XXXX
VOLUME 2
IN STORES OCTOBER 2008
© Project .hack 2002 - 2006/KADOKAWA SHOTEN
TEEN AGE 13+
SCI-FI
BASED ON THE HIT VIDEO GAMES!
ALSO AVAILABLE:
.hack//Legend of the Twilight Volumes 1-3
© 2002 Project .hack / KADOKAWA SHOTEN
HALF A MILLION COPIES SOLD!
.hack// Another Birth Volumes 1-4
© 2004 MIU KAWASAKI / KADOKAWA SHOTEN